THE COLOUR

Rose Tremain's last novel *Music and Silence*, won the Whitbread Novel of the Year Award. Her work has been translated round the world, and she is a best-selling author in Britain, America and France. She has won the James Tait Black Memorial Prize and the Prix Fémina Etranger (*Sacred Country*), the *Sunday Express* Book of the Year Award (*Restoration*, also shortlisted for the Booker Prize), the Dylan Thomas Short Story Award (*The Colonel's Daughter*), a Giles Cooper Award (for her radio play, *Temporary Shelter*), and the Angel Literary Award. She lives in Norfolk and London with the biographer, Richard Holmes.

Rose Tremain

THE COLOUR

VINTAGE

Published by Vintage 2004

2 4 6 8 10 9 7 5 3 1

Copyright © Rose Tremain 2003

First published in Great Britain in 2003 by
Chatto & Windus

Vintage
Random House, 20 Vauxhall Bridge Road,
London SW1V 2SA

Random House Australia (Pty) Limited
20 Alfred Street, Milsons Point, Sydney,
New South Wales 2061, Australia

Random House New Zealand Limited
18 Poland Road, Glenfield, Auckland 10,
New Zealand

Random House (Pty) Limited
Endulini, 5A Jubilee Road, Parktown 2193,
South Africa

The Random House Group Limited Reg. No. 954009
www.randomhouse.co.uk

A CIP catalogue record for this book
is available from the British Library

ISBN 0 09 9425157

Papers used by Random House are natural, recyclable
products made from wood grown in sustainable forests. The
manufacturing processes conform to the environmental
regulations of the country of origin

Printed and bound in Great Britain by
Bookmarque Ltd, Croydon, Surrey

Contents

For the Domino team,
with all my love

Gold diggings disorganise society, induce a moral blight, divert activity from saner enterprise and encourage a disagreeable immigration of the scum of China.

Lyttelton Times, New Zealand, 1861

Gold has been all in all to us.

West Coast Times, New Zealand, 1866

PART ONE

The Cob House. 1864

I

The coldest winds came from the south and the Cob House had been built in the pathway of the winds.

Joseph Blackstone lay awake at night. He wondered whether he should dismantle the house and reconstruct it in a different place, lower down in the valley, where it would be sheltered. He dismantled it in his mind.

He rebuilt it in his mind in the lee of a gentle hill. But he said nothing and did nothing. Days passed and weeks and the winter came, and the Cob House remained where it was, in the pathway of the annihilating winds.

It was their first winter. The earth under their boots was grey. The yellow tussock-grass was salty with hail. In the violet clouds of afternoon lay the promise of a great winding-sheet of snow.

Joseph's mother, Lilian, sat at the wooden table, wearing a bonnet against the chill in the room, mending china. China broken on its shipment from England. Broken by carelessness, said Lilian Blackstone, by inept loading and unloading, by the disregard of people who did not know the value of personal possessions. Joseph reminded her gently that you could not travel across the world – to its very furthest other side – and not expect something to be broken on the way. 'Something,' snapped Lilian. 'But this is a great deal more than something.'

Her furious voice dismayed him. He watched her with a kind of familiar dread. She seemed lost in the puzzle of the china, as though she were unable to remember the shape of ordinary things. She kept moving pieces around and around, like letters which refused to form a word. Only occasionally did she suddenly discover where something fitted and dare to smear a shard with glue. Then she would press this shard into place with a kind of passionate, unnecessary ardour and her lips would move in what might have been a prayer or might have been a silent utterance of the only French word in Lilian Blackstone's vocabulary: *voilà,* which she pronounced 'wulla'. And what Joseph saw in all of this was an affirmation of what he already knew: that by bringing his mother here to New Zealand he had failed her, just as he had always and always failed her. He had tried all his life – or so it seemed to him – to please her, but he couldn't remember any single day when he had pleased her enough.

But now he had a wife.

She was tall and her hair was brown. Her name was Harriet Salt. Of her, Lilian Blackstone had remarked: 'She carries herself well' and Joseph found this observation accurate and more acute than Lilian could know.

He turned away from his mother and looked admiringly at this new wife of his, kneeling by the reluctant fire. And he felt his heart suddenly fill to its very core with gratitude and affection. He watched her working the bellows, patient and still, 'carrying herself well' even here in the Cob House, in this cold and smoky room, even here, with the wind sighing outside and the smell of glue like some potent medicine all three of them were now obliged to take. Joseph wanted to cross the room and put his arms round Harriet and gather her hair into a knot in his hand. He wanted to lay his head on her shoulder and tell her the one thing that he would never be able to admit to her – that she had saved his life.

II

After their arrival in Christchurch, Joseph had supervised the purchasing of materials for building the Cob House, and had hired men to help him, and horses and drays to lug the tin and the pine planks and the sacks of nails and bales of calico, and at last made ready to set off north-westwards, towards the Okuku River.

Harriet had asked her new husband to take her with him. She clung to him and pleaded – she who never whined or complained, who carried herself so well. But she was a woman who longed for the unfamiliar and the strange. As a child, she'd seen it waiting for her, in dreams or in the colossal darkness of the sky: some wild world which lay outside the realm of everything she knew. And the idea that she could build a house out of stones and earth and put windows and doors in it and a chimney and a roof to keep out the weather and then live in it thrilled her. She wanted to see it take shape like that, out of nothing. She wanted to learn how to mash mud and chop the yellow tussock to make the cob. She wanted to see her own hand in everything. No matter if it took a long time. No matter if her skin was burned in the summer heat. No matter if she had to learn each new task like a child. She had been a governess for twelve years. Now, she had travelled an ocean and stood in a new place, but she wanted to go still further, into a wilderness.

Joseph Blackstone had looked tenderly at her. He saw how ardently she wanted to embark on the next stage of their journey, but, as always, there was Lilian to think of. As always, the choices that he made were never simple.

'Harriet,' he said, 'I am sorry, but you must stay in Christchurch. I'm relying on you to help Lilian to become accustomed to New Zealand life. A choral society must be found for her.'

Harriet suggested that, with the help of Mrs Dinsdale, in whose neat and tidy Rooms they were lodging, Lilian would be able to find the choral society on her own. 'And then,' Harriet added, 'she will have no more need of me, Joseph, for it is her voice that sings, not mine.'

'There is the strangeness of everything,' said Joseph. 'You cannot comprehend the degree to which this new world is disconcerting to a woman of sixty-three.'

'The Rooms are not strange,' insisted Harriet. 'The jug and basin are of a pattern almost identical to the pot your mother kept under her bed in Norfolk . . .'

'Different birds sing outside the window.'

'Oh but still they are *birds* singing, not monkeys.'

'The light is other.'

'Brighter. But only within a degree of brightness. It will not harm her.'

On and on it went, this conversation, for it was not a conversation but a war, a small war, the first war they had ever had, but one which would never be quite forgotten, even after Harriet had lost it. And on the morning when Joseph set off towards the ochre-coloured plains, Harriet had to turn away from him and from Lilian so that neither of them would see how bitterly angry she felt.

She ran up the wooden stairs to the Rooms, went into the green-painted parlour and closed the door. She stood at the open window, breathing the salty air. She longed to be a bird or a whale – some creature which might slip between men's actions and their forgetfulness to arrive at its own private destination. For she knew that in her thirty-four years of life she had never been tried or tested, never gone beyond the boundaries society had set for her. And now, once again, she had been left behind. It would be Joseph who would make their house rise out of nothing on the empty plains, Joseph who would build a fire under the stars and hear the cry of the distant bush. Harriet yawned. In the tidy parlour, she felt her anger gradually give way to a deep and paralysing boredom.

III

Settlers from England were known as cockatoos, Joseph was informed.

Cockatoos? He couldn't imagine why. He couldn't even remember what kind of bird a cockatoo really was.

'Scratch a bit of ground, take what you can get from it, screech a bit and move on. Like a cockatoo.'

Joseph thought of a parrot, grey and morose, fretting among seeds in a cage. He said this wasn't appropriate to him. He said

he wanted to make a new life near the Okuku River, make his
acres pay, strive for things which would last.

'Good for you, Mr Blackstone,' the men opined. 'All credit
to you.'

What Joseph did not say was that, in England, he had done a
disgraceful thing.

'You're a thoughtful one,' the men said when the building of
the Cob House began. They were mashing mud and grass for
the walls, breaking stones for the chimney and they were
stronger than Joseph, who rested more often and was observed
staring down at the plains, known here as 'flats', wide plains
with hardly any trees, stretching to infinity below him, staring
as still as an owl.

'Penny for them? Missing home?'

'No.'

'Wouldn't blame you, Mr Blackstone. Homesickness: we
know a lot about that here.'

'No,' he said again. And took up his knife and sharpened it
and returned to his task of the grass-shredding and made
himself whistle so that the men could read his mood correctly,
his mood of optimism. Because what he felt as he surveyed the
flats or turned and looked up towards the distant mountains
was a sudden surge of hope. He was here. He was in the South
Island of New Zealand, the place they called Aotearoa – Land
of the Long White Cloud. Though he had done a terrible thing
in England, he had survived. The future lay around him, in the
stones, in the restless water of the creek, in the distant forest.

And with Harriet's help, he told himself, he would contrive
to live an honest and prosperous life, one in which Lilian would
eventually feel comfortable and cared for and some day put her
hand on his cheek and tell him that she was proud of all that
he'd achieved.

IV

The Rooms let to Harriet and Lilian by Mrs Dinsdale in

Christchurch smelled of the resin which seeped from the matchboarded walls and of linen sprayed with hard water and scorched with burning irons.

Mrs Dinsdale had come to Christchurch from Dunedin and to Dunedin from Edinburgh. In Edinburgh, she said, there had been no creases in her laundry.

She was Lilian's age and a widow like her, but with an obstinate prettiness which had not quite gone away, that kind of prettiness which suggested that Mrs Dinsdale might soon become – even at her age – Mrs Somebody-Else.

Lilian said to Harriet: 'I do believe she's a coquette. Is that the word?'

And in strange contrast to her savage way with the smoothing iron, Mrs Dinsdale seemed to be such a light and gentle person that it was not long before Lilian found herself sitting on what Mrs Dinsdale called 'my best verandah', drinking lemonade and confiding many of the sorrows and embarrassments of her former life.

Under her steel-grey hair, parted in the middle and whipped round her head in a stringy plait, Lilian Blackstone's face was as white as dough as she described to Mrs Dinsdale her 'struggles' with her late husband, Roderick. Barely paying attention to Mrs Dinsdale's observation that 'marriage was always and ever a rare battle of wills', Lilian whispered to her new friend how Roderick had possessed one vice and this vice it was which had caused his embarrassing death.

At the word 'vice', Mrs Dinsdale's blue eyes took on an eager glitter and she moved forward a fraction in her wickerwork chair.

'Oh, vice,' she said.

'Some would not call it "vice",' said Lilian. 'But I do.'

'And what was the particular . . . vice?'

'Curiosity.'

'Curiosity?'

'Yes. Roderick could leave nothing alone. If he had been able to leave things alone, he would not have died and I never would have been manhandled across the globe like this.'

Mrs Dinsdale took the beaded muslin off the jug of lemonade and refilled the two glasses. In this little action, Lilian saw, in drawing her attention to the way the sun scintillated so satisfactorily, so un-Englishly in the pale liquid, Mrs Dinsdale was reminding Lilian that Christchurch had its charms and that she should not refuse to notice them.

'I do not mean any criticism of New Zealand,' said Lilian hastily. 'All I mean is that I had the life I wanted, in the village of Parton Magna in Norfolk, and I would not have chosen to leave it. It was my son's idea, to abandon the Old World. And once that idea had come into his head ...'

'Oh yes. Once an idea has come to them, they will not be turned aside.'

'Exactly.'

'And as a widow you had inadequate means, perhaps?'

'Miserably inadequate. Roderick had not expected to die.'

Mrs Dinsdale crossed her feet, shod, Lilian noticed, in very choice little brown boots.

'So, it was his curiosity, then?' said Mrs Dinsdale, her eyes still wide and expressing sparkling interest. 'But how can curiosity kill a man?'

Lilian sipped her lemonade. She had never liked it very much, but, here, you were at risk from scurvy if you did not drink it, someone had told her.

'Ostriches,' she whispered.

'Ostriches, Mrs Blackstone?'

'Yes. I really cannot bear to say it out loud because people are so mocking. But I can whisper it to you: Roderick was killed by ostriches.'

After Joseph had gone away to build the house, Harriet began her scrapbook. She told herself that she was making it for her father, Henry Salt, (a teacher of geography who had never travelled further afield than Switzerland) but she also knew that she was making it for herself.

In her first letter to Henry Salt, she said that she did not expect the scrapbook to contain 'much of irresistible interest' at first, but that when the Cob House was built, when they were living there, out in the middle of nothing, 'then I think I will find something to intrigue you'.

She had been surprised to discover a very beautifully bound

leather book in a shop in Worcester Street, with pages stiff and creamy as starched pillow-slips. She was tempted to ask for her name to be inscribed on the cover in tooled gold lettering, but Joseph had warned her not to spend money on 'anything dear or inessential'. What she had of currency was going to be used to buy vegetable seed, poultry, fence posts, wire and a dairy cow. She knew she should not really have bought the book itself, but it was her way of marking a line between her new life and her old.

The first thing Harriet put into the book was a leaf. She thought it was a maple leaf. It had fallen out of the sky on to the ship in the middle of the Tasman Sea – or so it had seemed. She named it *Leaf out of sky on board the* SS Albert. The second item was a label from a box of Chinese tea she had bought at a shop called Read's Commodities. On the label was a drawing of two herons, with their necks entwined amid some Chinese writing, and Harriet thought it beautiful and strange. She labelled it *First purchase of tea.*

She added some photographs of boats at anchor in Lyttelton Harbour, found in the shop where she bought the book, and some New Zealand stamps with Queen Victoria's head on them. Neither of these last things did she find interesting, but she saw that the leaf and the tea label on their own did not convey the idea of the coming book.

And it was this that excited her, the scrapbook filling up with all the elements of her future life. To her father she wrote:

> *In Christchurch, I do not feel as though I have yet arrived. Where Joseph is, there will I encounter the true Aotearoa, there will I feel the extraordinary difference of things. There will I see flightless birds and glaciers shining in the sun.*

To pass the time, while Lilian and Mrs Dinsdale sat on the 'best verandah' drinking lemonade, Harriet designed a vegetable garden for the Cob House. She wanted to put wooden fencing round the plot, but she had been told that wood was expensive and that they could afford wooden windows and doors for the house, but nothing else. So she enclosed her garden with stones. She imagined the warm touch of the stones in the summer sun and the icy touch of them in winter. She put in carrots and parsnips and kūmara, the sweet potato which was a staple of their lives, said Mrs Dinsdale, 'as vital as bread'. In among her peas, beans and lettuces, she sketched lines of dandelion. The farmers of New Zealand, she'd heard, fed their pigs on a diet of dandelion leaves and snails and these pigs were as healthy as any pigs in the world. They were frisky in their movements and their tails were bristly and pert and their flesh tasted like veal.

There would eventually be pigs on Joseph and Harriet's farm, but where, Harriet wondered, can one be certain of finding the snails?

V

Meanwhile, the Cob House took shape around its stone chimney.

The iron hinges of the door glinted in the heat. The tin roof was nailed down. Inside, the earth was soaked and tamped and beaten smooth and hard, but there were no interior rooms, no closed and private spaces, only partitions made with stretched calico.

Joseph sat with his back against the cob wall, smoking a brittle pipe, and congratulated himself for finding the right spot for the house, where the afternoon breeze shivered in the beech leaves and set the calico gently swaying. Though the men had advised him to build lower down 'deeper into the flat, Mr Blackstone, where you won't feel the winters so bad', he'd resisted them. He wanted to build high, near the straggly trees. He wanted to feel the bush at his back and the flats beneath. He was a Norfolk man, the son of a livestock auctioneer, whose clerk he'd been, travelling roads and farm tracks in all weathers. Winter held no terrors for him. And the chimney was well shaped and solid. Harriet and Lilian would be warm in the Cob House when the snows came – if the snows came. And whenever he looked out of the nicely crafted wooden windows, he would see the great sweep of land that belonged to him, the first land he had ever owned and for which he had paid a mere £1 an acre. In time – in not very much time at all – that land would be transformed. It would be fenced and planted with hedges and trees. He would dig out a pond for ducks and geese. Willows would lean towards the pond, as they leaned towards a Norfolk mere. The tussock grass would be ploughed up and the land sown with clover for the horses and wheat for the household. There would be a mill.

Joseph worked so hard on the Cob House that, in the hot nights, listening to the melancholy cry of the weka, he fell without difficulty into a stunned, dreamless sleep. He lay near the creek, rolled up in a striped blanket that smelled of camphor, with his head in the crook of his arm. He was thirty-five, a lean and stringy man with pale eyes. His hair was dark and his feet were large and narrow. Already, he'd formed the habit of stroking his sparse black beard when he closed his eyes.

The noise of the water usually woke him at dawn, but seldom before dawn, as if the river settled into a silent pool for all the hours of darkness and only gathered strength to start flowing again in the morning.

The men told Joseph that this particular creek had no name 'for the plain reason that no one has stopped here long enough to name it'.

So Joseph decided to call it 'Harriet's Creek' because he knew how much this would please his new wife. He imagined her sitting at the old mahogany table carted out from England on the *Albert* and writing to her father, the geography teacher, telling him how fast the water rushed over the stones, 'and don't you think this is very romantic of Joseph?'

After the time of my disgrace, I gave my wife a river.

Lilian wouldn't be happy about this, of course. Joseph knew that his mother would prefer to have the river named after her, to know herself to be at the centre of everything, even if this everything now consisted of a calico tent within a house made of mud. But in time, he told himself, once the pond was there and the willows, and the land was fenced and the animals began to thrive . . . then surely Lilian would become susceptible to the beauty of this new world? Surely, she would begin to feel that her only child had done the right thing? And, if she didn't, well at least he would break his back trying.

A determined bloody cockatoo, the men began to call him among themselves. And they told him cockatoo stories in the dusk, round their fires. 'You know a cockatoo can imitate a hawk, Mr Blackstone? He does it to scare the fowls. He does it for the fun of it, to see the fowls run away squawking! And it can laugh, too. Anyone tell you that? Fowls all scuttle away or drop dead from fear and old heartless cockatoo, he laughs like a hyena.'

Joseph smiled, because he was expected to smile, because he wanted to stay on good terms with these people who were helping him and teaching him the skills he needed to survive. But the word 'heartless' made him shiver. He drew closer to the fire. He clung to thoughts of Harriet, evoking as consolation not her silky hair or her strong body, but a single tooth of hers that showed and was not meant to show when she smiled. Without this flaw, this little ivory flaw in what he thought of as her impenetrable hardness, perhaps he would not have had the courage to marry her? It was the tooth which had given him hope, that here was a woman he would grow to love. And loving her as he would and living sensibly with her, without loathing and without damage, then he believed, his past would slowly vanish. He would be able to grow old without it, just as, if a man is careful, he can grow old without yearning.

The only thing he dreaded was that Harriet would pester him to father a child. He'd never said anything to her on this subject, but he hoped she sensed it: he hoped she understood that a child was not part of the bargain they'd made. She was a clever woman. He prayed she understood that it would have to be the two of them and Lilian and whatever they could make of that; the two of them and that until the end.

VI

So slowly the summer passed for Harriet Blackstone. In January, when temperatures in Christchurch were so high that

Lilian twice fainted on Mrs Dinsdale's stairs, buildings were rumoured to be collapsing all over the town. Some people said that the mechanics of construction were not sufficiently understood in New Zealand and that there could be an epidemic of collapse before the year was out.

Harriet examined the walls and ceiling of her room. She never heard them move or creak in the darkness. Though resin continued to bubble out of the boards, there was no other outward sign of any precariousness, but how was one to know – someone like her, who didn't understand the mechanics of construction – how was she to be sure the roof wouldn't fall down and crush her while she slept?

She went to McArthur Street and looked at a building that had fallen. She tried to imagine where, in which exact spot – through all the months of the building's existence – the earth had tugged and called and beckoned to the rafters. She knew that this was a fanciful, womanish kind of a thing to imagine, that the heavy earth tugged and called and beckoned to every single thing upon it for all eternity and in time every single thing would fall. Yet she found herself hoping that Joseph was paying attention to this in the building of the Cob House, that he had imagination enough to listen to the earth.

Joseph Blackstone. She didn't know him yet. She saw – what she had known from the first but had not particularly minded – that he was rather an ordinary man. She knew that they had almost passed each other by. And then, for no reason that she could determine, he had come back, hurried back in a stumbling way one autumn evening, as though he'd suddenly remembered what it was he wanted to say or do, as though part of him had been missing when he first met her and then he had rediscovered it.

He wooed her with dreams of escape. She sat on the hearth rug with her head on his knee and he described to her the paradise he would create on the other side of the world. It was his words that made her cling to him when he touched her. And, feeling the warmth of him and the smell of his clothes, which reminded her of the scent of tree bark, she saw how sick of her life as a governess she was, how weary of owning nothing and going nowhere and spending her days by other people's meagre fires. So she knew in a very short time that she was happy to go off with Joseph Blackstone, to buy a trousseau for a new world, to stare at the sky and imagine the altered constellations of a different hemisphere.

Barely time to have the wedding, though. Barely time to put on the ring. Barely time to lie in a tall bed while he did what he did with his hand over her face (so that she might not see it?) and withdrew just before he came to his pleasure. And then, in a frenzy of endeavour, in a kind of fury, he was running her from shop to shop, pulling out of his fusty pockets orders and measuring tapes and money. Boots, shawls, stockings, woollen dresses, and aprons: these workaday clothes appeared to be the currency of her marriage, not kisses – or not many – not whispered confidences, nor laughter.

But he went on talking about New Zealand and she went on listening and while she listened she liked to be lying close to him and feeling the rise and fall of his breath.

One night, he told her about the First People. They were known as the moa hunters. They killed the giant Moa Bird and lived off its flesh and built huts with its bones and went to sleep wrapped in its feathers. They hunted it to extinction and then looked around them in disbelief. They did not know how else to live, except from the Moa, and so they sickened and died. 'And this, Harriet,' said Joseph, 'teaches us a valuable lesson. We will not cling to familiar ways. We will imagine ourselves reborn over there. On the acres I am buying, everything will begin afresh.'

They were lying in his bedroom in Lilian's house and the darkness of Norfolk pressed on them at the half-open window. Harriet liked her new husband's use of the word 'reborn'. She took his hand and drifted into a dream of sleep, wrapped in the feathers of a brown bird.

When she returned to Mrs Dinsdale's after staring at the fallen building, Harriet examined her face in the mirror. Her hair was curly in the afternoon heat, her cheeks red and moist. She had not often looked quite like this, so wild and agitated and damp. But then, everything in her life was changing. Less than six months ago she had not known Joseph Blackstone; now she was his wife and bore his name. Somehow, like the earth that called to the breaking rafters, he had called to her and she had answered.

Though Lilian complained that it was 'too hot for singing', she went off with Mrs Dinsdale on a Wednesday evening to the recently founded Laura McPherson Glee Club.

The club had no premises of its own yet, but met in the store-room of a clothier's shop, where Mrs McPherson had been allowed to rearrange the piles of hat boxes and armoires of linen-wrapped coats and dresses 'in a more acoustically favourable way'. It was a dark space, cool as a church, into which a small upright piano had been squeezed. Laura McPherson walked round and round it, adjusting the position of everything, including the clothier's fire bucket and his ironing table. Then she dusted off her wide shelf of a bosom and stood before the assembled women and sang to them in a sweet, throaty contralto, 'Jesus, Hear My Song in the Afternoon'.

Lilian listened and was moved. She felt herself to be back 'in civilisation' and let out a long, melancholy sigh. She hoped her own voice would be considered good enough. She hoped that these women would befriend her as dear Mrs Dinsdale had done. She even dared for a moment to wonder whether they might intercede on her behalf with Joseph and say to him that really and truly a person of her age and background (she had always considered herself – the daughter of a vicar – superior to Roderick, the livestock auctioneer) could not be expected to set off into the hills or bushes or flats or whatever the wretched places were called, to play her lonely piano and sing, unheard, to the birds and the wind . . .

Then she remembered money. Almost everything that remained to her and to Joseph had been spent on their passage on the SS *Albert* and on the 'farm'. The rest would be eaten away, as though by weevils or dust-mites, by the dreary purchase of corn seed and poultry and pigs. There would be nothing left for her to live on in Christchurch. And to beg or to borrow, to stoop to any kind of charity, was beyond Lilian Blackstone. She had her pride. *Wulla.* It would go with her into the wilderness. It would be the one thing that nobody would take away.

All she could do for now was to pop a throat pastille into her mouth and join in the handing out of music sheets. She put on her spectacles and saw that the first piece they were going to attempt was 'Hold High the Fiery Banner'. She remembered singing this in Cromer. It had been a time of storms. She had seen the sea rise up in a grey wall and come towards her.

As the women formed themselves into a smart line and began the difficult two-part harmony of 'Fiery Banner', Harriet opened the door of Lilian's room and went in.

She stood on the Persian rug and looked around. By Lilian's bed was a pastel drawing of a child wearing a dress. Harriet picked this up and saw from the dark curls and the little frown on the face that the child was Joseph. He was sitting in a large armchair and his baby fingers clutched its padded arms, as though the huge chair were a carriage, moving joltingly through some precarious, new landscape. She replaced the picture on Lilian's night table beside a bottle of eau-de-Cologne and a linen handkerchief-sachet. Spread out tenderly – as if for someone else, not for herself – on Lilian's bed was a white woollen shawl in which, at night, she liked to wind herself. Harriet touched a corner of it and smelled her mother-in-law; a mixture of rosewater and something like peppermint, a sharp smell which you knew you would not be able to tolerate for long.

Harriet sat down on the bed. The room was very tidy. Everything seemed to be in its rightful place, including, on the far wall, a palm cross stuck into the matchboarding with an unobtrusive nail. Near to this was a framed sketch of the Market Cross at Parton Magna, Norfolk.

On the front of the wardrobe hung Lilian's second-best bonnet, its ribbons creased where she'd tied them sternly under her chin. And, looking at these things, Harriet thought how hard it is to get old and to nail up a fragile cross on your wall and stare at a little boy in a dress and not know . . . not know what time remains or whether the man who was once the child is going to take care of you or not . . .

Poor Lilian.

Poor unhappy Lilian.

Harriet sat very still and prayed that, before her own life began to move towards such an uncertain ending, she would have seen or known at least one extraordinary and unforgettable thing.

VII

It was already autumn when Joseph returned. Autumn in April.

He looked thin and the skin of his face was lined and brown. But he was triumphant: the Cob House was built. There was a paddock for the donkey and hen-houses made of rushes and wire. The evening clouds over the flats were the colour of red clay.

Lilian wept. Some part of her had believed the house would never have an existence except in Joseph's mind. But now it did. She took out a clean lace handkerchief ironed by Mrs Dinsdale and held it, still neatly folded, to her face. Joseph stared at her in dismay. Then he attempted to put his arm round her shoulders, but she pushed him away.

Lilian thought of Roderick's grey marble grave at Parton and his name on it so blackly chiselled, so resistant to the sunshine and the rain.

Harriet left the room and waited for Joseph to come to her. Her heart was on fire with the red-clay clouds and the white Cob House waiting for her in its shelter of stringy trees. When, after some time, his hand crept over her face, she removed it. For Harriet wanted to see him now, in his nakedness, in his fussy strivings – her husband who had built a house on the edge of the world and survived. She brought his face down to hers and he kissed her like a stranger, a hard, dry kiss. Then, just as he was about to withdraw from her, he whispered to her that he'd named the river Harriet's Creek.

'Yes,' she said. 'My creek. Mine!' And she clung to him.

She wanted to leave for the farm straightaway. Drays to cart the furniture and Lilian's china could be hired without difficulty. But Lilian refused. She wouldn't even consider it. The Laura McPherson Glee Club were giving their first public concert on the nineteenth of April and she had given her word she would participate, for there was one high note in 'Fiery Banner' which only her voice, her voice alone in the fledgling company, could veritably reach.

'One note,' said Harriet to Joseph. 'Are we going to sacrifice a season's planting for one note?'

He told her gently there was little they could plant in autumn, that for the first winter they must live on what they could take with them – tea, flour, biscuits, pilchards, sugar and hams – and on mutton that they would buy from the Orchard Run, the biggest sheep-run on the Okuku flats. He also admitted that he needed to rest. His feet were blistered and his hands cut and raw. His neck ached from lying in the crook of his arm.

So they lingered at Mrs Dinsdale's Rooms for another three weeks, making lists: twenty-five laying hens and a cock, one dairy cow, a donkey, oats, corn seed, saplings, fence posts, wire . . .

They were together in everything now, scribbling and counting, feverishly bargaining, sifting, rejecting and acquiring. While Lilian's singing voice, in defiance of its coming separation from the edge of the civilised world, seemed suddenly to gain a new, maddening perfection, Joseph and Harriet walked away out of earshot of it, arm-in-arm from one end of the town to the other. They were recognised, now, in some of the Christchurch stores, the tall Joseph Blackstone and his tall, excitable wife.

Harriet remembered the frenzied buying of clothes in England and told Joseph how much she preferred this, this 'farm business', and how, at last, she could visualise their future. She was so proud of him, she said. She looked at him with a new feeling of desire. Running her long-fingered hands over the blade of a scythe in McKinley's Hardware Store, she said: 'Joseph, we should not let this life of ours merely arrive and then slip away.'

Slip away? What did she mean by this?

Oh, she didn't know, exactly, she said. But she thought there should be something – *a marker.* 'It will have to have a purpose,' was what she decided to say.

Joseph thought that he would strive to find 'purpose' in every day of it. In the dawns which would arrive at their backs, threading light between the blue-green leaves; in the never-ending rush and swirl of Harriet's Creek; even in the cold nights when they would hear the flightless birds calling, calling from their holes and hideaways. He would strive and he hoped he would succeed.

But then he stared at Harriet, at her face mirrored in the polished blade of the scythe. Was she talking about something else? He waited, holding himself still and straight, disguising a sudden, boiling-up of pain in his chest.

'Well?' she asked.

'Of course it will have ... purpose ...' he stammered.

'And,' she said lightly, turning to him and touching his arm, 'after us?'

This was it. The question he feared. Now it was here and would be here always.

'After us?'

She laid her face, just for a moment, against his shoulder. There was a smell of dust on him in this store, of cinders or ash, of something burned and gone.

'Don't you think there could be a child?'

Now, more than ever, he tried to hold himself tall, never to let her see that he longed to squirm away, to knead the area of his heart until it no longer hurt him. He tried to swallow, but his spittle stayed in his mouth and he had to tug out a handkerchief and wipe his lips.

'Harriet, I had never ...' he began.

'Never what?'

'I had never imagined that. I always thought your age –'

'I'm thirty-four, Joseph.'

'Exactly.'

She could have told him how profusely she bled each month, how so many wretched rags had to be soaped and slapped and rinsed and hung out where they wouldn't be seen. But she didn't know him well enough to talk about this. She let go of the scythe and walked on down the long row of bright implements stacked against McKinley's makeshift walls, and he followed her at a distance.

Beauty's Coat

I

Harriet knew that Joseph lay awake at night. In their calico room which trembled, she heard him sigh.

'What is it?' she kept asking.

He couldn't tell her that he thought the house was in the wrong place, couldn't possibly say that he'd been too stubborn to take advice from the men who had helped him. Because he needed to win her love and respect. In these lay his salvation.

He said only that he was worried about Lilian, who, when she stirred the washing in the heavy cauldron, had begun talking angrily to the underwear. She asked it why one soaping and rinsing couldn't suffice for a longer time, why it 'took dirt so easily'. When she hung it out to dry, she beat it with a wooden paddle. At other times, tired perhaps from scolding something which never answered her, she sat still and absent in her chair, rolling a darning egg in her palm.

'We must do more for her,' Joseph said.

'What more?' asked Harriet.

He didn't know. He wanted Harriet to tell *him*, to light on something. Women understood each other, or so he assumed, for someone must understand them and he knew that he did not. Only that they longed for things. And their longing seemed to be so tenacious that it could lead you to behaviour you had never ever imagined yourself capable of. It could destroy you ...

But it wasn't difficult to understand what his mother longed for. She made no effort to conceal it: she longed to be away from here. And Joseph saw, in the way she scowled at the calico walls and looked pityingly at her familiar pieces of furniture stranded like embarrassed guests on the clay floors, that she didn't even bother to plead with this longing; she just let it be.

'I don't know what more,' he said. 'Except that you might be a closer companion to her. I mean that you might be indoors with her, instead of out ...'

'Joseph,' Harriet said, 'I have spent my life indoors. What do you imagine a governess does all day but sit and read and write and breathe the indoor air?'

'I know. But I worry that Lilian is alone too much.'

'When my vegetable garden is planted. Then, I will be with her more often. But you know that she could come outside and work with me if she chose.'

Joseph said nothing, only turned over on the hard bed. Harriet lay quite still beside him. Above her, a soft rain made the tin roof gently sing.

They had a milk cow, but no horse. Joseph said they would not be able to afford a horse until the following year, when they would have wheat and corn and young animals to sell. So the plough was yoked to a donkey, heavily blinkered, and Joseph and the donkey walked up and down and back and forth all day and the tussock grass was slowly lifted and turned in wavering lines.

Lilian said: 'I thought a field was meant to be a straight and square thing.'

'I am trying to make it as straight and square as I can,' said Joseph.

'Well,' said Lilian, 'it looks a drunken shape to me. I'm glad that we have no neighbours to remark upon its peculiarity.'

Joseph allowed himself to smile. He reminded his mother that 'everything we're undertaking here, we're undertaking for the first time, but slowly, we shall learn'.

'I am not at all certain,' said Lilian, 'that I shall ever learn to cook on this range.' And she gave the old iron cooker, on which she was boiling a kettle, a spiteful kick. Fired with smouldering lignite, the range didn't seem eager to bake the loaves that Lilian put into it, only to steam them. They barely rose to the top of the tin and could achieve nothing better than the consistency of suet. Slices cut from them left a disappointing film of moisture on the knife. In Parton Magna, Lilian's bread had been crusty and ample and irresistible to Roderick Blackstone, who had adored the way it scratched the roof of his mouth, and had devoured great quantities of it, spread with beef dripping, on the morning that he died.

'In this godforsaken place,' said Lilian, 'everything is worse.'

Harriet hurried away. She hurried to the back of the Cob House, where her garden waited. There was nothing there yet, only a rectangle of tilled earth, where birds she didn't recognise parleyed in the early mornings when the sun rose over the valley and the beech leaves glinted like oil. Slowly, she was picking the stones from the soil, dividing the ground into squares with planks of totara pine, fencing it with tin. 'A stone wall round a plot of these dimensions', Joseph had told her, 'is pure make-believe. Have you any idea how long it took three men to build a stone chimney?'

Harriet had imagined the stone wall, but it could wait. She painted the tin white, nailed it to sapling stems. There was no gate. The tin enclosed the garden all the way round. Whenever Joseph and Lilian came out to see it, they stood watching Harriet from the other side of the wall, as though she were a prisoner they were not allowed to visit. They saw her working with her hair tied up in a kerchief, stooping over her planting, her apron bunched full of her seed potatoes, her boots clotted with mud.

'Is she happy doing that?' asked Lilian.

'Yes,' replied Joseph. 'She is.'

Lilian sniffed. 'It looks like convict work to me,' she announced.

The creek came snaking down behind Harriet's garden, noisy after a fresh, rattling the stones, carrying with it stems of red matipo and black beech from the high bush. Harriet had never touched nor tasted water of such icy sweetness. When the afternoon dusk fell and she saw the first glimmer of Lilian's lamps at the Cob House windows, Harriet stood at the creek's edge, listening to her new world. If the wind had died a little, she might hear an owl far away in the trees, or the mournful *kooo-li kooo-li* of the weka, which Joseph had taught her to recognise. Sometimes, she would spread out her muddy apron and kneel on this, rinsing her hands, then scooping water into her mouth. Often, she stayed here, with her face close to the water, for so long that when she stood up she discovered that an absolute darkness had come on.

II

In her first letter to her father, Henry Salt, Harriet wrote:

> *We eat mutton and more mutton: legs of mutton, mutton stews and chops, mutton pies and pasties. I think we smell like sheep.*

Then, she told him about the cow, whom she and Joseph had named Beauty

> *because her nature is so nice and her eyes are like pools of amber and the curls on her head appear quite as though they had been set in curl-papers.*

Beauty had no stable or barn. But from an old rug and some lengths of twine, Lilian had manufactured a coat for her. This had been the one task Lilian Blackstone had done with something like enthusiasm and now it was a strange and tender sight, to see a cow wandering about wearing a human garment as it munched the yellow hay.

When the sun shone and they had forgotten to take off Beauty's coat, steam rose through the wool. The smell of Beauty, Harriet thought, was almost as delectable as that of any person she had ever known and she imagined that her own children might smell like this, of milk and earth and warm wool.

Milking Beauty was her favourite task. The cow would stay perfectly still, while Harriet's hands, which were red and rough from her work in the garden, tugged at the warm, rubbery teats.

Only Beauty's flank twitched from time to time and her curly head turned and her heavy-lashed eyes stared into the sunset or the rain.

Sometimes at night, wearing her coat, Beauty lay down by the Cob House wall and Harriet could hear her breathing. To Henry Salt she wrote: *My nights are full of sighing; the wind and Beauty's breath and Joseph's anxiety.* But she knew that he, the geography teacher, would understand what this sentence was: not a complaint, just part of her evocation of her world, so that he would be able to use her letter like a map, to see and hear her in her new landscape. And at the end of the letter she drew for him pictures of objects she particularly liked: her hoe, the donkey-plough, the milking-stool, the butter churn. Of the churn she said:

> *Waiting for the butter gives me such excitement. The extraordinary change of colour! I think I have always been enthralled by any process by which one thing is transformed into something else. I can understand the obsession of the alchemists of the Ancient World.*

Her scrapbook was beginning, very slowly, to fill. In between the heavy pages were leaves of gossamer-fine paper, almost transparent, and sometimes Harriet looked at her entries through the paper, as though they were already almost vanished and part of the past. For this was what the book was, she knew: a catalogue of the passing of time. Already the maple leaf that had floated down on to the SS *Albert* in the middle of the Tasman Sea was faded and brittle, the Chinese tea label very slightly yellowed, and the Queen Victoria stamps smudged with dust or dirt of some kind, as though they'd endured a long journey on a letter.

On the third page of the scrapbook, Harriet added a square of calico, labelled *A piece of our wall,* a ground plan of her vegetable garden, a spiky green frond from a ti-ti palm, a brown weka feather, and a curl from Beauty's head. She glued them in with minute drops of Lilian's china glue. She noticed that near her, on the dresser, a Spode tea-service was slowly piecing itself back together again, shard by shard.

Remembering her old life as a governess, she wondered what she would have collected into a scrapbook across twelve years: curls, perhaps – not from the head of a cow who looked so sweetly foolish draped in a rug in the New Zealand winter – but from the heads of her English pupils, curls that darkened as they grew and were sent away to school and forgot her; drawings and pages of writing they were proud of; pieces of knitting or squares of cross-stitch they had made.

And perhaps a solitary banknote, a ten-shilling note, given to her by Mr Melchior Gable, to be spent on gloves she was supposed to wear when she visited his bank on the occasion of its summer open day. On this day, visitors were shown a fine collection of weights and measures, a display of Roman coins and early examples of the 'Gable Safe-and-Sound', a patented brass lock which thieves were supposedly incapable of breaking. But Harriet hadn't been among the visitors. The ten-shilling note had never been alchemised into a pair of gloves. Mr Gable's love-letters to her had stood in a pile, hidden inside a cracked washing jug – hidden from the world and from Harriet herself, who had no wish to read them again and would shortly feed them to the fire.

She had tried to return the ten-shilling note to Melchior Gable. She had sent it round to the bank with her handwritten refusal of his proposal of marriage. But it had come back. She had asked her father to post it to him and he had done so, but once again it returned. So she kept it in a box and never spent it. She used to look at it sometimes – her alternative life, the land where she had not gone. And then, on the day she married Joseph Blackstone, she burned it.

III

When the donkey needed rest, Joseph worked at digging his pond.

He thought of the pond as soundless, a place that the wind would barely touch and around which the distant bush would soon seed itself – if only the seeds were not blown away.

Though he'd imagined Norfolk willows, he'd be perfectly content with cabbage trees and manuka scrub.

He sited the pond in a dip in the fold of hills. A long, curving trench would be carved out to let water into the pond from Harriet's Creek and then out again by some means that Joseph couldn't precisely envisage. He found himself wishing that he were more of an engineer.

Lilian came out of the house, wrapped in a shawl, and stood watching Joseph. The ground was as hard as wood. Lilian stared at her son's booted foot on the shovel, heard the repeated knock of the hob-nails against the shovel's edge. Though he was tall, in the surrounding panorama of yellow grass he appeared oddly insubstantial, almost as if he were a figure her mind had conjured. Perhaps, when she next looked at him, he would no longer be there. She asked herself whether she had ever really *seen* him or understood who he was.

For how was it possible that the Joseph she thought she'd known – from baby boy in a hand-sewn dress to gawky man with raven hair and a commanding voice – now believed that his future and hers could be lived out here in this desert of grass? What had put this preposterous idea into his mind?

It was a day of light wind with a sun that came and went and showers that seemed to fall straight out of a brilliant rainbow. For the first time in a long while, Lilian raised her face towards the horizon. She liked rainbows, for they behaved as God had told them to behave: 'I do set my bow in the cloud and it shall be for a token of a covenant between me and the earth.' But Lilian examined this one critically, as though she believed a New Zealand rainbow might somehow be disobedient to God's law. She counted the colours, verified the precision of the arc, qualified the brightness. She barely listened as Joseph began to describe the pond to her; she was intent on the rainbow. It was too big, she decided after a while: in its vastness it had no humility. She distantly heard Joseph say that when spring came and green shoots snaked up through the mud at the edge of the water, the mallard and the native blue-duck would leave the creek and come to swim in his pond, in sweet domestic circles. But she felt obliged to remark. 'Your pond will not necessarily behave as English ponds do,' she said.

Joseph turned a tired face towards her. 'What do you mean?' he asked.

'I mean,' said Lilian, 'that nothing here is ever quite as one has imagined it.'

As she walked away towards the Cob House, Lilian remembered that she was, at least, working on a possible plan of escape. The plan was tentative and far too dependent on unverifiable factors, but it was a plan, and that was something. It was important in life, she told herself, always *to have a plan*. She should have planned for the eventuality of Roderick's death, but she had not and now she had lost her old life and the little daily diet of hope that had gone with it.

Sometimes, when she thought about it as generously as her mind would allow, she admitted that she could understand that, if you were young, as Joseph still was, if you had never attached yourself to anything too fiercely, this vast new empty country with its violent weather and its cheap land might seem to promise you something. She knew Joseph imagined himself, six or seven years from now, as the thriving owner of a big farm and a house built of stone and timber, with a verandah like Mrs Dinsdale's and a hammock where he would dream. To be fair to him, he had never pretended that the first months would not be hard and he had married the right wife for this kind of hardness. Somewhere inside her, Lilian admired her son's faith and Harriet's tenacity. Together, she thought, the two of them are all sinew and bone and obstinate will and if these things count for something, then they will succeed.

But she believed that it would be far better for them to be doing all this arduous work alone. For them, there was a future here and Lilian knew that most of what Man does, moment to moment, is for his imagined future, for the coming time, in which he will be happier than in time present. Merely, Joseph and Harriet had ignored the fact that Lilian, in this place, at the age she was, was so devoid of a future that she might as well be dead. Days and weeks and years would pass without an audience for her singing. The winds would scream in her head and muddle her thinking. Her china would break again along the same cracks she had glued together. Her spirit would fail.

So she tried to piece together her plan.

The next time Joseph set out in the donkey dray for Christchurch to buy supplies, she would send with him a letter to Mrs Dinsdale. She would explain to Lily Dinsdale that she owned a few items of value, inherited from her mother, the vicar's wife. They included a fine ivory fan, a tortoiseshell brush-and-comb set with a matching manicure case, a rope of pearls, a ruby brooch and several rings. These she proposed to pawn (she supposed that there were pawnbrokers in Christchurch because in any new place settlers will be at the mercy of seasonal poverty) and, with the money raised, to rent her old room at Mrs Dinsdale's for the few weeks that it would take for her to find some kind of employment in the town.

Though she had never worked at any 'outside job' in her life, she did not see this as an insurmountable obstacle. She wondered whether she could be taken on at the clothier's where the Laura McPherson Glee Club had their meetings. She was gifted at sorting and ordering. And it was perfectly clear from her observation of the clothier's piles of boxes that this business was in a muddle. She didn't know how much a person of her standing might be paid for this kind of work, but she supposed it might just be enough to keep her in Christchurch. And that was where she would remain. She wouldn't attempt to cross the vast, black seas to England. Her house in Parton Magna was gone anyway, sold to pay Roderick's gaming debts. The idea of renting rooms in England made her weep, somehow. And yet, in Christchurch, she would be near the shore. She would know what ships were coming and going from the Old World. While she established a bearable routine with Lily Dinsdale and Laura McPherson and their circle of friends, the possibility of a return to England would be constantly within her sight.

Lilian went to her room, which wasn't a proper room, of course, with proper privacy, but merely a kind of tent within the house, from which she could hear everything – everything – that went on inside it.

She took out her fan, her brush and comb, her manicure set and her jewellery and looked at them. It was an ugly fact of the world that when you tried to buy anything of value it cost more than you had imagined and when you tried to sell it, its value had always mysteriously leaked away. Where had it leaked to? Lilian wished she lived in a society where people knew the answers to such questions.

Laid out on her bed in this tent in the Cob House, Lilian's little valuables, on which her plan depended, suddenly appeared anachronistic, like a shrine to some deity who demanded the strangest sacrifices from you and then fled away. She re-arranged the pearls, the fan, the hairbrush and comb, the manicure set, but they still looked out of place and oddly worthless. For a long time, Lilian stared at them; then she felt such a deep weariness come over her that she pushed every-thing under her pillow and lay down on the hard mattress and fell instantly asleep. It was the middle of the afternoon and Joseph and Harriet were where they always were, out under the sky, and Lilian knew, as she closed her eyes, that she was probably gone completely from their minds.

IV

One evening at the beginning of July, the wind changed. A sou'wester began to howl, bringing with it a crawling, rolling mist, soundless and cold.

When Harriet went out to feed the hens, calling to them in the white gloom, she noticed a feeling of great weight in the air, as though it was now the sky which tugged at the earth. When she came into the Cob House, she said to Joseph: 'Something is going to happen.'

Joseph stood at the door. He felt the mist furl over him and shuddered. He fetched Beauty from the pasture and put on her coat. While he tied it on, the animal lowed at the strangeness of the air. And Joseph could hear the donkey braying in its compound. Not for the first time, Joseph felt the solitude and worry of the ignorant settler, who isn't able to read the signals in the wind. He wondered whether he should hitch the donkey to the dray and set out for the Orchard Run, where they would tell him what was coming in on the sou'wester, but he was afraid of losing his way and being overtaken by the night.

They ate a supper of mutton stew with carrots and some of Lilian's brittle cocoa biscuits and all the while they could hear the cow and the donkey complaining out there in the dark. 'I often wonder,' said Lilian, as she cleared away the cutlery, 'why God gave the animals such ugly voices.'

In the night, the snow began to fall.

It fell stealthily, while the three people slept, piling up on the tin roof of the Cob House, drifting before the wind on to the windows, sealing up the door. Though Joseph and Harriet woke at dawn, they turned over and closed their eyes when they saw the darkness in their room, which they mistook for the continuing night. Lilian, who, more and more, was developing a passion for sleeping – a positive ardour for it, as if sleep were opium – also drifted back into her dreams, where she often found herself on stage in one of the great opera houses of the world.

When Harriet woke again at last, as the roof began to bend and creak under the weight of snow, it took her a moment to understand what was happening. She woke Joseph and they stood in their nightshirts staring at the strange grey light of the room. They dressed hurriedly, rubbed their hands uselessly on the insides of the blind windows. They went to the door and struggled to move it, but it opened only a bare inch. They listened for the sounds of their animals and heard nothing.

Joseph's thought was: *I escaped a coffin in England. Now, Nature builds another one round me.*

But there was that inch of light outside the door. He had no tools inside the house, but he had his hands and his ingenuity.

Lilian was up now and Joseph instructed her and Harriet to build up the lignite fire in the range and put water on to heat. He would melt the snow that had drifted against the door. He prayed that there had been enough warmth left in the chimney during the night to keep it from being sealed up by the snow. He took up a stick and with this began working to move the door: two inches, three inches, four . . .

The lignite refused to burn. It smouldered like damp turf and in moments the low room filled with smoke. Harriet and Lilian, covering their mouths with their aprons, came to the door to take breaths of freezing air. The cold and dark in the Cob House seemed to be increasing all the time. Lilian lit the oil lamps. She and Harriet worked on at the fire in the range, riddling out the charred clinker, trying to coax a flame with sticks, a minute flame which flared and immediately went out.

They persevered, while Joseph scraped and kicked against the high drift against the door, until Lilian was seized by a choking cough so violent, she thought she might fall dead on to the earthen floor. Outside, through the slowly widening gap beyond the door, her bulging, weeping eyes could see that the snow was still falling: fat snowflakes, sticky as porridge, like none she'd ever seen. She cursed silently as she struggled for breath in the smoky tomb of a room.

Fetching water for her, Harriet suddenly understood how foolish all of this was. Three minds at work and all of them had overlooked an obvious thing.

Harriet handed the cup of water to Lilian, then snatched up the heavy iron cover of the range and slammed it down on the smoking lignite. She went to one of the windows. The snow on the sill was piled to seven or eight inches, but the window opened wide enough for Harriet to stretch out a hand and start pushing the snow away. She leaned out and looked at a white world in which nothing was visible, nothing moved except the snowflakes, so soundlessly, yet in a kind of hectic clamour, like a mute gathering of people anxious to reach some already crowded destination and find some last remaining space.

The smoke in the room began to disperse, eddying between the window and the door. Tugging her shawl round her, Lilian sat down on a chair and wiped her mouth. She stared first at Harriet, who was hitching up her skirt and clambering up on to the window sill, then down at the cold floor, on which she had just managed not to die.

Harriet climbed out of the window and jumped down into the snow.

The snow came over the top of her boots and melted against the warmth of her legs, and the pain of the icy snow-melt on her feet was fierce.

She began calling to Beauty.

Joseph struggled to follow her through the small window,

folding and unfolding his long limbs, snagging his coat on a splinter, cursing as he heard it tear. He uncovered a shovel propped against the wall, and he and Harriet began to dig a pathway – with the shovel and with their hands – round the Cob House towards the door. New falling snow began to cover the path again as soon as their backs were turned. And the weight of the snow was like mud or like sand, its appearance of lightness a deception.

Harriet's hair hung loose and there was sweat on her head and bright colour in her face, but her expression was determined. From far away, they heard a bray so they knew that at least the donkey was alive, but no other sound came out of the silence. Resting for a moment, Harriet said to Joseph: 'Even if Beauty is lost, we will go on.'

'We will go on, Harriet,' he said, but he didn't pause in the arduous work and Harriet saw that this was the kind of man he was: that once he was embarked on a thing, he wouldn't rest.

She began shovelling again. No snow in England had ever fallen as fast and as stealthily as this. And coming on the unexpected south-westerly wind, a wind they were unable to understand, it had drifted almost waist-high against the south wall of the Cob House – as though it had been falling for a week without end.

'Beauty!' Harriet kept calling, for the cow was obedient, and always tried to reach them when they shouted into the vast emptiness of the air. 'Beauty!' And then listening in the white silence for the sound of her lowing. But it didn't come.

They had reached the end of the west wall now. Harriet was thirsty and held a handful of snow in her mouth and let it melt against her teeth.

Inside the Cob House, they could hear Lilian coughing. Then, as they turned and began to dig their way towards the door, Harriet saw Beauty's coat – a smudge of tartan just visible on a mound beside the front door.

'There she is, Joseph!'

They began to wade through the drifts, thigh-deep, Joseph leading, trying to clear a path for his wife, towards the mound that was Beauty, who had simply done what she often did in the cold nights, come to the Cob House wall and lain in the shelter of it, seeking some warmth.

Harriet thought: I used to hear her breathing, but last night I heard nothing. The snow smothered every sound.

They uncovered Beauty's head. Furiously, they cleared the frozen snow from her nostrils, slapped her neck, put their faces close to hers, giving her their own breath. But the flesh of her muzzle, flesh that had been warm, supple, drooling, had become hard and set. Her amber eyes had rolled backwards under the long-lashed lids.

Harriet knelt in the snow, tears brimming, one hand helplessly tugging at the ridiculous tartan coat. What she felt, more strongly than anything else, was admiration for an animal who could die so slowly, so patiently, without a sound.

The Orchard Run

I

Toby Orchard was a big man who had always felt confined and hot and unhappy in his job in the City of London.

A voice inside had called to Toby night and day: *Set me free, set me free, set me free.* As his girth expanded and the buttons of his finely tailored coats kept bursting off, his dreams of owning his own horizon became more and more ardent. His brown eyes restlessly examined the sooty roofs and spires of Threadneedle Street and London Wall and found them fearful. He longed to ride strong, unbreakable horses and shoot guns and shout at dogs under a monumental sky. He thought he would die of this longing, if he did not satisfy it.

He set sail for New Zealand in 1856, with his heiress wife, Dorothy, and they lost no time in buying land and stock, as much as they could acquire, and taking on the labour they needed. They put in so many miles of fence posts, they could no longer remember where the fence had begun or where it ended. On this part of the Okuku flats, all that could be heard above the sighing of the wind was the bleating of Orchard sheep. Toby thought of his land as a continent. Acres of tussock grass were ploughed up and sown with clover for his horses, which seemed to spend their days galloping in wild, unknowable circles, stopping only to sniff and nibble at the succulent clover when the moon came up and glimmered on it and the stillness of the night let them rest.

Toby and Dorothy Orchard built a house of surprising beauty out of the materials to hand: totara pine from the bush, slate from the gullies, lime wash from a hand-hewn quarry. Saplings of oak and maple, willow and poplar had been hauled across the miles of flat and planted in the wet seasons, and had flourished, and the earth around Orchard House had become cool and shady and kingfishers nested there.

Inside, the place was grander and more comfortable than its lime-washed wooden exterior suggested. The stone fireplaces, in which scented apple wood was burned, had been carved with rough approximations of the Orchard family crest. All Toby and Dorothy's wedding gifts – mahogany dressers and dressing-mirrors, Caroline day-beds and candle sconces, Regency silver-ware and fine French and German porcelain – had endured the same kind of journey as Lilian Blackstone's ill-fated tea-service and survived to embellish the large rooms. A servant whose name was Jane, but whom the Orchards idiosyncratically addressed as Janet – perhaps to make her particular to them? – kept things polished and neat. At Christmas time, Dorothy Orchard decorated the walls with ferns and made honey-coloured candles from beeswax, while Toby ordered geese to be killed and plucked.

'Our world,' Dorothy would whisper as, one by one, she lit the Christmas candles. 'Our world, our world, our *new* world.'

They were not alone in it. They had a son called Edwin, whom they had almost lost to a different world.

In the summer of 1856, Edwin Orchard had been lying in his rushwork cradle on the verandah of Orchard House. A hot, dry wind was blowing, bending the newly planted saplings, tugging at the sheets on the washing line and sending sudden swirls of dust into the air. Baby Edwin's Maori nurse, Pare, was watching over the cradle, but, little by little, her attention wandered from it and went towards the dust and the suffering trees. It seemed to Pare that the invisible god of the forest was close by and she was unable to stop herself from shivering. She felt light-headed, confused, as though the wind had entered her skull. She blinked and rubbed her eyes. The sun glinted on a nail at the verandah's edge and Pare was staring at this shining nail when she saw, at the edge of her vision, a green creature come scuttling towards her.

Pare screamed. She stood up, and, as though flayed by the wind, she went flying into the house, with Edwin in his cradle quite forgotten. She shut herself in the kitchen, stuffing towels into the crack between the door and the floor. Her mind filled with visions of the ngārara, the giant hot-tongued reptile which the Maoris told stories about and which had often crept into her dreams. She imagined this creature following her into the house and pinioning her beneath him and she knew that to be raped by the ngārara was the most terrible fate a woman could suffer.

Pare put her face in her hands. She could still hear the violence of the wind. It rattled the kitchen shutters and howled in the rafters overhead. And she thought now that this what the wind had heralded – the coming of the ngārara to the Orchard Run. She could not go back on to the verandah. She would have called for Toby Orchard to come and kill the ngārara with one of his shotguns, but she knew that he was out on the flats, miles away. Nor were Dorothy and Janet in the house, but out in Dorothy's carriage, taking oatcakes and tomato chutney to the vicar at Rangiora. Pare didn't know what she could do except to stay locked in the kitchen until somebody came home and saved her.

Meanwhile, the wind altered its direction just enough to begin to rock baby Edwin's cradle. Edwin Orchard always swore that he could remember this, the sudden marvellous see-sawing of the rush cradle in the southerly wind. And then, like a ngārara picking up a human girl, the wind scooped him up – baby and cradle and little embroidered coverlet – and hurled him off the verandah and turned him upside-down on to the parched front lawn.

He could never remember this momentary flight of his, nor his landing, nor the time that followed. He lay without moving for almost an hour, until Dorothy and Janet found him, with his little head lying in the dust. Dorothy wrapped him in her skirts and carried him inside the house, where Pare was locked in the kitchen. Dorothy could feel Edwin's heart still beating, but he wouldn't move nor open his eyes.

She laid him in her bed. Janet was sent back to Rangiora to fetch Dr Pettifer. He told Dorothy that none of Edwin's limbs was broken but that he couldn't say whether the baby would live or die. 'He is elsewhere,' was all he could pronounce, 'he has gone away from the here-and-now and may never return.'

That evening, Toby Orchard conducted a lizard hunt. In his fury and sorrow at what had happened, he shot at everything that moved or rustled within thirty yards of the house. He showed Pare the bloodied remains of a green gecko. Then he sent her away. He let her take water and food and a little money in her bundle of possessions, but he felt no mercy for her. He didn't care where she went or what became of her. He would have liked to have given her a whipping.

Edwin Orchard woke up five days later.

For a year, he seemed weakened by what had happened, his face pale and his eyes peculiarly large. But then he started to become like any other boy, except that he always wanted to be rocked and never grew out of it. At eight years old, he would still climb on to his mother's knee and say: 'Rock me, Mama. Rock me like the wind.'

II

When the snow melted in the warm winter sunshine that succeeded it, it was to the Orchard Run that Harriet Blackstone travelled.

She and Joseph had looked at what had happened – the loss of Beauty and of almost all their hens, the donkey grown thin and tormented by coughing, the tin roof of the Cob House buckled and leaking – and seen their own responsibility in these disasters, their own ignorance.

'We're fools,' said Joseph. 'We're blunderers. We're geese.'

He thought in his panic and pessimism that they wouldn't survive the winter. It was Lilian, with her belief that only the well-to-do could succeed in the world, who suggested the journey to Orchard House. Drying Beauty's tartan coat by the range, so that it could be put on to the suffering donkey, she sniffed and said: 'The only people who will set you straight are the Orchards. You will have to go cap-in-hand to them.'

Cap-in-hand? Joseph thought that all of that had been left behind in England. He'd seen how the squires of Norfolk had looked down on his father, the livestock auctioneer, and how few of them had bothered to attend his funeral or even send a condolence letter. He rounded on Lilian and snapped: 'I am never again going *cap-in-hand* to any living soul!'

'Well,' retorted Lilian. 'Then you are more of a fool than I took you for. *Wulla.*'

That night, in their calico room, Harriet took Joseph in her arms. She said she had always wanted to visit the Orchards so that she could see what grew in their vegetable plot and learn how they irrigated it in summer. She reminded Joseph that Dorothy Orchard, virtually alone in a world of men, was a woman who might enjoy discussing with her how to make a carrot cake or poach an eel.

It was a long time before Joseph said anything. On the edge of sleep, he muttered: 'You are not travelling all those miles alone.'

'Yes I am, my dear,' replied Harriet, wide awake. 'The donkey and I will go at a very slow trot, taking the cart so that I can return with some milk. We shall rest there for a day and a night, or a little longer. I will see what has been planted on the edge of the Orchards' pond.'

She travelled almost due south. When she reached the Ashley River, she stopped and stared at the hectic, jade-green water. A raft made of kanuka trunks, worked with ropes and pulleys, took carts and passengers across the Ashley, and this contraption was waiting there, under the charge of a ferryman, chewing tobacco and spitting into the water.

The ferryman saw Harriet hesitating. 'Bring him on, Miss! Bring him on!' he shouted. So Harriet tried to lead the terrified donkey to the water's edge, where the raft fretted at its mooring. But the donkey wouldn't go on. He attempted to rear up between the shafts of the cart. He brayed to the sky.

'Cover his head!' yelled the ferryman. So Harriet took off her cloak and tied it round the animal's face and thought that in this way he would go on, but blind as he was, he could feel the cold of the river and the tilt of the raft and again he tried to rear up and the cart tipped and almost fell and the ferryman swore and one of the shafts slammed into Harriet's elbow.

Trying not to cry out with pain, Harriet turned the donkey and led him in a circle on the dry bank, stroking his neck under the cloak and trying to soothe him with human words. He started coughing and she felt him shivering and some of his fear passed into her and she began to feel cold, but she had to bring him back to the river and this time the ferryman loped off the raft and helped her to pull the animal on, keeping his head low so that he wouldn't rear and trying all the while to steady the cart.

And so the donkey had a footing at last and Harriet held tight to the animal's neck, while the ferryman, always chewing, with his jaw muscles moving and twitching, tugged on the pulleys and the raft floated out into the surging river.

Harriet saw long-legged birds land on the further bank and stare at the approaching apparition. And she thought how, if everything capsized and all of them were drowned, the accident would go unregarded, except by birds she couldn't even name, and she said a prayer that she wouldn't die here, because she knew that her future life would contain wonders and she wanted to remain alive to see them.

The ferryman swore again as the rope tightened on its opposite mooring and burned his blistered hands. Harriet could see the water becoming shallow, and lifted her head when the birds flapped clumsily away.

The raft was nudging the bank now. It was tied up and Harriet coaxed the donkey on to the shingle and uncovered its head and then put on her cloak and pulled it round her. She rested for a few moments and ate some of the dried fruit she'd brought for the journey and let the donkey graze on a patch of straggly grass. She waited until her heart was still again before going on.

She arrived at Orchard House as dusk was falling. Eight-year-old Edwin, who had made his own house in a titoki tree, was the first person to see her, this stranger driving a donkey cart and the animal's head drooping from weariness, and he climbed down and ran to bring her in.

'Mama,' he said, as he escorted her into the sitting-room, where Dorothy was doing her household accounts, 'this is Mrs Blackstone and her hands are very cold.'

Dorothy Orchard looked up at Harriet, who was struggling to pile her brown hair back into the neat knot from which it had escaped, and said: 'Ah. Oh yes, what a nuisance long hair is in this country! What I advise is, cut it off. I broke my arm on a ride and could not, could not dress my hair, and so I gave Toby the scissors and ... oh but my goodness yes, your hands are frozen solid. Come to the fireside. And Edwin, take Mrs Blackstone's horse to the stables, dearest, and give him some oats.'

'It's a donkey, Mama,' said Edwin.

'Oh, a donkey. Well, take the donkey then, sweet boy. You rode a long way on the donkey, Mrs Blackstone?'

'No. There's a little cart ...'

'You crossed the Ashley?'

'Yes.'

'And you were not swirled away? They pretend that raft of theirs is safe, but of course there have been drownings. Now come along to the fire and I will call our maid, Janet, and she will bring us some brandy wine.'

Harriet looked at Dorothy Orchard, whose hair was indeed cut short and stuck out at a rebellious angle from the nape of her neck. Her face was wide and square and slightly flat, as though her jawbone were a sail, set squarely to the wind, but her eyes were large and beautiful. When Harriet began apologising for arriving unannounced, Dorothy said: 'You were not unannounced. That is to say, we heard from our cadet, from whom you bought your mutton, that you had built a house near the Okuku and that you were high up and I said to Toby when the snow came: "I think we shall see the Blackstones as soon as there is a melt". So I was not wrong, except that you came alone.'

She went to the door, then, and began calling to the maid: 'Janet! Janet!' then turned to Harriet and whispered: 'Her name is Jane, but we never call her that. It is very peculiar of us.'

Harriet smiled at Dorothy. Then she allowed herself to look round the large room. In its degree of spaciousness and comfort, it reminded her of places where she'd worked as a governess, places which she had never expected to see again once she'd set sail for New Zealand. She wondered how long it had taken the Orchards to create a room like this, with heavy curtains at the windows and a fine gilt mirror above the fireplace and newspapers folded in a rack.

'Now,' said Dorothy to Janet, who had come silently in, 'bring some brandy wine and three glasses, and some milk for Edwin, then make up a bed for Mrs Blackstone, and . . . what are we to eat for supper?'

'Pigeon pie,' said Janet.

'Very well. Make sure there is enough for us all.' Then she turned to Harriet as Janet slipped away. 'Troublesome to shoot, the pigeon,' she said. 'Flight like a spinning top. But Toby could shoot a flea. Sit down, Mrs Blackstone. Put your feet on this little stool and warm them.'

The pie was large and cumbersome. A whole flock of large pigeons seemed to fill it up, clustering together in a red gravy.

Harriet, yawning with hunger, noticed that Toby Orchard's enormous hands cut the pastry with surprising delicacy, as though he knew he had been put on earth to be the steward of everything physical in the world, whether these things were flying about, or growing at a creek's edge, or dead in a pie. She watched him as he cut the first triangle of pastry and laid it on top of the pie and scooped up the spicy meat with a heavy spoon, then transferred the pastry to the brimming plate that he handed her. Compared to Joseph, Toby Orchard was a giant. His hair and beard were yellow and wild and his face had a high colour, as though he had just run a race or fought with a tiger. His clothes were noisy as he moved inside them.

When he had served out all the portions of pigeon and mumbled a grace, he fell triumphantly upon his food. He tore bread in his hands and drenched it with gravy and swallowed everything down – pigeon flesh, pastry, potatoes, sauce and bread – so fast that the pattern of roses on the plate seemed hardly to have been covered up before it appeared again, shiny and clean. And Harriet understood that while Toby was in this first euphoria of his eating, he expected no one to talk to him. Dorothy smiled benevolently upon him between her own meagre mouthfuls. Edwin quietly recited to his mother a poem he had made up that day; it was about a hippopotamus. Harriet savoured the food and the fire in the room and waited to tell her story of the death of Beauty in the snow.

When she began her tale, the three faces stared at her as though at a waterfall, wondering at its downward precipitation. She supposed they were trying to imagine what kind of ignorant people could put a rug on a cow. Edwin's eyes were sorrowful as he asked: 'Why did you not put Beauty in her shed?'

'Because there is no shed,' said Harriet.

'That was the trouble,' said Dorothy gently, 'as it is with sheep when a southerly blows like that. There is never enough shelter.'

Toby Orchard began slapping crumbs from his coat-front. He did this impatiently, tidying himself up before beginning to speak.

'When we began here on the run,' he said at last, 'we lost livestock with every southerly gale. Sheep can be blown clean off a hill or they can cough till their hearts burst or cluster under the river-banks and drown. But what I said to Dorothy then, and what I say to you now, is *never give up.* Keep building. Make a barn with cob. Roof it with ti-ti leaves. Anything. You're high up near the Okuku, and the southerlies will bring in more snow this winter than you ever saw in Norfolk. Consider the latitude of the South Island of New Zealand! Nigh on fifty degrees south. Spend money on another milk cow and you will lose her too – unless you bring her in under your own roof.'

While Dorothy nodded and Edwin watched his father gravely, Harriet tried to imagine what Lilian would say about sharing the Cob House with an animal. ('I simply will not do it, Joseph. So why do you not put the cow in my bed and I will go out and sleep in the snow!')

A smile touched the corners of Harriet's mouth as Toby continued.

'We can sell you milk,' he said. 'In this kind of cold, it will keep fresh for quite a few days. When you've made the shed, scythe last year's tussock instead of burning it and dry it on the dry winds. No straw on the flats, of course, but tussock will do and cows must have plenty of it to keep them warm.'

Harriet nodded.

Edwin said: 'Poor Beauty.'

'No fleece on a cow,' Toby went on. 'And nostrils too large. Breath freezes and blocks the air passage, then they try to breathe through their mouths and the cold burns their throats. You must wait until spring in October.'

Harriet said: 'Joseph thought he knew livestock . . .'

'No use,' said Toby, 'no use at all, unless you also know the weather.'

The maid Janet removed the remains of the pigeon pie and brought in a trembling white blancmange, which she placed without hesitation in front of Dorothy, apparently knowing that a blancmange was not a real or pungent enough entity to engage Toby's attention. When served his portion of this confection, Toby wrapped his big hand around a spoon, lifted a few morsels to his mouth and then abandoned it, pushing his plate away and wiping not only his mouth, but his nose and his eyes with the table napkin. Dorothy regarded him watchfully.

'Toby is out on the run from sunrise to sunset,' she said softly to Harriet, 'and by supper time he is very tired.'

'Forgive me, Mrs Blackstone,' Toby Orchard said, getting to his feet and stretching. 'I shall go to bed now and listen to the night birds.'

Then to Dorothy, he said: 'Perhaps you will show Mollie to our guest?'

'Certainly I will, dear,' said Dorothy.

'Good-night, Papa,' said Edwin.

Toby came round to where his son sat, still eating his helping of blancmange, and put his wide hand tenderly on Edwin's head. 'I heard your hippopotamus,' he said. 'I thought him very good.'

Dorothy and Harriet sat in front of the fire, into which they both stared.

'You will discover,' said Dorothy, 'what a minute world you have come to. Vast outside. So vast it takes our breath away. But our concerns are so very small: the health of the sheep, a dry shipment of chestnuts, firewood that doesn't spit, a servant girl who can make mashed potato without lumps ...'

'Oh,' said Harriet, 'but when I stand by my creek and look towards the mountains ...'

'Precisely,' said Dorothy, 'they are grand. Nature is grand here. But too grand. To survive in New Zealand, we all have to re-create, if not the past exactly, then something very like it, something homely.'

Harriet saw the branch of apple wood she was watching break and fall and a high flame spring up and begin to consume it. She said: 'Our Cob House is not like any home I have been in.'

'Not yet,' said Dorothy. 'But if your farm prospers, then your husband will build a larger house, a house like this one, and you will serve tea in it, tea from China, but the rest of the world will have clean vanished from your head.'

'Well then,' said Harriet, 'I hope we may stay always in the Cob House, always listening to the river, always walking out at night to see the stars ...'

'No,' said Dorothy. 'Take my word for it. We are not strong enough for rivers and stars. We think we are at first, but we are not.'

'What do you mean, Mrs Orchard?' asked Harriet.

'I think you might call me Dorothy and I shall call you Harriet, if I may? What do I mean? I mean that inevitably we make a small world in the midst of a big one. For a small world is all that we know how to make.'

Harriet was silent. Here in this room was indeed a comfortable little piece of England reassembled. It was pretty and welcoming and outside were English trees moving in the dark.

'But then,' she said, 'we are not tested.'

'Now it is my turn to ask you what you mean.'

'Well, I am not sure I know what I mean. But when I am working in my vegetable garden, on my own, and I look up at the mountains, that is where I long to go.'

Dorothy Orchard ran her hands through her cropped hair.

She looked at Harriet, at her muddied skirts and her slender feet in their brown boots, and tried to guess her age. 'The mountains, as you call them, the Southern Alps are as fearful in their way as anything in the world. I've heard them called "the stairway of hell". If you don't want your children to lose a mother, then stay away from the Alps.'

'I have no children,' said Harriet.

'Ah.'

Dorothy paused for an anxious second or two, but then went hurriedly on: 'But you have a husband and you would not want him to be left alone.'

'No,' replied Harriet. But it came to her at that moment that there was a part of Joseph which, even in their bed, remained resolutely alone. This was not a thing they would ever speak of, but it was nevertheless true.

Dorothy stood up. 'It is getting late,' she said, 'and we shall go to bed, but Toby made me promise to show you Mollie, who, at the moment, is a resident of the airing cupboard.'

The two women went slowly up the stairs of Orchard House, Dorothy leading the way with a candle burning in a silver candlestick. They arrived at a landing from which they could hear Toby snoring.

Dorothy opened a small door and a warm, acrid smell made Harriet's nostrils flare. 'Toby is very proud of the airing cupboard,' Dorothy whispered. 'Heat from the range rises and warms the stones, so this is where we dry clothes and air the sheets and now if I shine the light down a little, you will see Mollie.'

Harriet saw two yellow eyes staring at her over the rim of a rushwork basket.

'Mollie the collie,' said Dorothy. 'Edwin named her and of course Toby thought this very droll. He used to make Edwin say "Mollie-the-collie must not be mollycoddled!" But now look beside her, there. Two pups. Born eight days ago, so we let her live in here with them until she weans them.'

Harriet knelt down and gently put a hand out to the dog. The pups came clustering to the edge of the basket.

'Good girls,' said Dorothy. 'Brave girls.' Then to Harriet she said: 'Mollie is the cleverest dog we've had. Knows every inch of the run. Knows which sheep are the strayers and the slowcoaches. Toby will keep one of the pups – the one Edwin has named Baby – and train her. But we never keep more than two dogs. We shall find a home for the other.'

In among the dogs' pungent warmth, Harriet's hand caressed them gently. She thought affectionately of her father's old wolfhound, a grey stumbling creature who was never fond of walking or running but preferred to lie all day across his master's feet in their heavy, polished shoes, with one eye closed and the other on its own reflection in the fender. Without thinking further, she said: 'May I ask Joseph if we could buy the other puppy?'

The snoring in Toby Orchard's room stopped suddenly and Harriet imagined that he might at any moment appear – to deny her request, not wanting a dog of his to live in so poor a place as the Cob House, a place where animals died because the people were too new to the landscape and had no understanding of the sky. But the snoring resumed more quietly and Dorothy merely said: 'Yes, by all means ask and I will ask Toby. But collies must work, you know. They must work or they are not happy.'

'We can put her to work,' said Harriet. 'And I believe things might go better for us if we had a dog.'

She and Dorothy said good-night and Harriet walked towards her room, a room with solid walls and a Dutch bed and a silvered looking-glass.

As she opened her door, she heard Dorothy say: 'The dogs are all named by Edwin. The one you want is called Lady.'

III

Harriet slept for a long time.

When she woke up, there was sun at her window and no sound at all inside the house. Harriet lay still and looked at the room, which had been painted the colour of cream and hung with faded samplers:

The Orchard Run

Mary Jane Orchard: Her own work: Aged six.
Augusta Eliza Orchard: 1811: Redeem the Time.

Her body ached. She knew she should go back to the Cob House, taking milk and Toby Orchard's instructions to build barns for the animals, but the task of returning – the long, slow miles over the flats with the donkey and the cart, the perilous crossing of the Ashley – suddenly filled her with desolation.

Shivering, Harriet poured cold water into a bowl and washed herself and put on her muddy dress. As she laced her boots, she thought with dismay: The desolation doesn't lie in the journey, nor in the crossing of the river, but in the return to Joseph. And then her fingers and the dirty laces fell into a muddle and didn't move.

She understood for the first time that Joseph Blackstone was a selfish man. She saw how he moved about in the world, deciding who should go where and when, with so poor an understanding of what they wanted. She saw how he refused to share himself, even with her, shying away from the subject of children, as though he couldn't bear to be responsible for anything beyond his own desires. But what *were* his real desires? Why, when he made love to her, did he cover her face? Harriet had thought, at the beginning, that perhaps his passion embarrassed him, that he didn't want her to see him in those moments. But now she wondered whether he was smothering her features so that he wouldn't see them; whether even in their bed he took himself elsewhere, to the private place of his desire, and never minded that she was left stranded and far behind.

Harriet returned to the task of lacing her boots. She saw that her hands were shaking. For what was going to happen to her if she couldn't love Joseph Blackstone? What was the purpose of all their arduous work? She'd told herself that, here in New Zealand, love would come in like a quiet change in the seasons, that she wouldn't have to strive for it; it would become as easy to her as breathing. But she saw now that it wasn't easy, that it hadn't thrived as she'd expected.

A knock on Harriet's bedroom door halted for a moment the terror into which she was plunging. She straightened up. She'd heard no footsteps in the corridor, but it was Janet who came in, carrying a jug of hot water.

'For your morning absolution, ma'am,' she quaintly said.

Harriet thanked her and she went out. Jane or Janet? Jane, the real name; Janet, the name the girl had to answer to here. But how much did a name matter? Harriet Salt. Harriet Blackstone. What was going to happen to her now that her name had irrevocably changed?

Harriet stared stupidly at the hot water. Slowly, she removed her bodice and began to wash herself again.

Dorothy fed her with coffee and bread and honey and told her she wouldn't be able to leave the Orchard Run that day because 'your poor donkey is lying down on a bed of straw and refusing to get to its feet. If you try to lead it home, you will certainly both be swirled to your deaths in the Ashley.'

Edwin took Harriet to the stable. He sat by the donkey and fed it sugar and washed its face and eyes with a rag.

'How does a windmill work?' Edwin asked.

A windmill. Harriet leaned against the open stable door. She thought: Life has turned and brought me here. I could become Edwin Orchard's governess and never return to Joseph and Lilian.

Harriet said to Edwin: 'A windmill is built on a platform that is able to turn, so that the sails may always face into the wind. The sails revolve and a ratcheted wheel revolves with them.'

'But where is the grinding stone?'

Harriet laced the fingers of her two hands to show the action of the interlocked wheels, one revolving right to left like the hands of a clock and the other turning on a vertical axis like a spinning top. 'Here is the grinding stone,' she said, indicating a point just below her elbow, and Edwin nodded, pleased with the information and his understanding of it, pressing the palms of his hands together to mill imaginary grain. 'In four years' time,' he said, 'I shall go to school in Christchurch. Papa says that by then I must know how things came to be as they are.'

'It may be impossible to know how everything came to be as it is.'

'Why?'

'Because to know a thing, you must know the principle and root of it and sometimes these are hidden from us.'

'Why are they hidden from us?'

'Either because they are too far away, like the stars, or because our minds can't imagine them.'

'I can imagine everything,' said Edwin. 'I know Maori things, too, which Mama and Papa do not know.'

'Maori things?'

'Yes. Do you know what the word maori means?'

'Native?'

'No. It means *normal*. The Maoris were in New Zealand before us. They call it Aotearoa. When we came, they thought we looked funny. They thought they were normal and we were strange.'

Harriet nodded. 'How did you learn this, Edwin?'

'Pare told me.'

'Pare?'

'My nurse, when I was a baby and the wind blew my cradle.'

'Your mother told me she'd been sent away . . .'

'She was sent away. But sometimes she comes back. She hides in the toi-toi grass and I talk to her. She can make the grass soft by plaiting it and then we sit down.'

'Do your mama and papa know that you talk to Pare?'

'No,' said Edwin. 'And you mustn't tell them. They could send her away again.'

Because the day was bright, after the bitter fog and snow, and because the donkey couldn't lift its head from the floor, Dorothy pronounced that she, Harriet and Edwin would ride to a sheltered place on the run known as Pukeko Creek after the swamp-hens which nested there. They would take lunch in a basket and ale for Toby, who would meet them down by the water. At Pukeko Creek there was a shepherd's hut and they would make a fire and eat a picnic. Toby might shoot some hens. Edwin might try to catch the muddy ika which swam in the green shallows.

So they set out under the wide sky, the horses frisky and longing to gallop. They hurtled over the flats, skirting the clover fields, sending sheep running and bleating in random directions. Strands of Harriet's hair unfolded themselves from the knot she'd made of them and buffeted her cheeks and whipped themselves round her neck.

She had never ridden at such a speed. The land spread out at every corner of her vision. Shadows of white clouds caressed the valleys and sailed on. Ahead of her, Dorothy's chestnut mare and Edwin's grey pony raced through the bright air faster and faster, until Harriet could no longer hear the sound of their hooves and they became smaller and smaller, a tiny, shimmering cluster of colour on the fawn palette of hills.

And the further away from her they moved, the more exhilarated Harriet became. To be alone here, alone with a strong horse in all this magnificent vastness! Alone and alone and alone, with no one guiding or leading. Alone in a desert of hills that lay between the mountains and the sea ...

She began to rein in the horse, slowing it to a canter and then to a trot. She pulled it at last to a stop and it remained still, sneezing and blowing and tossing its mane in the wind. Sweat ran into Harriet's eyes. Her heart pulsed with a rhythm unrecognisable as its own. She wiped her eyes with her sleeve, patted the horse's neck, heard her breath tearing at her lungs.

She didn't dismount, but stayed in the saddle, looking from horizon to horizon and finding no one and nothing but herself and the horse and their shadows and the shadows of clouds. A bird turned above her, against the cold blue of the sky. Harriet saw it as the majestic witness of a sudden happiness and she knew that in the time to come she would remember it.

She knew also that, in a little while, Dorothy and Edwin would return, worried that she had fallen. In fairness to them, she must gather the reins and urge the horse on. Yet she didn't want to move, didn't want to join the picnic and the fishing. She wanted to remain where she was. She wanted the dusk to come on and then the darkness. She wanted to ride alone through the hours of the night with a silent escort of stars.

The Tea Box from China

I

While Harriet was away, Joseph walked down the line of the creek to the place where the Cob House should have been built – to the place where he rebuilt it in his mind.

There were no trees here, no scrub, no ferns, no features at all, only a level plateau of tussock grass and stones. But the plateau was protected by a south-facing spur. When you arrived here, you could feel the air sweeten. The terrible sighing and pounding of the wind in your ears suddenly ceased. The men who had called Joseph a cockatoo had been right and he had been wrong; this was where the house would eventually have to stand.

Joseph paced out the plateau, measured its distance from the creek, tried with his bare hands to pull a grey boulder out of the earth. When the summer came, he told himself, if any money remained to buy timber, he would lay down the foundations of a new building. Years, it might take, for he would be alone in his task, could afford no more hired labour. But at least he would have begun, he would have admitted his error. In the new beginnings of this second house would lie his hopes for the future. All life, he thought as he tugged at the boulder, is a flight from mistake to mistake.

Joseph sat on the hard ground and looked up the line of the creek to where the Cob House stood. While working on it, in his first euphoria of construction, he had thought up names for it: Hope Farm, White Cloud Farm, New Paradise Farm, but as yet, he hadn't burdened it with any of these. It was just 'the cob house' and in this anonymity lay his admission that it was contingent, that for Lilian's sake, if for no one else's, he would have to build something better than this one day.

Joseph Blackstone longed to do something that would please his mother. Something definitive. Something which would undo all that he'd done wrongly or inadequately in the past. He thought that if he could achieve this, then he would rest. He didn't know precisely what he meant by rest.

Now, as he sat on the hard ground of the sheltered plateau, he remembered how, as a child, he used to scream. He screamed at things that moved towards him: a ball thrown or a hoop bowled, the sudden flight of a bird out of a tree in the garden. He screamed at a red-and-yellow spinning top given to him for his seventh birthday. The way the red and yellow merged, as the top spun, to become one indescribable colour, the way the top changed direction without warning, these things made him scream.

Lilian couldn't endure this screaming of his. She would clamp her hand over his mouth. Sometimes her hand smelled of potato peelings and sometimes it smelled of chocolate or eau-de-Cologne. She threatened to glue his lips together. She told him screaming was 'vulgar'. She told him poor people screamed but not the son of a livestock auctioneer, not the grandson of a vicar.

One evening, Lilian and Roderick Blackstone took Joseph to a circus and he saw acrobats swooping through the air. He felt Lilian's hand clamp itself across his mouth. He tried to be quiet. The costumes of the acrobats were spangled, as though they were made of glass and might shatter. Then a man with a whip came into the ring and round the man paced three snarling tigers and it seemed to Joseph that there was nothing anyone could do, in the face of these tigers, other than to scream at them.

Lilian took him by the collar and marched him out into the darkness, marched him all the way home along the moonlit lanes and tied him into his bed and bound his mouth with an old sash which smelled of camphor. She told him that if he screamed any more he would no longer be her son.

After that night of the circus, he tried never to scream at

anything, to keep all strong emotion locked inside him. When he felt a scream coming on, he would run away and bite his arm or his knee. Sometimes, he hid in the cupboard under the stairs, where the brooms and brushes were kept, and he would stare at these things and long to be them, or long to be, like them, something which had no feeling.

When his father died, Joseph felt his old desire to scream returning. He could master it only by refusing to think about the ostriches and the mutilated body in the field. So he gradually fell into the habit of suppressing, both to himself and to others, the actual manner of Roderick Blackstone's dying, referring only to 'his last sufferings' as though his father had expired from a protracted illness. And in this way, he was able to remain mute and controlled.

Joseph stood up. Today, the sky above the Cob House was a deep and startling blue, a rarefied un-English blue that made him yearn for the return of summer. He walked to the creek's edge and squatted down and put his hands in the icy water. Swollen with the snow-melt, Harriet's Creek was now a rushing torrent. Once the channel was dug to his pond, it would fill very fast. Joseph had heard that Tasmanian trout might be bought somewhere along the Ashley and had decided he would stock his pond with these.

Joseph wiped his hands on the tussock and began to walk back towards the Cob House, following the creek. Where scrub roots clung to the very edge of the further bank, the water, in its new frenzy, had taken a different course, revealing a sliver of muddy shore, on which some blue-duck were wading. Joseph stopped to watch the birds. As the winter progressed, he knew that he would have to take out his gun and begin shooting what wildfowl he could track down to keep the three of them fed.

But now, hearing the cry of the ducks, he felt his mind return to an autumn morning in Norfolk, waiting with his gun for mallard and widgeon, watching the haze begin to lift off the river, fumbling with his bag of cartridges, feeling the cold and his own solitude and then seeing, approaching through the mist, Rebecca wrapped in her brown cloak, her face oval and white in the mauvish light of dawn.

She called to him: 'Brought you griddle-cakes and tea, Joseph

Blackstone. Gave my mam the slip.' And she came and stood by him, holding her little basket of food, and his hand on the gun barrel began shaking. He tried to turn away from her, but she touched his arm and he moved his head and saw her laughing, her mouth open and wet and her fascinating crooked teeth like a taunt, a provocation . . .

The blue-duck launched themselves into the bubbling creek and bobbed out of sight. Joseph rubbed his eyes. There was a glare on the water, but beyond the glare, something else, a flicker of colour in the grey mud where the ducks had stood. As his memory of Rebecca began to slide away – back into the darkness where he wanted it to remain – Joseph concentrated on this colour. For a few moments, the sun disappeared behind a cloud and, in the shadow, nothing of it was visible, only the shingly mud and the herringbone imprints of the ducks' feet. But Joseph knew that he'd seen something. He stood without moving, waiting for the sun to come out again. It returned and sparkled on the water, dazzling him. He had to close his eyes for a second and when he opened them again, he'd forgotten the precise spot where the colour had revealed itself. Then, he saw it once more, a minute patch of shining yellow dust.

Joseph removed his heavy boots and his woollen socks and began to wade across the icy creek. Almost unbalanced by the current, he stooped and clung to stones, making his way to the mud-bank like a four-legged animal. He felt glad he was alone, felt the excitement, in fact, of being here alone with his discovery. And when he arrived on the further shore, he sank down on to his knees, not caring how his trousers would be soiled. With trembling hands, he scooped into his palms a spoonful of grey mud dusted with gold.

All day, he worked, combing the earth and stones. He gave no thought to Harriet, away on her journey to the Orchard Run, nor to Lilian, asleep in her room, oblivious to the sun and the blue sky. Once, he returned to the Cob House and found a shallow casserole dish the approximate shape of a gold-pan. Then he went back to the creek, taking this and a tin jug. Scooping mud into the dish, drenching it with creek-water from the jug, swilling it about so that the fine particles of sand

and clay were washed away, leaving behind the heavier grains of gold, he was able to believe that nothing escaped his sight. On the dry ground under the scrub, he spread out a handkerchief, and by mid-day a little mound of bright dust, a mound the size of a man's thumb-nail, lay there. Joseph knelt over it, put a finger into it and saw the tiny particles adhere to his skin. Tenderly, he brought his finger close to his face, caressed the gold with his eyes. He felt a scream rising in his heart.

His head was full of hectic planning. He knew he was going to keep his discovery secret. Later on, if a great fortune was waiting for him here along the creek bed, then he would talk about it, share it, but not yet. The creek, low down here on the undulating flat, wasn't visible from the Cob House. So he would come to this place alone and unobserved when Harriet was working her vegetable plot or stirring the washing in her copper and when Lilian was sleeping or mending china. With his rudimentary tools, he would patiently work every inch of mud. Then, towards summer, as the level of the creek fell after the freshes of spring, more and more of the little shoreline would be revealed and he alone would know what he might find there.

He reasoned also that secrecy was a prudent measure. If he told Harriet that there was gold in her creek, then somehow (because she was a woman and women liked to reveal what was in their hearts) she might let slip this information to the Orchards and from the Orchard Run it would stream outwards – carried far and wide by the shepherds, even whispered by the Maoris in their sing-song tongue – and sooner or later there would be a Rush; the hordes would come, the men who had found gold in Australia in the 'fifties and then in Otago at the beginning of the new decade and were only waiting (who knew where?) for the next discovery. They would arrive with their pans and cradles, their sluice-boxes and their picks. All along the creek, their shanties would appear, their grog-shops, their latrines and their filth. What had been Joseph's land would be annexed by the Canterbury Government and Miner's Rights sold by the hundred. The farm would be destroyed, the gold dredged and shipped out and he – who had begun it, who had been the first man to see the colour on the sliver of mud, *his* mud, *his* river – would be left with nothing.

Joseph folded the handkerchief, tied a knot in it so tightly that not a scintilla of gold dust could escape and put it in the pocket of his muddy trousers. It was only then that he became aware that, all around him, the light was failing and the winter dusk was coming on.

II

The following day, Harriet returned.

The crossing of the Ashley River was less terrifying on the homeward journey, the donkey quieter and more obedient, as though it knew it was returning home. The cart was loaded with milk and mutton and some pots of peach jam made by Dorothy Orchard. And Harriet felt buoyed up by her expedition, by the fast ride over the acres of empty land, by the idea of cropping her own long hair, by the promise of the dog, Lady.

The sun was low in the sky as she drove up to the Cob House. As she got down from the cart, she heard the wind sighing in the beeches and felt her buoyancy diminish and then slip away. She lifted the milk churn from the cart, unhitched the donkey and led it to the pasture, where it grazed for a moment or two and then lay down by a fence post and closed its eyes. Harriet walked slowly back to the house and went inside.

Silence reigned here. No lamps had been lit yet. The white calico of the rooms moved almost imperceptibly with the opening of the door.

Harriet didn't call out. She supposed that Lilian was asleep and that Joseph was working on the pond. She moved to the kitchen and set down the heavy milk churn, thinking how, with a dog to greet her, a homecoming would not be quite like this, not quite so sombre.

To cheer herself, Harriet lit a lamp, banked up the range,

drank a mug of the cool, fresh milk. Her back ached from her journey, so, unbuttoning her cloak as she went, she decided to lie down on her bed for half an hour.

She was amazed to find Joseph asleep in the calico room. His body was buried deep under the eiderdown, his head barely visible. One pale hand clutched the eiderdown's edge.

Harriet's entry into their bedroom with the lamp didn't wake him and, although on the point of uttering his name, Harriet remained quite still, deciding to say nothing, remained exactly where she was, staring at Joseph and remembering that moment in Orchard House . . . that moment when, tying her boots, her hands had let the laces drop . . .

She didn't know why Joseph was lying here in the afternoon. She thought that a loving wife would have felt concern, would have woken him to ask him whether he was ill, would have hurried to make tea for him, would have kissed his head. But Harriet merely stood there with her lamp, unmoving. She knew that, at that moment, she felt no pity for him, no pity and no love.

The terror of these feelings created such a pain in her chest, it was as if a weight had lodged there. She asked herself how or where she could unburden herself of this weight. She clutched at her breast. The sight of Joseph's pale fingers repelled her and she went hurriedly out of the room.

She sat alone by the range, hoping that neither Joseph nor Lilian would wake up for a long while. She decided that what mattered was to find a way – any way – of being able to carry on, for what else was there to do? She closed her eyes. She must hide her feelings, she thought desperately, hide them, banish them, consign them to some place where they would never come to light. But how could one consign or banish what was inside and had no way out?

After a while of sitting completely still, Harriet walked to a high shelf in the kitchen and took down the Chinese tea box, bought at Read's Commodities in Christchurch. The decorated label, depicting the two herons' necks entwined, had been pasted into her scrapbook, but the box remained, still smelling of tea, kept because it was the kind of object she might one day find a use for, a finely made box of cheap wood, the lid fastened with nails.

Harriet prised the lid open with a knife, the nails lifting easily and cleanly. She stared at the empty box, which must have crossed the Pacific on some interminable sea-voyage from Canton. Tea and silk. Opium and ebony. Chinese settlers hoping for money and gold ... All these, like her with her dreams of land and children, had made their way to Aotearoa, to the Land of the Long White Cloud, to a new world.

And there was only this now, this new world. She had to make of it what she could. So there and then, as the dark of the afternoon gathered at the windows, Harriet imagined that she was consigning to the box all the weight of her dislike for Joseph, and that this box – this object of no account – would enable her to go on with her life. She embodied the weight as a lump of some unknown metal which fitted the box so precisely that it might have been made, not for tea, but only and ever for this. She knew that what she was doing was childlike, but she didn't mind.

If it helped her to go on, what did it matter?

Harriet nailed down the lid of the box and placed it exactly where she had found it on the high shelf. And then she went to Joseph and woke him gently. He took her hand in his, which was burning hot. He told her he had some kind of a fever, foolishly got, he said, by staying too long by the river, getting cold while trying to work out where the channel would run to bring water to his pond.

That night, while Joseph sighed and sweated in the bed, Harriet slept beside him on the earth floor. Twice she woke when he cried out, trying to piss into a flask and feeling his urine come out of him like fire.

She brought him water, turned his pillows, wiped the moisture from his face and returned to her place on the ground.

She didn't mind the hardness of the earth. She dreamed she was miles from here, in the mountains, alone with the sound of rushing water and the silent brilliance of the stars. Not far from where she lay stood a tall horse, motionless, as if keeping watch.

III

Joseph's fever had come on very fast.

Returning with the gold knotted in his handkerchief and worrying about where to hide it in this house that was not really a house and in which he had no corner to call his own, he'd begun to shiver. He put more lignite on the fire of the range and sat leaning towards it, but, though his cheeks burned, he couldn't get warm. His legs twitched and ached. There was a pain in his bladder.

Lilian had made a meal of pilchards and onions, but Joseph couldn't eat this. He felt as though he were going to fall on to the floor from some colossal height. He remembered the glass spangles on the costumes of the circus acrobats and saw the people hurtling down and everything breaking apart in the dust. He crept to his bed, the gold still scrunched in his pocket. He couldn't bear to take off his clothes. Lilian brought him a bowl and a rag and sat by him for a while. 'The trouble with this pioneer life,' she observed, 'is that it does not allow for human frailty.'

Joseph's dreams were mad. He saw ostriches dancing like music-hall girls, revealing petticoats of feathers. He saw his father, wearing his hard top hat, beat at the ostrich-girls with a whittled stick, and one by one they fell down. He knew in the dream that his father had stolen his gold dust and concealed it in his pocket watch, where it sullied the well-oiled mechanism, and brought the watch to a stop.

When Harriet returned and woke him, Joseph was still wearing his shirt and trousers and his coat, damp and muddy from the river. The bed was soaked by this cold moisture and by Joseph's sweat. As tenderly as she could, Harriet helped him to undress and put clean sheets on the bed.

His coat, where the gold lay concealed, she folded and placed on a chair and Joseph was too weak to discover some way of asking for it, to have it near him – so that he could hold on to it until he had thought of a proper hiding place. He merely lay there, fighting sleep, watching the chair, until his dreams swept him away.

In the night, pissing into the flask, tortured by pain, Joseph saw the coat still there on the chair, but beside it, so close to it that she could easily reach out and put her hand into the pockets, Harriet's makeshift bed on the floor.

'Give me my coat, Harriet,' he said, when she returned from emptying the flask.

'You don't need your coat, my dear,' she said gently.

'I want it, to cover me.'

'I can fetch another coverlet . . .'

'Pass me the coat!'

She didn't argue, but brought the coat to him and laid it over the top of the eiderdown and at once he could smell the outdoors on it, the moss and the earth, as though it were made of these things, and he tugged it close to his face and held it there.

In the cold of morning, before Harriet was awake, he stirred and knew his fever had diminished a little. He tried to move, but could only lie there shivering, afraid for himself with the pains in his bladder, and afraid for the gold, which was rightly his, but which had to be hidden. He reached out his hand and found the coat pocket with the handkerchief and seized hold of it and brought it into the warmth under the bedclothes. He pressed it to his face, then clenched it into a ball in his fist.

He wanted to cry out with frustration and fear. If he could only find the strength to get out of this bed, to tiptoe across the room without waking Harriet, then the perfect hiding-place for the gold would reveal itself to him. Even in a house like this one, there must be somewhere – some ingenious somewhere – a place that was never visited . . .

He drifted to sleep again, then woke to find Lilian sitting beside the bed.

'What were you doing yesterday,' she asked, 'to make yourself so ill?'

He thought about this. Things arrive, he wanted to say; you, above all people, know this. Not everything is of our own making.

'I stayed at the pond too late,' he said. 'I had not noticed how cold the air had become.'

Lilian stared at him, her only child. There was a new salting of grey in his beard. The skin of his neck was beginning to pucker. While he had been outside catching this fever of his, she had written her letter to Mrs Dinsdale and hidden it under her mattress. She was impatient to send it, but knew that, at this moment when Joseph had been taken ill, sending it would constitute a betrayal of her son.

'It is all too much for you,' she announced, looking round the bare little room and sighing. 'In England, everything was to hand. We are not cut out for these terrible distances.'

Joseph managed to smile. 'We knew,' he said, 'that the first winter would be hard. In the spring and summer, we will start to see progress.'

Lilian blew her nose. She recognised how, since arriving at the Cob House, her belief in anything that anybody said had faltered. She thought that she had been a trusting person, until now . . . or perhaps not quite until now. She had been a trusting person until Roderick had died, and since then she had had to become far more vigilant, far more sceptical.

It was a shame, really, because Lilian knew that she didn't entirely enjoy this constant questioning of things; she'd preferred the time when she hadn't felt the need to question anything. Her days then had been so much easier to pass.

She made some broth for Joseph from chicken bones and began trying to spoon this into his mouth, sitting by him on the bed with the soup cup in her hands. He sucked in the broth like a child, his lips braced for the spoon, as if for some fearful kiss he had been forced to bestow. Then, after a few mouthfuls, he gagged and a look of terror came into his face. Lilian held a cloth under his chin, thinking he was about to vomit up the broth, but he didn't vomit, just turned his head aside, and Lilian could tell that some kind of panic had begun to overtake him.

'What?' she asked. 'What?'

He shook his head, then began searching for something under his bedclothes. 'What, Joseph?' Lilian said again.

'Go away,' he said. 'Let me be. Please let me be.'

'You must eat –' began Lilian.

'Take everything away,' he said, gesturing at the broth. 'Let me alone.'

So she had no choice but to do as he asked and remove the soup and the cloth, wiping his lips before leaving. As she returned to the range and served herself a bowl of the pale broth, she thought how those who are ill can exert a surprising power over those who are well and that illness might yet play a part in her plan to escape from this wilderness and return to an orderly life.

> *My dear Mrs Dinsdale. My dear Lily. I am writing to tell you that barely a day goes by in which I do not think about my very pleasant sojourn in Christchurch and find myself wishing that I was back there once more with you ...*

Joseph felt tears spill out of his exhausted eyes and roll down his face.

His handkerchief containing the gold had disappeared.

With frantic hands, he fumbled under the pillows, in the tuck of the sheet, beneath his body and in the sleeve of his nightshirt. With his feet, curved like a dancer's, he searched the crumpled darkness of the bottom of his invalid's bed. Then, bracing himself for the effort of this, he knelt and rolled the covers back and ran his hands over the surface of everything and then he lay down, the wrong way round, and hung his face over the edge of the mattress and his tears spilled and made tiny dark stains on the earth floor.

As Joseph searched, he told himself that if he had found this much gold at the creek, then of course there would be more and so this handkerchief of yellow dust wasn't important; as soon as he was well again, he would resume his panning of the mud and, eventually, the precious thing they called 'the colour' would come ...

But he still couldn't stop himself from weeping. He wept for his lost secret. He knew that neither Harriet nor Lilian would put a handkerchief into the wash knotted like this. They would unfold it and discover what it held and so the knowledge of the gold would be out – out into the avaricious wider world. It would thereafter belong to them all – shared, known, talked about, divided. And this was what broke Joseph's heart. He saw that he now lived in a world where nothing – not even something which he and no one else had seen – belonged to him alone.

Exhausted, he lay down on his pillows again and pulled the eiderdown over his head and wiped his eyes. He sank into a haunted sleep. He found himself running through the lanes and alleys of some English town, poorly lit, pushing Rebecca in front of him, urging her forward too roughly, paying no heed to her protests, intent only at arriving on the appointed destination.

He woke quite soon, needing the flask again. His penis ached and burned. He looked round the room for the wretched flask and saw it near him on the chair. He reached out for it and with his other hand, intent on pulling up his nightshirt, discovered something hard in the tangled folds of the shirt between his legs. He pulled it out. It was his lost handkerchief.

Thereafter, he never let it go. It was always in his fist or beneath his long fingers under the pillow.

Only when he was well again, some two weeks later, did he consign the handkerchief to a place he considered safe – an empty wooden box high up on a kitchen shelf, which had once contained tea, but from which the label had been torn and which he now believed had been forgotten.

Joseph took the box, its lid carefully nailed down around its precious contents, to the small space between the stretched calico and the outer cob wall of his room and pressed it into the earth and covered it over. He was as certain as he could be that neither Lilian nor Harriet would ever discover the box here, for the simple reason that – because the calico represented a solid wall – their imaginations never travelled to the space behind it. It was, in effect, a space which did not really exist, a space which everybody pretended was not there.

Among the White Stones

I

When Edwin's Maori nurse, Pare, had been sent away from Orchard House, she had walked towards Kaiapoi, towards her tribe.

Going south-east, she arrived after several hours at a northerly tributary of the great Waimakariri River, and here she sat down as the sun came up.

She sat on a white stone, with her feet in the water, chewing some raisins she'd taken with her in the bundle of possessions Toby Orchard had allowed her to assemble.

In the liquid light of morning, with the birds beginning their song, Pare no longer felt afraid of the ngārara. She knew that what she'd seen on the verandah of Orchard House had probably been just an inquisitive gecko, and because of this – because of the terrifying wind and the power of an ancient *story* – she'd lost Edwin, a child who, in her childless life, Pare had begun to love as her own.

The raisins tasted over-sweet and were hard and indigestible.

Pare scooped up mouthfuls of the cool water of the river and drank and drank.

She hadn't been allowed to see Edwin after Dorothy had rescued him and laid him in her bed; she'd been sent away into the night with almost nothing: her clothes, her treasured greenstone pendant, her basket made of flax. But she knew that Edwin was probably going to die. The cradle had risen up off the verandah and tipped out the infant into the dust. Pare imagined Edwin's neck, that tender place she often kissed, being struck as if with a terrible blow from a matipo club, and his poor head hanging limp and dumb. Her tears began to flow, salty and bitter, and she knew that she would regret for as long as she lived that she had so offended the spirits.

As the sun rose higher, the birds quietened. Floating down towards Pare on the current of the river appeared a black-beech log. She stared at it. An uncomfortable feeling began to take hold of her stomach and she set the raisins aside and tried to alleviate this feeling by kneading her abdomen very gently, just as she'd sometimes done for Edwin when he screamed from colic. Nearer and nearer to her floated the black log. More and more cruel became the pains.

'Auē!' Pare wailed. 'What are you?'

The log arrived almost at her feet, caught behind a little spur of white stones. It glistened blue-black in the sun. 'What are you?' Pare asked again.

Then she heard a voice inside her. The voice berated Pare. It told her she was like Houmea, the Cormorant Woman who swallowed her own children, as a spotted shag swallows fish. It warned her that the pākehā baby would die – and she would also die – *unless* she returned and kept vigil over him. While the voice spoke, Pare felt something creeping over her lips and she reached up and brushed away a fly which landed on her knee and she saw that it was a blowfly.

Pare vomited into the water. The voice said: 'Now you see your own sickness. This is the beginning of your death.'

She lay under a cabbage tree and slept and when she woke, in its green shade, she wondered whether the voice she had heard had been the voice of a spirit, a taniwha. The taniwha could take many forms and this one could have assumed the shape of the black-beech log.

She got to her feet and walked unsteadily towards the water. The log was still there, but the current of the Waimakariri had moved it to the edge of the stone spur and now she saw it swing round and re-enter the fast-flowing river.

As it floated away, the voice seemed to whisper: '*Go back and keep watch*.'

Pare was hungry and weak. Her tribe lived no more than a

few miles from here, whereas to go back to the Orchard Run would take her hours – on feet that were blistered, on a stomach that was empty – and so she decided that, for now, she had to ignore the warning of the voice and return to her old home.

So she trudged on towards Kaiapoi. As she walked, she reasoned that if she had imagined the ngārara, so perhaps, in her sadness for Edwin, she'd imagined the voice inside her head? And anyway, the voice had asked her to do an impossible thing. If she reappeared at Orchard House, Toby and Dorothy would simply send her away.

Pare was ill for a long time. She grew thinner as the seasons passed.

It was her mother who at last understood that she was dying and asked her to try to remember anything in her life which could have caused this fatal illness of hers. When she told her mother about the black-beech log and the voice she had heard (long ago now) she put her hands together gravely. Then she laid around Pare's shoulders a soft cloak embroidered with kiwi tail feathers which was an heirloom of the tribe. She gave her water in a gourd and told her to return to the Orchard Run.

When she arrived within sight of the house, Pare waited, hidden amongst the scratchy toi-toi grass. The wind sighed all around her. She could hear the bleating of sheep and the barking of a collie dog.

From where she crouched, she could see the verandah and was able to recognise the exact spot where Edwin's cradle had been lying when the wind first started to threaten her. But now the verandah was deserted and she imagined Dorothy and Toby Orchard inside the house somewhere, staring at walls, completing tasks for which they had no enthusiasm, locked into a life's mourning for their dead son.

Pare sat with her thin arms round her bony shins. She was lighter than a child now, with no deep soft flesh on her body anywhere. She looked older than her forty years. Only her hair, which she kept oiled and plaited, was still thick and glossy.

She shivered among the stems of the toi-toi grass. She pulled her precious cloak close around her.

It was Pare's weeping that brought four-year-old Edwin to the place where she sat. He'd been lolling in his titoki tree, letting his pet brown caterpillar promenade up and down its branches, when he'd heard an unfamiliar sound. Pare's was a musical kind of weeping, and Edwin wondered whether this noise could be a giant Moa Bird crying for its lost ability to fly.

So then Edwin thought that he might be able to help the Moa, by lifting its wings, or something useful like that (his mother and father were always encouraging him to do 'useful' things) and he snatched up his caterpillar and came running towards the noise, dressed in a sailor suit for which he was very nearly too fat. And when he saw Pare, he didn't feel afraid. He was disappointed, for a moment, not to find a Moa, but he'd often been told the story of his Maori nurse who had been responsible for the accident and so he decided at once that this was who she was.

She looked at him, a pākehā boy with wide grey eyes, and opened her arms to him and said his name: 'E'win!' and without hesitation, he ran to her. She held him to her for a long time and he stroked the kiwi feathers on her cloak and breathed in the scent of her oily hair.

She told him that she would come here from time to time, to watch over him, but that he must never, never tell his parents. He asked her where she had come from and if she lived in a house made of flax. She replied that she lived in the pā with her tribe, and she had been ill, but now that she had seen him, in his smart blue suit, she would start to recover. He proudly showed her his caterpillar and how it would walk round and round his hand. She laid her forehead against his and touched his nose with hers and it seemed to him that he remembered this, this closeness of Pare's face to his and the shiny feel of her skin.

Then they heard Dorothy calling him and Edwin pulled away from Pare. She said: 'Always look for me here, in the toi-toi grass. Sometimes I will be here and sometimes I will be far beyond the river with my tribe.'

'Shall I look every day?' whispered Edwin.

'No,' said Pare. 'I cannot make such a journey every day. But you could call – always quietly, so that no one else can hear. Say "Pare, are you there?" – and if I am here, then I will answer.'

Pare's sickness left her and she began eating eels and kūmara and the meat of birds, and soft flesh now covered her bones. The years passed like this. But Pare now believed that her vigil over Edwin Orchard would have to last as long as her life lasted. Every month, therefore, unknown to Dorothy or Toby, she returned and sat in the high grass, wearing her kiwi cloak, and waited.

Sometimes she had to wait a long time, sleeping in the grass, making her existence there, always afraid of being discovered. But she was not discovered. The cloak seemed to protect her from inquisitive dogs and hide her from every eye. And then, eventually, Edwin's call would come: 'Are you there, Pare?' and she would whisper softly: 'E'win, I am here. I am here.' And then she and Edwin would sit on the grass she had plaited to make it soft and tell stories, and Edwin understood that the stories told by Pare were different from any others that he knew.

II

It was midwinter now. Midwinter in August.

Lilian Blackstone looked at her calendar disbelievingly as hailstones drove against the windows of the Cob House. She pictured the August light falling on the meadows and streams of Parton Magna and heard in her mind the fluttery, whistling cry of swallows.

She had progressed no further with her plan; her letter to Lily Dinsdale had never been sent. For, since Joseph's illness, Lilian had decided that she couldn't abandon him. Not now. For now, she would have to 'knuckle down' and make the best of things. *Wulla.* There were times when such a knuckling down simply couldn't be avoided.

Lilian also saw that the winter was beginning to sap the strength not only of Joseph, who walked about the empty land with his shoulders hunched, opening and closing his hands, like a pianist about to attempt some difficult piece of music, but also of Harriet. Harriet Blackstone's famous determination, on which so much had rested, had faltered, Lilian noted; there was no doubt about it. Sometimes, the young woman sat worryingly still at the table, some knife or implement in her hand, but the task in hand abandoned and her large eyes fixed on no object in the room but seemingly on some vivid internal landscape that seemed to have nothing about it that was consoling.

'Harriet?' Lilian would ask. 'Have you gone into a daze?'

'Oh no . . .' Harriet would reply, and immediately get on with peeling carrots or rolling suet crust or whatever it was that she had been doing. But she admitted to Lilian that 'the death of Beauty haunts me every day'. She said that she couldn't understand how certain things had been allowed to happen.

She was often to be found searching for something she refused to identify. Lilian could hear her arguing with Joseph about the Orchards' collie dog, Lady, which Harriet wanted and Joseph said they could not afford. She spent long, silent hours writing letters to her father, waiting for the day when they could be taken to Christchurch and posted. The unsent letters piled up, envelope upon envelope. *Henry Salt, Esquire, The Red House, Swaithey, Norfolk, England.*

In the nights, now, Lilian no longer heard her son making love to Harriet. In their calico room, they seemed hardly to speak to each other or murmur or move at all, but just lay still and soundless through the long dark hours and in the morning went their separate ways. They had been married less than a year. Rather to her own surprise, Lilian felt the sorrow of this estrangement. The revengeful part of her nature had wanted the farm to fail – as a punishment to Joseph for forcing her into a life for which she was not suited – but now that it seemed indeed to be failing, she felt it was a pity.

Though the monotony of the days tired Lilian, she tried very hard to retreat less often to her room and to resist sleep when it began to overwhelm her in her chair. Having decided that what the situation demanded of her was vigilance and a more willing hand, she told Joseph that she would even 'take her turn with the pig', a fat pregnant sow, bought from a farmer near Rangiora, and now so weighed down by the piglets she was carrying that her legs buckled under her and her teats scraped the ground.

The pig had to be fed with carrot peelings and stale bread and over-ripe kūmara and the scrapings from the soup kettle. Her sty, such as it was, had to be cleaned from time to time and this task was scarcely to Lilian's liking. What the sow's body couldn't absorb of the poor rations it was fed, she squirted out of her anus with a kind of venomous purpose, as though aiming at some target lurking behind her. Lilian found this rudeness quite shocking. It reminded her subliminally of the terrible behaviour of ostriches. She would have preferred to have had nothing to do with the pig, but she knew that they must not let it die, and so she took her turn at setting down the pans of food at one end and shovelling away the muck at the other.

And it was Lilian who found the sow, in a damp early morning, delivering herself of her brood. Three piglets had already been born and the sow lay panting with her snout resting on the earth, her vagina roped with blood and her breath hanging like a blue cloud in the moist grey air. Lilian stared. In her past life as the wife of a livestock auctioneer, she was used to thinking of the births of animals in arithmetical terms, but here, alone with the pig as the daylight slowly gathered, she felt its suffering and the feelings it might have of strangeness, of something progressing that had not ever progressed before.

Instead of walking back to the Cob House to fetch Joseph, Lilian sat down by the sow on some dry tussock grass and took off her apron. With the apron, she lifted the newborn piglets one by one and wiped the blood and white fluid from their snouts, then laid them near the sow's face, where their mother could lick them clean. Lilian had used the word 'vigilant' to herself. And now, she thought, as she saw the slippery body of a fourth piglet slide out on to the straw, I am going to keep my vigil here until they are all born.

The sky slowly whitened. Lilian felt the soft drizzle begin to saturate her hair and wished that she'd put on her bonnet before coming out.

III

As soon as Joseph recovered from his fever, he returned to the creek where he'd found the gold.

The waters were high after a snow-melt. Joseph understood that he and the river were now locked in combat, just as he had once been locked in combat with the girl Rebecca. The river could reveal to him the place he longed to find, or it could conceal and withhold it. The river could bring him satisfaction, or it could sweep him away.

He began to dig out a channel between the creek and the half-completed pond. In this way, he felt that he was both demonstrating his power over the flow of the water and covering his tracks. The piles of earth that soon lay around the new water-channel towards the pond made less noticeable the mounds of shingle which began to pile up at the creek's edge. For there was no other way of getting at the gold than by digging and panning what was known as the 'wash-dirt' or the 'pay-dirt'. Fossicking for the colour was a grimy business. For every tiny ounce of gold there was a huge, embarrassing pile of detritus.

The weeks began to pass. There was a difference between finding nothing whatsoever and the 'almost-nothing' that was a minute pinch of powdery colour, painstakingly rinsed from the soil and collected in a rag. And most days Joseph found nothing. Then he would experience a fury he knew was out of all proportion to his circumstances and he would bitterly recall his father saying: 'Joseph, in every life, desires may be frustrated. Try to be more accommodating to the world when it crosses you.' He found it very hard to accommodate the maddening absence of what he knew *had to be there* – if only he could see it. He would stare at the accumulation of earth and at his inadequate tools – his shovel and pick, the dented casserole dish, the tin jug – and feel the pain of a life that had always taunted him and refused to give him what he wanted. And what he wanted now was gold: nothing else. Joseph's hopes for the farm disappeared under the weight of this new yearning. In his mind, gold transformed the farm from what it was – a few acres of land blasted by the southerly winds, stung by hail and blanketed by snow – into a thriving homestead, with great trees sheltering it and money flowing to it from fleece and mutton and timber. Sudden riches would cancel the years of struggle. Joseph Blackstone had been resigned to these years – or thought he had been resigned to them – and now he discovered that he would do almost anything not to have to suffer them.

Sometimes, when Lilian was feeding the pigs and Harriet was working on her vegetable plot, he opened the tea box and untied the handkerchief and added a few more grains and looked at what was there. He found each and every particle of the gold astonishing and beautiful. It had come out of the mud and it was *his*, because he alone had seen it and recognised it for what it was. He didn't know how much the gold he had found was worth. But he wasn't stupid; he knew there was not enough of it to make any difference to his life. He imagined the tea box filled with it, filled to the brim, and only then would he go down to Christchurch and ask to see the manager of the Bank of New Zealand.

He played out the scene in his mind. He would lay down the box on the wooden counter and open it with infinite care. The bank manager would be silent, staring at something he had not expected to see, and then Joseph would be ushered into a private room at the back of the bank, a room where a fire burned, and he would be given a drink of whisky and scales would be bought out and guineas counted and he would walk out into the sunshine with all his years of toil cancelled at one stroke.

He found it difficult to complete other tasks. The digging and sifting of the wash-dirt preoccupied him at the expense of everything else. With the first green signs of spring showing among the faded grass, Joseph knew that he would soon have to begin sowing the strangely shaped fields he had so patiently ploughed with the donkey, but every morning he felt himself drawn back to the creek.

One evening, Harriet asked him: 'What are you doing to my river?' And before replying Joseph cursed himself for giving the creek Harriet's name. The creek – and all that it concealed – was *his* and he should have named it for himself. But he had his answer ready. 'If we are to put trout into the pond,' he said, 'then they must have a shingle bottom on which to feed, or they will not thrive. So I am extracting shingle which, when I have dug deep enough, I shall lay into the pond.'

When I have dug deep enough.

Joseph had no notion of how far or how long he would have to dig by the river until he found what he was looking for.

When he worked with the dish and the water scoop, he had to be vigilant the whole time, watching the valley for the arrival of Harriet or Lilian and then, if necessary, hiding his tools under earth and stones. And this was exhausting and distracting. He began to feel that it was the constant fear of discovery that made his eye less sharp and his senses less keen. He knew that on the American and Australian goldfields it had been said that certain miners 'had a feel for the colour'; it wasn't a thing you could explain or even describe, but it had to do, perhaps, with concentration upon the particular shades of black and brown and red and yellow in a clodful of earth and upon the way it fell from the shovel, but also with something else – with the messages sent from a man's will towards the thing he desired. And Joseph understood that his will was cramped by the near presence of his wife and his mother. He dreaded to see either of them there, walking towards him, with the wind billowing their skirts. He went so far as to feel that the very shape of a woman on a hillside appeared to him now as an ugly and oppressive thing.

He conceived a plan to get the women away from the land. He went to Harriet and told her that he would relent about the dog, Lady. He would give her money for it and she and Lilian would go together to visit the Orchards, and perhaps 'stay there for a few days and go riding, as you did before', and then bring the puppy back.

Harriet looked at Joseph sharply. He saw questions forming in her mind and prayed she would not ask them. Quickly, he said that he had been too severe on the subject of the dog 'only in my belief that a dog is not a necessity and that our lives here must rest upon what is necessary and only that'.

She nodded. She opened her mouth to say something and then closed it again.

'Yes,' she said at last. 'Thank you, Joseph.'

That night, lying on her back beside him, she said: 'I was fond of my father's dog. I would go so far as to say I loved it. Love for a dog is not necessarily a sentimental thing.'

IV

Through the winter, Harriet had added only three objects to her scrapbook: a brown weka feather, a shard of greenstone found in her vegetable garden and a paper jam-pot cover from Orchard House, on which Edwin had done a drawing of a windmill.

Whenever Harriet opened the scrapbook at the first page, she stared at the entwined necks of the herons on the label and thought of the tea box.

The box had vanished.

Harriet had searched for it on every shelf and surface in the Cob House and had not found it. She dreamed that Joseph had understood exactly what it contained and had burned it. She did not dare to mention it. She half-believed that it was still there somewhere in the jumble of pots and tins in the kitchen but that she was somehow incapable of seeing it. In her mind, it grew unbearably heavy. She thought that if, one day, it did suddenly reappear, she might be unable to lift it.

She felt her spirits falter. She began to think – for the first time since deciding to marry Joseph – that she should have stayed in England, sitting in her governess's chair, with her pencils and her books, with children she was able to grow fond of, with a father who loved her. Only the sight of the distant mountains, the sheer size and beauty and *mystery* of them, kept her from falling into a deep melancholy. When the spring came, Harriet promised herself, she would go into the mountains – with a strong horse if she had one by then, or with the donkey, or even on foot. She would go into the mountains alone and rediscover her willingness to continue with this New Zealand adventure.

Meanwhile, she set off with Lilian for the Orchard Run. As she climbed into the donkey cart, Harriet saw that Lilian had dressed herself in her best bonnet and a smart black cape trimmed with rabbit fur. She smiled tenderly at her mother-in-law. She thought that it was not difficult to imagine these things floating away on the swirling current of the Ashley River and the long-legged birds raising their inquisitive heads as they passed.

V

Once again, it was Edwin who ran to greet the cart. Lilian didn't see him at first, so intense was her wonder at the tall trees that grew around Orchard House and the feeling of entering once again into a world she could recognise – a world where floors would have a shine to them, where the pattern on the soup tureen would match the ladle.

Then Dorothy came flying along the verandah and down the steps, with her cropped hair sticking out at its familiar capricious angle and Harriet saw Lilian touch her bonnet anxiously, like one who has turned up to a dinner wearing clothes too smart for the occasion.

'Harriet!' cried Dorothy, with evident delight. 'And the donkey is still alive!'

Dorothy reached out to take the reins, but Edwin, who had grown just a little taller since Harriet's last visit, already held them and was stroking the donkey's nose. Harriet quickly enquired after his caterpillar.

'It's gone,' he said, 'hasn't it, Mama? It's turned into something called a larva.'

'Yes,' said Dorothy, 'we have been discussing the great

question of metamorphosis. But my dear Harriet, you must be so tired after the Ashley and all of that. Come along into the house. Edwin, help the ladies down.'

Stiff-kneed, Lilian descended from the cart. Aware that she had been disregarded in the flurry of this arrival, she took Dorothy Orchard's extended hand only by its merest fingertips and withheld the smile she had felt on her lips only a few moments ago. The familiar feeling of being snubbed – a feeling she'd thought belonged only to England, where the disdain of the upper classes infected every encounter – made Lilian want to weep, or, worse, give Dorothy Orchard a vicious swipe across her badly coiffed head. Lilian was particularly vexed by the knowledge that she never understood exactly how people like Dorothy Orchard achieved their instantaneous mastery over others outside their class. It happened before you noticed it, like a perfectly executed card trick. It was done in an instant and what you were first aware of were the *feelings* it engendered, feelings it was designed to engender, of being 'put in your place', of being told (without any words being used) that you were of little account.

Though she couldn't help but admire Orchard House, with its sheltering gardens and its solid verandah, and wish that one day Joseph might build something similar to replace the wretched Cob House, Lilian walked into it with a heavy heart. Clearly, both Dorothy and Edwin had taken Harriet into their magic 'inner circle' and the three of them were now talking excitedly about the collie pup, Lady. And she, Lilian, the sixty-four-year-old widow of a livestock auctioneer, trailed behind, her knees trembling from the journey, her rabbity cape bouncing foolishly around her shoulders, her nose boiling in the warmth of the house after the bitter cold of the journey.

She wished, suddenly, to be dead. She felt that everything wounding had gone on too long. It was beginning to get dark and Lilian decided that she would shut herself in whatever small room Dorothy would select for her and lie down and sleep and hope that she would never wake up.

She dozed for a while with her eyes open, staring at her discarded bonnet. The bed was soft and she felt grateful for this.

The room was painted blue and contained an old mahogany armoire that creaked as the dark came on.

She heard Toby arriving back from the run with his dog, the mother of the pups, and calling to his wife: 'Dorothy! Doro!' The dog yelped.

A grandfather clock chimed six. All of this, thought Lilian, could be happening in Norfolk, on some large estate, to which poor Roderick would have made uncountable visits to inspect heifers and horses and never once have received an invitation to drink a glass of port or brandy with the squire.

She could hear the familiar southerly wind, but it blew more patiently here, rustling the bare branches of the tall poplars and Lilian lay there, with her nose pointing at the ceiling, praying that the wind would lull her towards some kind of eternal rest.

Toby Orchard returned to the house in a good mood. The lambing season was just beginning on the run and every lamb he had visited today had been alive and inclined to suckle. Toby often boasted that mortality on the Orchard Run was low and when he discovered anything that contradicted this boast it made him feel intensely worried – as though he were a schoolboy again, at the mercy of a bully. But on this day, all was well and Toby felt exactly as he liked to feel – the lord of everything he could see. He'd stood alone by the river and smoked a pipe. He could hear the watery bleating of the new lambs trickle from valley to valley.

When he strode in and was told that Harriet and Lilian had arrived, he decided to open two bottles of good claret and told Janet to warm them near the range. He buttoned himself into a new waistcoat he'd bought in London long ago and never worn because Dorothy considered it 'too horribly shiny', but now, he thought, he would damn well wear it – because his lambs were thriving, because there would be three women instead of one at his supper table, because the spring was almost here.

Dorothy recognised this mood of Toby's, this overflowing of his big, contented self. It both amused and irritated her. She thought it childish and foolish and hoped it wouldn't go on too long, but at the same time, she knew that human happiness is fleeting and that Toby Orchard was a good man and should be allowed his share.

At supper, she watched him carefully, without seeming to do so, with the merest glance, as he filled and refilled his glass and smoothed the front of his ridiculous yellow waistcoat. And she saw him gradually work his charm upon Lilian Blackstone, so that her austere face took on a softer look and her hands, which at first kept rearranging the cutlery and moving her wine glass here and there, became still.

They were talking about farming in England when this transformation overtook her. Lilian had begun to describe the arduous life of her late husband, the livestock auctioneer, when Toby said: 'Ah. A livestock auctioneer. Now there is a group of people for whom I have the very greatest admiration.'

Lilian's disbelieving stare flew at Toby like a bullet, but he barely recoiled and pressed on in a loud jovial voice. 'When I was a boy,' he said, 'I spent all my holidays on my grandfather's farm and I was always enthralled by expeditions to the livestock auctions. For I heard a new language there, one I couldn't begin to comprehend, but I knew that those who did comprehend it were very clever.'

'Well,' said Lilian, aligning her pudding spoon carefully with the edge of her table mat, 'it is a language of abbreviations, that is all.'

'No,' said Toby, 'it is a language of mathematics, a scientific language.'

'Perhaps "scientific" is too grand a word?'

'Not at all,' said Toby. 'It is not too grand a word. For the auctioneer must, simultaneously and at great speed, sing out the bids expected and made, and appraise every sinew of the animal in front of him, and how is this appraisal arrived at? Through scientific knowledge.'

'Roderick would have been flattered to hear himself called a scientist,' said Lilian.

'Yet he might, after consideration, have thought it appropriate. All of us underestimate the knowledge that we possess, for although the getting of it may be hard, once it is got, we think it innate, as though we were born with it. Am I not right, Doro?'

Dorothy, who had been feeding a morsel of rabbit to Mollie

under the table, looked up and smiled generously at Toby. 'I expect you are right, dearest,' she said. 'Although certain ordinary things can continue to seem difficult when they should not.'

'The skill of the livestock auctioneer is not "ordinary", however,' said Toby and turned his big face, beginning to be pink from the claret, away from his wife and fully towards Lilian. 'It is quite exceptional, in my opinion. We live in a slow and cumbersome world and wherever I encounter that which is quick and adroit, I am disposed to marvel.'

The word 'marvel' seemed to have a wonderful effect upon Lilian. Though her hand had been creeping back towards her pudding spoon, to move it half an inch *away* from the mat, this hand now joined with its partner in a little impulsive, prayer-like clench. 'I think that you're being too generous, Mr Orchard,' she said, 'but on the other hand, I know that Roderick sometimes felt himself to be ... under-appreciated ...'

'That is a very great shame. The English used to show some reverence for skill of all kinds, but I fear they are now too much lost to the degrading spirit of commerce.'

'That was certainly what Roderick perceived,' said Lilian with an intimate sigh and Dorothy saw in the look she gave to Toby the trace of some long-ago flirtatiousness she had probably thought dead, but which was not so completely dead that it couldn't be reawakened.

'Are we finished with the stew?' asked Dorothy. 'Shall I ask Janet to bring in the pudding?'

Toby nodded and went on: 'In my former life, Mrs Blackstone, I lived and worked in the very heart of the commercial world. The City of London. But I can tell you that there was not a day that passed when I did not long for some other way of being. And I found it. Tomorrow, I will show you the new lambs on the run and perhaps you will feel some of the joy that I experience ...'

'Oh,' said Lilian. 'I am certain that I will!'

Dorothy now suddenly felt that she had had enough of the spell Toby was working on Mrs Blackstone and in calling loudly for Janet she hoped to break it. What she could not know was that, on this particular evening, it could not be broken. For Lilian, who had felt snubbed on arrival and near to death from too great an accumulation of misery, now felt her heart beating wildly with joy. Her late husband had been reinstated to a position of honour in open company. He had been described as a 'scientist' and Lilian Blackstone knew very well what weight, what marvellous respectability resided in this word.

She raised up her chin defiantly and smiled. Then she lifted her wine glass and sipped the delicious claret, remembering to hold her little finger out at an angle while she drank, as her own mother had always done when taking tea. That Toby Orchard did not know – when he made his scathing references to the degradations of commerce – about Roderick's disastrous debts to his bookmakers seemed not to matter at all to Lilian at this most exquisite moment.

VI

The next day dawned so bright that a vivid remembrance of summer came into Edwin Orchard's mind as he washed his face and he thought of Pare with her golden skin. He hoped she might come today and call out: 'I am here, E'win. I am here.'

Edwin decided that he would take Harriet with him to the place in the toi-toi grass where Pare always waited. They would set out with Lady and he would pretend he was giving Harriet a lesson on how to make Lady obey her. He would tell his parents that no one else must come with them, or Lady would be too confused to show any obedience at all.

He thought that Pare might gather Lady into her cloak and stroke her nose with the precious kiwi feathers and laugh her laugh that was as musical as her weeping.

Edwin waited until his father and mother had set out with Mrs Lilian Blackstone to show her the new lambs and then he took Harriet's hand and they walked slowly and quietly, with the black-and-white puppy bouncing at their heels, in the direction of the clumps of toi-toi. The sun was still shining, but from the north a dark grey cloud was beginning to move across the sky.

'When we get near,' instructed Edwin, 'you mustn't make any sound. You must stop Lady from whining or barking or anything. And I shall call out: "Are you there, Pare?" And then we will just wait and see if any answer comes.'

He called several times and they stood and waited, while the huge dark cloud advanced upon the sun.

'Are you there, Pare? Are you there?'

But there was no reply, only the wind moving in the grass. Harriet looked at Edwin and saw the intensity of his expression.

'Sometimes, I can tell,' he whispered. 'I can tell she is there before she has answered, even though I cannot see her.'

'But she isn't there today?'

'No. I don't think she is there. But we could go to the place where she sits, and wait and she might come.'

They moved forward and the scratchy grasses touched their arms and prickled the puppy's inquisitive nose and made her yelp. Edwin walked in a straight line for some distance, then turned right and left, as if following some hidden path. A brown bird flew up and fluttered away. Harriet saw Edwin standing still now – so still that he seemed to cast no shadow. Then slowly he beckoned to Harriet and, as she walked towards him, he crouched down and was hidden by the toi-toi.

By bending the harsh stems carefully, folding them one over another (in exactly the way that Pare folded them), Edwin contrived a soft and comfortable place for them to sit and the puppy lay down beside them.

Harriet didn't speak. She saw Edwin looking and listening intently still, as though Pare might yet be there or else moving closer to him, invisible in her feathered cloak, and waiting only for the moment when he would call to her.

The sun disappeared and the place where they sat felt suddenly dark.

Edwin looked up at Harriet and said: 'Shall I tell you a secret?'

Harriet waited a moment before saying: 'You shouldn't tell me anything you've been forbidden to tell.'

'No,' said Edwin. 'Not forbidden. It's just Mama or Papa . . .'

'Is this is one of Pare's secrets?'

'Yes. Pare knows things before the pākehā people know them because the Maoris listen to the earth and they listen to the birds and the rivers. And in the rivers there are Maori spirits called taniwha who sometimes speak to them and the taniwha know everything in the world.'

'Everything in the world?'

'Yes. And one thing they know about is greenstone.'

'Greenstone?'

'Yes. You mustn't whisper this to Mama, but Pare told me that there's gold at Greenstone Creek. It would have been Maori gold, but they sold their land to the pākehā. Long ago.'

'Whose gold will it be, then?'

'Pare says thousands of men will come. She says gold can make everybody do things they'd never normally do. She says people will die trying to cross the mountains.'

At this moment, the darkness which had settled on the landscape after the disappearance of the sun became still more sombre and hail began tumbling out of the black sky. Edwin and Harriet fell silent as the icy stones stung their heads and bounced all around them on the flattened grass. The dog stood up and went in a circle, trying first to shake the hailstones away and then snapping at them as though they were a swarm of white bees.

Edwin held out his hands, cupping them to catch the hail and then showing Harriet the perfect round white stones in his palm.

'I like weather,' he said. 'Don't you?'

Harriet nodded and smiled. The puppy looked from her to Edwin expectantly, but neither of them moved.

The Preservation

I

In November, with his small, irregular fields sown with wheat and lopsided cob shelters built for the animals, Joseph went down to Christchurch to buy a new milk cow. He took Lilian with him in the donkey cart.

On the journey, she talked about English trees. 'You should put in willow saplings by the pond and poplars to shade the house, Joseph,' she said.

Joseph didn't say anything, but Lilian went on: 'And I do think that a laurel hedge between the west window of the Cob House and Harriet's vegetable patch would be agreeable to the eye, wouldn't it?'

'Yes,' he said, 'it would be "agreeable to the eye".'

'What I mean,' continued Lilian, 'is that now that the spring has come, it is surely time to make everything nicer?'

Joseph said nothing more, only muttered to the donkey, spurring it on. He wanted to say to Lilian that the day would arrive when he could give his attention to 'niceness'. He wanted to tell his mother that once the creek had yielded up the gold that he knew was there, then he would rebuild the house lower down the flat and that the second house would be built of stone and wood and slate, with a large verandah sheltered from the winds. He longed to reassure Lilian that she wouldn't end her days in a room made of calico and he was on the point of telling her simply to have faith in him, for he knew the future would be bright. But he couldn't say any of this because this brightness was not yet assured in his mind. For gold is deceitful; this he was beginning to understand. It is as duplicitous as a girl. It shows itself and beckons. Within its first gleam lies the promise of more, much more, and so men go forward, cajoling the earth, breaking their backs and their hearts, but very often they're rewarded with nothing – or almost nothing: just the very little needed to keep hope and longing alive.

'Box,' Lilian mused. 'How sweet a low box hedge would be beside the door, Joseph.'

'Yes,' replied Joseph, urging the donkey to a faster trot, 'the scent of it would remind you of Parton.'

Lilian hoped, in Christchurch, to stay with Mrs Dinsdale, but to her chagrin, a large sign had been hung on Mrs Dinsdale's window, which read NO ROOMS AVAILABLE HOUSE FULL.

'It cannot be,' Lilian said with a sniff. 'It is merely Lily's way of selecting the genteel from the riff-raff. I will go in and find her and she will give me my old room.'

Lilian descended from the cart. The soles of her feet ached as they touched the ground. She rang the bell and waited. She noticed that Joseph had remained sitting, holding on to the reins, as though preparing to drive away.

Lilian remembered Lily Dinsdale's house as a place of quiet and salubriousness, but now, as she stood in the street, she could hear noisy laughter – men's laughter – coming from an upper room, and she noticed that the step on which she was standing had a patterning of mud on it, which could only have been made by heavy boots. She tried to peer, beyond the lace curtains, into one of the downstairs windows. Her heart lurched with the terrible thought that perhaps Lily Dinsdale was no longer here, indeed had died of some tropical infection brought from Fiji or Samoa, which no one knew how to cure. How ghastly life seems, she thought, when a person on whom we have depended in our minds goes suddenly missing.

The door opened and a young girl, wearing a creased and stained pinafore, stood before her. 'No rooms, ma'am,' she said and was about to close the door in Lilian's face when Lilian reached out and held it ajar.

'I am an old friend of Mrs Dinsdale's,' said Lilian, standing as straight and tall as she could on her painful feet. 'Will you fetch her, please?'

The girl stared at Lilian, rudely looking her over. The male laughter which Lilian had heard in the street now came cascading down the stairs, causing Lilian's eyelids to flutter with revulsion. Then she heard Mrs Dinsdale's voice calling to the girl: 'Tell them we are full, Hetty!'

'We're full, ma'am,' said the girl, again trying to close the door, but Lilian pushed past her into the hall and called out: 'Lily! It's Lilian Blackstone!'

There was a moment's pause, during which the laughter above burst out with new intensity. Laughter like gunfire, Lilian thought. And then Mrs Dinsdale appeared from the parlour and the two women stared at each other in shocked silence, both recognising that some kind of calamity was occurring. For the Mrs Dinsdale who stood before Lilian was really not the 'dear Lily Dinsdale' who had been so kind to her and so very friendly on her first arrival in Christchurch; she was definitely some other Lily Dinsdale, not 'dear' at all, a Lily Dinsdale dressed in a tight black satin dress, cut low above her white breasts, with, instead of her habitual lace cap, coquettish bows adorning her hair and tumbling in a silken tangle almost to her shoulders.

It was she, however, in all her conspicuous finery, who recovered before Lilian. Indeed, Lilian decided she was seeing something from which she might never recover and so she could only stand there and gape while her former friend began offering her apology.

'It is the Rush,' said Mrs Dinsdale. 'I am so sorry, Mrs Blackstone. The Rush has altered everything. You see? I expect you have seen what is happening on the road to Lyttelton Harbour . . . ?'

Lilian tried to say that she'd seen nothing, that she and Joseph had driven straight here, to this door, where they thought they would be welcome and had planned to lay their heads for the night, but she found herself unable to speak.

At this moment, a man's voice called down the stairs: 'Lily! Lily-my-dainty! We're thirsty here!'

'Ale,' said Lily Dinsdale, with a frail little smile. 'That is what they all bleat for. I have told them I am not an ale-house. I have warned them they should get used to hardship and deprivation, but they take no notice.'

Mrs Dinsdale seemed to hope that Lilian would say something now, would see what her position was in a man's world and take her part, or at least release her from shame. But Lilian Blackstone was incapable of uttering a syllable; she stood there with her face hard as flint, remembering the letter she had almost sent here, remembering how, to this very day, the house of Lily Dinsdale had always featured in her plans for her own salvation. And realising now that *there was no salvation*. There was only this rowdy house of men and Lily's ridiculous clothes and the dabs of – what was it called? – *rouge* on her face.

Mrs Dinsdale gathered herself for a last effort at smoothing down what could not be smoothed down. 'I am very sorry if you were hoping . . .' she said and then stopped and then began again. 'I truly am sorry if you were expecting . . . but a Rush, you see . . . it will change everything. It will turn us all upside-down.'

At the word 'turn', Lilian took some kind of desperate cue and whirled away from Mrs Dinsdale, striding the few paces to the door, where Hetty still stood in her greasy apron. She gave the girl a venomous shove which almost knocked her off her feet and walked away from the house, slamming the front door after her. She climbed into the donkey cart with an agility born of shock and fury and instructed Joseph to drive on.

Joseph found a tea-room and, tying the donkey to a post, installed his mother there with a bun untouched on a plate in front of her, until he saw a little colour return to her cheeks.

'Eat the bun,' he said kindly.

Lilian took a tiny, sugary nibble, but found chewing difficult. 'Gold,' she said, when she had swallowed the small mouthful. 'Is that what she meant? A Gold Rush?'

Joseph said that, on entering Christchurch, he'd noticed groups of men – men alone, dressed in working clothes – moving restlessly about the streets. He'd noticed grog-shops that had not been there before. On the side of a cart piled high with canvas, he'd read the words *Buy your tent here Best prices*.

He didn't say that at the sight of these things and knowing what they might mean, he'd felt a terrible unease. He didn't say that, until this particular afternoon, he'd imagined himself to be the sole possessor of new gold in all of New Zealand and that now he knew that he had been deluded. He didn't say that he had begun to pray – pray and pray to a God he hardly ever talked to – that whatever gold had been found, it was a long way from his own creek and that his secret (such as it now was) could remain safe. All he did say was: 'Something has happened here.'

He suggested that he should leave Lilian in the warmth and relative comfort of the tea-room while he searched for information and found them somewhere to stay.

'There will be nowhere to stay,' Lilian said bleakly.

'Then,' Joseph said, 'we shall buy a tent,' and hoped to see a smile cross his mother's face. But it was as if Lilian Blackstone had decided she would never smile again, that she would put that particular muscle of her face to sleep and never call on it to move any more for as long as she remained on the earth.

'If only . . .' Lilian began. And then faltered.

'If only what?'

'If only she had not pretended to be my friend. To suggest we had so much in common . . . She even had the temerity to remark on the similarity of our Christian names . . .'

Joseph nodded. Then he said: 'People change according to the times in which they live, that is all.'

'It may be *all*,' said Lilian, 'but it is also a great deal.'

Joseph stood up. The afternoon was already darkening and he knew that he had much to do. Not only did he have to find somewhere for his mother to sleep; he also had to discover where everyone was going and what this Rush portended. And he knew that he couldn't begin on the search for a room in this suddenly crowded town until he understood what was happening. First, then, he would go down to the market. Already, he'd begun to hope that the men he had seen were here to take ship out of Lyttelton to Nelson or down south to Dunedin – far from the Okuku Valley.

Let them go.

He had no wish to follow or take any part in a mass Rush. He had gold on his farm.

He walked through the dusk. As he came within sight of the market, he could hear a fiddler playing and the reckless little cries of people dancing. As he turned into Diamond Street, he found himself suddenly becoming part of an immense crowd, men and women both, but mainly men, wearing leather hats and moleskins, pushing carts or carrying on their backs the primitive tools of the miner: picks, shovels, pans, billy-cans, boots, and sacking. Money was changing hands at a brisk rate for the purchase of tea, flour, rice, candles, knives, canvas, brandy and a hundred other commodities men wanted to take with them into whatever wilderness they were going to. And there was a haste and an intensity to this commerce – with hands reaching and grabbing and coins counted at extraordinary speed – as though the coming night were going to place a curfew upon it and the wares had to be got now or for ever put beyond the people's reach.

Joseph stopped in front of a counter advertising itself as the Survival Stall. Others pressed around him as he watched a man in a sacking apron take a live eel from a bucket, lay it on a wooden block and slice off its head. The head lay still, but the body moved until it had almost slithered off the block. 'Don't you dare, my boy!' said the stall-holder and spat on to the floor. He snatched up the eel and with a dexterity which astonished the small crowd, slit it in half and removed both backbone and gut and threw these away. He laid out on the block the two halves of the eel, pink and a little bloody, with tender care, like a jeweller laying out a ruby necklace for a rich customer.

'Now,' he said. 'Watch this. For this is the Preservation. This is the thing that will keep the meat sweet. And without it you may die.'

The people moved closer. Joseph could smell the eel flesh and could see, in the sagging pocket of the man's apron, a fine fistful of money.

The man laid on the block a jar of salt, reached into it with his bloodstained hand and spread the salt along one half of the eel.

'Work it in,' he said. 'Smother your eel in it. Pretend it is snow or ice. For snow and ice are the Preservation, too, but snow and ice you may not have, for they melt away. But salt you can keep.'

The eel, smothered with salt, was now sliced into pieces, which the stall-holder began to lay carefully in a pickling jar. Joseph had seen his mother preserving herring in just this way and was about to observe out loud that there was nothing new in all of this when the man turned his attention to the second half of the eel. He reached under his bench and brought out a second large bucket and a second jar. The bucket was filled with yellow-brown bladder wrack and he took up a fistful of the seaweed and held it aloft.

'Now you thought that without salt you would have no Preservation, didn't you?' he said. 'You were imagining lugging blocks of salt on your backs through the swamps of the Grey, weren't you? Well, salt is the finest Preservation, but wrack will do. And wrack is to be found all along the shore.'

The second fillet was sliced and laid in the jar with the bladder wrack packed closely round it. 'Burst the blisters of the wrack on the flesh of your fish,' the man instructed. 'Tamp it down. Pack it tight. You will have a brine.'

The lid of the jar was screwed down as tightly as it would go and bound with strips of damp canvas, split and tied at their ends like a bandage.

'*Voilà*! As the Frenchies say,' the eel man concluded triumphantly. 'You have your Preservation. A shilling for the eel. A penny for the lesson.'

The eel was bought and everyone in the cluster around the Survival Stall, including Joseph, dutifully handed over a penny piece. It would not have been difficult, thought Joseph, to slip away without paying, but in such a case, as the eel man knew only too well, some superstitious worry impels you towards an act of honesty.

As he moved away and realised that night was coming on very fast now, Joseph turned to faces all around him and asked: 'Where is the Rush? Where is everybody going?'

Some laughed – as at the one fool in the company who is without the essential knowledge. But the person nearest to

Joseph, a large man with the seamed and weathered face of a seasoned digger, pointed in the direction of the Port Hills. 'The *Wallabi* waits at Lyttelton,' he said. 'She's north-bound for Nelson and then – if the saints and the wild winds agree – for Hokitika.'

The word 'Hokitika' acted like magic on Joseph, like a healing balm. His creek was safe, then. These men would set off with their jars of eels and their sluice-boxes, but they were travelling to the West Coast, to the other side of the South Island. They wouldn't come anywhere near his land.

Joseph began to retrace his steps towards the tea-room where he had left Lilian. He wouldn't bother to seek other accommodation. He would simply bribe the owner of the tea-shop to let his mother sleep there and, if the bribe was good enough, no doubt she would eventually agree. And as for him, he didn't care where he slept. He thought he could lie down anywhere and get a night's rest, just as he had done when he was building the Cob House, listening to tales of cockatoos in the firelight, with his head resting in the crook of his arm.

II

It was the time of year for burning the tussock. Though the land would be blackened and hideous for a while, new, succulent shoots would be summoned into existence by the fire and for a brief season, the dun-coloured flats would be dusted with green.

Dorothy Orchard had told Harriet that she loved 'setting the fires and seeing the flames creep forward so obediently'. She whispered that she always set her fires at dusk 'and watch them until they are embers in the dark. And then I'm afraid there is a smell of roasting meat that arrives on the wind and it is all the grasshoppers and the lizards cooked in the flames. And even this, I find to be almost thrilling.'

Alone with the dog, Lady, after Joseph and Lilian had departed for Christchurch, Harriet marked out an area for burning below the new cob shelters and the half-completed pond. 'Even pigs', said Dorothy, 'love to munch the new green tussock and it will keep them healthy, so you might burn your tussock, too, even though you have no sheep. But never choose a day of high wind.'

This November day was gentle, almost warm. Harriet waited until the afternoon began its drift towards evening and then started lighting her tapers. It had not rained for some days and the tussock was dry and brittle. Fires sprang into life at the first catch of flame – nine or ten small fires devouring the faded grass as they moved forward and fanned out and joined and divided and joined again, running downhill at a cantering kind of speed. Harriet thought that she had never seen fires that looked so contented. They made her smile; small fires, but busy and thorough.

Lady barked at the little flames and, believing them alive, would have chased them as she could already chase sheep, but Harriet kept her close on a lead and together they followed them at a distance as the air began to fill with smoke. Like Dorothy, Harriet was enjoying her task – the more so because she was alone with the dog and Joseph and Lilian were far away and she could do whatever she pleased. Though the area of the fire was safely bounded by creek and plough, she had set the flames a single puzzle: in their path lay one cabbage tree, taller than a man, with its dragon leaves a bright, striking green against the pale colour of the flats.

What would the fires do? Would they circle the tree to carry on with their task of burning the tussock or would the tree prove irresistible? Would they climb into it, inch by inch, and devour it?

Harriet waited and watched. She glanced at Lady and saw that the yellow-brown eyes of the dog had taken on a strange brightness as the light of day drained from the sky. And it seemed to Harriet that already, the dog could feel her mood and tune its own way of being to hers.

The smoke stayed low over the valley, so that the top of the cabbage tree was still just visible above it when the first flames arrived at its feet. Harriet knew that these trees held dense moisture in their stems and she thought this would repel the fire. She saw it trying to climb the stem, thrusting itself upwards towards the giant leaves, then falling back, while all around the tree the busy fires on the ground scuttled on. Then, for a few moments, the direction of the wind veered slightly to the west, and smoke obscured the cabbage tree. Would it be burnt, or would it remain? Harriet thought how, though men and women struggle day and night to tame the world and make it theirs, so also do they long to see wild and random things and marvel at them and carry their memory away.

The tree began to burn. A single flame seemed to travel through it, splitting it like a spear and when this spear of flame caught the leaves, it burst into a fountain of yellow fire. Against the darkening sky, this fountain was of a colossal brightness, a biblical brightness, and both Harriet and Lady shivered with the wonder of it.

Later, in the dark, two kea came and feasted on roasted insects and lizards. Harriet, walking out with a lamp to make sure that the fires were extinguished, heard them squabbling and then watched them picking their meal from the cinders of the valley.

She watched them for a long time, attentive to the strangeness of them. Then she went indoors and began cutting off her hair.

The hair she cut smelled of the smoke and she thought how, in the hours that had just passed, alone with the dog, she had been entirely happy and that everything in the world around her had seemed beautiful to her. And it was this that she longed to preserve – this sense of a beautiful world. In cutting off her hair, she believed that she was preparing herself for all that was coming in the new season, so that she would see everything clearly, as clearly as she had seen the burning cabbage tree.

But this 'everything' didn't pertain only to what Harriet called 'the beautiful world'; it included all that Joseph was doing in secret.

She had been down to the creek. She had found her casserole dish, buried under shingle. She'd stood and stared at the mounds of soil at the creek's edge. She'd been amazed that Joseph thought her so stupid that she was incapable of deducing what he was doing. It made her furious – not that he was fossicking for gold in her creek, but that he was doing it like this, under the pretence of digging the gully to the pond and laying down a shingle bottom for the trout.

What made him lie about it? Had he found any gold? There was so much work to be done on the farm that surely Joseph would not have been turned aside from it, except by a discovery which had taken him by surprise and which he had not been able to resist? And then, for reasons which Harriet couldn't deduce but which might have to do with the egotism she saw in him, or with some *habit of lying* that he might barely recognise in himself, he had decided to keep everything secret.

The excavations at the creek were ugly. There was something obscene about them. But as Harriet contemplated them, she thought that perhaps they were no more 'obscene' than the workings of her own mind and heart in relation to Joseph. For day by day, she kept secret from him her own lovelessness. It piled up in her. At times, it was not merely lack of love that she felt; it was hatred of the blackest kind. And though she struggled to conceal it from him, perhaps she succeeded no better than he did with his blatant heaps of earth? In the nights, she often awoke at first light to see him staring at her, his eye close to hers, his fists clenched around the sheets. Did he know that she did not love him? Did he understand all too clearly that she loved the wilderness he had brought her to, but not him?

Harriet peered at her face in the glass. She thought that it seemed larger now that her hair had been cut away, with its every expression more exaggerated and more transparent. From now on, her mind would surely be easier for Joseph to read?

After sweeping up her hair and throwing it into the range, Harriet began her search for the missing tea box. She was also looking for Joseph's gold.

One by one, she took down every kitchen implement, every pan and tin and sack, every china pot and glass jar, every sachet and square of folded muslin. All were clean, dry and empty and she replaced them exactly as they had been found. She stood in the kitchen, staring. Her candle burned with an even flame. Lady slept in front of the fire.

She took up the candle and moved into the calico bedroom. She lay down on the earth floor and peered into the dark space under the bed. She tugged out a pair of Joseph's boots and saw the mud of the creek still on them, dried to a bluish colour. She put her hand into each of the boots and shivered as she imagined that she felt there some vestigial warmth of Joseph's feet, but the boots were empty. Harriet turned them over, examining the mud, bringing the flame very near to the soles of the boots and trying to see whether there was any speck of yellow dust adhering to them. But there was nothing and she replaced them in the dark square under the bed. Then she went to the old trunk where Joseph kept his few possessions and slowly opened the lid.

She'd never looked in this trunk. She knew that Joseph hadn't brought very much with him to New Zealand; only his clothes and his books, and perhaps a few objects that had belonged to his father. And having little, she believed he was entitled to keep this little locked away. Even now, Harriet hesitated to search the trunk. She knelt, with her hand on the lid, looking quickly for any sign of the tea box and not finding it. But she knew also that she was memorising the contents of the chest and the precise arrangement of things, so that she could take everything out and put it back exactly as it had been found.

There were Joseph's clothes with their frayed pockets and worn collars. There was a Bible and a hymnal and a volume of poems by Andrew Marvell and another by William Words-worth and a map of the world. There was a leather-bound fishing book, filled in with Joseph's handwriting and containing mainly disappointed entries: 'A poor season.' 'River low.' 'Bitterly cold.' 'No mayfly.' 'Fish very choosy.' There was a small, ornate pistol in a wooden box and Harriet took a long time examining this, even looking down its barrel to see if anything had been concealed there.

At the bottom of the trunk were laid Joseph's fishing rods and hand-tied flies in a glass case, every one labelled in its own small compartment: *Iron Blue, Sawyer Nymph, Lunn.* Harriet opened the lid of the case and looked at the flies, which were the flies of an English river and might delude no fish in Aotearoa, but she thought them clever in their mimicry of insects and oddly beautiful. Harriet was about to replace the fly box when she noticed that one of the tiny compartments contained, not a fishing-fly, but a curl of human hair. She picked up the brown curl and stared at it: a memento so precious to Joseph, he'd hidden it away in the fly box in order to bring it with him to New Zealand.

Harriet felt breathless. She considered burning the brown curl, as she'd just burnt her own hair – burning it to punish Joseph, to let him know that she knew his secret. But, in truth, she did not know it and *did not want to know it.* She understood that there was nothing to be done with the curl except to put it away where she'd found it.

III

The owners of the tea-shop agreed to lodge Lilian for the night, but explained that their three bedrooms were already occupied and that she would have to sleep in the parlour that lay behind the tea-room itself.

The parlour was dark and cramped and contained nothing much except a sideboard and a small sofa, so plumply upholstered that it looked as though it would burst under the least impress of any human weight upon it. Lilian imagined how this ridiculously stuffed thing would bounce her bones from position to position all through the hours of darkness and never give them any rest. She let escape from her chest a deep, shuddering sigh. The day had been vile: the long journey in the small cart, then the terrible encounter with Mrs Dinsdale ... and now the night promised to be quite ferociously as bad.

But she had no choice. She was told that every room in Christchurch was taken by people awaiting passage to Nelson and the West Coast on the *Wallabi*. Rooms that were not even rooms were taken. People were bedding down in stables and warehouses, in lofts and closets, in cellars and pump-rooms and bars. At the words 'pump-rooms and bars' Lilian fanned herself with her gloves and informed her hostesses that she would gladly take advantage of the offending sofa. 'Luckily,' she said, 'I am not very tall.' 'My husband was tall,' she added for no reason that she could explain (and Roderick Blackstone had not been particularly tall), 'but I am not.'

Joseph bought a bag of hay for the donkey, then took supper with Lilian and the tea-shop owners and was shown the silk eiderdown that would cover his mother while she slept, as though this were an exhibit they were planning to offer at the local museum.

The supper was a meagre one of cold mutton cutlets and pickles and with this in his belly Joseph left them and walked away into the night. The donkey stood in the road, between the traces of the cart, sorrowfully munching its hay.

Joseph walked north-west out of the town, the way they had come, on the road to Okuku. He didn't want to be among the crowd of would-be gold-seekers heading towards Lyttelton. He didn't want anybody to inform him that on the Hokitika River there was the colour waiting in miraculous quantities or to hear how lives would be changed and fortunes made; he wanted to be alone and quiet and dream his own dreams.

Then, on the road, an awesome weariness overtook him. His legs felt as though they had walked across the world, from the Orient to the Alps. He wished he were lying by a fire with the beeches sighing on the empty hill and his vision of the Cob House still untainted by its reality.

He saw a barn in the distance and thought he would go in there and lie down. He didn't mind whether there was any straw or hay. He had his cloak. He would cover himself with that and fall instantly asleep. But as he approached the barn, he heard an agitated barking and whining coming from it and understood that the barn contained dogs – not the collies the run-holders used, but poorly fed hounds, by the sound of them, of the kind cockatoo farmers kept to kill weka and pukeko and retrieve pigeons. So Joseph skirted the barn, drank from a water butt, but didn't go inside, only settled himself by the barn wall, in the shadow of its roof, and watched the moon skim in and out of the clouds.

All night long, he could hear the dogs, sometimes near him scrabbling at their confinement, and sometimes in his dreams. He knew they could smell him – this human trespasser. They howled at his obstinacy in remaining there, pressed up against the wall, and he thought how he had heard this fury of theirs in his own mind for a long while – fury against himself, fury for the past which had been spoiled and for his audacious belief that he could begin everything afresh.

He woke at first light, when the dogs had fallen silent at last and with the grey pallor of the sky hung out like a sheet that never stirs in the wind. He walked on the wet grass, back and forth, to wake up his limbs and then set out to look for some breakfast before he began his round of purchases for the farm.

Though he prided himself that he was a man who seldom felt the cold, he found himself shivering on his walk back into Christchurch. Other men joined him on the way, moving, each aloof and alone, like ghosts without shadows in the overcast dawn. And although Joseph kept his head low and began no conversation with anyone, he noticed that the faces of these people looked wan, as though they had been coaxed into banishment by relatives in England or Scotland who were weary of them and who didn't care what became of them, just as long as they didn't return. And now they were going to try to sail to the West Coast, where no safe harbour existed, where ship after ship had been wrecked on the sandbars and hundreds had drowned in the violent surf. In their solitude and in their determination, these were people who had nothing to lose, but Joseph did not dare to pity them because he saw himself as one of them.

He drew his cloak tightly round his chest and moved with them towards the next moment, the next hour of the fast-approaching day.

In Hudson's Utilities, a cavernous, dusty store that smelled of chaff, Joseph saw that the usual stock of farm implements and seed had been shouldered to the back of the shop by a large consignment of gold-mining equipment.

He walked slowly along an array of pannikins, picks, shovels, knives, boots, hats, flasks, buckets and tents. He stood still and stared at these objects. Then his eye was caught by a hand-scribbled sign: *Change your fortunes with this cradle!* A contraption made of wood and iron, not unlike a small sleigh at first glance, stood underneath the sign and advertised itself as *The One and Only Otago Sluice-Box.* Joseph understood at once that this was an object of considerable ingenuity.

An upper section, a tray made of metal slats, could be moved back and forth by hand (very much as a hand rocked a cradle) as water was played over it. Stones and coarse shingle would be trapped in the slats and most of the fine sand would be washed away by the play of the water. But beneath the slats was a shallow box, lined with pleated sacking, and on to this sacking any small but heavy particles would fall. Piles of dirt could be 'washed' through this sluice-box and then the sacking picked over inch by inch. And all that had fallen would be preserved in the sacking, held by the pleats. If gold was present in the wash-dirt, there it would be.

Joseph looked at the *Otago Sluice-Box* for a long time. He wanted to buy it and load it into the donkey cart, hidden under the sacks of provisions he had yet to acquire. But he felt the morning brighten outside. He knew that the box was too cumbersome a thing to hide in the open air.

The Line

I

It was almost night once again when Joseph returned to the
Cob House. He had to walk most of the way, holding the
donkey's bridle, with the new milk cow tethered behind,
swaying along at a slow pace. In the cart, Lilian slept with her
head on a sack of coffee beans and didn't notice the sun going
down and the gradual obliteration of the path by the gathering
dusk. When they arrived at the farm, she woke up and asked:
'What time is it, Roderick?'

A dry wind was blowing from the south-west. Harriet had
worked all day at washing sheets and cloths, shirts, drawers and
petticoats so that she could peg them out before the wind
changed its mind. Her knuckles were bleeding and she could
see a rash beginning to creep between her fingers. The only part
of the arduous business of washing that she liked was turning
the mangle. The rest of it was a purgatory. While she soaped
and slapped and pummelled the soiled garments, she had
wondered aloud how much of life was repetition. During her
long years as a governess, it had been the year-by-year
recapitulation of the same historical or mathematical facts that
had sometimes made her want to scream.

In the night, when Joseph lay down beside her, she took his
hand.

He turned his head and looked at her and said: 'You should
not have cut off your hair.'

Harriet lay still and replied: 'I did it to see clearly, that's all. And now I see why you're digging by the creek.'

She felt him tense along the whole of his exhausted frame, but he said nothing, only turned his head away.

She said: 'I understand that we have to keep some secrets from one another, Joseph, but I think gold is too heavy a thing to hide.'

She waited. She imagined her washing, like ghosts, flapping in the moonlight.

After a long while, Joseph said: 'There is no gold.'

She didn't believe him. She said: 'Yet you continue to look for it. What makes you continue?'

'I saw ... what I thought was the colour. Some particles of dust. If I had made a proper find, I would have told you.'

'Where is the dust?'

She felt him tense again and he removed his hand from hers. 'Washed away.'

'There's nothing gleaned from all your work, then?'

'No. Nothing. And now I know that I was mistaken to search here. The gold is on the West Coast.'

'And in the south, on the Arrow. So Dorothy told me.'

'The Arrow is finished. All of Otago is finished. They say only the Chinese are still there, picking over the tailings.'

'Yet if there was gold in Otago and now on the West Coast, perhaps there will be gold in our creek? Perhaps there is gold to be found everywhere in New Zealand?'

Joseph lay still and silent. He was dog-tired. He didn't want to be interrogated. He closed his eyes and prayed that sleep would overtake him before Harriet said another word.

He had just begun that gentle see-saw between consciousness and darkness when some little noise reached him from beyond the calico wall and he knew that Lilian had cried out. 'What is the matter?' Joseph said, without moving. But no one answered him.

II

Now, the summer began to come in.

The tussock was springy and bright. The cow, which had no name, meandered over the flats, munching without pause, and her milk was plentiful and thick with cream.

When Harriet found snails creeping over her first lettuces, she gathered them into a bucket and fed them to the pigs, who crunched them eagerly, making her smile. She saw, suddenly, that not only the pigs but everything else was beginning to thrive. Even the wheat Joseph had sown in his oddly shaped fields was appearing, a bit sparse and thin, but there nevertheless, a combing of pale green on which the sun came and went as the clouds allowed.

Harriet planted and hoed. Dorothy Orchard had given her strawberry plants and currant and gooseberry bushes. She cut tea-tree stakes from the bush to make a scaffolding for her beans. The stems of her onions were like neat green fountains against the dark of the earth. White flowers began to bloom in her potato patch. The first carrots were pulled and were sweet enough to eat raw. There was a sudden scent in the vegetable garden, which, on certain evenings, reminded Harriet of England. It was the scent of something which had begun to have permanence.

For the first time, they were no longer cold in the Cob House and often ate their mid-day meal with the door open, to let the sun dry the earthen floor. They could hear crickets beginning to chatter on the flats and the songs of birds they couldn't yet recognise. On a flax bush under one of the windows, orange buds started to open. When the rain fell, it was copious and warm.

Lilian got out her sewing machine and began to make curtains from a bolt of blue cloth she had bought 'very advantageously' from the owners of the Christchurch tea-rooms where she had spent her night on the sofa. She leaned over the machine so closely that her pointed nose almost touched the N of the word SINGER inscribed on it, while her white hands guided the material into the perfectly turned seams she had been so proud of in the days in Parton Magna where she made chair covers from green brocade.

That there was nothing on which to hang the curtains troubled Lilian only fleetingly. She would nag Joseph until he had come up with some solution to the absence of poles and rings. She reminded him that 'this whole enterprise turns upon ingenuity' and said she would not let him rest until the poles were up. 'You made the windows,' she added crossly, as though this addition had been somehow reckless and unnecessary.

Christmas came in the middle of a hot spell. Lilian hoped for an invitation to Orchard House, so that the day would have some feeling of amplitude and grace and the dirty plates be taken care of by Janet, but the Orchards invited only the people who worked on the sheep run at Christmas time and had no room for anyone else.

Harriet decorated the kitchen in a simple way. Strings were nailed up and pulled taut just under the ceiling, and armfuls of green ferns were pressed behind the strings and arranged this way and that like a garland. The smell of the ferns was pungent 'and not unpleasant' remarked Lilian. She made ribbons from her bolt of blue cloth and tied bows along the strings. The ribbons, too, turned out to be the solution to the hanging of the curtains. Joseph set tea-tree poles above the windows and the curtains were looped to these.

'They draw very slowly,' said Lilian, 'but I suppose this does not matter. Time is the one thing we have too much of.'

On Christmas morning, the Cob House kitchen looked as much like a proper room as it was ever going to look and as Harriet banked up the range in preparation for cooking two wild duck, she let herself feel proud of everything they had done. Soon, they would be able to trade vegetables and hams and butter for mutton and coal. Joseph had begun to talk about buying a horse and Harriet dreamed of this horse while she worked. She would ride it towards the mountains. She would see red-crowned parakeets flying in the forests.

As she seasoned the ducks, rubbing salt into their skins and folding them over where their necks had been, Harriet remembered the herons of the tea-box label and then the tea box itself, which she had never found. Joseph's secret, his digging for gold, was in the open now, but her secret was not.

She thought it pointless to torture herself with these matters and yet they came and went from her mind every day, usually towards evening, like rooks gathering at dusk. She longed to confide in somebody. She thought that perhaps what she longed to hear was that almost every life was arranged like this, around a void where love should have been and was not, and that her predicament was therefore an ordinary one.

She wondered whether Dorothy Orchard might tell her that she didn't love Toby, saying something like: 'This is perfectly all right, Harriet. It is even *convenient*, because love makes people so wild and thoughtless. So really it is better to live quite outside it.'

Imagining this conversation comforted Harriet, but she didn't think it would take place, because she believed that what she saw, quite to the contrary, whenever she went to the Orchard Run was Dorothy's passion for Toby. When Dorothy heard his loud voice in the hall, his booming shout of 'Doro! Doro!', her hand would fly up to her hair and try to smooth it down from whatever strange angle it was in, and when he entered the room, a smile formed on her lips, as though he were the one man in all the world who amused her.

Harriet found herself envying Edwin, who talked in secret to Pare and could tell her everything that was on his mind. She thought fancifully that this was what she longed for: an encounter with a stranger wearing a cloak of feathers.

Meanwhile, she cooked the ducks and the three of them sat down to their Christmas meal, with the blue curtains keeping out the sun and the ferns smelling of the earth. They exchanged no presents. When the light in the room faded and cooled, Lilian sang to them. 'Jesus Occupies My Soul'. 'Silent Night'.

III

They began to long for rain.

Day after day, the hot northerlies blew and dust streamed off the tilled land and the wheat began to look poor.

'We have the creek,' said Joseph. 'We must dig new channels for the water and contrive some system of irrigation.'

The earth was hard under the tussock. Joseph made sketches of where the channels should run and, dutifully, they tried to follow these, but the distances were so great, it was difficult to imagine this task having any end. Harriet wrote to her father: *Our life is digging now. We dig from sunrise to sunset and all the while above us the sky is an empty blue.*

The garden flourished because Harriet was able to water her vegetables with buckets and cans, filled at the creek's edge. She husbanded everything for the pigs and chickens, every snail and worm, every feathery carrot stem, every onion stalk and damaged lettuce leaf.

By her wheelbarrow sat Lady, swishing her black tail and watching Harriet's careful hands, and when they took the garden gleanings to the pigs, Lady darted round the animals, tidying them into an orderly group, like a flock of sheep. Lady was no longer a puppy and Harriet wrote to Henry Salt:

> *Lady can out-run the dust. Up rises a plume of it, from the poor fields, and off it streams towards the hills, all golden in the sunshine. And then Lady sees it and gives chase and I marvel that sometimes she is faster than the wind.*

Late one evening, with Harriet's task of watering her vegetables almost complete, Lady began to bark. Harriet looked up and saw two men moving out from behind the beech trees towards the creek. One of them was pulling a cart, piled up with possessions, and the wheels of the cart squeaked – an unfamiliar, disturbing sound in the silence of the valley.

Hearing the dog, the men looked towards Harriet. They were almost at the creek and Harriet saw them hesitate, but their thirst called them on and they reached the water and squatted down and drank.

Lady began to run towards the men and she heard one of them yell: 'Watch out! Dog's coming for us!'

Harriet began to move up the hill, calling to Lady. Never, in all their months here, had strangers walked across their land and Harriet would willingly have had Joseph at her side to confront them, but Joseph was far away by the pond and so she had no choice but to go on, wiping her hands on her apron, striding boldly forwards in her dusty boots. Lady wouldn't return to her, but nor did the dog go right up to the men, only cowered a little way off, barking and growling. Harriet reached her and put a hand on her collar and calmed her. The men stood by their cart. They wore wide-brimmed hats against the sun and so their faces were in shadow.

'Your run, is it?' said one of the men. 'But we can take a drink, can we, miss?'

Not since her days as a governess had Harriet been called 'miss'.

She thought that – just as she was wondering who these strangers were – so they were wondering what a woman was doing out here on the flats alone.

'Certainly, you may take a drink,' she said. 'But I fear you must be lost. You are a long way from the road.'

The younger of the two men looked at the other, who was the one who had spoken and now this same one said: 'Short cut. Through to the dray road at Amberley. But we're too westerly, are we?'

Harriet had never been to Amberley, but she knew it was some way from here, towards the sea.

'If you carry on as you are going, you will get into the mountains . . .'

'Saw that, didn't we, Bunny? We saw we'd be blocked off.'

Harriet looked at the cart, piled up and covered with sacking. The older man wiped his neck with a rag and said: 'We'd beg some oil, if we could. If you have any . . . ?'

'Some oil?'

'For the blessed wheels. Just come on, this squeak. Come on to torture us.'

'Aye,' said the younger man. 'Abandon it, we almost would.'

'But we can't,' said the other. 'Key to our fortune, you see? If you meet us in time future, coming the other way, we'll be rich men.'

Lady had stopped barking and had begun to whine, frustrated that she wasn't allowed near the men, to sniff them out, to round them up . . .

'Nice dog, a collie,' said the younger man. 'I'd like one of them for myself.'

Harriet held tightly to Lady's collar.

'No dogs allowed on the fields,' said the older man with a grin. 'Just the curs of humanity!'

'On the fields?' said Harriet.

'At the diggings. Didn't guess where we were bound?'

'Amberley.'

'The dray road. Takes you to the Hurunui or just short of it. The Waitohi Gorge. Then you're on your own. Across the Saddle and it's downhill, but they say the downhill is the worst of it. They say the downhill freezes your soul.'

Now Harriet looked in admiration at the men. They were planning to struggle across the mountains, all the way to the West Coast. They had nothing, it seemed, no horse, no guns, just a handcart. They were going to attempt the 'stairway of hell' and they believed they could survive.

'Come down to the house,' said Harriet. 'We can oil the wheels of the cart and you can take some supper with us before you go on.'

Their names were Hopton Fellwater and Bunny McGee. Hopton may have been near fifty and Bunny fifteen years younger, but they had come out from Peebles in the Scottish Border country together, 'each of us having no wife nor bairns'. They said they'd arrived too late for the Otago diggings, where there was 'nothing left but a wee pasty bit of colour along the Clutha', but they'd heard that on the Grey and the Hokitika there was 'real true gold'.

They'd worked as sheep-shearers on one of the Canterbury runs and as porters on the Dunedin docks. They'd lived rough and didn't mind it because, they said, 'there's promise here. You can smell it in the air.'

Harriet heated mutton stew for them and Lilian made suet dumplings to make the meat go further. The presence of strangers in the Cob House somehow brightened the atmosphere, thought Lilian, even if they were rough-and-ready Scots. She liked listening to their voices and laughed with them when Hopton described one of the shacks where they'd lived on the sheep-run: 'Leaky plank walls and do you know what they were papered with? Copies of the *Illustrated London News*. I never learned the art of reading myself, but Bunny, he used to lie in his bunk and read to me, about the Queen's spaniels and the sayings of Lord Melbourne!'

'And on the goldfields, where will you live?' asked Lilian.

The men shrugged their shoulders. Bunny wiped his mouth with the linen napkin Lilian had provided for him. 'A Gold Rush, ma'am,' he said, 'is pure and absolute chaos. We saw it in Otago – and that was the last breath of the main Rush. So you really cannot say at all where you will live. Some nights, you have to lay your head on a stone.'

'Aye,' said Hopton. 'That's right. You cannot say at all. You might be snug in a tent on terra firma or you might be perched on a rock ledge with a south-westerly trying to blow you to hell.'

There was a short silence while more of the mutton stew was going down, then Harriet said: 'Why don't you take ship from Lyttelton, if the mountain route is so difficult?'

'If you told us we were mad,' said Hopton, 'you wouldn't be the first. But the way we see it, there *is* a way over the Hurunui Saddle. It's a treacherous way. They say sunlight never creeps into some of those deep gorges, but what are a few days of darkness if you're moving towards a bright gleam?'

'We cannot afford the ship,' said Bunny flatly. 'That's the truth of it. Cost of a passage rises every day. The Hurunui is our only chance.'

Joseph, who had remained silent during the meal, now raised his eyes and looked anxiously at the men and they took this as a sign of sympathy with their dilemma, which it was, but it was also more than this. It was his sudden realisation that men such as these – men who couldn't read, men who had been ragged and poor all their lives – might, in the coming season, before another winter had come and gone, overtake him so far in material wealth that everything he now possessed would seem pitiful to them in comparison. They might be able to buy his farm and the Cob House and everything that it contained five times over. It had been said of the goldfields that they were 'a fine force for levelling out in society', and Joseph now saw how true this could prove, for it wasn't the rich who went to the swamps and the river-beds and broke their backs filling and emptying a sluice-box from dawn till nightfall, it was men like Hopton Fellwater and Bunny McGee. And it might in the end be they, not him, who became wealthy men.

The question that Joseph began to ask himself as the supper went on was this: was he being obstinate and foolish to trust in his own creek? Should he forget about the scratchings of gold dust he had found there and follow the Rush? He glanced over at Lilian, who seemed – quite contrary to what Joseph would have expected, especially after the disasters of their visit to Christchurch – somehow entranced by these men. He wondered whether she was thinking these very same thoughts, that he, Joseph, should join the gold-seekers before it was too late, or whether ... and here he paused and stared harder at his mother ... she was only enraptured by the idea that these people were about to walk to their deaths in the mountains. Very often, Joseph could tell exactly what Lilian was thinking, but tonight, he couldn't.

As a dessert, they munched on some chocolate flapjacks Lilian had made two days before and drank a pot of tea and by the time they had finished, it was beginning to get dark. Hopton Fellwater looked towards the windows draped with the blue curtains and then at Bunny, who was yawning. 'Time to go,' he said.

Bunny obediently stood up and looked around for his hat, yet everybody fell silent, because this didn't seem to be quite right, for the strangers to walk out like this, into the dark flats, into the huge, featureless night.

Harriet was the first to speak. 'Why not wait till morning?' she said. 'Don't you agree, Joseph? Then Joseph can direct you towards the Amberley road ...'

'Oh no,' said Hopton, 'we won't trouble you.'

'It's no trouble,' said Harriet quickly. 'You can sleep here on the floor. Lady will watch over you.'

'I agree,' said Lilian, who sounded, to Joseph, as she sometimes used to sound in Parton Magna when Roderick over-filled her glass of rum cordial. 'I most certainly agree. Look at Mr McGee. He can barely keep his eyes open.'

'I shall be well, ma'am,' said Bunny, but Lilian laid a firm hand on his arm, as though to guide him to some child's bedroom where a nightlight was burning and a musical box would lull him to sleep. 'You need rest,' she said. 'In the morning, you shall go on.'

Harriet lay in her calico room and listened to them snoring. She thought that maybe snoring was something only the carefree did because those who were not carefree slept a hunched-over sleep with their noses buried in the pillow.

She tried to imagine what it was like to be Hopton Fellwater and Bunny McGee, headed for the vast shaded forests and the long silent valleys of the Taramakau. They had no overcoats. The cart they were dragging would break apart long before they reached the West Coast. Yet she envied them. They would walk across waterfalls. They would see the sacred kingfisher. They would live on fern roots and minnows. They would sleep in greenstone caves.

Harriet planned to be awake before they left, to fry a hunk of bacon for them and watch them walk away beyond her garden, going towards Amberley and the dray path. But they departed like ghosts before it was light. They left behind them a little patterning of oil on the dusty floor, from the silenced wheels of their cart.

IV

Joseph stood and looked into the pond. The water, which had at first stayed clear above the shingle he had laid in, was now muddy and his plans for stocking the pond with Tasmanian trout had come to nothing. Toby Orchard had reminded him that trout needed a fresh, running current and would survive very little time in this kind of confinement. So the pond remained empty. No trees had been planted at its edge. It was just a crater in the landscape.

It was getting towards evening and Joseph could see gnats, lit by the amber light of the sun, dancing just above the water.

Then, something disturbed the surface of the pond and a circle of ripples expanded briefly before disappearing. Joseph stared at the spot where the ripples had been. On a Norfolk river, he would have seen this as the sign of a fish rising, and it occurred to him that when he had let in water from the creek to fill the pond, perhaps a fish had been swept along with it and was now swimming in slow circles there. His fisherman's eye checked the movement of his own shadow on the water and he moved slowly round the pond until his shadow fell behind him. He waited.

A slant of sun still caught at the gnats' wings. Then came another flick, another rippling of the water, unmistakable to Joseph as the feeding of a fish on the surface. And he thought, with a strange, intense pleasure, that Nature now and again idly fulfils a man's desires – by fortunate accident, by a confluence of time and matter that could not have been predicted.

Joseph walked back to the Cob House and found it empty of people. For a while now, Lilian had taken to helping Harriet with her evening watering and he could hear the two women talking companionably together in the garden. He felt glad that he didn't have to talk to either of them.

He went to his trunk and opened it and took out his favourite fishing rod and a selection of flies. He stared at the brown curl once cut from Rebecca's head and his hand moved towards it for a moment, then away. He closed the trunk and walked out, feeling the sun still burning on him as he made his way back to the pond.

He had no idea which fly to choose. Everything was different in New Zealand. He tied on a Nymph and began casting, enjoying the familiar movement of his arms and the delicate swish of the line. He wondered whether, when he was old, his life would permit him to be idle and spend his days fishing by some quiet river. But he recognised that these wonderings were futile, because the river that he imagined was in England and this was the one place to which he would never be able to return.

He moved silently round the bright side of the pond, taking care with shadows. His skill in placing a fly very delicately on the water had not deserted him. Nothing moved.

The fish he imagined in the depths of the pond was a silvery blue. He thought it would have the muddy-tasting flesh of a trout and weigh three pounds or more. He wanted to hook it cleanly, bring it in adroitly. He looked around for a rock to break its skull, felt a pull on the line. His heart was beating fast, but he wound in the line as gently as he could. The pull was still there, the rod bending as it took the weight.

So few things excite us.

We are dead, as dead trees. Then a sudden green shoot breaks free . . .

Playing his fish, even though he couldn't see it, playing it with his old, beautiful skill, Joseph felt himself slide into previous time and the thrill of it tugged at him. He didn't want to go there, but for the first time since coming to New Zealand, he felt himself returning . . .

Vividly, in the golden evening, he saw the girl, Rebecca, sitting astride the gate, showing him her brand-new brown boots. He saw her bunch up her skirts and the hem of her petticoat and display the shine on the boots and their smart new laces, but he looked only glancingly at the boots because he had seen blood on the petticoat, a startling red smear of fresh blood. And it was this knowledge that she was bleeding, that it was her time and that he knew this intimate thing about her, which excited him. He longed to put his hand under her skirts, in among the rags, and feel the blood oozing there. And then he wanted to lay her down on the field, just where she was by the iron gate, and put his hand around her arching back and pull her towards him and find release in her, *release with no consequence*, because she was bleeding and she had shown him this.

He saw that, at sixteen, Rebecca Millward was already full of wickedness. She had deliberately let him see the stain on her petticoat. And look at how she sat there, with her legs wide apart, sat there smiling at him with her crooked teeth all on display, luring him on . . . But here was the beauty of it; he would be saved by the blood from having to love her . . .

Joseph remained sunk in his past for enough time to discover, when he returned to the present moment, that his back and his arms were aching. Something still tugged on his line, but it seemed to lie deep down in the pond and never showed itself near the surface, and so his image of what it was began to change. Instead of seeing a nimble fish like a trout, he saw some black, writhing creature like a water-snake. It felt heavy and thick. He gave a deliberate jab to the line, trying to free the hook. The descending sun disappeared behind a cloud and the water of the pond was suddenly flat and without shadow. Joseph jabbed again, but the hook stayed in. Now, he regretted fetching the fishing rod. He wished he'd never opened the trunk and thought only with intense sadness of the curl he kept in the fly box.

He kept jabbing on the line, something he never would have done on any of his trout-fishing expeditions. He thought what a fool and a madman he must look, pulling helplessly on his line, and wished he had a knife with him so that he could cut himself free. He looked around him, as though he might find something at the pond's edge to make the cut, but there was nothing except the dry earth and the yellow tussock bleached by the south-west wind.

Backwards and forwards Joseph walked, hoping to free the line by altering its direction, but the thing on the end of it also moved. There was sweat, now, on Joseph's face and he felt a panic in his heart. He felt that he would never be able to outwit the creature that had taken his Nymph. He could wrestle with it till nightfall and it would stay down in the mud of the pond, as though it were luring him towards it, as though it might suddenly pull so strongly on the line that he would be thrown into the water.

Joseph knelt and laid the rod down and took up a section of line and began tearing at it with his teeth. The line was made of gut. He knew how strong it was. But Joseph clamped his teeth on it and tugged and tugged until he felt it begin to fray. And the fraying line tasted salty and bitter. It almost made him retch, but still he endured it and clung on until he could feel only a tiny thread against his tongue. And then it snapped and he spat it out and watched as the line drifted out on to the water and lay for a moment on the surface before disappearing.

Bargains

I

Lilian now worked hard in the vegetable garden. When the spinach she'd sown and faithfully watered came clustering up above her boots, she ran her hands through its bright green leaves and said: 'Harriet, you know this looks better to me than anything we grew at Parton.' She sat on the ground, eating carrots out of the earth, spreading her skirts in the sunlight. She didn't tire of picking snails from the lettuces for the pigs. Sometimes, she went out before sunrise, so that she could hear the bellbirds singing.

Lilian Blackstone was reconstructing Roderick's life and death in her mind and it was this reconstruction 'along scientific lines' that enabled her to feel more comfortable with her past and more resigned to her future in New Zealand. Tormented by the idea that she'd spent thirty-five years married to a mediocre and irresponsible man who, by dying an untimely and ridiculous death, had consigned her to an unendurable fate, Lilian now tried to see everything pertaining to Roderick in an altered light.

Toby Orchard had expressed his admiration for the livestock auctioneer's sophisticated grasp of mathematics; now, Lilian understood that mathematics, or what Toby had called a comprehension of 'scientific language', had also played a part in Roddy's gambling enterprises.

He'd often described these enterprises as 'experiments'. He had sometimes tried to explain to his wife the rules of the law of averages and the 'indisputable frequent reappearance of the only even prime number, the number 2, in any random selection of numbers, such as those designated to horses entering the Winners' Enclosure at Newmarket'.

In games of poker, Roddy told her, he would seldom discard a low 2, 'because the 2 can be a magnet, attracting a pair or even a third replica of itself' and he claimed that he had won more than a few games by 'trusting solely in the Even Prime'.

At the time when he had explained this, Lilian had understood not one word of what he was talking about, but now she saw clearly that Roderick had at least had a *system* and that his betting was not quite the random venture she had taken it for. He'd always claimed to 'study form' on the racecourse and had kept, Lilian remembered now, a notebook with more than a hundred horses' names in it and their placings in successive races. She had never entirely seen the point of this. She recalled saying: 'Because something has occurred in the past, Roderick, this does not mean it will necessarily occur again.' But it was clear to her now that she had been wrong to be so sceptical about the Form Notebook. For not long before he died, Roddy's luck on horses had begun to turn and he had seen this as 'a combination of my adherence to the Even Prime and the growing sophistication of my form book'.

What Lilian now chose to believe was that her husband would have emerged from his mire of debt, had he not been killed by scientific curiosity. He was on the way, she told herself: I should have trusted in his systems. He would have pulled us free.

And as for the death itself, here Lilian made a bargain with memory: she would force herself to think about it, to look it in the eye, to relive it as far as was possible, given that she hadn't actually witnessed it, provided she was able to give it a different frame of reference.

The stark facts remained: Roderick Blackstone had been killed in a field by ostriches. The peculiar birds belonged to an enterprising Norfolk farmer, who had planned to make a fortune by selling their plumes to the millinery trade and by 'introducing the delicate taste of ostrich meat to the discerning people of the county, including Her Majesty Queen Victoria herself at Sandringham'.

Invited to inspect these creatures he'd never seen before, Roderick Blackstone's curiosity had been roused by the sight of their long necks and startled eyes and fluttering feathers. Instead of remaining on the other side of their fence, while the farmer went away to attend to a ewe caught in a bramble hedge, Roddy climbed into the ostrich field and approached the birds.

Inquisitive as they were, the ostriches immediately surrounded Roderick and began pecking at his top hat. They were known (it was later said) to be fascinated by hard, shiny things and no doubt what Roderick should have done was remove the hat and run as fast as he could away from them. But he didn't remove his hat. He died with his hat *on.* And the question of why he hadn't removed it had always taunted and maddened Lilian. Surely, he couldn't have been so stubborn as to believe, when his life was threatened, that propriety or convention required that he keep his hat on in the middle of a meadow? The ridiculousness of this notion made her want to cry out with fury.

There had never been any proper explanation of the hat business – until now. But here it was at last: Roderick had simply been so altruistically curious – as a scientist – about the behaviour of the eccentric birds that he hadn't understood their intention until it was too late, until after one of them had jabbed at his face and taken half his nose away in its long beak and he had fallen down, screaming with pain and covered in blood and the birds had pecked him to death.

Lilian now chose to see that Roddy's actions, far from being foolish, had been brave. Her gratitude to Toby Orchard for suggesting to her this new way of thinking about Roderick was overwhelming. She dreamed of going back to the Orchard Run and confiding everything to Toby – the gambling, the ostriches, all of it. She imagined Toby putting his arm round her, as she shed a tear. She remembered the comfortable, blue room at Orchard House and the creaking mahogany armoire, and predicted how well she would sleep in it now, with the presence of Toby just along the landing.

But for the time being Lilian had to content herself only with her new feelings of optimism. Neither she nor Harriet nor anyone could make the journey to the Orchard Run for the simple reason that the donkey was no longer capable of pulling the cart.

The donkey walked with ever more faltering steps and brayed all day at the flies. It stood in the little patch of shade afforded by the new cow barn and stared at the ground.

Harriet tried to cosset it, feeding it soft radish leaves from her palm and stroking its neck. She would see its eyes close, as if the touch of her hand gave it some longed-for permission to sleep, or even to die. Joseph swore that the donkey had croup and would recover, but both Harriet and Lilian disagreed. They knew that the donkey would never survive another winter. And one night, in the hot silence of their room, Harriet said to Joseph: 'What we must buy in the autumn is a horse.'

Joseph made no reply. She heard him sigh, as if everything she said wearied him, as if she were a child begging him for hoops and skittles and dolls with china faces.

II

Edwin Orchard didn't know that Harriet couldn't use the donkeycart to make the journey to Orchard House and he hoped she would arrive soon so that he could confide to her his worries about Pare.

Pare had not come to the meeting place in the toi-toi grass for a long time – a longer time than Edwin could ever remember. In this time, his caterpillar had hatched out of its cocoon as a scarlet-and-black butterfly and fluttered away; the spring lambs on the run had stopped kicking and prancing and started bleating like ordinary sheep; his mother had cut off his ringlets; Toby had shot twenty-seven weka; a family of moreporks had hatched in one of the barns; and Janet had made a blue blancmange, the like of which no one had ever seen before.

Edwin longed to tell Pare about the moreporks and the blue blancmange. He felt lonely without his caterpillar. He wanted to hear about the gold at Greenstone Creek and to stroke the kiwi feathers of Pare's magic cloak. Every day, now, he walked into the grass and called softly: 'Are you there, Pare?' But there was never any answer, only the hot wind sighing and the grasshoppers scratching, and the bleating of sheep, far away.

The thing that worried him most was the possibility that Pare *had* come one day and seen him without his ringlets and not recognised him and gone away, thinking that some other boy lived on the run now. For he saw that he looked completely different. 'You should not have done that cutting, Mama!' he said angrily to Dorothy. And his mother's reply surprised him and worried him yet more. 'I know, Edwin,' said Dorothy. 'It almost broke my heart to lose my baby. But it was time for a transformation.'

Time for a transformation.

Edwin looked furiously at Dorothy. He wanted to take a cruel bite out of her hand. He knew what a transformation was. It was what his caterpillar had undergone. It was one thing becoming something else. 'I did not *want* that!' he said.

Edwin drew a picture of himself on a slate, with his hair sticking straight out, like his mother's. He didn't know whether Pare could read, but under the drawing he wrote on the slate: *This is not a koko nut this is me now Ewin.*

He laid the slate on some white stones in the toi-toi grass. He hoped the dry weather would last.

III

As the drought continued, the mounds of earth at the creek's edge hardened and cracked and whitened. Joseph thought that they began to resemble a range of miniature mountains and that, like mountains, they would be there for ever because he didn't possess the strength to break them up.

The level of the creek was falling. More and more muddy shingle appeared and every day, Joseph dutifully shovelled and sifted it, but he found nothing. He began to feel the terror of a future without gold and without water.

Channelling the river so that it flowed, almost unimpeded,

into his pond, he consoled himself with the thought that at least all the work he'd put into the pond had not been in vain. What had started as a sentimental attempt to contrive a corner of English landscape might now be the thing that would save the farm from ruin. He hoped the flow into the pond wouldn't stop. He dreaded to see the level of the pond fall and the great black worm he knew lay in the mud underneath the water be revealed.

But the slow drift of Joseph's mind was towards the Hokitika and the Grey. He began to feel that he'd been wrong to trust in his own creek. It was proving obstinate and valueless, but these vast, inaccessible rivers of the West Coast would be yielding and rich. They would gradually give up their colour. They would turn from gold to silver to brown as the men who had had the resolution to approach them – ordinary men like Hopton Fellwater and Bunny McGee – washed the gold from their banks and saw their lives change and happiness come in.

So intensely did Joseph long for happiness that, to ease his mind, he began to plan what he would do once he possessed his share of the gold. He thought he would send money to Rebecca's family, enough money to repair their roof, to build a new privy, enough to let them buy a forest, if that was their desire, or set themselves up in the lucrative business of rearing pheasants. He would make sure the money reached them anonymously and that they would never know its sender nor its source.

And then I will be free from guilt.
Then I will have made amends.
Then I will have done enough.

This was how Joseph's thinking went. And what he hoped might come in the wake of these actions would be a rediscovery of his feelings for Harriet. For he knew how cold he was. How could he not know?

He remembered her laughing with delight over their first purchases for the farm, and taking his arm in the street and kissing his face ... he could remember these actions very vividly and yet he saw that he had somehow sent them away, sent them out of his life like children punished by being sent out of a room.

And he recognised that this was lamentable and shocking. Harriet deserved his love and yet he couldn't give it, not only because he'd *never* loved her as much as he'd hoped to, but because, now, his mind had gone towards gold. And this drift towards gold had somehow opened a door on to the past, a door he had thought was closed for ever, but was not.

The rain came early in February. It fell in torrents from a black sky and, to Joseph's astonishment, began to dissolve the 'mountains' by the creek's edge, letting the earth slide back into the river.

Harriet stood by the wall of her garden, listening to the rain on her bean leaves. Then she turned and saw Joseph coming up towards her and knew that he had something to say, something which the longed-for rain had released in him.

He began by admiring the vegetable patch: the tiny stems of fruit on the currant bushes and the wine-coloured stalks of the beet tops. Then, he said: 'I have made my decision. Now that the rain has come I can leave for a while and not worry that everything might die or fail. So, if you agree, I shall buy a boat passage to Nelson, then on to Hokitika.'

Harriet stood very still, with the dog by her, with the moisture making silvery cobwebs in her hair. She didn't look at Joseph, but kept a watch on the earth, noting places where the rain didn't reach or where puddles were forming.

After a while, she bent down and stroked the dog's damp head, then straightened up and said: 'And if I don't agree, what will you do?'

Joseph took off his hat and shook the rain from it and put it on again.

'I must go,' he said. 'I must go before all the gold is gone.'

'And if there is no gold?'

'Men are not risking their lives for nothing, Harriet.'

'Men are risking their lives *in the hope of something.* That is all.'

'I have dreams about the Grey River. I shall come back with enough ... enough gold to transform our world.'

They were getting soaked, standing out there under the dark sky. Harriet hadn't minded this a moment ago, but now she saw how stupid it was; it was stupid because they were frail. 'What have we been doing for all these months,' she said, 'but endeavouring to "transform our world"?'

'Yes,' said Joseph. 'And we have. We have made the garden and the pond . . .'

'But you've lost heart in these things?'

Joseph hung his head. He didn't want to say that he'd lost heart in them on the morning in late winter when he'd first seen the colour at the creek's edge, that from that moment he'd begun to see them as small and of very little account. He reached out and tentatively took Harriet's hand. 'I want more,' he said.

She let him hold her hand for a brief second before pulling away.

'And *I* want more!' she said crossly. Then she called to Lady and began to walk away from Joseph down the hill.

Later, when they were lying in bed in their calico room, Joseph, who couldn't leave the subject alone, began to plead: 'If I don't go, then I'm less than men like Hopton Fellwater. Everyone in the South Island will be rich and we shall be left out, because I was too cowardly to go.'

'Is that what you believe?' asked Harriet coldly.

'Yes. It's what I believe.'

'And if you go, what happens to the farm?'

'You will manage,' Joseph said. 'I've seen what you can do. You will take care of everything. And Lilian will help you. Then in the winter, I'll come back. I'll come back with the gold. And we shall begin again.'

Harriet now wanted to say that she didn't believe in the gold but saw that this was not quite what she meant. She certainly believed that gold had been found and indeed Edwin Orchard had already told her what Pare had said about the discoveries at Greenstone Creek. She could imagine, too, that Joseph would work heroically, work until he died, to find the colour at Hokitika and bring it out of the earth. What she decided she meant was that she didn't believe in Joseph's vision of the gold as something which would bring them happiness. She thought that happiness lay hidden somewhere, in a place just out of reach, and that one day it might reveal itself to her, but she didn't think that it would be contained in lumps of gold.

So she lay silent for a while, finding nothing to say. And in this silence, she began to imagine what her days and nights would be like without Joseph. She saw in not much time that she wouldn't mind his absence at all, just as she hadn't minded when he and Lilian had gone down to Christchurch and she had set her fires and seen the flame in the cabbage tree.

And Harriet soon understood another thing: by agreeing to what Joseph wanted, she could get something for herself, something which had constantly been refused her. So now at last she turned towards him in the bed. She touched his cheek more tenderly than she'd touched it for a long while.

'You're right,' she said. 'You should go, Joseph. There was certainly no gold in England. None.'

'No,' he said. 'None.'

'So you should take the chance. Follow the crowd. See what you can get. It would be wrong of me to try to stop you.'

'I will come back in the winter.'

'Yes.'

'And now that the rain has come . . .'

'Yes. Now that the rain has come.'

'Your bean crop will be good . . .'

'How will you live, in Hokitika, Joseph?'

'I have no idea. I shall do what the others do.'

'But first and foremost, you will need supplies.'

Harriet waited to hear what he would say to this, because now she was nearing the thing that would be her part of the bargain. For they both knew that the donkey couldn't take them in the cart to Christchurch to fetch supplies, or even to Rangiora, and that, even if Joseph was prepared to walk down to Rangiora to hire a dray, Harriet and Lilian shouldn't be left alone at Okuku with no means of leaving the farm or reaching a town.

'I shall make sure we get . . . from one of the farms lower down the flats . . . we shall find someone to sell us another donkey,' said Joseph. 'and hope it will be in better spirits.'

'No,' said Harriet. She removed her hand from Joseph's cheek and sat up. A candle still burned near her side of the bed and now her shadow loomed up large and dark against the white calico. 'I want a horse,' she said. 'If I can't have a horse, then I simply shall not let you go.'

'Harriet . . .' Joseph began, but she cut him off.

'A horse is strong enough to swim the Ashley, roped to the ferry, but a donkey is not. If there were any accident to either of us, a horse can take us in the cart very fast to a doctor at Rangiora. So it is a horse, Joseph, and nothing else that we must have.'

Joseph looked at her, her skin brown and dry from the days of burning heat, her eyes very black in the candlelight. He thought how she tricked him or manoeuvred him into giving her what he didn't want to give and what they couldn't afford: first the dog, Lady, who seemed attached to her and to no one else and now this, the tall horse she said she saw in her mind and about which she had begun to pester him.

He sighed. He felt chilled from having stood out so long in the rain and knew that, on this particular night, he lacked the will to argue with her.

'Very well,' he said at last. 'But if we buy a horse, we will have almost no money left. I suppose you understand that?'

IV

A week later, Joseph and Harriet trekked on foot to Rangiora and waited for a dray to take them to Christchurch.

Lilian sat alone in the Cob House, with Lady whining and turning in circles, searching for Harriet. 'For goodness' sake,' said Lilian to the dog, 'try to be still.'

But she was glad to have the dog with her. As night fell, everything outside the Cob House seemed to grow in immensity: the clouds moving across the moon, the distant mountains, the flat grassland all around. Lilian knew that she had never been as far removed from any other human being as she was now. It was as though she were aboard some strange conveyance, taking her further and further from small familiar things, into a universe of shadows.

She spent her evening mending broken plates, making sure that the tiny pattern of flowers was not disturbed by the joins, but as she worked, this feeling of travelling into vastness increased to a point where Lilian became dizzy and faint and had to lay her head down on the table.

She stared at the objects in the room: the chair by the range, the towels drying on the airing frame, a cheap almanac on a hook. And she wanted to gather these things to her and cling to them as she flew through the enormity of the night.

D'Erlanger's Hotel

I

There were no cheap rooms available in Christchurch. On his own, Joseph would have walked out of the town and slept in a field, as he'd done before, but he had Harriet with him. Though his money was running very low, he told himself that all the expense he was incurring now would seem trivial at some future time.

The place he found was called D'Erlanger's Hotel. It employed two bellboys, dressed in blue-and-red uniforms and smart little boxy hats.

One of the bellboys showed Joseph and Harriet to a room with a four-poster bed, hung with muslin. The bellboy opened the window on the sunny afternoon and stood by it, whistling for his tip.

As evening came on, Joseph heard the sound of a concertina being played downstairs and he thought what a long time it was since he had danced. On the bed, where the muslin moved softly in the draught from the open window, Joseph laid out his father's pistol and a box of bullets and told Harriet that he wanted her to have them while he was gone.

She said she had never fired a pistol, so he showed her how to load it and close it and unlock the safety catch and how to aim, looking straight along her outstretched arm. She said: 'We look like some Gang of Two, planning our crimes.' And she smiled at him, still holding the pistol, pointing it at a mahogany wardrobe, and he saw once again that pearly tooth of hers which showed and was not meant to show when she smiled.

The concertina music was melancholy but warm and Joseph stood up and drew the curtains and thought he would let himself give in to the unexpected sweetness of the moment, because it might never come again.

He took the gun from Harriet's hand and laid it down. Then he brought her to the bed and pulled the muslin round them and kissed her mouth. Her skirts were muddy from the walk to Rangiora, but Joseph didn't remove them, only bunched them up so that the mound of them lay under his belly. He wished he could spread her hair out on the pillow, as he'd done in the early time of their marriage, but her hair was too short to spread. He tried to move in time to the music floating up the stairs and he felt her move with him. She smelled of the muddy flats, of dry leaves and sweat and earth.

He had to withdraw from her more quickly than he'd wanted. The music stopped and the only sound that Joseph could hear as he lay there with his wife was the thudding of his heart and he found this condition of silence intensely painful, as though everything in his world were about to cease.

Harriet's arm circled Joseph's back and her hand touched the hardness of his shoulder blades and she realised how thin he'd become from all his arduous work by the creek. Yet his body, lying on hers, felt very heavy, as if his bones were made of lead, and she wanted him to move away and walk through the muslin curtain and be gone.

But she lay there, unmoving, and suffered the weight of him because she saw how mean her thoughts were and how lovelessness carries with it a kind of shame, which grows more and more fearful as the days pass.

On a night-table by the bed, Harriet could see the gun. She stared at it. She thought how easy it would be to pick it up and put it against Joseph's head and muffle the shot with the pillow. She saw how death would arrive with mundane simplicity in a single moment and how nothing in the hotel room would move – only the thin curtains in the afternoon breeze – and how, in a little while, the concertina music would start up again.

She imagined walking out from D'Erlanger's Hotel in a clean dress and soon becoming lost in the crowds and going in search of some food and a horse and then riding away from Christchurch in the moonlight. She would eat her food and let the horse graze on the tussock and then she would lie down on the ground and sleep, with the horse tethered to a stone. And all the while, Joseph's body would lie on the bed, his brain bleeding into the pillows, and no one would discover it until morning, when the chambermaids arrived with their brooms and pails. And by then, she would be far away, asleep in the emptiness of the flats. She would ride to the Orchard Run and have breakfast with Dorothy.

She didn't know if anyone would track her down, arrest her, try her, condemn her, hang her. She thought that here, in New Zealand, murder might be one of a thousand crimes which could remain unpunished for years, the identity of the culprit lost in the immensity of distance.

Harriet heard Joseph's breathing change and knew that he'd gone to sleep, lying on her, on her damp skirts. She knew she would always remember this room in D'Erlanger's Hotel, with its open window and its elegant bed, and the sun on the face of the bellboy as he'd stood and whistled for his money, and the concertina music waltzing up the stairs.

Experimentally, she moved her arm and began to push aside the muslin drapes, so that the gun was within her grasp. She knew, if she decided to kill Joseph, how easy it was going to be to lie to Lilian, telling her that Joseph had boarded the steamship in Lyttelton Harbour and waved to her from its crowded deck as it sailed away.

'What did he take with him?' Lilian would ask.

'The thing they call a swag,' she would reply, 'a rolled canvas bag secured with two straps and with a sling for carrying.'

'And in the swag?'

'Oh, provisions. Tall boots for the swampy ground. Money.'

'But what for the diggings?'

'Knives, a mallet, a pannikin, rope to peg out his claim. A little tent for when the winter comes.'

'When the winter comes? He said he would be back by winter-time.'

'Oh yes. Unless his finds are very good. Or unless he has no luck at all. In either event, he might stay longer . . .'

So easy to lie to Lilian. On and on through the seasons the lie would share their house and breathe the air they breathed. On and on, until sufficient time had passed and Lilian began to suspect that something terrible had happened to her son. But even then, she would believe that Joseph had died trying to dig gold from a river-bed and never in the world imagine that Harriet had killed him in a Christchurch hotel, for no reason other than her inability to love him.

The gun was within a few inches of her hand now, an irksome little gun, Harriet thought, ornate and mean. She didn't like it. Because it was when Joseph had showed her how to use the gun that he'd become aroused in just the way that he used to be, wanting his pleasure with an embarrassing desperation, arranging her body under his, pushing and pulling at her thighs, with no thought for what she was feeling, and it was this – only this, she now saw – which had brought on her murderous thoughts. If Joseph hadn't touched her, if the weight of him hadn't felt so great, then the idea of killing him would never have entered her mind.

Downstairs, the concertina music began again. Joseph woke up and moved off Harriet's body and lay with his back to her, listening to the tune.

The bed was soft and he congratulated himself on having found a comfortable hotel. He was still half in his dream, which was a dream of Rebecca. He was dancing with her at the Parton Magna fête, in a hall strung up with flags, and her breath smelled of cider and she took his hand and laid it on her breast, under the tight bodice of her dress.

Joseph felt Harriet turn over and move towards him. She put a hand on his neck and whispered: 'Can you hear people laughing?'

II

They stayed two nights at D'Erlanger's Hotel and on the day in between set about their purchases, which reminded Harriet of those early times when they were buying seed and utensils for the farm and when she still believed in the possibility of their love.

Joseph's passage to Nelson and Hokitika on the old *Wallabi*, which should have cost £4, had risen to £15 because of the clamour of people wanting to get aboard. There were no berths left on it; Joseph would have to sleep on deck, among the chicken coops 'and pray for a fine night, sir, or else get a drenching'. But he knew that, despite the expense and his poor place on the ship, he was lucky. All over the town, men worked, trying to save up their fares for the steamboat. They worked as porters and carters, or set up in small enterprises, selling canvas or knives or grog, or fashioning sluice-boxes out of beech planks.

The Survival Stall was still there in the market, the live eels being split and sliced and packed in bladder wrack, but Joseph heard a bystander remark that the eel preserver didn't need to cross the sea to the goldfields; the 'Preservation' was his gold. And Joseph understood how a whole new economy can spring up around gold and fortunes be made by those on the periphery of the diggings, and he thought how, in his entire life, he had never had anything to sell, only his mundane skills as a livestock auctioneer. But he told himself that in the time to come, he would sell his gold for more money than he and his father had ever earned in their lives. He would become the kind of man who inspired envy in other men and longing in women.

He packed a swag with tea and tobacco, ham, flour and sugar. He added two jars of the salted eel. He bought a billy-can, a tent, an axe and a box of nails, strong boots and two pairs of moleskin trousers. When he put on one of the pairs of the trousers, he imagined himself already at work in a wide gully, pegging out his claim. He spent a long time looking at the sluice-boxes or 'cradles' with their iron slats and their layer of canvas beneath. He loved the ingenuity of them, but they were heavy and cumbersome and Joseph thought that, when he arrived, he would make his own cradle out of wood and nails and fit it with a wheel, so that he could push it like a barrow along the beaches or through swamps or into the dark unending world of the bush. He'd already built a house with a stone chimney and windows that didn't leak; he was surely capable of making a simple device for sifting earth?

He sat in the bar of D'Erlanger's Hotel, drinking beer and making sketches of his sluice. He felt his readiness for his adventure creep all through him, like a strange fever.

III

Harriet had thought she would call her horse 'Sentinel'. In all her dreams of the horse, it stood on a high ridge, keeping watch.

But the animal she liked the look of, a chestnut gelding with a high-stepping trot, answered to the name of Billy. 'You can change the name if you want,' commented the stable-owner, 'but he won't know who in the world you're talking to.'

Harriet smiled. She now saw that Sentinel was a portentous kind of name and she thought how, in her dreams, she made herself astonishingly grand and singular. 'Billy,' she repeated. 'I'll call him Billy if that's his name.'

She led the horse into a muddy, fenced paddock and the stable-man helped her into the saddle, sitting astride with her skirts tucked round her, and she walked Billy on, holding the reins loosely and patting his neck so that he would start to feel comfortable with her. Then she shortened the reins and spurred him into a trot and despite his high step, his gait was easy and his mouth sensitive and obedient to the bit. Already, she could imagine the horse in a flowing gallop across the flats, the birds flying from the grass as he came on.

She bought Billy for less than the price of a passage on the *Wallabi*. She paid for him to be re-shod and said she would collect him the following day and ride him home. Then, she returned to D'Erlanger's Hotel and wrote a letter to her father:

> *I have a horse and I shall keep reminding everybody that he is mine.*

Except that I do not know who this 'everybody' might be. When Joseph has left me tomorrow and I return to the Cob House, I shall be alone with Lilian and the animals.

IV

The *Wallabi* ploughed slowly northwards out of Lyttelton, towards the high winds of the Cook Strait. The ship smelled of coal and grease and the crowded deck was as noisy as any boat's deck could be. It was crammed with men: 'new chums' like Joseph and 'old returners' – diggers who had been in Otago three years before and were going back because the colour drew them back, like a lover. Around and in between the groups of men, a company of hens in wicker cages kept up a tuneless serenade to the sky.

Joseph set himself to endure it. He sat on a wooden crate in the stern, with a view of the flagpole and the Red Duster whipped sideways by the wind and the wake of the ship, flowing backwards towards everything that he was leaving. He stared at his hands and the dirt in the cracks of them and then at his swag, to which he was already attached, and he kept tightening the straps that held it together. Around him, games of cards and drinking began and laughter, but Joseph remained aloof from all of this.

He thought about Harriet riding home and hoped the horse wouldn't stumble or fall. At the quayside, as the *Wallabi* had begun to shudder and smoke in its readiness to depart, and its bell was rung, summoning the last passengers, Joseph had held Harriet to him – as he might have held a friend, closely, but with no passion – and she had looked at him with sadness. The look was not devoid of affection, but it was such as a mother gives to a fond child who has disappointed her. And then she asked: 'Do you think that we shall see each other again?'

He kissed her cheek, the hard, tight skin of her cheek under its high cheekbone. He thought her question melodramatic. But he told her calmly that he would certainly come back. He told her to look at the map of New Zealand to see that he would not even be very far away, but only just on the other side of the mountains.

'Ah,' said Harriet. 'The mountains that cannot be crossed.'

'Men have crossed them.'

'But I cannot, Joseph, and nor can you.'

The bell was clamouring and it was time for Joseph to turn and walk on to the gangplank of the ship, but he searched for something else to say because he didn't want to let the parting end like this, in a dishonest way, as if it what had never seemed final were suddenly afflicted with finality. He was tempted to make the promise that he'd sail back with his swag full of money and begin work on a new house . . . the new house of his imaginings in a sheltered valley where the winds wouldn't reach. But, out of superstition, he said none of this and instead asked: 'When I return, why don't we meet at D'Erlanger's Hotel? And I shall buy us a fine dinner.'

He hoped she would smile; he wanted to be left with this – the sweetness of her flawed smile – not her showy kind of sorrow. But her look didn't alter as she nodded and replied: 'Yes. Why not? A fine dinner. I shall give you back the gun.'

And then he was gone, and he stood and watched Harriet on the quayside as the moorings of the boat were untied and it began to move away through the water. He saw her waving to him, standing very tall and still.

A boy of fifteen or sixteen now came to sit down near to Joseph on the *Wallabi*'s deck. The boy took out a penny whistle from his jerkin pocket and began turning it over and over in his hands. He had no possessions that Joseph could see, only the whistle. His boots were worn and the jerkin frayed at the cuffs.

'Why do you not play something?' Joseph said gently.

'On the Arrow, I played,' said the boy. 'Played my whistle and done all kinds of service and got a little gold, but I was cheated of it in the end.'

'But now you're trying again?'

'All I can do, mister. Try again. Play my whistle again. Do my services again. Hope not to die again.'

V

Harriet rode to the Orchard Run. Billy's gallop was frisky and he held his ears high. Harriet loved the sight of his fast-moving shadow on the ground.

She found Dorothy and Edwin whitewashing the stables. Dorothy, who was wearing a pinafore and a frayed old straw hat, said to Harriet: 'Why do we like white so much? Is it the blankness of it?'

'I am white now, Mama,' announced Edwin.

Harriet and Dorothy looked at him and saw his face and arms covered with the chalky wash. 'Oh, so you are,' said Dorothy. 'Do you like being white, or shall we put you in the tub?'

'I like being white,' said Edwin.

Dorothy's fondness for picnics decreed that the whitewashing would be 'suspended' and saddle bags packed with cold pigeons and cheese 'and any bottle of wine that Toby will not notice is missing' and that the three of them would ride to the river and have lunch sitting on the grass. 'The dogs can come with us,' she said. 'They like to bite minnows out of the water.'

They let Billy rest, after his ride from Christchurch. Edwin combed the sweat from the horse's neck and put a rug on his back and Harriet was reminded for a moment of the old tartan rug with which they'd covered Beauty.

Edwin said: 'He's pretty like this, on his own.'

'On his own?'

'I mean, not attached to the cart.'

'Sometimes, he will have to pull the cart.'

'Your donkey can pull the cart.'

'The donkey walks very slowly now.'

'Pare used to walk very slowly,' said Edwin.

Harriet looked around to see whether Dorothy was within earshot, but Dorothy was striding towards the house, calling to Janet to prepare the picnic.

'Have you seen Pare?' Harriet asked.

'No,' said Edwin. 'I think that log came back and her voice told her not to visit me any more.'

'Suppose she came today, while you were white?'

'She won't come. She never comes.'

Together, they led Billy into the stable and put feed into the manger. Edwin's face had a powdery, ghostly look. Through the powder, a single tear snaked down his cheek. He wiped it away.

'Shall I shall tell you what has happened to me?' Harriet asked gently.

'Is it something bad?'

'I don't know yet. It's about Joseph. He's gone away to look for gold.'

'Gone away to the West Coast?'

'Yes.'

'Papa said yesterday "the West Coast is a terrible madness". But I don't know what he means. Sometimes he says "there is a terrible madness in these sums of yours, Edwin".'

Harriet stroked her horse, smoothed a tangle from his mane.

'Perhaps your Papa means that all these things are difficult to understand?'

'Gold isn't difficult,' said Edwin. 'You get a pan and fill it with mud and water and slither it around and everything falls out except the gold. That's what Mama taught me.'

'Yes. But sometimes there is no gold in the pan to remain after the rest has fallen out.'

'Then there is no point in it.'

'There is the same kind of point as there is in going to the toi-toi grass to call to Pare. For a hundred days there may be no one there, just as, for a hundred days there might be no gold in the pan. But on the hundred-and-first day ... there she will be.'

Edwin looked solemnly at Harriet. After a while, he said: 'I'm going to begin counting.'

They sat by the river and the sun shone on the water. The pigeons were tender and tasted of something earthy, like fungus or like damp dead wood. The wine Dorothy had stolen from Toby's store was sweet and cold.

While Edwin played in the creek with the dogs, Mollie and Baby, Dorothy talked about what it could mean to find riches in the earth. She said: 'I have no right and Toby has no right to

criticise anybody for going to the goldfields. My father owns a
tin mine and almost all of what we've been able to build here
comes from that money . . . that tin money. Chance arranged it
this way. But for the men who work in my father's mine . . . for
them, every day is hard. I have seen them in the cold English
winters, standing up to their knees in that icy, reddish water.
And I think that on the West Coast, in the swamps and in the
gullies, everything will be very hard indeed.'

Harriet rested on her elbows and looked at the sky. She felt
stiff from her ride. 'Joseph isn't afraid of hardship,' she said.

'No, I know,' said Dorothy. 'Building your house out of cob
must have been extraordinarily hard. But I wonder what made
him go now, when there is so much work to be done on your
farm?'

Harriet started to explain about the creek and Joseph's
fossicking for gold there. She said: 'He began to dream about
gold. He couldn't let it go. And the things Joseph wants, he has
to try to have them then and there and cannot wait. That seems
to be the way he is.'

When Dorothy said that she understood this and that every
human life hurtles too fast through time 'with too much
spinning off and being left behind for ever' and how we fly this
way and that trying to catch those spinning things, Harriet's
mind returned to the brown curl she'd seen in Joseph's fly box,
and the person to whom it belonged, whoever she was, the
person who had been left behind.

She looked over at Dorothy, still wearing her ancient hat,
with her legs sticking straight out from her muddy skirts and
seemingly with no thought for elegance or vanity, and saw in
her a confidante whom she thought would be silent and true.
She took a breath and said: 'Joseph fled away from England.
There were his father's debts, but it was not only these. I think
there was something else. Something he never talks about.'

Dorothy picked up her wine glass. She was a woman who
liked wine very much and who thought every single sip a
marvellous pleasure. After a few moments had passed in silence
and pleasurable sipping, she said: 'I have never supposed that
men have no secrets. I discovered a postcard in Toby's
dressing-case which said *Fondest love from Scarborough*. I

couldn't read the signature, the writing was too poor. But it was Maud or Mabel or some name like that. It gave my heart a jolt. But then I thought, what does it signify? We can't pretend the lives of men begin or end when we marry them – just as ours do not either. All we can hope is that nothing too hurtful has been done.'

Harriet picked at the grass. She found that her appetite for the cheese which lay beside them on the dry tussock had vanished.

'And suppose something hurtful *has* been done?'

Dorothy's wide face, in the shadow of the hat, looked at Harriet intently. 'Then I imagine, in time, it will come to light, because most of what we think is buried away for always seldom is. But you should not create a myth of wrongdoing, Harriet. I am sure that Joseph Blackstone is a good man.'

VI

Joseph was trying to sleep on the windy deck of the *Wallabi*. Near him, the boy with the whistle, whose name was Will Sefton, lay and slept with his head on a coil of rope. Now, Joseph could see the holes in the soles of Will's boots. He took out of his swag an old woollen jacket and covered the boy with this. There was something about Will Sefton which reminded him of Rebecca's brother, Gabriel, and, after gazing at him for a while, Joseph looked away.

Not far from where Joseph sat, in the shelter of the ship's housing, two Chinese men were boiling rice over a tiny spirit lamp and the fragile blue flame of the lamp, which would have had a little warmth to it, soon began to tease and torture Joseph. He couldn't take his eye from it. He wondered whether he might approach the men and ask to warm his hands. He would try to explain that this was all he wanted, that he wasn't begging for rice, but only to warm his frozen hands, so that he could go to sleep.

The Chinese men were whispering in their language, which was like a language of percussion, Joseph thought, each with an instrument on which he sounded a strange and startling measure. Joseph listened and watched. He could smell the rice beginning to boil. Lit by the small flame, the expressions on the faces of the men seemed neither cheerful nor sad, but to have about them a strong degree of resignation, as though the world had pestered them – like a mosquito or like a fly – pestered them for so long that they could no longer be bothered to swat it away, but just let it settle quietly on them.

Joseph remembered Mrs Dinsdale referring to a Chinese family who ran a market garden nearby as 'the Celestials' and when asked why she had coined this name for them, saying: 'Well, I did not coin it. It is a general term. John Chinaman has his head in the heavens, owing to the opium he smokes, so I suppose that is how it came about. For there is nothing else celestial about them, even though they believe their Emperor to be divine. They are quite filled with degradation, so I have heard tell. And I, for one, would certainly think twice before purchasing a lettuce from them. One would not be able to tell what might be lingering on the leaves.'

On the *Wallabi*, the two men whom Joseph was watching so intently seemed to have crept into visibility only as the darkness had come on. They were barefoot but warmly clad in padded coats. They surely had no berth on the ship and so must have been there on the deck all the time, but Joseph hadn't noticed them. It was as if *no one* had noticed them. Yet now, there they were with their lamp and their hot food, hunched quietly together, while all around them men lay and drank or snored, with their backs turned.

Joseph began to wonder how, in the crowded and competitive world of the gold-diggings, the Chinese would survive. He saw in them some quality of patience, which he envied. He knew how ardently, with what breathless expectation, he was rushing towards gold, but he also believed that it was that very desire which would sustain him, through disappointment and cruel weather, and which would ensure that he persevered until his fortune had been secured.

Without desire, nothing is made.

And yet he also knew, from the hours and days that he had worked sifting mud at the edge of the creek, that gold-mining is pure drudgery: a drudgery of the body and of the mind. And so perhaps the miner who is patient and resigned and goes about each day with so small a portion of hope that it is almost no hope at all can ferret out from difficult ground, or even from ground abandoned or overlooked by the multitude, nuggets of the precious colour nobody else would ever have found.

Joseph kept watching as the Chinese stirred their rice. He didn't move from where he was, only tried to warm his hands on his own body. He understood that even here, on the open deck under the stars, these people had fashioned a private world for themselves around the minute flame of the lamp and that they would resist any intrusion into it.

Joseph closed his eyes. The *Wallabi* was a coast-hugging boat and the seas wouldn't be rough until they reached the strait. He tried to empty his mind of everything that he longed for and let the rise and fall of the steamer lull him to sleep. At the edge of his internal vision he saw something white moving like a waterfall or like the muslin curtains he had drawn around himself and Harriet in the bedroom at D'Erlanger's Hotel.

PART TWO

The Riser

I

Out of Nelson, the *Wallabi* ploughed north into the Tasman Sea with a strong southerly wind in pursuit, helping to speed it on. But as the old steamboat rounded Cape Farewell and turned south-west into the roar of the wind, it seemed to the passengers of the *Wallabi* that they had entered an altered world.

Now, they felt the true and heartless immensity of the sea. Through the mist and spray, they could see land, still, and they turned their eyes again and again towards it, wanting to glimpse some refuge there, in case the struggle of the ship against the high waves began to be lost. But what they saw on the shore were mountains rising into view, one above the other, straight from the water's edge, and it seemed to them, on this West Coast, that the land had set its face against them.

They kept searching for a place where a boat might put in if it had to, but none appeared. The cliffs were implacable, the dense bush clinging to every inch of their fantastic height. The men on the boat could only hang on to the *Wallabi*, to those objects that were bolted down, objects that should have been immovable, but which now seemed to alter position as the ship pitched and rolled. They were heard to curse as a taut rope suddenly went slack, or the ship's rail – even this – reared up and bruised them on the arm or the jaw. A perpetual ache lodged itself in them. They felt as though they had walked a hundred miles.

Joseph stared at the mountains. He thought back to the

journey from England on the *SS Albert,* and the hope that had seemed to shine then on the blue-green waters and the triumphant feeling that he'd had of sailing away from danger. He could barely recall days of cloud and cold, though there must have been some on that first voyage, but in his memory, all across the Indian Ocean, as week followed week, the seas had been bountiful and bright.

Hours he'd spent, staring at the wake of the *Albert,* seeing distance accumulate between him and the things that had almost destroyed him, and it was as though the sun were following him, moving southwards as he moved, and in the nights the stars came crowding to his eye.

But here, after Cape Farewell, both sun and stars disappeared, as though for always, as though the *Wallabi* were moving irrevocably beyond any ordinary or comforting thing into a place from which nobody on board would ever return.

Joseph and the boy, Will Sefton, held to the ship's rail in the stern. The boy was pale, sunk in silence, shivering in the raw cold. When something white and slick floated up and was borne along for a moment in the wake of the boat, Will stared at it until it disappeared. Then he began to tell Joseph how he'd spent two years working for an undertaker in Queenstown.

'The job I had,' he said, 'was the filthiest job on earth. Sucking out with tubes the foul stuff from the dead man's gut and pumping in the chemicals.' He said: 'If you want to know what I think, Mister Blackstone, I think the living body is ninety per cent dead matter and only some little spark in us keeps the rest of it alive.'

Now, he mumbled to Joseph, as the spray rose and drenched them for the hundredth time: 'I feel I'm dead, Mister Blackstone. All through me.'

Joseph urged the boy to endure, for that was all there was to do, to carry on existing. Either the *Wallabi* would be engulfed by the waves and they would all drown and their bodies be hurled against the hard roots of the bush at the edge of the land, or the paddle-wheels would keep turning, inching them on against the onrush of the sea, until the mouth of the Grey River was passed and the level ground of the Hokitika plain let them in.

But when Joseph contemplated the shore and let his gaze rest on its green vastness, he felt for the first time that the struggle to dig gold out of such a wilderness would be greater than any vision he'd ever had of it. He thought that his arduous work on the Cob House, cutting tussock grass and mashing it with earth, would seem as nothing compared to what would be asked of him here and that perhaps gold was the only thing that could lure men to a place where Nature asserted so supremely her disdain for anything unable to exist in the darkness of the forest floor or in the high branches of black beech.

To the boy, Joseph said: 'How shall you survive these miles of bush, Will?'

Will stared out and up at the mountains. His eye rested on the tops for a moment, then on the sky above, where now and then they could spy a bird circling, but his expression didn't alter. 'Same way as I survived on the Arrow,' he said. 'Do my duties. Keep silent. Wash my arse in the river.'

There was sickness on the ship, with men vomiting and spitting and some howling like dogs in their misery and fear. And most of them thought, while these days lasted, that no cradleful of gold was worth the terror that had rushed in on them with the southward turn of the ship. They wished themselves back in Christchurch or wherever they had come from. They longed for warmth and stillness and a soft place to lie. They found it difficult to breathe in the salt air. They complained that they had not been warned that, on the West Coast, there was nothing but mountains – mountains on land and mountains of dark water rising up in the winds against the dark sky.

Joseph, too, was sick. As he clung to the rail, retching, his body felt so weak, it was as if it had capitulated again to the fever that had arrived on the afternoon when he'd found gold at the creek and from which it had taken him so long to recover. He lay down on the deck and Will covered him with his blanket and he was grateful for this little kindness and he managed to fall asleep, even in the teeth of the wind.

Hour after hour, the *Wallabi* limped on, round the cape and on, past the mouth of the Grey River and then at last the passengers saw the change in the shore-line they had waited for. It was as though the mountains had moved, because in this place, there seemed to be nothing that was not moving and altering from moment to moment; the mountains had stepped aside and shown them a scrub-covered plain and a long grey strip of beach.

And now, the steamboat was turning and slowing. Joseph woke and felt stronger and stood up and saw that they were making for the shore, where the beach came slowly into view. Will produced a stale ginger biscuit from his pocket and gave it to Joseph and he ate it gratefully, glad of its sweetness.

Closer and closer came the beach and a cluster of low buildings could be seen along the estuary edge. The mist had turned to rain when two of the exhausted crew pushed through the crowded decks to the prow, where they dropped a lead-line and stared down into the depths of the sea, shouting instructions back to the wheel-house. The passengers, soaked and weak and shivering, clustered round them, sensing that something new was happening and the danger wasn't over yet.

'What?' they asked. 'What have you seen?'

'Seldom anything to see,' replied one of the crew men. 'But it's there.'

The word went round: it was the Hokitika Bar, a long snake of sand and shingle that shifted with the tides, sometimes swelling up into a solid mass, lurking a mere two fathoms beneath the surface of the water. It lay in wait for incoming ships, calling to the keels of ships like a magnet and breaking them apart. One rumour had it that only the Maoris knew the moods and alterations of the bar and that, in their shallow mokihi, they whispered to the sand, whispered death to the pākehā on their tall, keel-heavy boats. On the grey beach, among the driftwood, the men aboard the *Wallabi* could see the empty hulls and broken masts of ships wrecked on the bar. 'Every tenth day, on average, there's a drowning at Hokitika,' said one of the diggers, with a satisfied smile. And all had the same thought: could we swim to shore from here if the steamship strikes the bar? So a conversation began. How cold was the water? How great was the pull of the undertow? How powerful were the breakers?

'I'd swim,' said Will Sefton to Joseph. 'I wouldn't care if I was drowned. Rinse me out, that salt sea. Rinse away the maggots in me.'

Joseph thought of how in his life he had very often got near to something and then lost it. Now, he was face to face with the landscape where his future lay waiting in some harsh stone gully or beneath the roots of the manuka scrub. But this capricious last stretch of water still lay between him and the hard ground of his hopes and he dreaded to die here, within sight of it, but never reaching it. He swallowed the last crumb of the ginger biscuit and said a prayer: Let me come to riches, let me come to the happiness of riches before I am taken away.

'I'd swim,' he said to Will. 'I'd fight my way through.'

But the steamship was still making headway. Everyone was waiting for the moment when the keel would strike the sandbar, but the moment never came. The *Wallabi* had a draught shallow enough to elude the tentacles of the bar on this cold day and sailed gamely forward, pressed on by the breaking waves. At last, Joseph and Will and the other passengers felt the wind die and the rain miraculously cease as the wide arms of the Hokitika River took the *Wallabi* in and let it glide towards a safe mooring.

II

It was barely there yet, the town of Hokitika: a place so lonely and far from everything, it looked as if it had never expected to become a town or anything resembling a town, but had imagined itself soon enough breaking adrift from the coast, like a raft, to wait for the tides to carry it away.

There was a wide wharf, buttressed against the unknowable rise and fall of the water, and along the wharf a cluster of low shanties. But now, muddy streets were beginning to straggle outwards from the quay, backing hesitantly towards the bush, surprised by their own existence. These were yards and alleyways brought into being by the gold-diggings: stores offering tents and picks, fishing rods and matches; a bakery;

two banks; a hotel with a flagpole already rusted in the salt winds; a warden's office, painted yellow, selling miners' licences for thirty shillings.

As night fell, the arrivals on the *Wallabi* crammed into the hotel and paid a few farthings for hot water and a place to lie down and sleep. Some of them already had their licences clutched in their hands; others had felt unable to undertake the simple transaction of parting with thirty shillings and told themselves that their lives were somehow suspended, that there would arrive, in due time, some necessary tomorrow in which they would be resumed, but it was not now. All that *now* contained was rest and the knowledge of firm ground under their bones. They washed themselves and ate each a meagre plate of stew and lay down to sleep. They spilled out from the bedrooms into the passages and public rooms, lying on thin mattresses, wrapped in grey blankets, and the sound of their snoring was like a snarling of their souls, disgruntled at having found themselves so near to being lost.

Joseph lay among them for a while, but he couldn't sleep. He'd been one of the first to hurry to the warden's office and buy his Miner's Right, and now he took the licence from his pocket and stared at it in the dark. It entitled him to peg out a seventy-two-foot claim and work the claim 'for a period of one month'. His name was written on it in fine calligraphy: *Joseph Blackstone*. And this had thrilled him, as though the licence were itself a bank bond of substantial value. But now, in the darkness, Joseph understood that what it resembled most was a ticket in some enormous lottery. For no one knew precisely where the gold was to be found. Greenstone Creek on the Taramakau had yielded the colour to the first comers but, as others arrived in the Rush, the gold had begun to vanish and now Greenstone was declared 'exhausted' and no one remained there, except a few hardy fossickers, picking over the tailings other men had left.

Rumours now were all of Kaniere, five miles upstream on the Hokitika River and most of the new arrivals would head there when the next day came. But Joseph understood that the men of a Gold Rush were like moths, going towards a golden light and in time – inevitably – that light began to die, and so they hurried blindly on to the next and the next, always hopeful but always aware of the enormity of the pursuing dark.

Joseph got up, with his blanket wrapped around him, and made his way among the sleeping men to the door of the hotel. He walked out into the dirty street and, following the sound of the breaking waves, arrived once again on the beach, where the grey driftwood lay all around. The big pieces of wood reminded Joseph of the dead, lying in attitudes of ecstasy or torment, as though some final and terrible human conflict had taken place here on the sand. A half-moon was up and glimmering on the roaring sea, and Joseph thought that he'd never seen any place on earth like this or felt the power of it in his heart.

Though the wind was cold, he was glad he'd left the hotel. He walked to the sea's edge and stared at the water and remembered that he'd travelled this ocean in a paddle steamer and survived. To the wind and the waves he said: *Let this not have been in vain.*

He stood unmoving for a long while and then he searched for a sheltered spot and made a fire from grass and twigs and sat by it, feeding in small grey limbs of driftwood, until he'd achieved a blaze big enough to warm him.

Then Joseph Blackstone lay down on the sand, swaddled in his blanket and began to cry. He wasn't crying because of what he'd suffered on the *Wallabi*, nor because he knew now that his dreams of finding gold had led him to this place with nothing in his pocket except a piece of paper that was probably worthless. He was crying because he understood, now and for ever – or so it seemed to him – that the person he had loved was Rebecca Millward, truly loved her, as much as any man is capable of loving anyone outside his insistent self. Joseph was crying because he knew, as his driftwood fire blazed up and hurled sparks out into the sky, that he should have given in to what he'd felt and honoured it instead of denying it. He was crying because it was too late; he should have married Rebecca. But he had not married her: he had killed her.

Joseph slept a little and woke as it began to get light.

His fire was out. As the sun rose, he felt the bite of the sandflies on his neck and hands.

He returned to the hotel, where he found his fellow-passengers from the *Wallabi* eating a breakfast of porridge, tea and fried herring. He took a bowl of porridge and a mug of tea and sat down with the men. Their mood was loud and jocular and their talk was all about Kaniere and the finds there.

'A riser,' they told Joseph. 'A good riser.'

'A riser?'

'You're a new chum, eh? Never heard the term "riser"? Better than tucker ground, mister. On tucker ground you can pay your fees and get something for yourself, for your stomach and your thirst, but not much else. With a riser, you could make a good bit more. Send a few pounds home, or where you will.'

Joseph drank his tea, which was strong and bitter. He had no appetite and let Will Sefton eat his porridge as the men began to leave the hotel to walk to the warden's office for their licences or begin their trek up-river to Kaniere. He told Will to follow the diggers and not wait for him, but Will shook his head, wiped his mouth on his sleeve and said quietly: 'I heard a tale, Mister Blackstone. Heard two of them whispering in the privies. Kaniere may have a riser, but something's happening at Kokatahi. Trapper killed a blue-duck there. Found a lump of gold in its gizzard. Lump the size of a beech nut! So that's where them two pissers are headed.'

Joseph nodded. He saw that Will Sefton had adopted him. He didn't know whether the boy was giving him protection or seeking it, but he thought that this didn't matter.

'How far is Kokatahi, Will?'

'Beyond Kaniere. Further up-river. Wet-flat ground, they said. Nothing there but birds and bush rats. So, if we're lucky the Rush may not come.'

This was what Joseph wanted and Will had understood it: to be apart from the horde. He felt inclined to marvel at the boy's ability to read his mind, but then at once became aware of his own naïveté: for wasn't this exactly what every gold-miner longed for, to be in front of all the others, to strike out and strike lucky on his own and keep his finds to himself? Perhaps,

only latecomers to a Rush were truly happy men? The miner in
the vanguard saw all his patient workings brought to insignificance by the invading havoc around him.

'Shall we get some gold before the night, d'you think?' asked
Joseph.

'Don't know, Mister Blackstone.'

'Or shall we stay here and not trouble ourselves after all?'

'We should trouble ourselves or we shall get nothing. And I
know what that *nothing* can do to a digger. I know a song from
the Arrow and it goes:

'Where it be
There it be.
But where it be
There aren't I.'

'Where it be, there aren't I?'

'Yes. And I've seen that: some who peg out claim after claim,
thirty shillings a time for the Right, and they find nothing.
Only a little dust.'

Joseph remembered his creek. He put his hand into his
pocket and touched the handkerchief containing the scant
accumulation of gold dust, hidden for so long in the tea box
behind the calico wall of his room in the Cob House.

'I want more than dust, Will,' he said.

'Then we should make a start. Begin our journey. We should
hurry on, Mister Blackstone.'

Joseph bought a handcart, like a barrow with a single wheel
made of wood and rimmed with iron against the hard ground.
He found a sluice-box, on sale for three shillings, which had,
instead of canvas on its collecting tray, a piece of faded green
velvet. He imagined how the gold would shine, lying on the
velvet, and thought this box might bring him luck, so he bought
this, too, and found that he didn't seem to care any more about
the cost of things.

He discovered Will staring longingly at some fishing rods.
With a rod, the boy said, he could catch 'all the fish in the river
and us live like pigs in clover', so Joseph, who now cursed

himself for leaving behind his own rods and the fly box with its hidden curl, bought a rod and a can of maggots. 'This is called a grub-stake,' said Will. 'I'll owe you some gold for this, if I find any.'

Joseph lingered, pushing the handcart, among the shanties of Hokitika.

A girl called to him from a doorway, and he stared at her and met her eyes for a moment, but passed on. All the while, he could hear the roar of the sea and it was as though he was afraid to leave it and go into the silence of the hills.

III

Joseph and Will Sefton followed the Hokitika River in its south-westerly course. Along its length, they saw diggings begun and abandoned among the scrub. Near the mounds of wash-dirt, they saw broken shovels and picks, crates which had once contained hens, sacks of flour left out in the rain and turned to glue and scraps of newspaper blowing about in the wind.

The ground became steeper, and to their left the forest crowded in between them and the sky, and their pathway by the river became narrow. They heard the sweet song of the bellbird.

Now that they were finally moving towards their destination – or at least towards some destination that Joseph could envisage – he began to feel better. His stomach settled and he and Will rested a while and chewed a piece of bacon. And, in the wake of his night of weeping, he felt calmer than he'd felt for a long time, as though the persistent fever in him had broken and gone.

As they approached Kaniere, Will stopped and told Joseph to listen.

'Sounds of the Rush, Mister Blackstone. No other noise like this under the sky.'

Joseph set down the cart. He wiped the sweat from his neck with a rag. The walls of the valley were still steep, throwing echoes into the air, and now he could hear what sounded like a wild orchestra assembled among the scrub, beating out music on the stones and in the tall trees.

'Cradles,' said Will. 'You hear them? Rattling back and forth?'

'Yes, I hear them.'

'And picks striking the flint. There's a windlass, too, I reckon. I can hear the shrieking of a wheel.'

'Bring the wash-dirt up with a windlass, do they?'

'Yes. Or use it for draining their shafts. Gold lies on the blue-clay bottom and it's that bottom you have to find. But sometimes the water's your enemy. Fills your shaft and keeps filling. You can see the blue, but you can't reach it.'

They walked on. The narrow track was gently rising all the time and Joseph had begun to feel the weight of the loaded cart in the ache of his arms. He would have gladly stopped at Kaniere, but this was not what he wanted, to peg some 'duffer' claim among the hordes. He wished that he and Will could skirt round the diggings, but they had to follow the river until it divided and they saw the open pathway to Kokatahi. So they went forward at a slow pace and the winds that tormented the coast began to drop and the sun was warm on them. In the fast-flowing water of the Hokitika River, they began to notice the rubbish of the mine – the stirred mud of the pay-dirt, slices and ends of rope, greasy wrappings of stale food and tobacco, old bottles and jars – borne away towards the sea.

And then the Kaniere goldfield opened up in front of them: the scrub uprooted and burned, the trees felled and stripped down into saplings and planks for the windlasses and for the flumes on stilts that carried water from the river to the hillside claims. The ground had a pocked and tousled look. Tents stood on this ground at tilted angles, in untidy rows. The scene, thought Joseph, resembled a field hospital for the remnants of some small, forgotten army. Slab huts, roofed with ti-ti leaves and barely larger than dog kennels, had also struggled into being: shelter for those who'd had no money to buy rope or canvas. These were hovels held together with nails and flax, and Joseph saw men sitting in their narrow shade, puffing on pipes or brewing tea, or just staring into vacancy, nursing the pain in their arms from their ceaseless work, like convalescents.

Everywhere, the rattle of the sluice-boxes bore witness to that work: for there was no other way to get gold here but through the digging and washing and sifting of the earth, and all around the diggers of Kaniere, the earth spoke to them and insinuated itself into their dreams and wouldn't let them rest.

No one paid any attention to Will and Joseph. The Kaniere miners knew the Rush was on and that, day by day, more and more people would arrive and the claims would spread out wider and further, right up to the implacable bush-line. In the nights, by their fires, the men would drink and tell stories, but the daylight was a precious commodity never to be squandered in words. It was thirty-shilling light.

'We could try our luck here, Mister Blackstone,' said Will, 'if you want to.'

Joseph stared at the scene before him and found it hateful. A memory of his father, trapped against iron rails by a squealing cartload of pigs, holding high his precious gold-edged auctioneer's ledger, came into his mind. Afterwards, Roderick Blackstone had been embarrassed by the smears of pigs' slobber on his black trousers, but had been 'victorious', he said, 'absolutely victorious because my ledger has no trace of my ordeal upon it'.

'No,' said Joseph. 'We will go on, Will. We must get up-river of all this, to where the water is clear.'

It was much further to Kokatahi than they had imagined and the sun was already going down over the mountains when they heard, in the misty distance, a mouth-organ being played:

'Speed, bonny boat, like a bird on the wing,
Over the sea to Skye ...'

'Scots,' whispered Will. 'There's our signal, isn't it? The pissers I overheard in the privy were Scotsmen.'

Though the melancholy tune was consoling and seemed to lure them on, Joseph set down the cart where he stood, at a good distance from the music. He waited for a moment, looking about him, feeling the dusk coming towards him and aware of how exhausted he was.

He told Will to search for twigs and wood for a fire while he set up the tent he'd bought such a long time ago. His back and arms ached as they had never ached on the farm, but he set out the tent with as much patience and care as he could muster. The music stopped and, in its absence, Joseph could hear again the glide and fall of the river. As he hammered in the tent pegs, he realised the ground he was standing on was much softer than any ground that they'd passed that day or any that he'd imagined.

In the night, after some hours of a deep sleep that seemed as though it might have no end, Joseph woke to a strange sound.

Will Sefton lay beside him, and the boy was naked with his blanket pushed aside and he was playing his penny whistle, making short repetitive sounds, like a bird.

'What are you doing, Will?' Joseph asked.

'Playing my whistle. Like a bellbird, ain't I?' said Will. 'Just as sweet, ain't I? Just as sweet?'

'Yes,' said Joseph, his voice thick and slow with sleep. 'Just as sweet.'

'I only whistle in the night,' whispered Will. 'Always the middle of night, because I like it that way, in the darkness. On the Arrow they called me Whistling Willie! Apt as any name could be. But they knew I would only do it in the darkness.'

Joseph lay on his back and stared at the boy and he thought then that he'd known all along that this moment would come.

'What way do you like it, Mister Blackstone?' Will said. 'For I've learned they like it different ways and it's all one to me.'

'All one to you?'

'All one. Told you. Do my services. Get my pay ... Some liked me to kiss them and I'd even do that. Kiss their lips like a girl. And that'd craze them sometimes and they'd call me tender names: Willie-my-sweet, Will Sefton my lovely boy ...'

Joseph reached out a hand and touched Will's thin shoulder. He opened his mouth to say to Will that he didn't want his 'services', that he hadn't befriended him for that reason, that, if he found gold, he would give a share to Will because Will and he had travelled together and that travelling together was better than travelling alone. But he felt too stunned, by all that he'd endured and by what he knew was happening now, to form these words, to form any words. So he just lay there, touching Will and staring at him and understanding that Will would leave him the next day – leave him to take up with another man who would want his 'services' and pay handsomely for them – and that his own gift of the fishing rod would count for nothing. And he saw his own approaching loneliness as something unendurable.

It seemed to Joseph that a long time passed without either of them speaking or moving, but only looking at each other in the dark.

Eventually, Joseph heard himself say: 'Kiss me like a girl, then, Will. Kiss me gently like a girl.'

A Neat and Tidy Room

I

On the Canterbury flats, after the heavy rain of early February, which the land drank fast and forgot, the drought came in again on the hot wind.

The Maoris of Pare's tribe saw a season of hunger approaching. They stared at their kūmara plantations, which were yellow and sickly, and they prayed to the spirits of the air to send rain. Some of them saw the spirits turning cartwheels in the flames of the sunset, but still no rain clouds appeared in the sky.

Pare sat alone in a corner of the pā that was seldom visited and looked out at the dusty earth and heard the fury of the wind and knew that she was responsible for the drought. She had offended the gods of the the natural world. She heard their anger in the trees, saw it in the cracks which began to split the furrows of the fields, felt it in her stomach and in her heart. They had already commanded her – or so she believed – to cease her journeys to Orchard House – and she'd done what they asked. But now she saw that this was not enough. It was as if the Maori gods understood that Pare's love for Edwin Orchard was stronger than her love for her own people and they were determined to punish her. To make this punishment yet more bitter, they were visiting suffering upon the whole tribe.

Pare stared at her legs. She noticed they were much thinner than they had once been. It frightened her to know that her old sickness had returned. She felt intensely aware of the ever-moving, ever-changing nature of the world, realising that no minute of existence is identical to that which precedes it nor that which follows it. She saw herself being hurried faster and faster through time, towards her death.

The sun was going down and Pare could smell fires and roasting meat, but she had no appetite. Even in the sheltered place where she sat, the wind discovered her and blew her hair across her face. She held her arms out to the wind, to Tane, the fierce God of the Forest, and prayed to be forgiven. Then she began to ask herself what she could do to appease the gods. Her head burned with a fever and her thoughts were confused, as though insects were swarming inside her skull or the skull itself were turning to dust. The darkness settled quietly round her and she didn't move.

Pare dreamed that she stood again at the river's edge, where she'd seen the taniwha so long ago.

In the dream, the tea-brown water rose and slopped about her naked legs and it was icy and she felt its intention, to pull her down among the weeds and the black eels. But she knew that it was not to drown her there, but only to make her search for something in the darkness of the mud. So she let herself be carried down and down into the depths of the cold river and her hands explored the oozing mud of the river-bottom. She didn't know what she was looking for, yet she knew, even though her lungs were hurting and the eels were winding themselves around her arms, that she had to remain there until she found it.

Then, at last, there was something solid in her hand. Pare clutched it. She unwound the eels and pushed them away and swam to the surface and when she reached the surface, she saw that the sun had risen and was sparkling on the water and touching the leaves with silver and she knew that she had found the answer to her puzzle. In her hand lay a piece of greenstone.

The next day, Pare told her mother she was going on a journey to find greenstone for the gods. She was going to walk across the mountains to the place where the pākehā were digging for gold, for gold and greenstone often lie along the same lines in the earth. And when she had found the greenstone and offered it to the spirits, the rain would come and all the seasons revert to what they had once been and there would be no more drought or suffering.

Pare's mother stared at her daughter. She touched her nose, her glossy hair. She reminded her that the mountains were treacherous and cold. Then she went and fetched her few precious things: a shark-toothed knife, a wooden pot filled with poroporo balm, a coloured blanket, a phial of red ochre, a paua shell and a coil of fishing line with ten hooks. Pare already had the small greenstone pendant, which had in turn been worn by her mother and her grandmother before that.

'Take these,' said Pare's mother. 'Break up the shell into little pieces that will resemble minnows in the water and tie them to your hooks, and with these you will catch large fish. And you will survive.'

Pare hung the greenstone pendant round her neck and wrapped the other objects into a bundle, which she would carry on her back. Then she swept a corner of the pā and shook out her flax mat and folded this into the bundle. Where her mat had lain she placed a small circle of stones. Before leaving, Pare arranged and rearranged these stones several times until each one seemed perfectly settled in the place where she'd put it. She knew that, in the cold silence of the mountains, she would dream of her life here in the pā and long to return to it. And, to comfort herself, she would imagine the stones, waiting for her, untouched and unmoving.

II

In the continuing drought and in the hot winds, something irreversible was happening to the Cob House: it was turning to powder.

Harriet stood low down on the flat and looked up at her home. Silhouetted against the evening sun, she could see an unending swirl of dust blowing off the Cob House walls. Mixed with the dust was a speckling of dry, mashed grass and Harriet understood now why everybody had said that cob was 'temporary', 'contingent', 'unstable'. With every gust of wind, the house was beginning to crumble.

She and Lilian tugged out a ladder from the cow barn. They went back and forth from the creek, filling cans with water and then Harriet climbed up the ladder and poured water down the walls and with their hands the women tried to tamp down the brittle cob and press new handfuls of mud into the places where gaps were appearing.

Wiping this mud from her hands, Lilian commented: 'Some unorthodox girls of my acquaintance, when I was young, had a fondness for the pottery wheel, but I was never among them.'

Harriet smiled. Less and less did Lilian dress herself in fine clothes or bonnets; she wore smocks now, and sacking aprons, and pushed her grey hair into a net under a crumpled linen hat to keep off the sun. She said that she was 'getting quite attached to the pigs' and even her struggles with the smoky range seemed to vex her less than they had done. Her bread became crustier, 'more', she said proudly, 'as Roderick would have liked it', and sometimes she and Harriet were so hungry after their day on the farm that they consumed an entire loaf, smeared with dripping, between them. 'If only,' Lilian said one evening, as she sat contentedly sewing, 'there could be no return to winter.'

Harriet, who was working on her scrapbook, placing in it a shrivelled ear of wheat and a turquoise kingfisher feather, looked up at Lilian. She wondered whether this slow arrival of cheerfulness owed itself to Lilian's hopes for Joseph's expedition. Was her mother-in-law simply dreaming of the way their lives would alter when her son returned as a rich man? For even the fact that the Cob House was disintegrating did not seem to dismay her particularly. Perhaps poor Lilian felt so certain that a new dwelling – one more resembling the Orchards' magnificent place – would be built at last that she was perfectly resigned to patching up the walls of the old cob shack for a little while. For they wouldn't be there for very long. One winter? Or, at worst, one winter and one spring? Harriet supposed that Lilian comforted herself with a vision of polished floorboards, marble mantelpieces, carpets from Chengchow.

And who was she to say, if Joseph was alive and working on the goldfields, Lilian might not be given them one day?

Harriet preferred not to think about Joseph.

She discovered that almost every memory she had of him produced in her a feeling of disquiet. Though she had to work harder, she found life much easier without him. In her bed, she let Lady lie in the space where Joseph had been. In her dreams, Joseph and the odious Mr Melchior Gable became indistinguishable in her mind.

Yet, she also lay and wondered about her life. She hoped that something else awaited her, beyond the drudgery of the farm. *Better that we never know*, she wrote to her father, *what lies beyond the next hill.*

> *For the answer might come back 'nothing'. And I confess, that having travelled across the world, I do not feel I would be content with that 'nothing'. My habit of looking at the mountains has not gone away. They are so fine. I wish that I could paint a picture of them for you. And they contain a mystery: that is what I feel. And I ask myself: is the mystery they contain the mystery of my life?*

She rode every day now. She thought Billy the nicest horse she'd ever encountered. His gallop was skittish, earnest, like a pony's, but his heart and lungs were strong and he never seemed to tire. Harriet wished she could reward him with the grass of a green field, but she let him graze by the pond, where the tussock was still moist, and fed him carrots from her vegetable plot. She talked to him as she groomed him and he would sometimes turn his head and rest it against her back. She told him that the task of keeping all the animals alive was getting harder and harder as every day passed. Yet she knew she wasn't unhappy. She told the horse this as well. She told him she was happier than she'd been for a long time.

The first rains arrived early in March.

They were gentle at first, almost invisible, like an English rain. Then the wind veered due south, bringing a freezing torrent towards them from the Antarctic.

'Spiteful rain', Lilian called it, a rain that whipped and beat at the faces of the two women as they struggled out to feed the hens and collect eggs for their supper. And, in its spite, the rain seemed intent upon completing what the drought had begun. The cob, made so brittle by the heat, now turned to mud. Holes appeared in the walls near the stone chimney. No sooner had the women patched the holes, with rags or paper or wood or whatever they had to hand, than they reappeared, and the rain came through and began pouring down the kitchen wall.

Harriet and Lilian asked themselves what Joseph would have done, had he been here, but they agreed that neither of them knew. Joseph had never been the kind of man who dreamed up ingenious solutions to things.

'Roderick, on the contrary, *was*,' said Lilian firmly. 'Roderick was a veritable inventor because his mind had a scientific disposition. But Joseph didn't inherit it, not that I can see. Joseph too often relies on the visions of others.'

'So what would Roderick have invented for our present predicament?' asked Harriet. And Lilian said she would think about this, said she was sure that poor dear Roddy would 'come up with something'.

Lilian's head filled with imaginary solutions: walls of stone rising miraculously around the cob, to enclose it; a solid wooden frame attached to the cob somehow and totara planks nailed to the frame. But she knew that none of these materials was to hand and that they had no saw to cut planks nor any heavy hammer to break stones. And they were women, after all, Lilian Blackstone told herself. There was a limit to their strength.

Then, one night, she remembered a time of autumn floods in Norfolk and how Roderick had built a wall out of sacks of sand, to keep the water away from their door. She could see it so very clearly: Roddy patiently filling bag after bag and laying them one on top of the other, in a plaited kind of pattern, almost up to window level. Hours and hours of arduous work, but entirely successful because all her carpets had been saved and hers was the only door-mat that had remained dry in Parton Magna.

'Sacks!' she announced the next morning to Harriet. 'Do we

not have very many empty flour sacks and potato sacks and sacks of all kinds and sizes? We shall fill these with sand and press them up against the wall on the chimney side, as high as we can possibly go.'

Harriet thought about this and said: 'Where are we to find sand, Lilian?'

'At the creek!' replied Lilian triumphantly. 'For what are those mounds Joseph left but heaps of shingle and sand?'

Harriet seldom went to that place. It felt to her like a landscape of the dead, as though the mounds were graves, as though she would find bones in the earth. What she saw there was Joseph's secrecy of soul.

'It is a good idea, Lilian,' she said, 'but I think the material is not right.'

She would do it herself, Lilian decided. She would save the Cob House. She would begin the next morning, before Harriet was awake. If the rain had let up, then good, the task would be almost enjoyable, but if it hadn't, she would simply get a soaking and not care to mind about it. She would pretend she was a Foot Guard at the Battle of Waterloo. She would endure until victory had been won.

The morning dawned dry but very cold. It was difficult to imagine the hot days that had passed. Lilian wrapped a scarf round her neck and put on her linen hat and took a barrow and a shovel and a pile of sacks down to the creek's edge as the sun came up.

She began work. The rain had loosened the shingle mounds, but she knew that this stony sludge was heavier than sand. She decided to hang each sack on to the front of the barrow by two nails, counteracting its growing weight by stones laid in the back of the cart. When the sack was full enough, she heaved it backwards into the barrow. This was scientific, she thought proudly. This was a *system*.

She returned to the Cob House towards eight o'clock to eat porridge with Harriet, telling her she had been walking out on the flats in the fine morning. She had filled five sacks. Up and down her spine ran a shiver of pain, but she didn't mention this. As she poured milk on her porridge, she found herself wishing she had the bones of the young girl she'd once been, who had walked on her hands five times round the nursery. This was how she had to think of herself, she decided, part Foot Guard and part ten-year-old girl with her toes pointed towards the ceiling and her white drawers falling backwards down her legs.

She set off again, as though to continue her walk, knowing Harriet would be occupied with the animals all morning. She hoped the pain in her back would diminish soon, for now she had to push the barrow uphill to the house and lay the filled sacks round the chimney in a careful pattern, just as Roderick had laid them round the door at Parton Magna. She allowed herself to imagine that, when Joseph returned, Harriet would tell him that she, Lilian, had saved the house single-handed with her fine 'sack artifice' and there would be no day when it was not gazed upon and admired.

Pushing the barrow was 'terrible, quite terrible' and, with each difficult step, Lilian cursed the house for being so far away from where it should have stood. But she arrived at last and wheeled the sacks round to the chimney, where she saw some creature – a mouse or a rat – scuttle out of one of the holes in the cob. My remedy, she thought, has come not a moment too soon.

Once she had leaned for a moment against the wall and caught her breath and wiped her face, she began hauling the sacks out. But she found she couldn't lay them in a sensible pattern, as Roddy had done, she just had to let them fall in a heap, then push and kick them into position. And when she'd laid them she saw that the distance between them and the worst of the holes was colossal. *Colossal*. The Cob House had always seemed so small. She remembered that snow had almost smothered it in one night. But now, Lilian could swear that it had grown taller. The wall dwarfed her and her labours. But she told herself that that was how life was arranged: things made you small. What you had to do was fight against insignificance.

Lilian went back to the creek. She worked so arduously that she didn't feel the cold, except in her feet, where they stood at the river's edge.

Nor did she really notice when the rain began to fall once more. She just kept on until – from one moment to the next –

she felt that she could go on no more. She let her shovel fall. She told herself that in a while she would wheel her second – or was it her third? – barrow-load of filled sacks up to the house and continue the 'wall' she'd begun. But now, she felt herself fall into a kind of daze. It was like no daze into which she had ever fallen before and one part of Lilian's mind was fascinated by its strangeness. She thought she would sit down, exactly where she was, between two of Joseph's shingle heaps, and think about what kind of daze it could be.

So she sat and the rain fell on her and stained her linen hat and ran into her pockets and trickled through the eyeholes of her muddy boots.

She looked about her, not recognising anything. Aloud, she said: 'Is it Waterloo?'

Lady found her in the early afternoon and began whimpering and Harriet came running as fast as she could over the flats. Lilian was lying by the creek and her white face looked oily in the rain.

Harriet knelt by Lilian and felt a faint pulse. She saw the barrow half filled with sacks. Sorrow for Lilian made her utter a little cry. She pulled Lilian into her arms and stood up and laid her gently on the barrow.

She whistled to Lady, who was drinking at the creek, and the dog followed her as she slowly pushed the cart back to the house.

Harriet undressed Lilian and dried her and wrapped her head in a towel and put her favourite flannel nightgown on her. All the while, she was trying to decide what she should do: stay with her and nurse her herself, or ride to Rangiora for Doctor Pettifer before night came on.

She laid Lilian in her bed and covered her with as many blankets as she could find. She kept patting her hand and her cheek and saying her name, but Lilian didn't open her eyes. Outside, Harriet could see the light of afternoon beginning to wane.

She stood up. She wrote a note to Lilian: *Gone to Rangiora for doctor*. Then she found Lilian's favourite darning egg and wrapped the note around this and pressed it into Lilian's hand. She told Lady to stay and went running out to find Billy.

Lilian woke and found herself in the dark.

She had no memory of filling sacks with stones. There was a burning pain in the area of her heart and there was something binding her head, which she took to be a helmet made of iron.

She thought that perhaps she should pray, but she couldn't remember the words of any prayer or hymn or psalm or anything connected to God except the word God. So she said this. *God. Dear God.*

She was in a furnace. She couldn't see any flames, but they were there, she could feel them, they were all around her and in her and the heat of them was greater than any heat she had ever known. She was in a furnace, wearing a helmet made of iron: she was in hell.

God. Dear God.

She tried to move her hand and found that she could move it and thought that if she could move her hand, then she might be able to climb out of hell and ascend to heaven by some light and beautiful ladder made of muslin. So she reached up and saw that she had arrived in a familiar room.

She would have recognised it anywhere: it was her room. She couldn't remember the name of the place where this room was, but she knew it was hers. There was a small window, where the sun came in between chintz curtains, and under the window an oak chest-of-drawers with, arranged very neatly on it, a selection of photographs in cherrywood frames.

The room was papered with a yellow striped wallpaper. On a wash-stand stood a china jug and bowl, made by Paines of Stafford. And next to the jug and bowl was a glass vase of flowers and Lilian could smell these flowers and imagine the place they'd come from, which was a green meadow.

Her room.

She hoped it was tidy. She'd taken pride in neatness.

It looked tidy enough. In the shadowy part of it, she could recognise the familiar wardrobe, with, carefully folded on its top, the tartan rug she placed on the bed in winter. But Lilian didn't think that it was winter now, or summer either, now she came to think of it, because there was no burning heat in the room of the kind that she'd felt a moment ago. No. The room was, in fact, exactly as she liked it to be, not cold, not too warm. And so Lilian let her hand fall back on to the pillow. She could rest now, she told herself. She was in her room in England and it was springtime.

The Torn Painting

I

As Harriet rode through the gathering darkness towards Rangiora she thought that, all in all, life had asked very little of her compared to what it demanded of many people, but now, on this night, it was asking something important: it was asking her to save Lilian.

When she knocked on Dr Pettifer's door, she was told by his wife that he was out delivering a baby. At first, Harriet said that she would wait for him, in the little low street, but then, suddenly afraid that a difference of half an hour's delay might mean the difference between Lilian's life and death, asked Dr Pettifer's wife whether she might go to the house where the child was being born and catch him there.

She was directed to a shop, Parsons & Co., which sold tea and coffee, and told to ring the bell. She tied Billy to a post and stared in the shop window, and saw candles flickering on the counter and near it a trestle table on which was lying the scant remains of a meal, and she thought how the child about to be born might always remember this in his future life: eating his suppers by candlelight in the tiny store where his parents worked all day. She rang the bell, but nobody came. After ringing a second time, Harriet opened the door and went inside.

The smell of coffee was like the smell of a wood fire, she thought, because both spoke to the human mind of some pause in the onward rush of events, some parenthesis in which the body could be comfortable and still. And so – just for a moment – Harriet sat down on one of the chairs half pulled up to the table and breathed in the scent of the coffee beans, which were piled up in sacks all around the room, and let herself rest.

She knew that she was a trespasser in this house, and should have waited outside until someone answered the ringing of the bell, 'but it seems', she told herself calmly, 'that I just did not do this, and I do not exactly know why'. And she considered for a moment the idea that her life might have been full of such small transgressions, which she had never brought to her own attention.

Now, she could hear, in the room adjacent to the coffee counter, a woman's voice calling out: 'Lucas, where are you?' and then other voices consoling, urging, and the creak of a wooden bed and a fit of coughing and then again: 'Lucas, let you come near.'

Harriet stood up and called softly: 'Dr Pettifer?' Yet she half expected that nobody would hear her and she also knew that she couldn't go into the room where the labour was going on. She was a stranger who had no right to be here.

She sat down again and, to her own shame, picked up a piece of bread from a plate on the table and put it into her mouth. She reached for a pickled onion and ate this and then her hunger came roaring at her like a wolf and she was unable to stop herself from eating every single thing that had been left in front of her: bread, cheese, onions, shards of fatty ham, a fold of black treacle on a spoon. And all the while, as she ate, she could hear the voices next door and the coughing and the sudden moments of crying and calling out to Lucas and the movement of the wooden bed on the slab floor. And it was as though her hunger were in a race with the birth of the baby and if the baby were born too soon, then it wouldn't be sated.

All urgency, Harriet realised, had somehow drained out of her mission to get the doctor to Lilian. It had been obliterated by her terrible desire to gobble food and she felt ashamed of every bite of everything that she took, but she went on eating until nothing remained on the plates, and then she wiped her mouth and looked at the clock on the wall above the sacks of coffee and felt the night assemble all around her, pressing on the windows and altering the colour of the candle-flames.

*

She arrived back at the Cob House with the elderly Dr Pettifer towards one o'clock in the morning and lit a lamp and they went together into Lilian's calico room. Straightaway, Lady began whining and jumping up on to Harriet's muddy skirts. On the doctor's black coat there was a smell of iodine and ether.

Lilian was lying as Harriet had left her, with her head wrapped in the towel and her body neat and straight in the bed. One arm was raised and resting on the pillow, however, and Lilian's hand held up the darning egg, as though to demonstrate its usefulness or to show its marbled colours to the light. When Dr Pettifer took up the hand to feel for a pulse, the egg popped out of it and bounced on to the floor and Harriet saw the note she'd wrapped around it float down after it. As Harriet bent to retrieve the egg, Lilian opened one eye.

'Lilian,' said Harriet, leaning near. 'Lil?'

'She can't hear you,' said Dr Pettifer, who was now lowering Lilian's arm and arranging it by the side of her body. 'She's dead as can be. I'd say she went two hours ago.'

'She opened her eye . . .'

'Both eyes normally open in death. Unless there is a little rheum present, so that the eyelid adheres – which we have, I expect, in her right eye, still. I would estimate that death occurred at eleven o'clock.'

Harriet remembered that it had been at this hour that the baby had been born in the back room of Parsons & Co., a boy, and that the father of the child had appeared in the shop, in search of grog, and found Harriet sitting at his table. He'd shown no surprise, as if, on this night of the birth of his son, he'd expected strangers to be waiting there. Nothing was said about the stolen food, but Harriet found herself explaining that her mother-in-law had been trying to build a wall out of sacks when she'd fallen over.

'A wall of sacks?'

'Filled with shingle and sand. To keep out the rain.'

'Ah.' Then the man smiled as his hand lighted on the grog flagon.

'In New Zealand,' he said, 'you cannot keep out the rain.'

Now, Harriet stood up and looked down at Lilian. She

stroked the hand that had held the egg. She thought of Lilian's palm cross nailed to her room at Mrs Dinsdale's and her white shawl laid out ready for the night. She said to Dr Pettifer: 'If we had got here sooner, might you have been able to save her?'

But Dr Pettifer was already writing out the certificate of death and he was one of those self-important people who refused on principle to do two things – such as writing and talking – at the same time, and so he made no answer.

'Christian name of the deceased?' he snapped after a moment.

'Lilian,' replied Harriet.

'Other names?' he said with a long, exhausted sigh.

'Lilian May,' said Harriet, who had begun to unwind the towel from Lilian's head. 'Lilian May Blackstone.'

Harriet was told by Dr Pettifer that an undertaker would be sent from Rangiora 'in a few days'. How many days he couldn't say. And then he was gone, with his ether smell and his shabby coat and his tiredness, trotting away into the dark on his bay horse, and Harriet was left alone with Lilian.

She was glad that the heat-wave had passed. The cooler air of March would be kinder to the body. All she prayed was that the Cob House would endure and that the tin roof wouldn't come crashing down upon Lilian as she lay and waited to be put into the ground.

Harriet fed the dog and made tea and she and Lady sat by Lilian's side and the only sounds were the rattle of the teacup on its saucer and the grinding of the dog's teeth on a worn bone.

Both Lilian's eyes were closed now and her hair, in its wiry plait, was dry and smoothed back from her face. She looked as cheerful as she'd ever seemed. And Harriet remembered how, in the winter, she used to get into her bed very often and lie exactly like this, with her nose in the air, as though practising dying.

The night very slowly passed. Harriet kept vigil with a single lamp and Lady slept at her feet. Joseph was always on the edge of her thoughts and she knew that, although he seemed to be a man untouched by any strong emotion, he had tried to do his best for Lilian. And it was for Lilian, certainly, as much as for himself or for her or for any future they might have together, that Joseph was searching for gold.

Harriet didn't know how Joseph would receive the news of his mother's death. She thought he would be altered by it in ways that she couldn't foresee. And so she understood that the news had to reach Joseph as soon as possible, wherever he was, and that the news would have to be carried by her, because who else was there to take it? As his wife, she owed him this.

When the morning came, Harriet pulled the sheet over Lilian's face and went out to feed the animals. The sky was blue, but she could see clouds piling up on the southerly horizon and feel the wind rising again and smell the nearness of rain.

II

Harriet sat with Dorothy Orchard by the fire, while the rain drove against the windows, and described how she had dressed Lilian in her finest black bombazine dress and her favourite bonnet and put into her hands, as she lay in her coffin, the painting of Joseph as a child, which Harriet had first seen in Lilian's room at Mrs Dinsdale's.

'Poor woman,' said Dorothy. Then she asked: 'Was the coffin well made?'

Harriet shook her head. 'I felt . . .' she began, 'that its sides were too thin. I was afraid that when they lifted it up, it was going to bend.'

'Oh dear,' said Dorothy. 'I have heard just such a thing before, that the slabs they use are too insubstantial.'

'But Lilian wasn't heavy,' Harriet went on. 'I think that our life here had worn her out. She was carried safely into her grave.'

'And I suppose you were the only mourner?'

'Yes. But I managed to sing one hymn that Lilian liked: "Hold High the Fiery Banner".'

Edwin, who had been in a corner of the parlour, writing a

story about a Moa bird, now put down his pencil and asked suddenly: 'What is bombazine?'

Harriet turned and looked at Edwin. She noticed that, in the shadowy room, Edwin's eyes looked tired. She explained that bombazine was a kind of material, something between silk and worsted, of which mourning dresses were very often made.

Edwin said: 'When you die and go to heaven, do you only have one suit of clothes for all eternity?'

'Oh, of all the questions!' said Dorothy. 'But if children should die, I think that they would certainly have beautiful white robes and feathery wings.'

'I don't want white robes,' said Edwin.

'No?' said Dorothy. 'But then you're not going to die. Not until you're very, very old.'

'Yes, I am,' said Edwin. Then he sat down again at his story and began immediately writing: *One day, the Moa looked around and saw that he was lonely . . .* The two women glanced at each other and then they heard Edwin say: 'I will ask if I can have the wings and not the robes.'

Dorothy got up and crossed the room to Edwin and put her arms round him. 'Why do you say that you're going to die, my darling?' she asked. 'What on earth has put that into your mind?'

Edwin didn't look at his mother, but down at the drawing of the Moa he had made to illustrate his story. 'Do you want to hear my story so far, Mama?' he asked.

'Yes,' said Dorothy, 'I would very much like to hear your story. But first I want to know why you said that you were going to die.'

Edwin stared at his picture. He thought that perhaps the colouring he'd done was all wrong and that the Moa might not have been yellow and red, but a dull brown like the kiwi.

'Edwin,' said Dorothy, hugging him more tightly. 'Answer me.'

'The Moa wasn't red and yellow, was it?' he said.

'I don't know what colour it was,' said Dorothy. 'I want an answer to my question!'

Her voice had become cross, without Dorothy's intending this. And this crossness brought tears to Edwin's eyes, not tears for himself, but tears of sorrow for Pare who had vanished from his life. In his dreams, he saw Pare falling from a rock into a river and being swept away to her death, and in all of these dreams it seemed to him that she called to him to follow.

And now, in his waking life, Edwin Orchard believed that he *would* follow, at least in his mind, and that the calling of Pare would never stop until he reached her and that, to reach her, he would have to depart from his life here. He wouldn't be able to say a word to his parents about it – except to try to find ways of warning them as he had just done – but quite soon he would have to leave them.

Dorothy was shaking Edwin now and tears had welled up in her eyes, too. 'Edwin,' she kept repeating, 'tell me. Tell me. Tell me what you meant!'

Edwin knew that part of him wanted to follow Pare, but part of him wanted to stay here with Dorothy and Toby and the dogs and Janet's blue blancmanges. His tears fell on to the picture of the Moa and the red and yellow merged together in places, to form a peculiar orange. He tried to push Dorothy away. 'Don't hold me so tight, Mama!'

'I'll hold you tight until you say what you meant. I'll hold you and never let you go.'

'I don't *know* what I meant!' Edwin blurted out at last.

'I don't believe you. Why would you have said such a thing for no reason?'

'I only said I didn't want those robes ...'

'But why is there a question of robes? Are you ill, Edwin? Is something happening that you haven't told us?'

'No! I just *said* that in case.'

'In case? What d'you mean "in case"?'

'In case I fell ...'

'Fell? Fell from where? From your pony?'

'Fell anywhere. All I meant was, I'd like the wings by themselves and not those white things and not bombazine!'

Mother and son were both weeping now and clinging to each other and Harriet got up and slowly crossed the room to them and sat down opposite them.

'Harriet,' sobbed Dorothy, 'what in the world has brought this into his mind?'

'I think', said Harriet gently, 'that he may have had a dream. Am I right, Edwin? I think you may have been lying down somewhere comfortable, perhaps in your bed, or perhaps somewhere else like in the toi-toi grass, and then you went to sleep and had a dream about falling and dying. And now the dream won't go away. Am I right?'

Edwin turned his head from where it was buried in Dorothy's shoulder. His crying ceased. He said nothing, but only nodded and regarded Harriet gravely with his wide grey eyes.

'Is that it?' said Dorothy. 'Is Harriet right? You had a dream?'

'Yes,' lied Edwin. 'But now it's gone.'

After supper, Toby Orchard, puffing on a cigar, his wide frame nicely settled in his favourite chair, said: 'I have been putting my mind to how we can get word to Joseph and there are only two ways. The first way is that one of us must go to Lyttelton and make sure a letter is put into the hands of the captain of the *Wallabi* or the *Nelson* to be given to the commissioner or warden at Hokitika. However, I can't say when these boats may next be putting out, so very much time might be lost here.'

'Perhaps there is no particular haste?' suggested Dorothy. 'For this kind of news does not alter, Toby.'

'No,' said Toby, 'of course it does not "alter", Doro. But when a man has lost his mother, he should be told about it. Harriet is perfectly right on that score. So. Our alternative is that we ride to Amberley, to the dray road, and talk to one of the foolhardy crew going west over the mountains and entrust a letter to a stranger of our choice – and hope that he, and the letter, may arrive at his destination in one piece.'

'There is talk of a proper route being sought,' said Dorothy. 'Through one or other of the passes.'

'Yes,' said Toby, 'but that does not help us at the moment, Doro, does it?'

'No, I was merely remarking, there *is* to be a road one day.'

Toby looked critically at the end of his cigar, fearing it had gone out, but there was still a little glow on it and he concentrated on sucking this back into life while Dorothy said:

'What I keep thinking about it is how, when any letter finds its way to Hokitika, it may also find its way to Joseph. For where is Joseph now, Toby? We do not know.'

'No,' said Toby. 'We do not know. And I saw the goldfields in Otago and they were like a rabbit warren going on and on, with everywhere the same features and the same huts and shelters, and to find a man there would have been almost impossible. But Harriet might send a photograph – if she has one? And this could be passed around.'

Harriet replied that she had no photograph of Joseph, that he had not wanted a wedding picture, that the only likeness of him she had ever seen had been put into the ground with Lilian. And she saw in her mind's eye the enormous distance that was already beginning to expand between Joseph and the news that was so necessary to him, so that it wasn't difficult to imagine weeks and months going by, with a letter waiting somewhere, but never arriving in Joseph's hand.

'There is no certainty . . .' she said.

Toby and Dorothy both looked up at her, expecting this sentence to continue somehow, but when it didn't continue, Dorothy said: 'Distance is so mighty here. Not so much in miles, but in the *obstacles* we must contend with. Isn't that true, Toby?'

'Yes, Doro, it is true,' replied Toby. 'If this were America, there would be a railroad through the passes by now. But there are too few of us here to build it. We are too isolated and alone.'

In the night, Edwin crept into Harriet's room. She woke and saw him standing there with his candle and he was shivering, so she lifted the coverlets and the boy got into bed beside her.

'Now . . .' she said.

Edwin was silent for a long time. Then he said: 'Will you find Pare?'

Edwin's candle rested on a small table and the flickering light cast enormous shadows on to the wall. Harriet began stroking Edwin's head, but she suddenly saw the giant shadow of her hand as a strange, unwanted creature alighting on him and she asked herself whether the fondness she felt for Edwin Orchard was born only out of her own childlessness. She didn't know the answer and thought that perhaps she never would know it because her childlessness would never have an end.

'Is Pare with her tribe?' she asked.

'No,' said Edwin. 'She's in a high-up place, on a ledge sort of thing. And underneath her there's a waterfall going into a river.'

'And where is this waterfall?'

'I don't know. She calls to me all the time, but I don't want to go there because I don't want to leave Mama and Papa and Mollie and Baby, so somebody has to find Pare and tell her to come back, and no one else knows about her except you.'

'But how am I to find her?' said Harriet. 'How am I to know where to look?'

'Look in the mountains,' said Edwin. 'You could ride there on Billy, couldn't you? You told me you wanted to go into the mountains.'

'Yes. I did.'

'Please, Harriet. Just find the waterfall and call to her. Say "Pare, are you there?" Remember? *"Pare, are you there?"*'

Harriet was silent for a long while. Then she told Edwin that both Joseph and Pare were people who had to be found and that she would try to decide very soon how best this could be accomplished.

III

The Orchards persuaded Harriet to stay with them until the weather brightened and then she rode back to the Okuku flats, with Lady running beside the horse. The sun on Harriet's head felt warm and the wind had died.

She was counting the tasks that awaited her when she crossed the southerly arm of the creek and turned into the valley where the Cob House stood. And it was then that she saw that what the drought had turned to dust, and the rain to mud, the rain and wind together had finally broken apart.

Harriet reined in Billy and he slowed to a walk and Lady began running ahead, barking at the strange things she saw: the

sheets of red tin roofing resting in the tussock grass; the front
door, blown almost to the creek's edge, sticking into the mud
like a meat cleaver; and all the yards of white calico lying across
what remained of the walls and half covering the wild assembly
of objects with which Harriet and Joseph had tried to begin
their married life.

Harriet dismounted and walked slowly towards the peculiar
scene.

In the still air, almost nothing moved, not even the calico,
which was here and there stretched taut, attached to nails or
snagged on thorns.

Staring at this, it came to Harriet Blackstone that what she
was looking at was a painting of a life, a torn canvas which, at
the moment of cutting, instead of holding its colours flat and
fast to its surface, had spilled out what it had once depicted into
three-dimensional space.

In escaping the confines of the painting that had held them
together, objects had forgotten what purpose they were
supposed to have. One of the iron beds stood on its end, as
though offering itself as a perch for eagles. Pillows, lying here
and there in the tussock, had the appearance of mushrooms.
Broken shards of plates and cups decorated the ground like
flowers.

Harriet remained a little way off. Dorothy Orchard had once
said to her that men and women were destined always to make
'a small world in the midst of a big one' and she remembered
this now and saw that it was exactly what she and Joseph had
tried to do. They'd made their 'little world' for Lilian, with all
the possessions she'd so laboriously and so insistently carted
here from England, but also for themselves as well, because *that
was all they had known how to make*. In a cave of ice, Harriet
supposed, man would try to light a fire, carve chairs and tables
from the walls. For what other means of living did he
understand? What better thing could he aspire to if he wanted
to survive?

Lady had returned to Harriet and was looking up at her now,
for even the dog knew that some habitual arrangement of things
had been turned on its head. Harriet stroked Lady's neck to
reassure her, but she asked herself what reassurance was there

to be had on the empty flats? How could anything be put back together now? Struggling to save the Cob House with her sacks of stones had killed Lilian. Joseph was far away and knew nothing of what had happened and wouldn't return – not even when winter came – unless he had filled his pockets with gold. She was alone.

A mocking voice in her head reminded Harriet that this was the very state after which she had yearned – to be alone in front of the mountains and under the sky. But now that she was face to face with her solitude she could only feel its enormity.

She nevertheless swept aside any thought of a cowardly return to Orchard House. She knew that if she went there, she would probably never leave, because her affection for Edwin Orchard was greater than her affection for her own husband. And she didn't want to grow old as she would have grown old in England – as the caretaker of other people's children. Why travel half the world to arrive at a place almost identical to the one you had left? Better to return to England, to her father, and care for him at least, than to become a cuckoo in the Orchards' nest.

It was mid-afternoon and Harriet judged that there were four or five hours of light remaining. Before the night stole up on her, she must busy herself with inspecting what remained and seeing what shelter she might be able to contrive. She told herself that at such a moment, it was best to move from simple task to simple task, going slowly and keeping watch, like a mariner who prepares his small boat for the coming storm. Yet the mile upon mile of emptiness around her made her more afraid than she had ever expected and she found it difficult to move from the spot where she stood. She looked down at her feet, shod in dusty black boots, with the laces beginning to fray, and was struck by how small they appeared.

Dead Work

I

For Joseph Blackstone, the moment of pegging out his miner's claim – a moment he had imagined for such a long time – brought him to a torment of indecision. With thirty shillings, he'd bought a patch of ground seventy-two feet square. Every speck of gold that he found on this plot would be his to keep. But where should he peg it? How was he supposed to guess where the colour was lying?

He walked a little way from where he'd pitched the tent, towards the Scots diggers, and stood and watched what they were doing. He knew that sometimes, claims were 'shepherded'. This meant that newcomers to a goldfield waited to peg until they'd seen what results were coming from this area or that. Beyond the Scots' camp, four or five other claims had been pegged and were already being worked with sluices. Windlasses had been erected to speed up the business of bringing the dirt out of the ground, and the squeaking of the windlass, thought Joseph, was like the first sound of protestation here, the first lament for the alteration that was coming to Kokatahi.

It was early in the morning and misty. Joseph had instructed Will to boil a billy-can to make coffee and to cut up some bacon and he thought, as he walked away from the tent, how satisfying it might become to impose upon Will Sefton the tasks of a housewife. In the coming chaos, Will would keep the tent ship-shape and purchase supplies and cook trout from the river on fires that he'd made with his small hands. He would do the washing.

Joseph nodded to the Scotsmen, as he approached their claim. They were working as a team, one setting out the pegs, the other measuring and remeasuring the ground. Joseph saw that their pegs went right to the river's edge and he knew that diggers always had hopes of creeks and gullies and these would be the first claims to be taken up and worked here. Gold-mining needed water, too, for the sluice. Hill claimers had to buy water rights or pay for the construction of water flumes, but the gully men had all the water they could ever need – and more, when a fresh came and filled the shafts they'd dug and swept away their tents and their tools.

'What's the word?' Joseph asked the Scotsmen. 'How much colour has been found here?'

One of the men kept on with his task of hammering pegs and barely looked up at Joseph, as he stood there in the mist, but the other man straightened up and replied: 'All we heard tell: nugget this big ta'en out of a duck's throat.'

'If it was a duck, then it was from river ground, I suppose?'

'You can suppose it if you will. Ducks can fly, too.'

Joseph smiled. He indicated the workings further up the river, where the windlasses were turning. 'What have they taken out so far? Did they tell you?'

'Say it's only tucker ground. A few pennyworth. But when does a miner ever admit to anything else?'

Now, the second Scotsman removed his hat and wiped his forehead with his sleeve. 'Diggers are the biggest blood-curdling liars on God's earth, mister. Did naebody tell you that?'

'I don't need to be told ...' began Joseph.

'They are, *by their natures*, of a lying disposition. Every last one of them. We'll lie to you, too, when we find our share, eh, Hamish?'

'Aye. We'll lie to you and to everyone. And we don't want to be shepherded. You keep your distance. And tell your boy not to play his blasted penny whistle in the middle of the night.'

Joseph stood his ground. 'And your mouth-organ? You'll keep that quiet, too?'

'We'll keep it quiet at two in the morning, mister. But we'll play our songs. Songs of home. Englishmen never cared for our songs, never did care for them at all, so you move somewhere else, if they make you afraid.'

'They don't make me afraid.'

'Kaniere's full of English. Why don't you go back there?'

'Because', said Joseph, 'we heard about the duck. But what kind of duck was it? Did nobody tell you that, in New Zealand, there are very many birds who have *forgotten* how to fly?'

Joseph turned and walked away, pleased with his parrying of the Scotsmen's hostility, but, without looking back at them, he could tell that the men paid him no heed and resumed their work without glancing further at him. He understood that, wherever he decided to peg out his claim, it would have to be in a place where they couldn't see him, in a place where he could forget them as absolutely as they wanted to forget him.

The mist lay just above the river and wreathed itself in among the trees on the further bank and sometimes drifted to where Joseph sat, at the mouth of the tent, drinking coffee and gnawing biscuits and bacon. There was almost no wind, so Joseph could hear the dripping of the trees and began to feel the melancholy of this sound.

He didn't look at Will. He was glad that, from time to time, the mist thickened as it lifted off the water and almost masked Will from his sight. Because the memory of the night still seemed very heavy in him, as though some new weight were tugging him down. Images transfixed him as the trees dripped into the water: Will's mouth on his; the smoothness of Will's body; the wanton way he'd knelt above Joseph and held his own sex, to show off how it bucked and paraded in his hand. Joseph hadn't ever thought to find such a thing arousing, but now, even the mere memory of it made the blood come and the bones of his thighs ache – these altered, heavy bones of his. And he knew there was shame in this, shame that he didn't wish to think about.

So he kept his face turned away from Will, who sipped his coffee noisily and swore at the cold. And he prayed again to choose a good claim, to find gold so that he could bribe Will to stay with him. For he understood that Will Sefton could sell his 'services' to almost any lonely man between here and the mouth of the Grey River. In the night, Will had boasted that in Otago 'two miners had such a rivalry for me that they fought in the mud like dogs, like curs, like fighting cocks, Mister Blackstone, and one of them had his brains beat to pulp'.

'Were you proud of that?' Joseph had asked, coldly.

'Yes, I were proud of it,' Will had replied, taking up his penny whistle and caressing it softly with his lips, coaxing from it just the merest whispering sound, very close to Joseph's ear. 'Sign of my talents, it were. Sign I were the best at my trade. After that, I could name my price.'

In the dark, but with sufficient moonlight to make every shape and movement clear to him, Joseph had looked at Will's face and remembered his torn jerkin and his down-at-heel boots. 'And where did it go, then, the money you made in Otago?'

'Where did it go? Where does it always go, Mister Blackstone? On this thing and that thing and then it's gone.'

Joseph finished his coffee and stood up. He began to walk along by the river, in the direction from which they'd come the evening before, with his head lowered and staring all the while at the ground by the water's edge. To be far enough away from the Scots' claim, he had two choices: to press on southwards, inland beyond the further workings, or choose a spot here. He knelt and rinsed his hands in the water and saw it running clear and fresh now, but imagined how, in a short while, the detritus from upstream would come flooding down and muddy everything to a brown soup. He didn't want to see other men's leavings in his bit of the river. He wanted to be above them, for them to suffer *his* mullock, his tailings. And so this decided him: he would instruct Will to help him pack up the tent and supplies and load the barrow and they would trek further inland, nearer to rising ground, and not think of pegging out his claim until they could no longer hear the noise of the windlasses.

The trudge was uphill and in and out of the newly roped ground and, when the mist lifted and the sun came out and the bush began to shimmer near, the walking seemed vain and arbitrary.

Joseph stopped and looked around. He was waiting to see some sign, some instruction in the lie of the terrain, to tell him where to stake his claim, but nothing presented itself. He set the barrow down and listened. The trees still dripped into the river and some bird called from the shingle banks. In the distance, he could hear the sound of a waterfall. He took a shovel out of the barrow and dug it into the soft earth between two grey stones. He turned the shovel and lifted up his first heap of West Coast soil and looked at it.

Will set down the swag and came and peered at the lifted earth and then knelt and began to sift it with his hands. It was pale in colour but mixed with a dryish, dark grit.

'Easy to work,' Will commented. 'We could get down to the blue clay quite fast, through this, 'less we're flooded out. And there's pine up above for slabs.'

Now, again, the pain of indecision began to take hold of Joseph.

Had he been wrong to walk this far upstream? Did the men with the windlasses *know* the ground there was auriferous? Had he put himself beyond this vital knowledge for no sensible reason except his old reason of wanting to be alone, ahead of the Rush?

He let the shovelful of earth fall away. He turned in a circle and noticed that, behind him and to the left, there was a grassy plateau, level and dry and free of manuka, where the tent could sit.

'Pitch the tent there?' he asked Will.

'For you to say, Mister Blackstone.'

'Will,' said Joseph, 'I'm tired of all this *Mister Blackstone*! Call me Joseph, won't you?'

But Will shook his head. 'Never do that. Clean against my credo, Mister Blackstone.'

'Your *credo*?'

'Isn't that the word? Learnt that from an educated miner on the Arrow. Meaning my *policy*. Never say a man's precious name, see? Never let him be my darling. You understand, don't you? I'm sure you understand.'

Joseph stared at the boy. He saw that in the sunlight, his mouth looked very red, exactly as Rebecca's mouth had been red – red and moist, with the lips just slightly parted as though she were always and always about to speak or laugh. He looked away and down again at the earth.

'Yes,' he said. 'I understand.' And he felt, in that instant, that he couldn't walk any further, so he made a decision: he would peg his claim here. He took out from his pocket his Miner's Right, with its elegant rendition of his name, and he pressed it against his lips.

'Kissing it for luck, are you?' asked Will, laughing. 'Think that'll help you, Mister Blackstone?'

Joseph measured the ground he had chosen not once but several times. Where boulders lay on the periphery, he ran his rope round the back of these, so gaining a few inches here and there, for boulders could be prised out of the earth and the colour had been known to sit right underneath them, as though it had glued them to the ground.

When the task of pegging and roping was complete, Joseph stood and looked at his claim. Seventy-two feet square. It ran down to the north bank of the river, to a small shingle spur. If the southerly bank were staked by another miner, then Joseph would have rights over the water only to the middle of the current. But for now, this portion of the river was his, and a comfortable flat rock nearby would make 'a nice chair', so Will had announced, 'for fishing'.

Marking out the ground had reminded Joseph of his first days on the flats, when he'd chosen the site for the Cob House and felt the grandeur of the empty valleys and the watchful mountains, except that, now, he had backed himself into a narrow corridor of land between the dense bush and the sea, and the feeling of vastness here was of a different order. Only the prime, unanswerable question was the same: was the claim in the right place? On the Okuku flats, he'd put his house in the pathway of the winds; here, would he make some similar mistake?

He decided he would work the claim outwards from the river, leaving himself a firm strip of land, running north-south along the side of the claim, for barrowing away as much of the mullock as he could. He didn't want to work surrounded by his own leavings; he wanted the river to carry these away – down to the Scots' camp and beyond, to Kaniere. The thought of this gave him pleasure. He had put himself at the head of the Kokatahi workings.

A good part of the day remained, so Joseph set his cradle at the water's edge and then began to shovel in dirt and wash it through. Now, he thought, I'm a true gold-miner, a digger, a prospector, a new chum.

And it was as though everything that he'd done, everything he'd achieved in New Zealand so far had been a preparation for this moment. *Now*, he would make his fortune. *Now*, he would dig himself a new future. The sun shone on his neck and on his back, bent over the cradle, and he was happy.

In the night, Joseph heard a squeaking and scuffling outside the tent and knew that the bush rats had arrived. 'Dig a hole and put your stores in it,' a passenger on the *Wallabi* had said, 'and the bush rats will smell it from nine miles.'

But Joseph was too tired to get up, to look for his gun. Let them eat the bacon tonight. Tomorrow, he would begin sinking shafts in the ground, to get down to the blue-clay bottom. Tomorrow, he would contrive some ingenious way of out-witting the rats.

He closed his eyes and began to drift back to sleep. He could sense that Will was awake beside him, but he didn't turn to look at him.

In the mist that came again with the morning, they started cutting pine from the bush, to saw it into planks, or 'slabs' as the miners called them, to shore up the shafts. Joseph told Will he would contrive a windlass, too. He had no length of chain, but he thought rope would serve.

He knew that all this preparation was known as 'dead work'; it brought you nothing while it lasted, but you couldn't operate a claim efficiently without it and Joseph wanted his plot to be a model of its kind, tidily and methodically worked, so that every inch of ground could be excavated and sifted. And he realised

now – faced with the relative smallness of his seventy-two-foot
holding – that his first attempts at trying to find gold in
Harriet's Creek had been chaotic and wasteful.

As they hacked at the trees, Will began chattering about his
time as the undertaker's apprentice. He'd often helped, he told
Joseph, with 'dressing up the dead in their finery' and laughed
his mocking laugh when he recounted how 'sometimes, we
would find an instruction to put an old hag into her wedding
dress and it would be half rotted away or else we'd split it
trying to make it stretch across her, where her fat tits hung. But
a coffin conceals a multitude of sins, Mister Blackstone, for you
cannot see the *back* of anything, so there can be pins or tape
holding everything in together, but on the front side, where the
living come to have their last look, all appears neat and proper.'

'What about the men?' asked Joseph. 'What did they like to
be dressed in?'

'Black. Like as they were going to be guests at their own
funerals! But then sometimes, if you hadn't put the band round,
the mouth wadding would start to come out and you'd get
staining on the shirt or necktie.'

'The band?'

'It's like a buckram you tie round the jaw and up to the
crown of the head and pull it tight with hooks and eyes, to stop
the mouth from gaping. But my employer, Mr da Costa, he
used to pride himself on tipping the head back at just the right
angle, so you didn't have to display it with the band. For the
relations, they don't like to see any contrivance. They know it
is contrived, or some do, but they just don't wish to see it.'

Joseph was silent for a moment, then he said: 'With some of
the short slabs, Will, why don't we make a coffin for our food?
In the night, I heard –'

'Rats,' said Will. 'You'll never outwit them. In Otago, I saw
men sleeping with sacks over their faces to try to keep the bush
rats away and that was one of the stupidest notions I ever came
across. For what had the sacks contained but oats or flour or
rice and so the rats came to lick what was left of this, and one
man had his nose bitten clean away. Yet he went on digging for
gold without his nose, and he found some, and he thought this

would buy him a bride, but no bride wants a man with only half a face, am I right?'

'I expect so. But with nails and planks we could build some kind of box for the stores and sink it underground ...'

'We can try, Mister Blackstone. But they'll still come, you wait. Not only the food that stinks, is it? It's us, too. And they smell that smell of the human from a long way off.'

It was soon after this that Joseph looked down towards the river, looked back at his claim and at the little tent which stood on the grassy plateau in the morning sunlight, and saw a figure walking along towards it.

The figure had come out of the bush. He wore a fur hat and carried on his shoulders a bamboo pole and at each end of the pole was strung a wicker basket and from the way the man walked, Joseph could tell that the baskets were heavy.

Will rested his axe and stared at the stranger. 'That's a Johnny, I warrant,' he said.

'A Johnny?'

'John Chinaman. A Celestial. A Chinky. Only the Johnnies carry baskets like that. Otago was crawling with them in the end. They used to come and fossick where the real diggers had already been. Didn't mind picking over what other men had left behind.'

Joseph and Will watched the man. When he reached their claim, he stopped and set down his baskets.

'Aye-aye,' said Will. 'Now, he'll try stealing something and popping it in his panniers. You see if he doesn't.'

Joseph remembered the Chinese men on the *Wallabi* cooking rice on their tiny lamp and staying apart from the crowd, as though in a different world, and he now saw that this man – even at this distance – had something of the same containment about him, in the way that he moved so quietly and in the way that he had struggled to hold himself tall and upright under the weight of the baskets. He watched the man walk a little nearer to the tent and heard him call out something which he couldn't catch. Then the Chinaman stood perfectly still, waiting, with the sun of mid-day shining on him and on the river as it flowed past him, clear and bright. And after a while, when no one came out of the tent, he shouldered his pole and the heavy baskets and walked away.

'He took nothing,' Joseph remarked to Will.

'No,' said Will. 'Not this one. But they do. And you cannot know them. That is what used to vex me on the Arrow. You can never read their thoughts.'

II

His name was Chen Pao Yi.

He'd been in Otago for a year and then he'd come here, not to dig for gold, but to start a little market garden and sell what he grew to the West Coast diggers. The diggers never called him by his real name; they called him 'Jen' (deliberately mishearing the name Chen) or 'Jenny' or sometimes 'Scurvy Jenny' because people said the vegetables he grew held that sickness at bay, but Chen Pao Yi suffered this without moving a muscle of his face and bowed to them when they handed over their money or a few grains of gold in exchange for his produce.

He was forty years old and there was grey in his hair, which he wore plaited into the traditional pigtail under his hat of rabbit fur, and he dreamed of his home, which was a small house on the shores of a lake called Heron Lake in Panyu County in south-east China, and he dreamed of his wife whose name was Paak Mei and of his son whose name was Paak Shui.

Paak Shui meant 'white water' and this boy had been named in honour of Pao Yi's parents, Chen Lin and Chen Fen Ming, who had died trying to rescue their neighbours in a spring flood on Heron Lake, when their boat had gone over a weir, throwing them on to a water-wheel and all the bits and pieces of their bodies had glided around Heron Lake for all the days of the flood and never come to shore until the eighth day and then Pao Yi had to go and gather them up – a leg, a hand, a severed foot, their precious heads bruised and dented – and lay them out on the reeds and try to piece them back together.

But it had been impossible to find every bit of them for there were fingers that had been eaten by fish and hair snagged on sow thistles and eyes lost among the amber-coloured shingle and so what Pao Yi buried was part of his parents and not all, and it seemed to him that all the while he remained in China, they called to him and begged him to find the missing bits of themselves and lay these bits in the burial site so that they could be whole again, with ears to hear the wind in the fir trees and noses to smell the plum blossom in winter and feet to carry them to Pao Yi's side and see his child, Paak Shui, take his first steps.

They had been poor. He and his father were fishermen on the lake.

And when Pao Yi saw other men leaving for the Gold Rush in New Zealand, he thought he would try to overcome poverty, because poverty and hunger tired him almost as much as hearing the calling of his parents' voices tired him and he saw that if he remained in his house on Heron Lake he would soon shoulder a burden of tiredness so great that he would be able to do nothing except lie down on his straw mat with his opium pipe and fall into an eternal sleep.

And then he discovered that, as he travelled south, the voices of Chen Lin and Chen Fen Ming began to grow fainter, as though the Pacific Ocean were too immense for even their powerful spirits to cross and he wondered whether they called to his son, Paak Shui, instead or even to his wife, Paak Mei, who had always been a dutiful daughter-in-law and cared for Chen Fen Ming when she'd been ill with a black fever and paddled her own little boat in the lake, collecting water-chestnuts to put in Chen Lin's favourite dishes.

But Pao Yi couldn't know, for no word could come from Paak Mei because she couldn't write, nor barely form the characters of her own name, 'White Plum Blossom', and it felt to Pao Yi after he'd been in New Zealand for a while, as if the voice of Paak Mei was becoming fainter, too, as though his wife had caught a chill and had trouble speaking above a whisper. Only in his dreams did he hear her clearly, hear her high laughter and remember the sound of her walk, which was a little ghostly shuffling on the heels and knuckles of her bound feet in cloth shoes.

'To walk is pain,' she sometimes observed, but in a neutral voice without complaint, as though she were observing the rain or the sunshine or the grey hairs in Pao Yi's pigtail, and it had been one of Pao Yi's self-imposed duties to unwind the bindings of Paak Mei's feet and hold them in his hands and try to soothe their agony with lavender oil. And when he knew he was going to leave for New Zealand to put an end to poverty in his family, he attempted to show Paak Shui how to care for these feet, but Paak Shui said he didn't want to do this, he liked his mother's small feet when they were bound up and in her shoes, but to see them unwrapped, with the bones of the toes broken and turned over towards the soles, like a bird's claw, made him feel queasy.

Pao Yi reminded Paak Shui that filial piety was his first duty in life because that life had been given to him by his parents and without them, he would have remained a mote of dust on a distant, treeless hill. He said: 'This pain likes to go where it will and do as it pleases. But it is afraid of lavender. The lavender oil is your weapon, but weapons are of no use sitting on a shelf or hanging on the wall. You must take the weapon in your hands to show duty to your mother and chase the pain away.'

Paak Shui protested that the pain was too headstrong for him. He was eight years old. He said that he could see and feel, from the queasy feeling he got when he looked at Paak Mei's feet, that the pain was wilful and cruel like the tail of a dragon; but Pao Yi put the pot of lavender oil into his hands and told him that wilfulness and cruelty must not be allowed to enter the house on Heron Lake. He said: 'In the name of your lost grandparents, Chen Lin and Chen Fen Ming, who sacrificed themselves for others, you must chase these things away.'

But now, Chen Pao Yi often wondered, as he dug and watered his vegetable garden, whether his son had been able to do what had been asked of him. He was a child. His favourite pastimes were making lures for fish out of broken shells and flying his kite in the wide sky above Long Hill in Panyu County. He loved things which moved in ripples and loops, not things which looked already dead, as his mother's feet looked dead to him. And Pao Yi was gradually coming to believe that the pain might be howling round Paak Mei's bed like a tiger and that it might be for this reason that her voice was becoming almost too weak to hear.

But he couldn't go back to China. Not yet. Not until he was a rich man.

To go back without the riches that he'd promised would be to lose face in his village and even with Paak Mei and her parents. He'd made a little money in Otago from his market garden there, but just as his enterprise had begun to prosper, so the Gold Rush had ended and the miners had drifted away and Pao Yi had been left alone in the ruined landscape with its abandoned shafts and box flumes and the old horse-whims which still turned on their own in the wind.

So, when the new Rush began on the West Coast, he had made his way here and thought to rent a plot of ground directly behind Hokitika, within sight of the diggings. But the Commissioner had informed him that all of this land was deemed auriferous and none of it could be given over to the growing of food. 'Go further inland,' the Commissioner told Pao Yi. 'Go towards Lake Kaniere and find a plot there and we will send the warden to tell you whether you can work it or not. Canterbury County is in favour of market gardening, but not at the expense of the gold. Now, shoo, Johnny, for we are very busy, and do not waste my time with any more talk of coastal land.'

So Pao Yi walked up the Hokitika River towards the bush-line.

He passed the Kaniere diggings and the tiny settlement at Kokatahi and then he walked on until he found a flat curve of land in the arm of the river and sheltered on its northern side by tall rocks. In the rocks was a small cave and Pao Yi crawled into the cave and buried his Otago money under a stone, then he lay still and quiet in the silence of the cave and felt that the cave was a beautiful place.

The rent for the land was fair. He counted it out and was given a piece of paper with a snarled signature on it, which he couldn't decipher, and he went down to the Hokitika mining stores where he bought himself new boots and his rabbit-fur hat. Then he returned to the cave and began to construct a tiny dwelling out of sacking and stones, leaning against the rock face and having the cave as its inner secret sanctum. He roofed it with ti-ti palm and laid his mat on the earth floor and dreamed of Chen Lin and Chen Fen Ming gliding over Heron Lake towards the weir. Endlessly, they glided towards it but, in this dream, they never reached it and when Pao Yi woke up from this dream he began straightaway turning the earth for his new garden and he saw that the soil was black and rich.

By the time Joseph and Will Sefton caught sight of Pao Yi with his baskets on his bamboo pole, he had been working on his garden above Kokatahi for a year. Once a week, he walked to the Hokitika diggings with his panniers full of cabbages, onions, leeks, turnips, radishes and potatoes. In the high summer, he'd grown lettuces, kūmara, beans and peppers. He was trying to nurture a plum tree. He caught fish in the river with lures made by his son.

In the long nights of March, he sat by his fire and smoked his opium pipe and said English words aloud: *river, potato, duck, woman, gold.*

III

Sinking shafts and slabbing them was arduous work.

'The blue clay's down there, must be,' remarked Will, after two days of digging, 'but you never know how far down.' And later on, he added: 'I've seen a digger cry like a woman when he thought he'd got to the blue and then hit stone. Cry for all that lost dead work.'

Soon, the first shaft on Joseph's claim went so deep that it was almost impossible to climb in or out of it. Joseph had to stop digging and fashion a ladder out of pine branches and rope. And still the excavation was bottoming on gravel and not on clay, and water was beginning to seep into it, making necessary a parallel drainage bore, sunk deeper than the shaft.

Standing on his makeshift ladder, Joseph examined the strata of earth, going down from the sandy turf, through a blackish silt, into a dull brown marl, with flecks of grey and white visible in it, but not a shard of the true colour. His anxiety that he had put himself beyond the gold line would be present at every moment, he knew, until or unless he had his first sighting of the colour. He kept reminding himself that on the Arrow and on the Clutha, gold had been found high up in the gorges. Gully workings had become bush workings. Miners had died falling from rocks and waterfalls, but many had dug their fortunes out of the mountains.

In the nights, when Joseph lay awake in the tent and wondered if his work here would all be in vain, Will Sefton would sometimes turn away from him, indifferent and aloof, and fall asleep in moments. Yet at other times the boy would read Joseph's thoughts and take up his penny whistle and play one of his melancholy tunes and then say: 'Forget the earth, Mister Blackstone. Go to a different place.'

The Road to the Taramakau

I

Harriet rode to Christchurch and hired a dray.

The big cart, with its melancholy drayman chewing tobacco and spitting into the tussock, made two journeys to and from the ruins of the Cob House. First, it took the pigs and the chickens to the little market in Rangiora, with the milk cow attached to the dray and trotting behind it, her udders humiliatingly swinging side-to-side and her eyes a raging, startled white. Then the dray returned and all the furniture which had remained intact and the china and glass which wasn't broken and all the kitchen utensils were loaded on to it, including the mangle and the butter churn. On top of these things were placed Joseph's clothes in his trunk and his fishing rods and his fly box and his poetry books and the tools he'd left behind and Lilian's bonnets tied up in a sack and her boots in a wicker basket.

Only the range remained. The solitary drayman swore blue at the idea of lifting it. 'Besides,' he pointed out to Harriet, spitting more tobacco into the dusty grass, 'the flue of it goes up into the stone stack, Miss. To get that out again would take more time than I've got to give you.'

Harriet saw that there was no point in arguing. So the range and the stone chimney stood alone on the flats and it made Harriet smile to think that a stranger could arrive here and light the range and then stand under the open sky and bake a cake.

The loaded dray would then make its slow journey back to Christchurch, to a place called Bloomington's Warehouse, not far from where Mrs Dinsdale lived. The clerk at Bloomington's, Mr O'Malley, had already explained to Harriet that the rates charged for storage were high at the moment. 'For what you have in New Zealand,' he'd said, 'is an epidemic of abandonment. Say the word "gold" and men will desert their dearest things.'

When the dray was almost ready to leave, Harriet pulled down what remained of the calico rooms and she and the drayman stretched the torn calico over the piled-up cart like a tarpaulin, and the dray set off, leaving Harriet alone, with the wind picking up again and blowing her short hair into her eyes and buffeting her skirts among the dry grasses.

She stood and watched the dray swaying slowly along until it was out of sight and then she turned away and went down to the donkey, still racked with a cough, waiting in the paddock. Harriet had got money for the cow, the pigs and the hens at Rangiora, but she knew no one who would buy the donkey, unless to slaughter it for its sinewy meat. So she had made up her mind what to do with it: she would bring it to paradise.

With a hammer, she smashed down the tin fence that surrounded her vegetable garden and kicked the pieces away, and she led the donkey here, where it could smell all the varied and succulent green. She left it untethered so that it could drink at the creek and graze all day on carrot tops and the stalks of beans and pale winter cabbage and the leaves of beets. She wondered whether, in all the empty landscape, it would know something of loneliness, and begin braying at the sky, but she thought that she was doing the best she could for it and she told herself that seldom is any 'best' so good that it could not be further perfected. But she liked to think that, after all her work, the vegetables she'd nurtured on her plot wouldn't rot in the ground. She stroked the donkey's neck and felt it shiver and saw its ears twitch forward and then she left it to eat its way to death in its own time. She didn't look back.

Harriet was abandoning the Cob House, not only because so little of it remained, but because she had found the tea box from China buried behind the calico wall.

At first, Harriet had thought the box was empty. Then she

had run her finger round the bottom of it, into its hard, dark corners, remembering what she herself had consigned to it. And what she found there was a shard of gold.

When Harriet saw this shard, the pity she'd been nurturing for Joseph in the wake of Lilian's death was replaced with a fury so cold it was like a weapon made of ice. She wanted to tear this weapon out of her and lodge it in her husband's neck. She felt that Joseph Blackstone had stolen her life.

She'd kept apart some food and a few possessions of her own and these she put into sacks and tied to Billy's saddle. Billy stood patiently waiting, flicking his tail at imaginary summer flies. Lady crouched in the grass, her yellow-brown eyes large and bright, her ears alert to the next command.

Harriet packed the gun Joseph had given her at D'Erlanger's Hotel and a compass that had belonged to her father and then she put on her cloak and a woollen hat knitted by Dorothy Orchard and climbed on to the horse. In the hat, she knew she looked older than she was, like someone who had survived a long time in New Zealand and understood how to read the signals in the wind.

Lady stood up and began barking. Back into the earth had gone the tea box, with its lid nailed down, just as she had found it. Inside it, a note to Joseph read:

> *The weather took the Cob House and we couldn't save it.*
> *I am coming to find you, for I know your secret. Lilian died on the 12th of March and is buried at Rangiora. The animals are sold. Your furniture is at Bloomington's, Christchurch. Ask for the clerk, Mr O'Malley. From your wife, Harriet*

Then she began to ride towards the mountains, skirting them to the south and turning north again towards Amberley. She let Billy canter or walk, as he had a mind to do, never urging him, and Lady ran along by the side of them, always keeping pace.

Five or six miles south of Amberley, Harriet picked up the dray road that went from Christchurch as far as the Waitohi Gorge, a dirt track, sluiced by the rains and sculpted with the ruts of heavy wheels and the imprints of men's boots. And it was not long before she was joined by a straggle of gold-seekers, some riding in drays, others pulling handcarts, some carrying almost nothing beyond a swag and a pick.

All were men. They stared at Harriet on her smart chestnut horse. She saw in their eyes disbelief mixed with something else, which might have been fear for her and might have been disdain, and she couldn't tell which.

'Stopping at Amberley, miss, aren't you?' one of them ventured. 'Not going over the Hurunui, are you?'

Harriet didn't want to have to engage in any kind of conversation. She wanted to be alone with her purpose, or at least alone with her thoughts, from which she was all the while trying to disentangle her purpose.

She replied that she was 'going some of the way' and hoped they would leave the subject at that. But a few of the diggers, with their faces set on what lay before them, liked to keep up a prattle about the terrors of the route to the Taramakau River.

'Men try to warn you off from going there,' they said. 'They tell you tales of boulders falling on you and drownings in the river and how the gorge narrows and narrows until you're in darkness. And what can you reply except that men *have* crossed the Hurunui Saddle. Hundreds have done it. All we doubt is that a woman could do it. That we do doubt.'

'Do you?' said Harriet.

'You won't do it, miss. Not a digger's chance! Yet it's no more than fifty miles. *Fifty miles.* And why should strangers cross from Australia and Celestials sail from China and get to what is rightfully ours in Canterbury County and we be denied it by a mountain put in our way?'

'Why indeed?' replied Harriet.

'The government should build a road. That'd be the answer. A proper dray road all the way to the gold. Then you could be comfortable in the cart and admire the scenery along the way! You'd prefer that, as a woman, wouldn't you? Wouldn't you?'

'Perhaps,' said Harriet.

'No "perhaps" about it. You'd prefer that. Keep your skirts dry, eh? But governments are too slow, see? Send surveyors, that's all. Send men to stare at the confounded passes. But still no confounded sign of a road from east to west beyond Waitohi.'

'No,' said Harriet.

'So we have to risk our worthless lives, like transports, to get there! Or die in one of those tubs they run out of Nelson. Either way, we could lose. There's a word for that, isn't there? A word to say that never can you win?'

'I expect so,' said Harriet. 'But, like you, I can't think what it is.'

These conversations grew tedious and Harriet wished she was once more alone until, after the stop at Amberley was passed, the road turned north-west and began to climb steeply and the air to grow colder and the high bush to close round them and the sun to glimmer and be gone. Then, she felt that to be part of this slow, shabby caravan was preferable to her earlier isolation. She could tell that Billy was nervous, trying not to slip or stumble on the steep path, and she could feel the dusk coming on and the way seemed visited by ghostly shadows.

She dismounted and pulled out a length of rope and tied this to Lady's collar and held it tight with the reins, for she saw that the dog could stray into the bush, chasing birds or small animals, and she felt on this road that all that was left to her in the world were Billy and Lady and that, whatever happened, she mustn't lose them.

But she got on the horse again quickly and rode on. She didn't want to be left too far behind the other travellers. Ahead of her, in the misty light, she could see the Puketeraki range of mountains, with their jagged tops, and behind these, the high peaks of the true Southern Alps, on which she'd gazed for so long.

II

On the plains of the Waitohi River, before the long ascent to the Hurunui, an enterprising man named Charlie Wilde had built two huts out of pine slab and tussock thatch. He charged sixpence a night for a mattress and a bowl of soup or a pigeon stew and was known among the diggers for the brightness of his fires, which he set in a pit of stones and which seemed to burn 'with a brilliant bloody flame'.

It was here, as the dusk turned to darkness, that the convoy stopped. There was a bit of grazing for the horses and the travellers sat by Charlie's fire, eating off tin plates and contemplating what waited for them beyond the end of the dray road. An area of manuka and cabbage trees behind the huts served as a latrine and Charlie Wilde noticed that many of the men about to go over the Hurunui kept going back and forwards from this bit of scrub.

Charlie had been to the edge of the Saddle and looked down the gorge and seen how the walls of the mountains seemed almost to close over the ribbon of valley, as though to crush anything that dared breathe there, and he had turned round and come back. He had lived in New Zealand for thirty-nine years, but nothing had ever terrified him as the sight of this abyss terrified him and he knew that no amount of gold would make him go down there. The men whose cramping guts forced them to trudge out to squat among the manuka hadn't yet seen what he'd seen, but they *knew* that it was waiting for them; they'd imagined the dizzying descent of the path and then the darkness and cold of the gorge and the freezing water and the high boulders and the echoes all around and the feeling of going in a circle and being lost. They were each one waiting to see what he would do and how he would hold himself together when he came to this place.

Only Harriet had no accurate picture of it. The Orchards had told her that trying to cross the Hurunui was 'sheer and absolute madness', yet what she saw in her mind was a continuation of the path very like the one she had travelled that day. Certainly, she thought, there would be some steep turns and she hoped Billy wouldn't stumble or fall or an avalanche of stones sweep her away, but she had never imagined 'the stairway of hell' as it truly was.

And so she was able to sit with the men and eat her plate of pigeon stew and warm herself by the fire and feel only the particularity of this night, which was the first night of her journey, and something like happiness began to creep over her. She found she didn't any longer mind the conversation of the gold-seekers, which turned now around the visions they had of themselves in a rich life 'once the colour's found'. It amused her that each and every one of them began by making himself into a philanthropist and swore he would never be 'tight-fisted and niggardly and mean as stone' but would share out his future wealth with brothers and sisters, cousins and nephews ...

'Do you not feel,' she ventured, 'that always, in advance of good fortune, men imagine how it will be so nicely shared around, but then, when that fortune comes, somehow it seems to them as though there is *not enough of it* to share?'

There was a simmering of laughter at this. 'That would depend,' said one of the diggers, 'on what you call a fortune. For the true fortune has to last. It has to have staying power against whittling away. So with a middling fortune, you might say to yourself that you were the one who got it and risked your confounded neck, and so you were the one who must rightly keep it.'

'I'd say a little poverty is a fine thing,' said another man. 'But only first time round! I can live on bush rats. But if I should get free of it for a while and get a taste for sweet lamb's meat and clean linen, and then all that is taken away, what will I feel?'

'Sick as a puff-adder!' said Charlie Wilde, and there was a chime of laughter around the fire.

Harriet slept in a corner of one of the huts, with Lady at her feet, and the men lay near her and snored and fretted through the night.

She woke when it got light and was cold, and made her way to the grove of manuka, which stank of death. And as she squatted down, she told herself to harden her heart, her mind, her sensibility and, from now on, to try to suffer everything that came her way or vanquish it and not fall under any spell of weakness. In the foul grove, it came to her that she was yearning – yearning beyond any telling – for something, but she couldn't identify what it was.

Charlie Wilde made a hot porridge on the remnants of the

fire and Harriet and the diggers filled their bellies with this and then set off on the last stretch of the road that led to the Hurunui Gorge. Here, the plains ended; here, the drays would turn back.

'You can count the minutes now,' Harriet heard one of the men say. 'Then hell closes in.'

III

Pare lay in darkness and listened to the waterfall.

It seemed to her, from where she was, in a narrow cavity of rock, that the voices of the world, of a hundred languages, from the throats of thousands upon thousands of souls, babbled in the falling water; if only she could lie perfectly still, breathing very faintly, then some words that she recognised might be detected and these words might comfort her and enable her to go on with her journey.

But Pare couldn't master quietness.

She was lying on a grey stone, covered with her blanket and clutching her bundle to her. She had rubbed poroporo balm into her feet and bound them with leaves, but the pain from these bruised and bleeding feet was so startling that her whole body was perpetually disturbed by it. She muttered to the pain, without meaning to, all the while, in fact, striving to be silent and failing and knowing she was failing, and the night wound on and the words in the waterfall kept tumbling and falling and vanishing away.

From time to time, she slept. She heard a cormorant shrieking in her dreams. She longed for the dawn to break, for with the coming of day she would resume her watch for travellers entering the gorge. Pare knew that the gorge, once glimpsed at the edge of the Hurunui Saddle – once truly seen by the measuring human eye – appeared as an Underworld, where the saddest spirits, left behind or shut out from some less melancholy place, snagged and rent their gossamer bodies on matador thorns and draped a veil across the sun.

But the West Coast gold had drawn men into these shadows

and now they would continue to venture here, to make their slow, terrified way, as she had done, back and forth across the river. Choosing where to cross and recross the water, when boulders or the overhanging cliff face blocked the path, required a knowledge of the river. But nobody knew this river. It was the unexplored heart of the South Island. And so, very often, they chose the wrong place and their feet were lacerated, as hers had been, or the icy water knocked them down and swept them away.

Pare knew that it was here that Death began to travel with the gold-seekers, as it travelled with her, and kept pace with them and refused to fall back. And they saw it everywhere: in every slippery stone, in every falling tree branch, and they felt it everywhere: in the air that was heavy and difficult to breathe and in their confused hearts. Yet they went on. They knew that the gorge had to have an end, that they were on the road to the level plains of the Taramakau River, that, if they could only survive, they would arrive at the swamps and the beaches and the sea.

Pare's hope was in these people. She'd seen one or two of them as she'd skirted the mountain lakes and come over the Saddle, before she'd slipped during one of the tormenting river crossings, and she prayed that others would pass this way and that she could barter her paua shell for a pair of woven sandals and fresh bandages, or food to sustain her while the cuts healed and the pain diminished. So she lay on her high ledge, from which she could see far up the gorge, almost to where the steep descent began, and waited.

She had waited for three days. Once, she climbed to where a silver fern was growing and dug it out with her shark-toothed knife and mashed its root and ate a few mouthfuls. She wanted to drink from the waterfall, but she didn't dare to go too near to it. She crawled back down to the river's edge, where the water seemed to protest all the while at its narrow confines, hurling up white spray in her face, and surging against her arm as she drank. Then she crept away, to a little patch of mud, and sat there and she could see the smears of blood from her feet colouring the ground.

IV

Harriet, leading Billy and holding fast to the rope tied to Lady's collar, now arrived at the edge of the Saddle, at the topmost point of the pass, and looked down.

She heard the men begin to swear. They stared at the abyss and the abyss revealed itself to them in all its unchanging darkness.

'God be damned, I'm for licking her!' announced one of the diggers. 'I'm for giving her her satisfactions. Then I'll be done with her and come to mine. This time tomorrow I'll be at the Taramakau.'

And this man, without any pause, but only clutching more tightly the handle of the little cart that he trundled with him, stepped off the ledge where they stood, as if into the void, but his feet holding somehow to firm ground, as the path fell away and spiralled downwards into the valley.

Harriet and the others watched him in silence. Nobody moved. Though the shadows were advancing on him, he was visible to them for a while yet and they could still hear his footsteps and the sound of his cart. Harriet remembered the drips of oil left on the mud floor of the Cob House after Bunny and Hopton had left and wondered what had happened to them here.

'Well?' said an elderly digger, when the man was lost to their sight. 'You're not going down there, eh, Miss Harriet? You don't want to die just yet, do you?'

The man coughed and spat and Harriet saw the gob of spittle land near her, flecked with red. She made no reply.

The wind, blowing in a curve up the funnel of the valley, was very cold here and Harriet realised that she was trembling. She held tightly to Billy's bridle and Lady's rope. In the sunless gorge, she now saw that a waterfall tumbled sheer for a thousand feet or more, and the roar of it came belatedly to her, as though sound travelled differently in this place. And she remembered Dorothy saying to her: 'We are not strong enough for rivers and stars. We think we are at first, but we're not.'

At her side, Harriet could now see the men slowly begin to prepare themselves to face what awaited them, adjusting the straps of their swags, retying their boot-laces, taking swigs of grog, slamming their hats more firmly on their heads, as though the hats might protect them from falling branches and rocks. And Harriet knew that, however afraid they were, they would all go down, all try their luck, because they'd come this far with their dreams of gold and *there was no other dream*. They were like soldiers in retreat.

But for herself, something else was clear to Harriet now: she might get down with Lady, but Billy would not get down. And this was all the justification she needed for her decision to turn back. For a few more moments, she stood where she was, trying to glimpse the tiny figure of the man who had already gone down, but unable to locate him. Then she turned Billy round and pulled Lady to her, out of the wind.

'A man's precious name'

I

Joseph lay alone in his tent and listened to the rain. He thought that the sound of it on the tent roof was like faint applause, heard from far off, acknowledging the achievements of others.

He was living desperate days. On his seventy-two-foot square plot, he had already sunk and slabbed seven shafts. Three of these had flooded and kept on filling with water, despite the painstakingly dug drainage bore-holes. In each one of the remaining four, Joseph had arrived at the blue-clay bottom and Will Sefton, nimble as a chimney-sweep, had gone down there to 'scrape up the gold, Mister Blackstone', gone down all eager and ready for each find, and then there had been no find at all, no trace of the colour, only bucketful after bucketful of the oily clay with its blue sheen, heavy and difficult to wash in the cradle.

Joseph thought of himself as a patient man. Hadn't he built the Cob House out of handfuls of this same wretched dirt? Hadn't he buried Beauty the cow in ground so hard it had broken his shovel? But now, he knew that patience wasn't enough; he needed *luck*. He would find the gold if it was there; but supposing it wasn't there?

The possibility that no gold existed anywhere on his claim created in Joseph Blackstone a dread so absolute it made his skin crawl. Each and every vision of his future assumed an alteration that could only be brought about by money. To return to a life no different from the one he had left when he boarded the *Wallabi* would be so painful, so terrifyingly unhappy, that Joseph now believed he would rather die here, on his thirty-shilling plot, and lie and rot in a blue-clay grave than suffer it.

For he saw very clearly, in the cold, wet light of the days he was living at Kokatahi, that without money, his farm on the Okuku flats would never amount to anything. Lilian would grow old, mending her china by the sooty range, and he would never manage to do the one thing that would please her at last. She would die despising him. And after that, he and Harriet might struggle on, but they would be for ever separate and secretive and cold, and hate would creep in and mark them with its eye and then they would be done for.

It was as though maggots were creeping up Joseph's neck and into his hair. He sat up and let a cry escape from him as he reached up with a hand, to try to wrench away whatever was crawling there. But there was nothing: only the dread in his mind that he couldn't overcome. He wanted to scream, as he had once screamed at birds or toys, at the three tigers in the circus ring. His longing to find gold was so intense, so unrelenting, that he considered getting up now, in the middle of the night, with the rain falling, and beginning work on a new shaft, just sinking it wherever he happened to find himself, with no regard to the lie of the terrain, and he imagined – even now, after the disappointments of seven barren shafts – that moment when, as the dawn arrived perhaps, there would be the first sighting of the colour and how his altered future would start spinning towards him.

But he lay down again and didn't move. Disappointment was tiring him out. He thought with sympathetic tenderness of his father who, on the days when he didn't have to visit any farm or be at the livestock market, with his ledger and his gavel, would often lay his head back in his favourite armchair and pull the white anti-macassar from the chair-back and crumple it in his hand until it half covered his face and fall into a fretful sleep from which he seemed not to want to wake.

Lilian complained about the crumpled anti-macassars. She clearly despised the use Roderick made of them. She said there was no earthly point in continuing to put anti-macassars on the chair-backs if he was going to do that to them.

'Let be,' Roderick had said. Just those two words: *Let be*.

And perhaps Lilian heard the pain in them, for the anti-macassars remained on the chairs, washed and ironed as frequently as was necessary, and Roderick Blackstone, before he met his death in a field of ostriches, continued to scrumple them up and pull them across his face whenever he felt in need of sleep to refresh his disappointed heart.

Joseph tried to settle himself into sleep now, but beyond the pattering of the rain he was listening for footsteps, hoping that Will might choose this night to return. Yet he knew that the hope was vain. Will Sefton had left him for the Scots' camp. An arrangement which Joseph had begun to think of as permanent – permanent for as long as it took to find enough gold to alter his life – had dissolved suddenly in violence and humiliation.

They'd begun a week ago – Will's complaints that he wasn't being paid for his 'services'. Joseph hadn't considered the complaints important at first. He reminded Will that he fed him, sheltered him in the tent, had bought him the fishing rod, with which he amused himself catching fish and cooking them on little fires at the river's edge. He'd believed that this was enough, that Will Sefton was 'his' now, for as long as this life at Kokatahi lasted, that they would wait it out together and labour together on the shafts and do what they did in the night whenever the urge took him (for Joseph admitted, now that he was in a world of men, that desire in men was like a hunger of the belly and had to be satisfied, and to moralise about this or that way of satisfying it could be left to pastors and to women) and then the colour would arrive and Joseph would be generous to the boy, as generous as his own plans allowed ...

But then word came up the river that the Scots had struck gold. On still nights, Joseph and Will could hear the jubilant Glasgow miners singing and shouting. And Will would go out of the tent and stand under the sky, as though moonstruck, and listen.

'I can *see* it,' said Will one morning, after a long night when he hadn't slept, but only day-dreamed about the Scottish gold. 'I can see it in their dirty palms. Not shavings or dust, but lumps of it, with that lovely weight it has ...'

Joseph and Will were standing side by side, resting from their work among the piles of mullock and the stacks of planking. Their crooked windlass creaked mockingly in the wind, like a clock beginning to tick for no reason.

'Their find raises our chances,' insisted Joseph bravely. 'Their terrain is almost identical to this. Our time will come.'

Will let his pick fall and blew his nose into his hand. 'Or it may never,' he said, wiping his hand on his trousers. 'And then my arse will have bled for nothing . . .'

Joseph cuffed Will across his neck. 'Don't use that language!' he said.

Will tottered for a moment, then righted himself and faced Joseph defiantly. 'What language do you want me to use, then, Mister Blackstone?' he said. 'Girls' language? Did you ever find a girl to let you do what I let you? Tear my flesh, you do, and never pay me – '

'Shut up! Or I shall never pay you! When we find gold, I shall give you nothing!'

'You wouldn't be the first,' said Will calmly. 'The things men promise when they're in rut aren't worth sixpence. I've sucked miners from Queenstown to Ten Mile, but am I rich?'

'I don't want to hear about it!'

'Jealous, are you? Think I'm your darling, or something, Mister Blackstone? Told you when I first played my whistle, I was nobody's darling and nobody is mine. Nobody on the stinking earth. I do this for the money, for the *survival*. But you, you have me digging in the ground night and day and slabbing and getting my feet frozen. But I don't like this work, Mister Blackstone. This mining work makes me choke worse than your slime in my mouth. See my skin? Wasn't it white and lovely when you first saw me and now I'm getting bruised and toughened and my hands are red and – '

Joseph hit Will again, this time across his ear, and the boy staggered and fell to his knees. With his heavy boots, Joseph wanted to kick him, kick him till he really hurt, but Will saw his intention and began to scrabble away from him through the mud. And seeing him cower like this, Joseph understood that he'd been wrong about Will staying with him and sharing his fate, wrong and naïve and pathetic. Will Sefton's heart was as hard as flint. He'd known this all along, but now it was making him suffer much more than he'd expected.

Will got to his feet and said: 'I always wanted to go to Scotland, Mister Blackstone. So now I shall. Something about the air, they say. Perhaps it's cleaner. Is it?'

So then Joseph, filled with dismay at the imminent loss of Will, approached him and tried to touch him and dissuade him from leaving. Will backed away from him, but Joseph followed, the two of them stumbling over the pitted earth. Joseph told Will he knew they would find gold soon on this claim 'and then', he said, 'you can name your own price. Your own price.'

'Oh yes,' mocked Will. 'Another fine promise! I've no use for promises any more. But the Scotsmen have the colour! They *have it*, Mister Blackstone, and now it will be mine: I have only to kiss their pricks – '

Joseph grabbed Will Sefton by the neck. Though the boy was strong, Joseph was stronger because all his arduous work in New Zealand had made him tough and lean. He twisted Will's arm behind his back and the boy cried out, but Joseph paid no attention. He pulled Will to him, so close that he could feel his sternum against his chest and the hard pelvic bone and the gristle of his cock pressing against his, and tried to kiss his mouth, the mouth that was pink and pretty and reminded him of Rebecca Millward. But Will clamped his jaw shut and they stood there, locked together in pain and fury, neither of them yielding, and Joseph felt all his anger and sadness at Will's parting turn to furious desire.

Keeping Will's arm locked behind him, Joseph undid the boy's belt and fumbled with his buttons and began to tug his trousers down. He now forced Will away from him, to kneel on the mud. They were in full daylight and only a few yards from them, sunlight glinted on the river as it rushed blithely on. Will attempted to stand, but stumbled over his trousers and now Joseph was kneeling behind him, unbuttoning his moleskins and bringing his own sex into his hand.

'Pay me!' yelled Will. 'You pay me this time, you dirty bugger, or I swear I'll kill you! You'll never sleep for fear of what I can do.'

'I'll pay you. I'll pay you, Will . . .'

Will kicked backwards at him, fighting him off. 'You pay me *now*!'

'I will. Just let me – '

'No! No, I will not let you!'

Will pushed himself up with his arms and spun round to face Joseph. He punched him hard in the belly, and Joseph doubled up and fell sideways, and all his breath seemed to leave his lungs and bile filled his mouth and everything around him – the rush of the river, the creaking of the windlass, the breathing of Will Sefton – was snatched suddenly away.

When he looked up he could see Will standing over him, as though preparing to punch him again. He blinked and spat. And now he saw that just beyond Will was another man. This man was as still and silent as a heron and Joseph knew at once that he had seen everything that had just happened. And he thought coldly: Whoever this man is, I am going to have to kill him.

Joseph tried to stand up. The man wasn't looking at him, he was looking away, but with something like a smile on his face – a smile which was not quite a smile – and Joseph remembered that he'd seen this kind of look before, this Chinese look, on the deck of the *Wallabi*. And he felt that to be regarded like this, in this state of humiliation and pain, by some self-satisfied Celestial was worse – if anything could be worse – than what had just occurred.

'*What?*' shouted Joseph, furiously buttoning up his mole-skins. 'What are you looking at?'

The man said nothing, only lowered his head. At his feet sat two baskets of vegetables and Joseph realised now who he was: he was Scurvy Jenny, whom they had glimpsed once before from high up in the bush, the market gardener, Chen, who made a living selling garden produce to the diggers at Kaniere.

'Wakey!' shouted Joseph, when Chen didn't answer. 'What d'you want? Think you can blackmail me for what you've seen? Is that it? Think you can take my gold? Well, I've got no gold, Jenny. I've got nothing and you've seen nothing. Savvy?'

'He's selling vegetables,' said Will calmly.

The man bent down and his long pigtail fell over his

shoulder. He took a cabbage from his basket and held it out to Joseph.

'What?' said Joseph again. '*What?*'

'You like this?' asked Chen Pao Yi. 'From my garden.'

Joseph wanted to take the cabbage and hurl it at the man's head. He wanted to drag his baskets to the river and send all the produce tumbling into the water. He tugged a shovel out of the heavy earth and brandished it like a weapon, all the while aware how foolish he was appearing.

'You leave,' he said. 'You vamoose, Jenny. This is my claim and I paid thirty shillings for it and you're on my land and I want you gone!'

He was ready to hit the Chinaman with the shovel, but to his surprise, the man obediently replaced the cabbage in one of the baskets and prepared to lift the baskets up on his bamboo pole and walk away.

But then Joseph heard Will pipe up: 'I'd like a cabbage, Mister Blackstone. Cure my diseases with fresh greens, couldn't I?'

Joseph stared at Will, thin and tattered and half covered with clay. He thought that he could kill them both – Will Sefton and the scurvy Chinaman – batter them to death with his shovel, and then he would be alone on his claim and the ground would hear his cries and yield up its treasure and all his world would be fine and bright. But he found that he had no strength left. No strength and no voice. He let the shovel drop. He searched in his muddy pocket and found a couple of pennies and he threw these at Chen's feet and Chen picked them up. Then the Chinaman selected the greenest cabbage from his basket and added a small bunch of radishes and gave these to Will.

'Ta,' said Will. 'Ta, Jenny. Now I shall get well.'

A week had now passed since Will had left to join the Scotsmen.

Though Joseph was getting accustomed to being by himself, he began to find that time moved much more slowly than before and hunger nagged at him, not just for food that he didn't have, but for the happiness that eluded him. He felt that contentment was present in every other creature and every other thing – in the water-birds which drank from the river, in the rats which scurried around his claim, looking for food, and in the songs the Glaswegian miners sang in the evenings. He alone lacked it.

And his nights were bleak. Sometimes, seeing moonlight beyond the tent flaps, he'd imagine he could hear the plangent sound of Will Sefton's penny whistle. He knew it was too far away to hear and yet he heard it just the same and kept wondering whose bed Will slept in now. One of the Scotsmen was called Hamish, but this was all he knew.

Never say a man's precious name, Mister Blackstone.
Never let him be my darling.

II

Chen Pao Yi liked to get up very early in the mornings.

Sometimes he slept in the hut of stones and sacking that he'd made and sometimes he slept in the dark cave beyond it, the cave that went into the heart of the mountain, and Pao Yi thought that the silence of this cave must be as absolute as any silence in the universe.

He liked to get up with the dawn and come out on to the hillside and see the brightness of the day beginning and feel the dew under his feet. It was April now and winter wouldn't be long in coming and the early mornings were cold, but he didn't mind. He knew how to endure cold. He would boil water on his fire to make tea, which he often drank scented with tarata leaves, and, while the water was boiling, inspect his garden and then sit by his hut and drink the tea and listen to the river and sometimes remember dawn on Heron Lake, when the clouds sat in white folds on the mountains and his red fishing boat moved quietly through the mist.

It wasn't that Pao Yi was homesick; he didn't feel any great longing to return to his other life, it was merely that his memories of this life – with Paak Mei and Paak Shui – were exceptionally vivid and full of a kind of tumultuous colour which his present seemed sometimes to lack. And Pao Yi liked to sit and admire this colour in his mind: the scarlet kites Paak Shui flew on Long Hill, the orange clay bricks of his house and its green windows, the brightly painted pictures of Chen Lin and Chen Fen Ming on the tiny ancestral altar near the cooking fire, the yellow and green glass beads of Paak Mei's tiny shoes, the shining silver of the fish in the lake. Nothing moved far nor changed in his imaginings. The scarlet kite was forever almost still, the fish swam slowly just under the surface of the water, Paak Mei stood quietly waiting in her beaded shoes. But neither did anything lose its vibrancy, and now, these days, it was beginning to dawn on Pao Yi that perhaps he had found his vocation as a market gardener. On his vegetable plot, he was replicating the colours of his past.

On the night after his encounter with Joseph Blackstone and Will Sefton, Pao Yi had had a terrifying dream in which he'd returned home to Heron Lake with nothing – no gold, no dollars, no gifts, *nothing* – and he'd knelt down and held out his hands to Paak Mei and they were empty and Paak Mei had begun to cry, and then the small room had filled up with members of Paak Mei's family, mother, father, brothers, sisters, cousins, and they all crowded round him and stared at him with pity.

He had lost face.

He thought he would have to kneel like that for the rest of time.

Some singing began, started by the brothers who sang with deep, resonant voices, and the song was about him, Chen Pao Yi:

‘Whose chosen name means Brother of Righteousness
But whose deeds are of no account
Lesser than the deeds of a frog
Lesser than the deeds of a cockroach a spider a snail
Yes lesser than the deeds of a snail . . .’

When Pao Yi woke up from this nightmare and discovered that he was alone in his hut above Kokatahi, lying on his flax mat, he felt such great relief that he got up at once, even though it was barely light, and went out to his garden and looked at the moon which was still visible in the morning sky. He was very fond of the moon. He'd tried a few times to compose a poem to it and the words of the poem had seemed quite satisfactory at first, even tinged a little, in a sentimental way, with the moon's beauty. But when Pao Yi came to transcribe his words on to paper, he recognised that his calligraphy was crude and he felt that the badly written Chinese characters had infected the poem with badness. In another life, he said to himself, in my *next* life, I shall study with a Master Calligrapher and compose letters for all the inhabitants of Heron Lake and carve the names of their ancestors on the tombstones on the south side of Long Hill. And I will write poetry.

Pao Yi made his tarata-scented tea and, as he drank it, remembered the things he'd seen yesterday: the man lying shamed in the mud; the half-naked boy. He wondered how their lives had led them to this moment and whether it could have been foreseen and prevented. Pao Yi's father, Chen Lin, used to say: We may avoid shame if we choose, for shame seldom takes us unawares, but has its warning cry and we can hear that cry as clearly as we can hear the coming of the north wind.

The man lying in the mud hadn't heard the coming of the north wind.

But Pao Yi didn't care to think about the man and the boy for very long, just as he didn't care to think about most of what he saw and heard on the goldfields, neither about the names men called him, nor about the way, wherever they went, the Chinese were looked down upon and mocked and threatened and their once great Empire forgotten or belittled. These things had to be endured. They were part of each day. They were part of Time. But to think about them for too long made Pao Yi's head fill with a kind of unendurable clamour, as though he'd been shut away in the engine room of a paddle steamer, where the air was black.

Here, on his hillside, drinking his morning tea as the sun broke through the mist, he was able to forget them or hide them away, just as his son Paak Shui hid his collection of stones in a hollow pine tree, covered up with moss. But he knew they were always there, the unendurable things which had to be endured. They were always more immediate to him than he would have wished:

I know where Paak Shui keeps his stones.

Paak Shui doesn't know that I know where he keeps his stones.

But I know.

Pao Yi ate a bowlful of mashed kūmara and started work.

He was planting out tiny onions, nurtured from seed. He knew what they liked, these baby onions, they liked a snug, soft bed exactly the right size for them, made with his thumb. So Pao Yi walked very slowly along the row of earth, following his planting string wound between two sticks, making the beds for his onions and putting them in. He would plant them all, then walk back down the row again and cover them with earth.

He'd made sixteen of these baby beds, when, on the seventeenth, he felt resistance from a flint underneath the pad of his thumb. Pao Yi liked to have all the onions perfectly spaced, one from another, so instead of making another bed a fraction further on, he dug down to remove the flint that was in the way. The flint was quite large – much larger than his thumb pad – and Pao Yi held it in his palm for a moment before throwing it away. But, as he threw it, he saw the sun catch it in an unexpected way, with a bright gleam, and so he turned to look at it, where it had fallen, and his eyes rested there. He didn't move: he remained exactly where he was, squatting down over his onion row, but regarding the discarded flint and formulating in his mind what – if anything – he wanted to say about it.

Chen Pao Yi had perfected a quality of stillness. He had learned it from his father, Chen Lin. It was a stillness of both mind and body, a stillness that had mastery over words. Perhaps almost any other man in New Zealand would have gasped out the word 'gold', but Pao Yi didn't do this. He refused to comply with any *naming* of the thing he had found in the onion row.

But he moved now. Very carefully, without hurrying, he finished planting the row. Then he stood up and walked to where the golden flint lay. He picked it up, noting its heaviness, and held it out, to let the sun touch it again.

He said nothing. He thought of the weir over which his parents had tumbled to their deaths and of their graves on Long Hill, which, perhaps, did not contain all that had been left of them. Then he thought of Paak Shui's scarlet kite above the hill and what a brilliant, beautiful speck it made in the sky. And then at last he thought about Paak Mei and how he might one day replace her beaded shoes with slippers encrusted with precious stones.

III

When the news of the Scottish find reached Kaniere, forty or fifty miners who had been toiling there for weeks for poor returns decided to cut their losses, buy new licences and make for Kokatahi. In the time that it took them to get to the warden's office at Hokitika and back, the Scottish strike had been talked up into a 'homeward bounder': a discovery so huge that it would change men's lives at a stroke and enable them to return home as rich men.

They came up the river in pairs and groups. They looked like a race apart, like convicts fleeing death, like a starving army. Many of them had fallen sick in the wet-flat swamps of Kaniere and couldn't eat and were as thin as wraiths, with their skin a waxy yellow and their eyes huge with pain and disappointment. Such clothes as they possessed were now so encrusted with mud that it had seemed to them pointless to try to wash them any more. 'The mud keeps us warm,' they quipped. 'Extra layer of insulation against the winter, it is. And it's camouflage, 'less there be crows waiting in the sky.'

When they reached Kokatahi, they saw that the ground was firmer here. Some of them hadn't stood or slept on dry ground for a month. But already all the river claims near to the Scots' camp had been bagged. The new arrivals from Kaniere could count twenty-seven windlasses and two horse-whims. The air was clotted with noise. The piles of discarded wash-dirt now made an almost unbroken embankment along the south side of the Kokatahi River.

Plenty of land was left on the northern side, well away from the water, good dry land where a tent would sit nicely, and where there seemed to be no sign of swamp rats, no itch of sandflies. The Kaniere men paused and set down their tools and looked at it and weighed up comfort against chance. They longed to recover their health, but what was health worth if they were going to remain poor? They knew that Hamish McConnell and Marty Brenner had made their strike close to the water, that what was now known as the 'Brenner–McConnell homeward bounder' was a river claim, and they also knew that gold very often lay in the earth in lines and seams and what the successful digger had to do was predict where the seam would go and stay on that same line. And so, although the dry grassland away from the Kokatahi seemed like heaven to them after Kaniere, not many men pitched a tent there. They walked on up the river.

Joseph heard them coming one late afternoon, as the light was fading. Then he saw them and he knew what they were: they were the unlucky ones. Perhaps they'd dug out a few pennyworth of gold dust at Kaniere, enough to keep them in grog and rice, but the way that they came shuffling and stumbling along the river-banks revealed to him their lack of fortune. They were like him.

And now they were going to invade his world.

Joseph stood on his claim and didn't move. He'd been at the head of the Kokatahi workings for almost a month, in his own universe, and now everything was going to change.

He hadn't yet made his fire. He knew that he must be almost invisible to the men arriving in the dusk and his instinct was to go into his tent, to hide from them, so that he wouldn't have to look at them or talk to them. But he stayed where he was. Hopeless as his claim was proving, he knew he had to defend his ground, defend his right to his section of the river, make sure that his ropes, which stole an extra foot or two by circling round rocks and boulders, weren't disturbed.

'How's it go, here?' called out one of the men to Joseph. 'You in on the Brenner–McConnell bounder, mister?'

Joseph could smell the men now, a filthy scalp smell, a stench of sore crotch and rotting feet.

'Got a prime claim here, eh?' said another man. 'Got a riser at least, haven't you?'

Joseph said nothing to this, but asked on impulse: 'Is Will Sefton with you?'

'Will Sefton? Who's Will Sefton?'

'My boy,' said Joseph. 'Went down to the Scots' camp.'

'The Scots' camp's like Piccadilly, mister. You can't hardly get near it. The Brenner-McConnell homeward bounder's known as far as Greymouth now.'

'I doubt it was a homeward bounder,' said Joseph.

'Why's that? I heard they dug out a lump the size of a man's fist. McConnell's bought a horse, did you know? Big expensive horse. And he's got women there.'

'Women?'

'From the Hokitika hotels. Wash their hair in his piss, they would, for an ounce of what he has.'

There was laughter and coughing. Joseph saw one of the Kaniere men kick out at one of his piles of wash-dirt and this man said: 'Work alone, do you?'

'Yes,' said Joseph. 'Unless my boy returns.'

'So, what've you found?'

He choked on the word 'nothing'. He had lost count of the hours he'd toiled, the slabs he'd fixed, the load after load after load of dirt washed in his cradle. He couldn't bring himself to admit out loud that all of this, every single second of it, had been in vain.

'Dust,' he said. 'Small grains. Nothing notable.'

'Diggers always lie,' said another of the men.

'I'm not lying,' said Joseph. 'I came here to be a bit away from the Scots, but you'd do better to go back there, peg claims as near to them as you can.'

'All gone, chum,' said a young miner wearing what looked like an old bowler hat. 'Not an inch of river left there. But they say the gold goes all the way up this line, right to where it narrows and becomes the Styx.'

'Who says this?' asked Joseph.

'Who says anything in this hell-hole? But one rumour's as good as another. And I'm too tired to go on, so tomorrow we're pegging here.'

These words were like a signal to all the others. They were tired, too, and the darkness was increasing all the time. They dumped their gear where they stood, just north of Joseph's boundary, and set up tents and hammered them in and began lighting fires and pouring grog and generally making ready for their night. Some of them splashed into the river and began washing themselves. The water that lapped round their thin bodies still had a glimmer of light on it and Joseph watched them until that light was gone.

The White Worm

I

Harriet was at Orchard House.

To Dorothy Orchard she admitted: 'You said we weren't strong enough for stars and waterfalls and you were right. I wasn't strong enough for the Hurunui Gorge.'

'My dear Harriet,' said Dorothy, 'you went all the way up that terrible dray road and slept in Charlie Wilde's hut and endured the men's snoring and so forth. And then you went to the very edge of that precipice. *The very edge*. All of that shows enormous strength, doesn't it, Toby?'

'Yes,' said Toby Orchard. 'It does, Doro.'

'Say it more forcefully, Toby! Don't merely agree with me. Tell Harriet how brave she's been.'

The three of them were sitting on the verandah of the house. The recent evenings had been cold, but suddenly this one evening was warm again, as though summer had barged in, like an old forgotten lover.

'Of course it was brave,' said Toby, sucking on his pipe, 'but it was also lunacy. It was suicide. And Harriet knows that.'

'I don't think she knows that, at all, do you, Harriet?' said Dorothy.

Harriet stared out at the garden, with its smell of pungent fern. She thought that if she'd been on her own with Dorothy, she would have tried to describe that feeling she'd had in the manuka grove, that feeling of longing – of yearning for a thing she couldn't identify, but which certainly wasn't death. But something in Toby's presence, the incontrovertible and solid *bulk* of Toby, allied to his probable disdain for words such as 'longing' or 'yearning', prevented Harriet from mentioning this.

'Harriet couldn't know what that gorge was like until she'd seen it, Toby,' continued Dorothy. 'Until you've seen a thing –'

'You don't have to *see* everything to know what it is, Dorothy. You've never seen the Himalayas, but you wouldn't think of attempting to climb them.'

'No, I wouldn't, but –'

'Toby's right,' said Harriet. 'I was warned. But the idea of mountains has always drawn me to them. I expect it's because I grew up in Norfolk!'

Nobody laughed or even smiled at this. The three of them merely remained silent for a moment or two, Dorothy moving her chair a fraction away from Toby's, to show him that she thought him too severe. She was about to point out to him, for the second time, what a beautiful evening it was and suggest that they shouldn't sully it by saying anything even passingly antagonistic when Toby said: 'I'm sorry if I sounded disagreeable, Harriet. As Dorothy knows, I'm all for women showing your kind of spirit. But we all have to learn the difference between what is brave and what is foolhardy. You showed great courage by turning back.'

'That's better, Toby,' said Dorothy. 'And of course he's right, Harriet. Imagine if we'd lost you.'

'Yes,' said Harriet. 'But I discovered that I didn't want to be lost.'

They talked of other things: of the new ice house being built beyond the pine spinney to store mutton carcasses, of the kingfishers Toby had seen that day at the creek. Then Toby finished his pipe and went to bed, leaving Dorothy and Harriet alone. Harriet was tired, but she felt comfortable in her verandah chair, breathing the night air of the garden, the scent of which floated to her more strongly now since Toby, with his man smell and his pipe, had disappeared into the house. She thought that, if she could just cover herself with a blanket, she could stay there all night and only wake up when some bird, startled by light, began its morning song.

Dorothy sighed. 'I'm sorry Toby was peevish,' she said quietly. 'He's so worried about Edwin that he can't concentrate properly on anything and so he doesn't feel the temperature of things.'

They were silent for a moment, then Dorothy went on: 'Edwin won't eat. Only blancmange. We've tried to force him, but he can't. He just vomits everything up again. So now we let him eat the blancmange. Janet makes them all colours and we try to put some good things into them – honey and lemon rind and so forth. We took him to the doctor in Kaiapoi. He said he thought Edwin has a worm.'

'A worm?'

'He prescribed some medicine. Bitter as aloe. We have to put the medicine into the blancmanges, too. He says the medicine isn't to *kill* the worm. A dead worm inside you will poison the blood. So now we must keep the worm alive and try to flush it out. We examine every stool.'

Harriet now felt that the air on the verandah wasn't as balmy as it had been a few moments ago. She pulled her shawl round her shoulders.

'I know what you're thinking,' said Dorothy. 'You're remembering that the last time you were here, Edwin started talking about wings and robes and said he was going to die.'

'Yes,' said Harriet. 'I was thinking about that. We thought he'd had a dream . . .'

'He still has them. He's terrified about something, but he will not tell us what. He says he cannot tell us, Harriet, that if we make him tell us he will die. So I said, "Will you tell the doctor then, Edwin?" But he refused. He said, "Mama, you do not understand about friendship." And so we're more confused than ever. What friendship is he talking about? Toby thinks the fears are all in Edwin's mind, but I believe that there's a connection, between those fears, or dreams, or whatever they are, and the wretched worm.'

Now, Harriet felt as though she were standing again at a precipice edge. She'd failed in her mission to find Pare. She had seen the waterfall (the very one where Pare might have been?) and she had nevertheless turned back, without giving Pare a moment's thought, and this was a betrayal of a kind. But what faced her now was a sickening fall from loyalty. She felt the pull of the ground far below, the implacable gravity of what she could reasonably call good sense or *right*. Because to stay silent and let Edwin die would be a criminal act, a wrongdoing far worse than the betrayal of a secret. And yet to fall so far from trust also seemed unforgivable. She hadn't asked to become Edwin Orchard's confidante, but he, in his lonely life as an only child on a sheep-run, had given her this role and she'd sworn to honour it.

Tentatively, Harriet said: 'Shall I try to talk to Edwin tomorrow? See if he will tell me? Because I know, from having been a governess for so long, that children will sometimes tell things to strangers that they can't say to their parents, not through any lack of love or trust, but because they're afraid to upset or anger them.'

Dorothy Orchard didn't reply immediately. She looked out at the night, moving her eyes from side to side, as though she had glimpsed something out there and was trying to identify it. Then she turned back to Harriet and said: 'The power of dreams can be very great, I understand that. And perhaps telling a dream helps to diminish its power, does it? Or if we tell our dreams, then perhaps we also tell our fears without noticing? I don't know about any of this. If you were brought up in a manor in Cornwall, as I was, what do you know about the world of the mind? You know how to tell when something is not really silver, but plate, simply by the weight of it. You know a thousand things like this, but you know nothing about *feelings*, or what I mean is, you know about feelings, but you seldom know where they come from or what to do with them ...

'But a worm. What a terrible idea a worm is! Could any *feeling* have put a worm inside Edwin? Could telling that feeling bring the worm out again? I just do not know, Harriet. I just do not know anything.'

Dorothy had begun the conversation in a whisper, but now she was talking very loudly, as if she were urging herself towards a scream.

Her hands were on the arms of her chair, gripping it, trying to knead it like dough. 'All I know,' she continued, 'is that if anything happened to Edwin, we would be lost. Toby and me. We would be drowned. We would not be able to go on because there would be no point in going on. So we have to do whatever it takes, whatever it costs, whatever, *whatever* to bring that worm out, but the most wretched thing of all is that I really do not know what to do and nor does Toby and every time Edwin is sick, I feel ... And all I can think of is blancmange. Make more blancmange ...'

Dorothy put her face in her hands. Harriet wanted to reach out and comfort her, but the set of Dorothy's shoulders suggested a carapace in which she wanted to hide and not let anyone come near her.

'You talk to him!' Dorothy burst out at last, running her hands wildly through her short hair. 'Try to find out what he means by "friendship". Why does it frighten him so? See if you can make sense of it.'

'I'll try,' said Harriet.

'And if ... if there is some secret that he doesn't want to tell us ... remind him that the only thing we care about is making him well. Nothing else is of any significance.'

Edwin Orchard could picture his worm.

He thought it was white and blind and lazy and lay coiled in him, barely moving, sucking up the sweet blancmange, becoming bloated and heavy. It had begun as something as thin as the stalk of a newly sown onion, but now it was much wider and longer than that. It was like a snake he'd seen in a picture book.

In his dreams, Pare on her ledge of stone talked to him in her low, anxious voice. She said that she knew he was suffering, just as she was suffering, and would have helped him if she could have reached him, but she couldn't reach him. She warned him that both she and he were probably going to die.

Some of the stories Pare had told Edwin returned to him, stories about people who leapt up to heaven on a bouncing rope, or killed their husbands and swallowed them like fish; about spirits who took the form of lizards or trees or cormorants or fire. He began to wonder whether his worm was one of these spirits. But one thing bothered him. He had no idea where this world of the spirits was. Edwin was a boy who liked to know exactly where things were. In the days of his caterpillar, he had been able to see it, at the corner of his eye, wherever it decided to wander – even when it made itself look like a twig or a little brown thistle – until it wandered so far away that it made itself invisible and became something else and then something else again. But he'd never *seen* the world of the spirits. Pare had never explained where it was or how it could be found. Was it under the earth or way up above the tops of the trees? And how could something from a different world which he'd never seen find its way inside him? He'd tried asking his father: 'Is there one world, Papa, or lots of worlds?'

Toby Orchard had been in an angry mood on the day Edwin asked this question because he knew that someone was stealing sheep from the run. He had no proof, but sheep were vanishing, so there had to be a thief working the run: some clever cockatoo, who knew his trade and left no traces.

'I don't know what you mean,' he'd snapped. 'Are you talking about heaven?'

'No,' said Edwin. 'I don't mean a different world when you die. I mean a different world here. A world you hardly ever see.'

'We all "see" things in our mind,' said Toby more gently. 'We can all imagine things ...'

'I mean real things, but you can't see them all the time.'

'Such as what?'

'Such as ... there could be a place where the Moa Bird is, couldn't there, Papa, but we can't see it?'

'No,' said Toby. 'There could not be a place where the Moa Bird is. The Moa Bird was hunted and killed until none were left. It can never come back.'

'I know. I know it can't come back *here*, but it could come back to another world, couldn't it? Couldn't there be another world where it hadn't died? And if we could go there –'

'No, Edwin. There is one world and one is quite hard enough to keep track of. You've got your thoughts into a bit of a muddle. Do you feel strong enough to get your pony? – You can help me see whether our sheep thief has left any clues lying around in the grass.'

Edwin Orchard liked to believe that, between them, his

mother and father knew everything there was to know. But he understood that there were certain things which Pare knew that were outside what they were capable of knowing. And this was what Edwin missed. Not only the smell of Pare and the feel of her forehead against his when she made her *hongi* greeting, but those stories of hers which came from another place and which made him shiver sometimes with a feeling that was not fear and was not delight, but something between the two.

He began to believe that Pare's present existence on the ledge was connected to that other world she talked about, but he also knew that she was still in the ordinary world, too, because she called to him in her ordinary voice. She spoke English. She pronounced his name: 'E'win'. She told him about the waterfall.

Sometimes, Edwin wanted Pare to be quiet. He felt so ill and tired. He wanted everything to be silent and safe and normal, as it used to be. But the days and nights went on and the worm feasted on all the imaginatively crafted blancmanges and the calling of Pare didn't stop.

At Harriet's request, Edwin took her to see the new ice house, built of brick and dug deep into the ground.

Edwin said: 'Some men are going to cut ice out of a glacier and bring it here on drays. Papa says it will be the coldest place in New Zealand, but he's wrong. I know where the coldest place in New Zealand is.'

'Where is the coldest place in New Zealand, Edwin?'

Edwin didn't reply to this. The ice house smelled of fern root and damp mortar. A little sunshine penetrated it now, but Edwin said: 'There will be a door there, where the sun's coming in, and then it will be all sealed up and dark and stay cold all the time.'

'It's ingenious,' said Harriet.

'What does "ingenious" mean?'

'Clever. The ice house is a very clever idea.'

Edwin walked around the ice house, running his hand along the walls. Harriet had noticed a growing restlessness in him, as though he was afraid to stand still or sit quietly anywhere.

Harriet felt herself shiver. She wanted to go back into the light above, but nevertheless she remained there, quietly watching Edwin. After a while, she said: 'I'm sorry I couldn't find Pare, Edwin. She may have been down in the valley . . . where I was too frightened to go.'

He didn't answer. Then he said: 'The ice will be put here. All the way round. Ice from the glacier.'

Harriet nodded, then said again: 'Do you think she's still in danger?'

Edwin stopped walking. He held on to the wall. 'I'm going to be sick again,' he said. 'You'd better not look. My sick is sometimes purple.'

Harriet crossed to him and held his shoulders while he vomited on to the floor of the ice house. Then, she took out her handkerchief and gently wiped his face with it. His face, in the subterranean ice house, looked as pale as a lily.

She led him out and felt him trembling and knew that he was glad of the little warmth there was in the sun. They sat for a moment on a pile of slabs near where the ice house door would go.

'Did Mama tell you about my worm?' he said.

'Yes.'

'It's never going to come out with that medicine.'

'Never?'

'Mama thinks it's going to come out of my bottom, but it won't, because it doesn't move downwards. It stays in the same place.'

'Where? Where's the place?'

Edwin pressed his gut, just above the hip bone. 'Here.'

'But,' said Harriet, 'the medicine will make it move and then it will come out.'

'No,' said Edwin. 'It won't.'

In the distance, Harriet could hear noise from the house: the barking of the dogs and Janet tunelessly whistling as she hung some laundry out to dry. These sounds seemed to draw Edwin to them and he began to walk towards them without glancing back at Harriet.

Before he had gone too far, she called out: 'I'm going to the goldfields, Edwin. By the sea route. North to Nelson, then down the West Coast to Hokitika. I could ask people . . . If

Pare is still in the mountains, I could go into the gorges from that side. I could try to find her . . .'

She saw Edwin stop. He looked round at her and said: 'She might be invisible. Like she was in the toi-toi grass. Then you would have wasted your time.'

II

Charlie Wilde was doing a good trade.

In the struggle between fear of the 'stairway of hell' and desire for riches, desire was winning. Most nights, there were men camped round Charlie's fire, eating his wild-bird stew, coming and going from the manuka grove. His sixpence-a-night charge for bed and food and fire was slowly building to a satisfactory small accumulation and it now occurred to Charlie Wilde to put the price up by a humorous little halfpenny that no one would begrudge him. He began to enjoy saying the words 'sixpence ha'penny'. They were words, he thought, which had a little dance to them. *Sixpence ha'penny la la la!*

Charlie kept the ha'pennies in a separate place from the sixpences and made separate plans for them. This was free money. Money no one noticed. So, one day, when all the gold fever was past, he would spend it on something extraordinary. The 'extraordinary' thing altered all the time. Sometimes, it was a Spanish girl with camellias in her hair. Sometimes, it was a boat with a scarlet sail. Sometimes, it was a strange and wonderful kiosk, tall as a minaret, from which he would sell . . . what? Jars of amber-coloured wine, lowered to his customers on a rope? Phials of opium? Homing pigeons? Hats?

Very often, Charlie Wilde drifted to sleep in the middle of formulating some new and astonishing idea for his ha'penny store. He was in no hurry to realise any of them. He understood, perhaps, that imagining them brought him as much satisfaction as ever they would bring when they had form and substance. But the ha'pennies were mounting up. Charlie enjoyed gazing at the pile. Now, for every twelve gold-seekers paying the extra ha'penny, he knew there was a thirteenth invisible gold-seeker (whom he did not have to feed) miraculously paying the former price of sixpence, too.

'I should have been in business,' Charlie Wilde told himself. 'Success in business consists of getting what is there to pay for what is not there, or, alternatively, getting what is not there to pay for something which is. I've missed my bloody vocation.'

III

While Harriet remained at the Orchard Run, two men from the Lyttelton wharves, John Shannon and Francis Fairford, arrived at the Hurunui Gorge.

Fairford was an immigrant from Dover, England, a man of fifty-four. The Dover docks had been his life until he decided, one February day, he'd had enough of the hail and the salt wind and the smell of herring and he bought a cheap passage on a ship bound for New Zealand. He'd never married nor had a child. He was 'hard', he told his mates, 'belligerent as a bloody seagull', and so he'd become known as 'Flinty'. But his legendary hardness now disguised a growing terror that he would die poor, with his pitiable wages spent long ago on grog and women and the feeling of a life lived in vain.

Shannon, usually called 'John-boy', had been born fatherless in Christchurch. He wasn't much more than twenty-three and ready to face down whatever had to be faced down to escape from the repetitive life poverty had imposed on him. As soon as he heard that men were walking across the mountains to the West Coast Rush, John-boy decided to try his luck with them. He smacked his beloved mother's arse in its cotton dress and told her he would bring her 'a pair of golden shoes'. Marie Shannon put her arms round the big hulk that her son was becoming and said: 'Take Flinty Fairford with you. He knows what's what. You need a hard head with you in the mountains.'

With a few others, Flinty and John-boy had paid their sixpence ha'pennies and stayed a night in Charlie Wilde's hut and eaten pigeon by his scalding fire. Both had guts of iron and slept like lambs, never needing to stumble out to the foul-smelling manuka grove and, when they climbed the Saddle and looked down, from the lip of scrub where Harriet had turned back, neither of them swore or even said a word. Because they had known how the gorge would appear. The gorge was the darkness of their heads made visible. The gorge was what Flinty saw every day at the moment of waking. The gorge was what John-boy knew when he imagined his father lying on his mother on an iron bed and leaving her before the day got light and never returning. But now, they were going to conquer it. Flinty and John-boy. They were going to crush the gorge under their boots, piss in its confounded river. At long last, they were going to master something.

They felt the cold and the dark creep towards them. They felt the stony ground break apart and slip under their weight. They heard birds shrieking somewhere in the freezing air.

They roped themselves together. Why not? Sometimes life throws you in with another and you accept it like you accept a free meal or a girl who happens to be by you when you're in need.

Roped, then, and each of them clinging to the rope – as though one end of it were tied to something unmoving – Flinty and John-boy came down towards the shadows. They tried to follow a track, where other gold-seekers had passed, but they found that in several places trees had fallen across the track, uprooted by the wind, and so thick was the bush that it was difficult to go round the fallen trunks and so they hauled themselves over them, snagging and tangling their rope, cursing as thorns picked at their arms and the weight of their swags made them stumble.

From the lip of the gorge, they'd been able to see the Hurunui River far below, but now they couldn't see anything, only the ghostly semblance of the track – or what their eyes wanted to believe was a track – weaving through the trees, leading them over termite mounds, around boulders, and to sudden unexpected precipices, where they just managed to stop before they fell, each pulling hard on the rope, and staring down and then looking about them for some other way. All the time, they felt stealing on them the certainty that they were lost.

'Keep on the descent and we'll be right,' said Flinty, who was leading, 'this path goes nowhere except to the river. Then we follow that.'

The deeper they went into the gorge the quieter it became. It was like a dusk falling – a noonday dusk – and every bird or creature vanishing with the onset of night. Yet, in the murky light, shapes of animals, of crouching figures, appeared to seep out of the trees, and John-boy's knuckles were yellow as ivory, so fiercely did he cling to the rope. He tried to choke back his fear, but he felt his legs go soft, as if gravity had lost its pull and, to Flinty, he whispered: 'Feels like . . . like the deep, eh Flinty? Like the bottom of the sea?'

'Stay on track. Stay on track,' said Flinty. 'Don't let yourself get confused.'

Alone, he would have been lost. John-boy knew this. He'd boasted that he – the younger man – would be the one to 'take care' of Flinty over the Hurunui, but he hadn't imagined the strangeness of it, this terrifying feeling he had now that he was walking into an underwater world and was going to drown. He'd lived through hunger and misery and he thought he could endure whatever life hurled at him and come through and see – somewhere in front of him – the light of something better. But now, as he and Flinty Fairford crawled on down into the depths of the gorge, John-boy Shannon felt himself drawn in to a world where there was no 'light of something better', where there was only confusion and a feeling of everything vanishing away.

'See the track, Flinty?' he kept on asking. 'See it, do you?'

And Flinty, hearing the terror in John-boy's voice, kept replying: 'I see it all right, John-boy. Hold to the rope. We'll be down soon.'

But both knew that these were empty words, not only because there was no track, but because *all* words were empty here, because the weight of the air pressed down so hard upon everything which breathed that sound could barely linger long enough to acquire meaning and it was becoming difficult to distinguish between what was spoken and what were hallucinatory musings of the mind. Flinty Fairford and John-boy Shannon were walking into a trance.

The Forest under the Earth

I

Joseph Blackstone was living in an altered world.

The Kaniere miners had pegged claims all along the river. They made fires on what had been Will Sefton's 'fishing chair'. The bush-line retreated as they felled trees for slabs and firewood. The river-bank piled up with wash-dirt and stones.

Bush rats arrived in countless numbers. For every man digging at Kokatahi, there now seemed to be four or five or six rats, living off flour and bacon and spilt rice and the oil from old pilchard tins. The rats were sometimes shot as food themselves and roasted, and their skins and tails thrown into the water. Only one of the Kaniere men would eat a rat's tail. He'd char it black and taunt the diggers by holding it up in the air like a delicacy before sucking the meagre flesh from the gristle. He said: 'If I never find gold, I'll make a living from rats. Change the name, that's all. Men will eat any breathing thing and I can get a million rats for nothing. All I need is a fancy epithet. "Water venison", I'll call it!'

There was a camaraderie among the Kaniere men which excluded Joseph. From the moment they'd arrived, they'd behaved almost as though Joseph wasn't there. They'd suffered together in the Kaniere swamps and now they'd moved on and this was their chosen camp, a paradise compared to Kaniere, despite the rats and the slow accumulation of rubbish, and they roped it to within inches of the water and straightaway began digging their shafts, setting up windlasses, rinsing and mending cradles, contriving latrines, lighting fires, shooting birds and talking, drinking, cursing and laughing far into the hours of darkness.

They seemed to give no thought to the man who had arrived here first. Perhaps they assumed that he'd soon decide to leave? Or else they saw, simply, that Joseph Blackstone had roped a duffer claim and would die working ground in which gold would never ever be found, and they wanted no part in his mistakes.

There were days when Joseph did no mining, never washed nor ate, never came out of his tent, but lay and listened to the noise all around him and was eaten up with a hatred of the world so deep he felt that he wouldn't survive it. He brought out his shotgun from his filthy swag and loaded it and lay it by him, within reach of his hand. He imagined the sweet silence of death, the absolution from failure, the rest from being. But something always kept him from taking up the gun.

Something.

It was a familiar memory and it still had the power to transport him to another place. It was a place on the other side of the world, but Joseph liked to imagine it as lying far down *underneath* him, as a place that could be reached, if only he could dig deep enough and wide enough for long enough. For long enough, harsh and lonely time ...

... He was walking along a Norfolk lane in June, going home to Parton with his auctioneer's ledger under his arm, wearing his brown suit and a tweed cap. The sun was beginning to go down.

He rounded the corner of Parton Woods and came to a green meadow where Lilian gathered mushrooms in September, and there she was: Rebecca Millward. She was sitting on the gate, sucking a stem of grass between her teeth. She was sixteen and her face was brown from the sun and there were laughter lines at the corners of her eyes. When she saw Joseph, she bunched her skirts up between her legs, so that Joseph could see her calves going down into her brand-new boots.

He glanced tenderly at these boots, was moved that she wanted to show them to him, show him that her father could afford them, that her father, the fishmonger, spoiled her.

'Mr Blackstone,' she said. 'Been at the market, have you? Glad I'm not a sheep or a heifer to come under your hammer!'

She tossed her grass away and laughed. He didn't know what to reply to this, didn't really know what she meant, except that she wanted to say something provoking, to show him she dared to tease him. So he said nothing, but of course he looked at her more closely, at her laughing mouth, at her curly hair falling round her shoulders ... and so, having got his attention, she contrived to show him something else: the smear of blood on her petticoat, to see what this would do to him.

Joseph supposed, when he thought back to this moment, that there may have been some conversation between them – some dull questions about the livestock market or the fish shop or about the weather or about her brother Gabriel who had an Irish sweetheart – but he had no recollection of any inconsequential patter on that first afternoon. He remembered only what he did next, there in the slowly declining sun of the summer day. He approached Rebecca and then stood between her spread legs, where she still sat on the gate, and kissed her, and the moment he kissed her, he knew that in his thirty years of life he'd desired no one as much as he desired her, this sixteen-year-old girl in her smart boots and her soiled petticoat.

What she whispered to him then was: 'If you want it, Mr Blackstone, we could go somewhere now and it would be safe. No consequence, you see? Just the pleasure of it. For I've always wanted you – so smart and tidy in that suit of yours – since the day I watched you sell my father's mare. I'd swear that mare was on heat for you, Mr Blackstone! The way she pranced about in front of you. But I know, for Gabriel says it, that what men want ... what men want is only the pleasure and no consequence nine months later. No foal! Tell me if I be wrong?'

He told her she wasn't wrong.

He thought it a kind of contract: *no consequence.*

It immediately became the thing that held him to her, the thing which made her different from anyone else, the thing which gave him a sweet tranquillity of mind.

But here, Joseph's memory began to be unstable, to slide about towards the time which followed, towards a time that he preferred to forget. For after that day, and the next and the next, and then again a month later when she had her bleeding again, how was there to be 'no consequence' to what they did?

He kept asking her. He expected her to know, but of course she didn't know. She said: 'What does it matter now, Joseph Blackstone, if you love me?'

He was distressed and confused. He replied that it did matter. He said it was part of the contract. But Rebecca whined that she didn't know what 'contract' he was referring to. She kept on with her tedious refrain about love until he felt that the very word 'love' would drive him insane.

And so he left her.

He thought that what he felt had nothing to do with love. He left her for two months and twenty-three days and tried to forget about her. Once, he saw her standing in the garden of Lilian's house in Parton, watching the windows, and he called out to her to go away. But it broke his heart to say that to her, because the moment he saw her all he wanted was to hold her in his arms.

She entered his dreams. He got no rest from his longing. He cursed her as a witch, a caster of spells. He despised himself for his need of her. He wanted to take a knife and cut her out of his heart. The world about him and every single person in it created in him a boredom so immense he thought he would suffocate. To drag himself round the farms or to the market with his father hurt his skull, put a stone in his chest. He couldn't eat the food his mother cooked, couldn't breathe when he lay down in his bed.

So in the autumn he went looking for her, where she worked with her father at the fishmonger's and led her, ladylike, on his arm to Parton Woods and before she could resist or cry out, he took her in her scut, in her little darling tail, and he was in heaven there and died when he got to his pleasure, died to the world, to everything but that.

No consequence.

Now, he could meet her whenever he liked. She protested that it hurt, but he didn't care if he hurt her. What was there on earth that had no hurt to it? he asked her. And she said in her innocence that there were plenty of things and started naming them, but this wearied him, her homely list of what she loved, so he stood up and buttoned himself and walked away, leaving her lying on the ground. The wind sighed all around her in the beech woods and a light rain was beginning and she added her tears to the rain, but he was unmoved.

When winter came, and she passed her seventeenth birthday and Gabriel married his Irish girl, she began to pester him to 'make an honest woman of her'. He refused. He said he didn't want a wife. All he wanted was what they had. And so she grew sulky and tearful and seemed never to laugh at anything or return his kisses and, worse, far worse than anything, wouldn't let him go to the place he craved. She sealed it off, the sorceress. She stuffed it with cotton: anything rather than let him do what he wanted to do there.

So he was in torment. He still told himself that he didn't love her, this brazen, stubborn girl, the fishmonger's daughter, and yet he knew that she had enslaved him. He felt that he would never be able to live without her, but knew that living with her was out of the question. For how could he, who tried so hard to please his mother, 'make an honest woman' of someone like Rebecca Millward or bring her to Lilian's parlour with the anti-macassars on the velvet chairs? Already, he was able to predict exactly what Lilian would say: 'That girl is a common minx, Joseph Blackstone! And don't you dare to let her ruin your life.'

He thought that Lilian was right. Rebecca was a minx. And yet he remembered what it was like to try to live without her. He remembered the tedium of days, the nights without breath.

So he trusted to chance. He let himself make love to Rebecca Millward as most men made love to their sweethearts or wives. He even let her get her own pleasure. The skin of his back was pierced by her stubby little nails. She bit his lips, his ears, his shoulders. And all went on as it had to go on until one day she came to him and told him she was carrying his child. And at that moment, it seemed to him that he woke up: woke up from his enslavement; woke to a nightmare; woke to *consequence*; woke to the inevitability, the necessity of a crime . . .

In his tent at Kokatahi, Joseph always managed to stop his

memories there – before any crime was committed, before any crime was even thought about.

He brought other events into his mind, which were pure inventions. He imagined marrying Rebecca Millward at Parton on a spring morning, with all her curly hair snowed by a muslin veil and a posy of pinks, bright as her mouth, in her fish-girl hands. He imagined dancing with her at their wedding and taking her to bed in some honeymoon inn, with a mad fiddler playing in the courtyard below, and undressing her piece by piece as he'd never undressed her, and looking at her body that was his and his only and would never belong to anyone else and never be hurt or damaged.

And these imaginings brought him a kind of rest. A rest from guilt. A rest from shame. They blotted out for a while the never-ending noise outside the tent, the squealing and scampering of the rats and the rattle of the wash-boxes and the whine of the windlasses turning and turning, and the wailing of the autumn winds.

But Joseph had to keep working. He couldn't keep hiding in his tent, scratching his skin, dreaming, aching, staring at death. He had to continue to mine for gold.

He was digging his eighth shaft. He had to bring out the dirt and sift it and then get down into the hole and slab it up and try to drain it. The earth was cold, iron cold. Joseph was reminded by the cold in the earth that his miner's right on this claim had expired and that, if he didn't want the Kaniere men to take it over as casually as they had taken over Will's fishing chair, he would have to go down to Hokitika to renew his licence.

Part of him now suspected that he'd selected a worthless claim. Perhaps, if the Kaniere diggers hadn't arrived, he would have moved on or tried to move back, nearer the Brenner-McConnell bounder. But part of him also believed that it was not the claim that was worthless, it was *he* who was worthless. He had no right to riches and so he found nothing. This was his punishment for wrongdoing. God knew what was in his soul. God had seen his cruelty towards Rebecca. God knew what he'd done with Will Sefton. But God was also a humorist, could make a Job of anyone he chose. It was quite possible –

even probable – that the moment he relinquished his plot at Kokatahi, and one of the Kaniere men began fossicking there, gold would be discovered.

So, one cold March morning, Joseph set out for Hokitika.

All along the river, now, right through to Kaniere and beyond, claims were being worked. At every moment, by every tent or shack that he passed, Joseph expected to discover Will, even found himself listening for the sound of his whistle above the noise of the picks and cradles, but there was no sign of him.

On the Brenner–McConnell claim, there now stood a neat hut made of slabs and stone and tussock thatch. Near this, a horse-whim had been constructed to pump water from the river into a box flume, so that all the land pegged by Brenner and McConnell could be washed without the need to cart water in buckets from the creek. This was successful mining, resourceful mining, mining with money behind it, and Hamish McConnell stood in front of his hut with his arms folded, wearing a clean shirt, smiling.

'How goes it at Kokatahi?' he called out to Joseph. 'Raised a colour yet, have ye?'

Joseph thought: The look of me, the scarecrow I've become must tell you the answer to that. He knew that his hair was wild and his skin grey and his collar bone was visible all along its length, like a clothes hanger.

'Not much to show . . .' he began, once again choking on saying the word 'nothing'. 'Not yet. But there's a good blue-clay bottom.'

'Good luck, then,' said McConnell, whose fine fortune had made him kinder than before.

'Sent money home to Scotland, have you?' asked Joseph.

'Aye,' said McConnell, laughing. 'Told my wife to find us a castle!'

As he trekked on towards the sea, Joseph thought that this was one more thing to torment him: he owned nothing but a mud house in the pathway of the winds, where his mother stared at the mended pieces of china and cried in the night; but Hamish McConnell would soon look out from stone battlements on to wide lawns and cedar trees. Servants would stand in a line to greet him when he returned. He would sleep in a high, four-poster bed.

Was McConnell a better man than Joseph Blackstone? Joseph didn't know. He saw only that misery could be endured in the midst of misery. But set adjacent to the good fortune of others, it became far, far harder to bear.

Joseph was glad to find himself once again on the beach at Hokitika, with its freight of driftwood and wrecked ships.

He stood and looked at the sea. He felt broken and brittle. But the bounding waves and the clean smell of the ocean reminded him that he wasn't trapped in the hell of Kokatahi. He could decide to leave. He still had a little money. He could admit failure in the Gold Rush and sail back to Lyttelton and try to pick up the threads of the farm. No doubt he wouldn't be the first to accept this kind of fate. And he thought that to be alone at his own creek, digging his own pond, would be very heaven compared to the rat-infested banks of the Hokitika.

But, when he remembered Harriet, a feeling of sickness spread right through him, right to the floor of his being.

He saw her on her vegetable plot, tall in her green garden – too tall for him, too clever, with too fierce a will – the wife he'd married to escape the snares of love. And he felt, as he watched the breakers come in, that the kindest thing he could do would be to stay away from her for ever. He'd send money – if he ever found gold. She'd married him in good faith and had a right to some share of everything he might still get, if his luck changed. But he couldn't go back to his life with her, that sham thing he'd tried so hard to live. Because he knew the truth of his feelings now. It was as simple as that. He understood what his true feelings had been and, more than this, he had also begun to believe that, in some way or other, he was going to have to honour them.

II

Six hours after they began their descent into the Hurunui Gorge, Pare saw them: two pākehā men, roped together, stumbling past the waterfall. They came on in silence, their faces moon-white in the dusk of the evening.

They were heading for the river, where Pare had crawled to bathe her feet, and she stayed very still because she knew they hadn't seen her, knew they could see nothing, after what they had been through, until they had lain down by the water and drunk.

She let them drink, let them sit up and slowly begin to unwind their rope. And it was then that she called out to them and they jerked their heads up and the younger man began screaming.

When they'd recovered from the shock of seeing Pare like a ghost at the river's edge, Flinty Fairford and John-boy Shannon slowly realised that they were in luck.

A Maori woman.

Everybody knew that the Maoris understood the bush, knew how the sun moved, knew where rivers could be crossed, knew which plants to eat, knew how to snare birds, soothe hornet stings and sandfly bites. It was said that the Maoris could start fires by rubbing the palms of their hands together, cure fever by laying their foreheads against yours. And so, once they realised that Pare was a Maori, the two exhausted and terrified men greeted her politely and after a while crossed the river to where she sat, bathing her feet.

It surprised Flinty and John-boy that she spoke English and was able to explain to them that she, too, had come over the Hurunui. She asked them tentatively for food and they gave her slices of bacon and made tea for her on a little fire. She ate hungrily and thanked them and said: 'You want gold? I can show you where there is gold. But I can't walk. You will have to carry me there.'

They looked at her, measuring her up. They saw that there was no spare flesh on her Maori bones. 'We'll carry you,' said John-boy. 'If you can show us gold, we'll carry you like a baby.'

They slept on Pare's ledge and heard the waterfall roaring in the dark. A canopy of stars hung above them and Flinty and

John-boy stared at the far-away light and felt triumphant that they had survived the descent of the gorge. Pare showed them how to cut ponga fronds to cover themselves against the cold and they slept like tired dogs.

They made a sling for Pare with her blanket and she rode on John-boy's back with her thin legs dangling down.

The way was dark and treacherous. The overhang of the cliff was so low in places that they had to crawl on hands and knees under it and all the while the river rushed onwards, and where they couldn't go round or under the overhang, they were obliged to cross the water. Before each weary crossing of the river, they stopped and John-boy set Pare down and she would kneel at the river's edge and stare at the water and try to gauge how deep or fast was the current and where the eddies swirled and what kind of shale or stones lay on the bottom.

Seventeen times Pare guided them over and back across the river, until at last the gorge began to open up and they reached the swampy flats of the Taramakau. John-boy set Pare down and untied the blanket and kissed her cheek. 'Good girl,' he said. 'Led us right to where we wanted to be! Eh, Flinty? Eh?'

'Not yet,' said Flinty. 'Not quite. No gold here, is there?'

'No gold here,' said Pare. 'Not here. When we reach Kumara, we go south. Two miles. Long ago there was a forest there. Now, it's underneath the earth. It sleeps and the gold sleeps in it.'

'In fifty-four years of this miserable life, I never heard,' declared Flinty crossly, 'of gold being found on the tops of trees!'

'The Maori know that gold is there,' replied Pare, 'in that sleeping forest.'

They were resting from the never-ending walk, sitting on soft tussock instead of rock for the first time in a long while. Flinty drank from his water bottle and spat on to the grass. He looked at Pare with his stoat's eyes.

'I don't believe you *know*,' he said. 'Do you? You've no

bloody idea where the gold is! You just wanted us to carry you through the gorge. You've tricked us fine and well.'

'Wait, Flinty,' said John-boy. 'Why's she come over the Hurunui herself, down that underwater hell, if she doesn't know where the gold is?'

'Ask *her* why. To be some gold-seeker's whore, I reckon. Get rich on a white man's work. Aren't I right, eh? Aren't I right?'

Pare didn't look at Flinty. His eyes frightened her. She looked at the river and all the grey boulders which tried to impede its desperate course.

'I must find greenstone,' said Pare quietly. 'I must find greenstone or my life will be lost.'

'What d'you mean?' asked Flinty. 'What the devil does that mean?'

'It means I promised greenstone to the spirits.'

'What's she saying, John-boy?'

'I'm not a mind-reader, Flinty. You fathom it.'

'If you're tricking us,' said Flinty, 'you'll be very sorry. Those bleeding feet of yours will be as nothing – '

'No tricks,' said Pare. 'I led you here ...'

'We could have got here ourselves! We only had to follow the river. The trekking down was the hard bit. We could have done all the rest without you.'

Pare felt cold. *Te riri pākehā: the white man's anger.* She'd seen it in Toby Orchard. It had damaged her life. She knew that in the North Island a land-war between Maori and pākehā was still raging. She knew there was no limit to the things this anger could do. She knew that she might not be able to survive it.

She forced herself neither to be afraid nor to sound as though she was afraid. To calm herself, she thought of the pā and the stones she'd laid out in a waiting circle.

She spoke slowly, looking again at John-boy, at his soft mouth, not at Flinty. 'I led you here because the gold is here,' she said. 'The Maori know that there is gold in the buried forest.'

'If they know there's gold, then they'll *be* there, won't they? There'll be a fine fat quantity of natives digging it up!'

'No,' said Pare. 'The Maori do not love gold. Greenstone is our treasure.'

III

Joseph lingered in Hokitika.

He paid for a hot bath and a small back room at the hotel, which he was lucky to get, said the owner, because a crowd of new chums was expected to arrive on the *Wallabi* any day.

Joseph had promised himself he would buy a woman for a few hours – any woman. But now the feeling of needing to be with a woman went away and he begrudged spending precious money on something he didn't really want.

He walked out from the hotel, along past the stores and shanties that he remembered, past the shop where he'd bought Will Sefton his fishing rod, past the banks and the grocery stores, in search of something, but not knowing what. He thought, after a little while, that he longed to hear music, some melodious sound, because all that had filled his head in the last weeks had been discordant and ugly.

There was no music on the Hokitika wharves, only the distant music of the sea, and so Joseph stopped and looked at this once more and noticed, after a moment or two of watching, a dark speck on the wide, grey water. He stared at it. It was the *Wallabi* coming in, slowly nearing the Hokitika Bar. And Joseph found himself wondering how his fortunes might have been altered if he'd delayed his journey, if he was even now among these gold-seekers, on *this* SS *Wallabi* which was and was not the *Wallabi* where he'd met Will Sefton and seen the Chinese men cooking rice on a lamp.

Life is a war that never ends between you and the intrinsic arbitrariness of things . . .

Joseph returned to the beach, to watch the crossing of the bar. The breakers were rougher than when his ship had crossed, but rough seas didn't necessarily mean that the bar was high. The bar moved and drifted all the time. The bar was the random and the unknown epitomised.

It was an overcast April day and the visibility wasn't good, but Joseph shaded his eyes and tried to see the people on the *Wallabi*, whom he knew would be clustered on deck, trying to make out what kind of a place Hokitika was, longing for the moment when land was reached but faced now with this new worry about the bar. He felt that he could imagine exactly what they were feeling. To be so near the end of their journey, to have endured the West Coast water, and yet cut off from the shore by some treacherous, invisible thing ... how could destiny be as capricious as this?

He could just make them out now: huddled figures crowding the ship's rails. And a new feeling of excitement that he hadn't experienced in a long while took hold of him, and it didn't take him long to understand what had brought it there: *he was hoping to see the* Wallabi *go down*. He wanted to witness a catastrophe of which he was not a part, wanted to see other men's fortunes brought to nothing, wanted to hear their anguish as they tried to swim to the beach – *his* beach, the beach where he'd cried for his lost life – in the churning, icy sea.

His heart beat hard against his chest, as though there were hardly any flesh left on his ribs to protect it. His mouth was dry. He saw the *Wallabi* turn, as though to leave, then come round for a different approach, so he knew from this that the bar was high, that the captain had seen its tentacles under the water, felt them with his lead-line. Joseph fancied he could hear a child crying.

Was it this that he'd been searching for along the Hokitika wharves? A glimpse of a fate worse than his own? Some sign from God that he, Joseph Blackstone, wasn't alone ordained to suffer and to lose?

He imagined how he would play his part in trying to rescue the men on the *Wallabi*. He thought that he would gladly help to save the few, in the sure knowledge that many would not be saved. And then, perhaps, after this, when he'd feasted his eyes and his mind on this, he'd be able to go back to Kokatahi, to the ruined land and the rats and the eight barren shafts slowly filling with rain? After he'd had proof that he hadn't been uniquely singled out for affliction. Once he'd seen this and stored the memory of it inside him like hard currency, then maybe he'd be able to go on with his search for gold?

Joseph wasn't alone on the beach. Silently, it seemed, all the inhabitants of Hokitika had come out to watch the *Wallabi* try to cross the bar. Small boats were being readied to go out to the ship, if it went aground. Ropes and life-buoys were being loaded aboard. Joseph turned and saw two men come out of the Bank of New Zealand, the place where he longed to go with his fistfuls of the colour, to see it weighed and measured and exchanged for more money than he'd ever possessed.

The men from the bank, dressed more smartly than everyone else, now stood watching, too, but a little apart from the rest, with their arms folded in exactly the way that the arms of Hamish McConnell had been folded across his brand-new shirt.

Black smoke streamed from the *Wallabi*'s funnel as it came in a second time, pursuing a more southerly course. Joseph held his breath, waiting for the thrilling moment when the keel of the steamer would strike the sand.

But the passengers were disembarking now.

There had been no disaster. No deaths.

And sure enough, Joseph experienced a kind of disappointment, a dull return to familiar boredom and pessimism, as he watched the new arrivals come off the ship. More than ever, he felt that everything was designed to cheat him of all that he wanted.

He eyed the men as they tottered, unsteadily, on to the quayside. Some carried with them all the cumbersome paraphernalia of gold-digging; some carried almost nothing. All looked pale in the cold light.

The hotel owner was calling out: 'Bed and board for a few pennies! Come and rest your bones at the hotel! Best accommodation in Hokitika!'

The bank employees had disappeared back inside the bank. The warden was handing reminders, printed on yellow paper, that Miner's Rights cost thirty shillings and that gold-mining without a licence was a crime punishable by fines.

Joseph was about to turn away, to return to his room before

some new chum stumbled into it and laid his flea-bitten body on the bed, when he heard somebody call his name.

He looked about him. The voice was high and light and, just for a moment, he thought that it could belong to Will Sefton.

Then Joseph saw the person he'd hoped never to go near any more: he saw his wife.

She was coming down the gangplank of the *Wallabi*, with her head wrapped in a shawl. She was moving towards him.

Instinctively, Joseph tried to back away, but there was no room to back away in the press of the crowd. So she came on, nearer and nearer to him, Harriet Blackstone, tall and full of purpose as she always was, leading her dog, Lady, and the dog saw him too and began whining as the memory of him – of Joseph Blackstone, who was master of nothing, not even this animal – traced a flickering pathway through its brain.

Harriet's face was white and bleak and unsmiling, her eyes large and tired. Joseph saw that her cloak was dirty.

He didn't move. He saw the seconds pass. He saw the inevitability of her arrival at his side and braced himself against her touch.

Now, the dog jumped up against his legs. Harriet tugged it away and bent forward to embrace him.

'Joseph,' she said.

He couldn't speak, couldn't say her name, couldn't even think about anything except that he had planned never to return to her and now – as though she'd read his mind – she'd boarded the ship and stood beside him on the grey planks of the Hokitika wharf.

She kissed his cheek. He remembered the smell of her, which had a tang to it, as of salts or sherbet. He knew that, somehow, he still smelled of Kokatahi, despite the bath he'd had, he still smelled of the blue clay and the soiled bedding of the tent.

She moved a little away from him and they were both elbowed this way and that by the crowd and almost lost their footing.

Then Harriet reached out and put her hand on his face and he endured the hand because he saw something serious and pleading in her eyes.

'Your mother died,' she said. 'Poor Lilian is dead.'

Distance

I

Chen Pao Yi examined the lump of gold he'd found in his onion bed. He examined it in sunlight and in the darkness.

It was about the length of his thumb and a little wider. Its weight was remarkable. He understood from what he'd learned in Otago that gold found near the surface of the soil often acted like a sample of merchandise, indicating the riches that lay underneath it. Pao Yi knew that the true gold-digger would immediately abandon the vegetable plot to begin sinking shafts. He recognised that, for many men, the growing of carrots and potatoes would now appear as a pathetic endeavour.

Pao Yi pondered this. He thought that, later on, the pathetic-ness of vegetable-growing might suddenly reveal itself to him, but that it hadn't done so yet. To tear out all the living and rooted things he'd planted was, at the moment, impossible for him. And he was wise enough to understand something else: the moment word got out that 'Scurvy Jenny' had struck gold on his market garden, the hordes from Kaniere and Kokatahi would arrive. They would try to squeeze him off his land.

In days, he would have destroyed his own world.

Pao Yi asked himself what that world consisted of and why he was there.

He knew that at the end of all his endeavours in New Zealand lay the journey back to Heron Lake. He had crossed the ocean only in order to return. Paak Mei and Paak Shui were waiting for him, waiting with their hands outstretched. But, just as he wasn't yet prepared to abandon his market garden for the sake of gold, so he wasn't yet prepared to abandon his solitude for the sake of Paak Mei and Paak Shui. He could picture them in their world, picture them fondly in that land around the lake where the water-buffalo moved so slowly, yoked to the plough, that from a distance they seemed hardly to move at all. He could hear the green frogs gurgling and calling from the rice paddies under a sea-grey wash of sky. He could see the hills behind the rice fields, rich with tombs. He could smell the tallow trees. He could see the men of the village, his old friends, treading the bamboo water-wheels, in times of drought, like dancers, hear the click-click of the one-wheeled carts on the rough cobbled streets. And the faces of Paak Mei and Paak Shui, waiting at the doorway to his house, were so vivid to him that he sometimes thought he could see them blinking.

He could even hear his own voice offering 'freshwater crabs, freshwater crabs' from the rickety quayside in the sharp air of evening. But it often seemed to him that the villagers, too, heard his voice and came scurrying out in their boots or in their cloth shoes to buy the crabs. 'Pao Yi, Pao Yi,' they babbled. 'Brother of Righteousness . . . why did you stay away so long?' And then he walked away, always walked away. It surprised him that he did this, but he always did it. He left the bucket where it was, told the villagers curtly to help themselves to the crabs, and walked away up Long Hill, past the tomb containing the incompletely reassembled bodies of Chen Lin and Chen Fen Ming, towards the highest slopes where the dragon spruce grew so thickly and where Pao Yi could lose himself in the blessed darkness under the trees.

He hid his lump of gold in the cave.

Forgoing the cave as a place to smoke and sleep, he took some time to haul stones and earth to its low entrance and arrange them there in such a way that the presence of a cave no longer revealed itself. Sticks and moss and a single fern pushed in amongst the stones completed the deception. But Pao Yi knew that – if he needed to reach his gold – the false wall would collapse with a mere few blows from his pick and he was disposed to be pleased with his own ingenuity. Yet there was something about the cave as a hiding-place which troubled him.

He thought it too conventional. He told himself that a man entering a cave *expects to find something*. He decided it would therefore be far better to hide the nugget in a place where nobody expected to find anything. But Pao Yi couldn't see exactly where such a place might be. He was living in a land where men expected to discover gold in every meagre handful of earth; indeed, he felt that expectation covered the entire landscape with a kind of invisible blight.

It then came to him that he should replace the gold exactly where he'd found it – under the baby onion. For, surely, when a man looks at an onion bed, all that he expects to find underneath the earth are the bulbs of the onions? The idea that there is something beneath what is beneath would very rarely occur to him.

Pao Yi dismantled the cunningly made wall at the cave entrance, climbed over the fallen stones and went into the cave. The sweetness of its darkness always gladdened him. He picked up the golden nugget and returned to the vegetable garden. A pigeon was feasting on a worm and flew away with the thing half eaten and had to land again almost immediately to swallow it down, and this made Pao Yi smile.

He walked slowly to the exact place, under the seventeenth baby onion, where he'd found the gold. The onion appeared to have done nothing since he'd planted it, but when he lifted it, he could feel the minute hairy roots clutch at the earth and Pao Yi was reminded that the inclination of almost every living thing is to cling on, to remain where it is, but that his own inclination – his own nature – suspended him always in a kind of no man's land between remaining and leaving.

With his blackened fingers, he gouged a well in the soil, laid the nugget in, covered it with more soil, then made a well in this for the onion.

He shored up the onion. Then, he fetched his hoe and swept away every trace of his own footprints in the earth.

He looked at all of this and congratulated himself for listening to his own anxieties. Now, he felt that his gold was safe. But Pao Yi also knew that his task wasn't finished and that, by perverse logic, he had to block up the entrance to the cave all over again. Though he knew that the cave now contained nothing, he felt a compulsion to wall up that nothingness. He knew that he was behaving as though the cave contained something after all, something which he hadn't yet seen. Half-way through his task of walling it up again, Pao Yi was almost tempted to take down the stones for a second time in order to go and look inside for the unseen thing. But he told himself that this was truly childish. He had to stop changing his mind, or else his tasks would never end.

He continued to rebuild the cave entrance and finished this within an hour or so. Nevertheless, almost a whole day had passed while Pao Yi went to and fro, to and fro like a water-buffalo, between the onion bed and the cave. Now, the sky was a deep violet blue and the vegetables were shadows in the ground. But he felt at last that everything was almost as it should be.

He expected to sleep very well. But his sleep was fitful and crowded with dreams.

He kept seeing Chen Lin and Chen Fen Ming, walking around with limbs missing from their bodies. Chen Fen Ming had only one eye, and this one eye flamed with a terrifying, intense anger, cursing her living son.

Pao Yi woke and lay in the dark of his hut. He knew how much he missed his parents. Filial duty had always played such a large part in his life, submitting to his father's bad temper, trying to become skilled as his father had been skilled as a fisherman on Heron Lake and to cast the nets in precisely the same way as Chen Lin; devising pleasant small surprises for his mother, letting her eat first, even when he was faint from hunger, kneeling beside her to take his turn at brushing her long hair and massaging her wounded feet.

He had tried in each and every thing to obey Chen Lin and Chen Fen Ming. Now, there was no one to obey, nobody to be filial to. And Pao Yi knew that the appointed order of things, with which he had been comfortable, was broken. He felt that a kind of chaos was lying in wait for him somewhere and he didn't know what he could do to keep it at bay.

He tried picturing Paak Mei, as she shuffled round his small house in her beaded slippers, but he found that this shuffle of

Paak Mei's, to which he'd thought himself perfectly attached, irritated him. Perhaps it had always irritated him and he had just never admitted this, or never noticed this before? He wished his wife could walk elegantly. He wished she could leap and run like a child. The sound of her shuffling was like the snicker of a broom, endlessly pushing little eddies of dust towards some ever-retreating dust-pan. It was ridiculous.

When Pao Yi slept again, he dreamed of dancers. They wore red silk skirts and satin shoes and they moved with a fluid and entrancing grace. Their feet were curved, with a high instep, but not broken. They could balance on the tops of their toes. They could leap and fly. And the surface on which they danced was made of gold and a big golden light shone upwards into their faces.

Pao Yi wanted to prolong this dream, but it evaporated with the sound of the wind rattling the makeshift door to the hut, and he lay there, marvelling at the scarlet dancers and waiting for the morning.

II

Joseph's room at the Hokitika hotel was small and contained one narrow bed. This bed, after the hard ground of Kokatahi, had felt, to Joseph, like the most comfortable place in the world, and when he understood that he was going to have to play the chivalrous husband and give it up to Harriet, he felt sick at heart.

He managed to procure a thin straw mattress for himself and laid this on the floor by the bed, but he felt stupid lying there, so much lower than the bed; felt like an infant, consigned to a lowly position, and when he looked up at Harriet, sleeping soundly, almost carelessly, in the place that was rightfully his, he hated her. The dog Lady began the night under the bed, but soon jumped up on to it and went to sleep lying contentedly across Harriet's feet. And this exacerbated Joseph's fury. Now, of the three breathing creatures in the tiny room, only he could feel the hard planks of the floor, breathe the dust that had been allowed to accumulate on the skirting . . .

I'm the cur kicked into a snivelling corner.

Joseph felt tears come to his eyes. He thought that he'd hardly ever cried before coming to New Zealand, but that now he wanted to weep all the time. The man who had built the Cob House – and had not minded where he laid his head and had not minded the way the men teased and mocked him as a 'cockatoo' – this man was gone, just as the Cob House was gone and Lilian was gone, and the creature who had replaced him was going mad with suffering.

He let his tears fall. Why should they not fall? Who saw them? Who cared whether he wept or not? His mother might have cared, but she was in her grave at Rangiora, in a cheap coffin made of totara pine, in a graveyard no one would visit . . .

Harriet had described Lilian's funeral. In Parton Magna, perhaps most of the village and half of Parton Parva would have turned out for the wife of the livestock auctioneer, but at Rangiora, there was hardly any village to turn out and no one had known who Lilian Blackstone was or seen the trouble she'd taken over broken china or remembered her love of singing or witnessed the neatness of her darning. The only mourner had been Harriet. Joseph could imagine his wife, 'carrying herself well' even here, and mouthing a few prayers, then watching silently as Lilian's body was put into a grave like a horizontal mine-shaft, a grave of blue clay.

'I didn't know what to give her, what to lay in the coffin with her,' Harriet had told him, 'because I really had no idea what object she loved the best. I thought about one of her pieces of Staffordshire, but in the end, I chose the pastel drawing of you as a child, wearing your little white dress. I think she would have wanted this with her. Was I right?'

Joseph had said nothing. He felt more than ever glad to have no child to humiliate in lace frills and white petticoats. He wished there had been a picture of him as a grown man, wearing a smart coat and a silk necktie.

'Was I right, Joseph?' asked Harriet again.

'I don't know, Harriet,' he said. 'Who can ever know?'

But he could imagine Lilian's thin hands folded neatly over the picture.

Indeed, he could imagine his mother dead very clearly and it broke his heart to think that now, whatever he did or however he succeeded, she would never be there to witness it, but always and forever remain dead in her coffin, her fingers decaying to bone as they lay on the ridiculous picture of him, done before his life was barely begun.

And there was one other thing which began to torment him.

He hoped and prayed that Lilian's coffin had had some lining or other, something to hold his mother in its grip, because she had been a person who had always inhabited her space very meticulously, keeping her knees side by side and her elbows in and her shawl pulled tight, and he couldn't bear to think of Lilian May Blackstone sliding around inside a wooden box: a state of affairs she would have detested.

Joseph wanted to ask Harriet whether the coffin had had a lining, but he was too afraid that her answer would be no. Because what he saw, when he imagined the small church at Rangiora, made of planking painted green and topped with a warped little bell-house, was a fearful kind of makeshift frailty. He saw things gaping, nailed together, splitting and buckling in the heat and cold; everything thin and shoddy and not built to last. He knew, therefore, that the chances of there being a coffin lining for Lilian were remote and so – lying on his mattress while Harriet and the dog slept comfortably on the bed – Joseph told himself that he was weeping for this, for the absence of a coffin lining for his dead mother, and that this was a perfectly legitimate reason for a man to cry.

The sea journey on the *Wallabi* had been long and cold and rough. Harriet was so tired by the time she reached Joseph's room in the Hokitika hotel that she felt sleep overcome her almost before she'd thought about sleep. She tried, then, to stay awake for at least a little while, to reflect on what she knew she should be reflecting – on the change in Joseph's appearance. He'd always been thin, but now he looked like . . . what did he look like? A scarecrow? A castaway? A convict? There was also, Harriet decided, as sleep kept creeping near her, stretching her thoughts into meaningless, weightless threads, something of a picture-book Jesus about him: his hair long and wild, his beard thick and curly, his suffering eyes too large for his face . . .

Fighting sleep, she asked herself a hard, sensible, well-made question: was this what gold-mining did to a man? When she reached the goldfields, would she see a hundred men looking as Joseph looked? Or had something else happened to him in the time that he'd been away? Harriet turned her head and looked down at him where he lay on his mattress. Joseph Blackstone. She hadn't yet admitted to him that she knew the secret of the gold at the creek and now she wondered whether she would ever admit it. For she felt that this might be just one among a thousand things that he'd concealed from her, felt as though secrets might have accumulated in him so thickly that they could never be unravelled. What purpose then, would any confrontation serve?

Harriet sailed into a sea of sleep so black and wide it had no features and no shape and was enlivened by no dreams. When Lady jumped up on to the bed, she didn't stir. People shouted in the corridors, banged doors, coughed, laughed and swore, but Harriet knew nothing of all this. And the sound of Joseph's crying? Perhaps, once or twice, she was woken by this, but never for quite long enough to hear it.

In the morning, as they ate porridge and eggs together, surrounded by the noisy new chums who had been aboard the *Wallabi*, Joseph said: 'I thought all night about what we should do now. I shall renew my licence and go back to Kokatahi, for two months at least, because I can't give up yet. But I won't take you with me. There are no women on the gold-diggings. And winter's almost here. You will have to return to Christchurch.'

Harriet said nothing.

Joseph wiped grey flecks of porridge from his beard. He longed to tell Harriet to go to Toby Orchard and persuade him to buy all the land he and Harriet had bought and all that remained of the Cob House and the barn and the vegetable plot. He wanted to announce that everything between them was at an end, that he was relieved the Cob House had been blown away in the storms, that nature had confirmed what he already knew to be true: the farming experiment in New Zealand had failed.

But because he couldn't see what lay beyond this 'end', he knew that it wasn't yet possible to pronounce the word *end*. Once he'd found gold, once he had money, then he would be able to make some plan which was fair to them both, a plan which was pragmatic and rational and which took account, somehow, of the hopes they'd both had at the beginning. But until this day came, when he had the wherewithal to devise a future, all he could do was to ask Harriet to let him be, to live some kind of quiet, inexpensive life far away from him, so that he wouldn't have to worry about her or even to think about her at all.

'I suggest,' he said, 'that you stay with the Orchards. I know that Dorothy is very fond of you ...'

'Yes,' said Harriet, 'and I am very fond of her. But I can't stay indefinitely with the Orchards, Joseph. I can't trespass upon them. And anyway, having come all this long way by sea, I want to see the goldfields.'

'No,' said Joseph. 'No. The goldfields are no place for you.'

'Why? Because they're rough? Because gold-mining is ugly?'

'It's no world for the likes of you.'

'The likes of me? I remember that you said something of that sort when you went away to build the Cob House. I was left behind in Christchurch.'

'For the sake of Lilian.'

'Very well. But Lilian is no longer here, is she?'

'You wouldn't be happy at Kokatahi, Harriet.'

'Why do you always mention happiness? As though that were the only thing to strive for?'

She seemed tall, even sitting on the hard chair, eating her breakfast. Joseph marvelled that he could ever have thought he could endure this: a woman who was as tall as he. When he'd taken Rebecca in his arms, her head had arrived approximately at his shoulder and he had been able to place his chin on her curls and smell the comfrey oil she used to wash her hair.

He wanted to say that he mentioned happiness because he

and it were strangers, just as he and Harriet were strangers now. And he was tired of living among strangers! So tired of it that he felt himself begin to stoop and lean down towards the earth like an old man. He thought of Hamish McConnell with his Scottish castle. He thought of Will Sefton getting rich on Brenner–McConnell gold. He felt a scream rising in his throat. He saw the three tigers pacing round the circus ring . . .

'The thought of taking me to Kokatahi wearies you,' said Harriet. 'I can see that it might. But I shall not stay long, Joseph. I've promised Edwin Orchard to search for a friend of his who is hereabouts somewhere. And when I find her, then I may get back on the steamer and sail away and she will come with me. But until then, I shall stay with you and help you on your claim. If I can dig a garden, I can probably dig for gold.'

Joseph put his face into his hands and looked at Harriet over the top of them. He saw that he couldn't order this woman he had married back on to the *Wallabi*. She was quite alone except for her dog, with no house to return to and all her possessions in a warehouse and every day now the winter was creeping on. By looking closely at her, he tried to ascertain what she expected from him. Did she, too, feel, as he hoped she did, that they could no longer touch, no longer admit to being people who had once touched?

He couldn't bear to hold his gaze on her for long. She looked too plain in the cold morning light, her hair too short, her nose too long, her skin too weathered by her days out on the farm and by the salt sea winds.

He wondered if he'd ever found her beautiful, but couldn't remember whether he had or not.

Joseph cleared his throat. 'If you are to come with me,' he said, in his auctioneer's formal voice, 'then you will need your own tent. Mine is too small for us both. We shall buy that and some better cooking pots and –'

'I am to cook for you? Is this all?'

'Cooking would be of great help. I've been half starved . . . Perhaps my luck would change if I were stronger . . . ?'

He wondered whether he should tell her about the bush rats. Perhaps he had only to describe the way the rats were always and ever crawling over the claim now and how they sometimes found their way inside the tent and how they could bite and the way they squealed and mated and burrowed and were shot for food and their skins thrown into the river; perhaps he only had to talk about them and Harriet would decide, after all, not to come anywhere near Kokatahi?

'I don't mind cooking,' said Harriet. 'But won't you let me look for gold, as well?'

'There *is* no gold!' Joseph blurted out so loudly that some of the new arrivals eating their porridge turned to look at him and there was a sudden shocked silence near their table.

'He only means,' said Harriet, turning politely towards the men, 'that there is no gold on his claim yet. I expect this is what Mr McConnell said the day before he made his marvellous find.'

So much is left unsaid, Harriet thought again, as she and Joseph set out to make their purchases in Hokitika. The distance between Joseph and me has become unbridgeable . . .

But now, she found at last that she truly had no urge to bridge it, that her curiosity about Joseph was dead. For it seemed to her that to know everything about another was very hell, that marriage was a wretched state if this was what it entailed. What human soul, bared to nakedness, does not look hideous – her own included? What fool society decreed that man-and-wife (so separate and different in their experience of the world and in their very natures) should be as one?

Let be. This had been poor Roderick Blackstone's lament, but he had been right to keep repeating it. Harriet had been told the story of the crumpled anti-macassars and now it appeared to her like a scene in a tragedy.

She was glad to buy her own tent. And it occurred to her that, with a tent, and with the gun Joseph had given her, and with Lady by her side and with some rudimentary supplies, she would be able to go where she liked. She decided, as she paid for the tent and a scarlet blanket which seemed both soft and warm, that she would stay only a brief time at Kokatahi. Then, she would leave Joseph. She would embark on the quest with which Edwin Orchard had entrusted her: she would go in search of Pare. And she knew that this search would take her into the mountains, going in a different direction towards the shadowy valley from which she had once turned back.

PART THREE

Towards the Fall

I

She was a curiosity: a woman at Kokatahi – just as she'd been a curiosity on the dray road to the Hurunui.

All the way up from Kaniere, diggers stared at Harriet as she passed. Those who knew Joseph's solitary ways made two assumptions, both of them mistaken. They thought he'd been morose because he'd missed her – this tall, almost beautiful wife of his, with her defiant look and her cropped hair; and they thought that he believed his luck would change now that she was by his side.

But when they watched Harriet set up her separate tent some distance from his, they returned to sniggering and whispering about him. They called him an 'odd eel', a 'singular bush rat'. Some had heard rumours of the boy who had been with him for a while. 'Now,' they joked, 'he's got no chicken and no fish neither!'

Harriet pegged down her tent at the very edge of Joseph's claim, furthest from the river, with her back to the scrub-line, where a narrow mat of grass was still green. But the stench of wash-dirt and human waste hung over the whole site, as though the earth had erupted from beneath, and spewed out all the rotten matter which lay around.

The tent was surrounded on two sides by huts and hovels and Harriet soon found herself staring, for long stretches of time, at the varied architecture of these constructions. Some were squared off and ship-shape, with slabs cut to length and doors or windows made of wire, hung with sacking. Others looked as if they'd been made by children or by beavers: low structures of indeterminate shape, roofed with thin branches of beech from which the wind began to tear the leaves away.

Harriet had seen face to face what the weather had done to the Cob House. She thought now that perhaps nothing at Kokatahi would survive the winter. One gale blowing down from the peaks, one snow-fall like that which had killed Beauty, one week of drenching rain to swell the river to a fresh: this seemed to her to be all that it would take to level the Kokatahi diggings.

Wrapped in her red blanket, lying on the hard ground, Harriet imagined dramatic endings to the Kokatahi gold-mine. She did this to lull herself to sleep above the noise of the men and the flicker of their night-time fires. She did it because, for all its ceaseless activity, she liked to think of this place as insubstantial as a sand-castle.

She decided that the wind would arrive first. It would come sweeping down the dark valley of the Styx and begin snatching at the tents and hovels as it had snatched at the roof of the Cob House and at the dust of its walls. Tents would bound away from their pegs, inflate, perhaps, for a moment like parasols torn from the gloved hands of women on a windy racecourse, then fall back to earth as rags of calico, chivvied into moving shapes, borne along to the river, where they would slowly sink. And against this wind, the fragile windlasses would have no resistance. They would simply topple over, subside into the shafts, the buckets clanking against shingle, then gone.

After the wind, the rain would begin to fall and bubble in the mounds of dirt, as in a hot spring. And all the while, in the mountains, the springs would be filling and filling, one day to burst out from the rock face as waterfalls. And then the snow would arrive. Harriet could remember the stickiness of the New Zealand snow, the fatness of its flakes, the way it accumulated so fast, so silently, the way it drifted and piled up and kept falling and filling the sky. Here, it would block the valley. It would rise up as cliffs at the river's edge, rise much higher than a man, higher than all the men, long gone, that fat snow .. It would be bent on the obliteration of all that had been tried here. The weight of it would level the earth. It would freeze to a seamless, sparkling crust.

When daybreak arrived, Harriet washed herself inside her tent and folded her red blanket and put on her clothes, which had begun to take on the smell of Kokatahi. She'd dug herself a privy hole among the manuka. Yellow flies, obscenely bright, clustered on the insubstantial evacuations her body produced. Bush rats squeaked among the manuka stems but Harriet didn't mind being stared at by the rats; it was the men's stare she dreaded, the stare which said: 'You're one of us now, you poor bitch, you digger's wife, you sorry helpless bit of flesh.' She tried to fan out her skirt as she crouched down, not merely to hide herself from the men, but to hide herself from herself. She felt that she'd come to a place where her body had begun to die.

She lit a fire in the mornings and made tea and she and Joseph crouched by the fire, eating bacon or salted fish, and Harriet saw Joseph's eye begin to wander over the piles of pay-dirt on his claim and on those adjacent to it, in case the colour had been there all along and somehow escaped his notice. He admitted to her that he had a dream of going blind. In this dream, he tried to read the earth with his hands, but all around him he could hear the laughter of the men. 'A blind gold-miner! Now, there's a peach of a joke!'

Washing became Harriet's chief task. This was what Joseph wanted her to do. Nothing else, really, as though he didn't trust her to search for gold: he just wanted her to make things clean again.

So she carted Joseph's stinking clothes and foul bedding up-river, out of sight of the diggings, and soaped and slapped them on a wide white stone and rinsed them in the icy water and pegged them to the trees. She asked no questions about the state of these things, not even to herself. She saw what she saw. She turned her face to the mountains or to the sky.

Harriet had questioned some of the Kokatahi diggers about Pare, but none of them had seen a Maori woman. They cackled at the idea of a Maori 'invading our diggings'. They told Harriet there had been Maoris at Greenstone Creek and one or two had been seen at the beach-workings, 'but not at Kaniere, Missus, and not here, no fear'.

But, while doing her washing, Harriet had thought she heard the sound of a waterfall. It was a steady, reverberating noise, as though the rock itself were roaring. And so, with the washing pegged and flapping in the breeze, and her hands raw and red from the river water, Harriet began to walk towards the sound.

The way was encumbered by rocks and boulders. The river had taken a tortuous course around everything that had fallen across its path.

After walking for thirty or forty minutes, Harriet realised that she could no longer hear the noise of the goldfield. She decided to mark the exact spot at which Kokatahi 'disappeared' into the air. And so she retraced her steps and when she found the place, she laid a stick across the path, to mark the line between the goldfield and herself. And she thought how everything in the world had its boundary and was finite, and her awareness of this cheered her.

She walked faster as the banks of the river began to stretch out again into shingle beach where a few long-legged birds pecked and sauntered. An hour or more passed. She grew thirsty and knelt to scoop up water in her hands and then stayed still, listening to the roar of the fall and to the wind.

It was at this moment that the sun came out and Harriet looked up and saw Chen Pao Yi's vegetable garden. She had to blink, to shield her eyes against the sun – which had lit up the garden on the other side of the river like a bright lamp lighting a darkened stage. She stared at the garden. She found it a model of what she'd being trying to achieve on the Okuku flats. The variety in it, the neatness of its planting, the dark soil patiently worked ... here, when her own garden had long ago been abandoned, was the paragon of what it should have been.

She noticed Pao Yi's hut, built of stone, tucked in against the rock face to protect it, neatly thatched with fern. She saw a fishing net, slung out between two trees in the shallow part of the river.

Though Harriet had drunk a good cupful of water, she was

aware of a residue of thirst, but it wasn't water that she wanted; her thirst was for some fresh green thing from this garden.

She took off her boots and began to cross the river. The current was fast and cold and tugged at her skirts and she knew that if she fell, she might be swept away, swept back down to Kokatahi to join the rats and the rubbish as they rushed on towards Kaniere.

She bent down, to pull her skirts out of the water and discovered a rope running along the shingle of the river-bed. When she lifted the rope, she saw that it was attached to a post at the edge of the garden. To arrive safely on the other side, all Harriet had to do was hold on to the rope.

She dried her feet on the grass and put on her boots. She stood where she was and called out, but nobody appeared. She saw a hoe with a red handle sticking into the earth of the onion bed. She noticed that the garden was divided up by narrow grass paths and that the edges of these paths were neat.

Along the western edge of the plot, the gardener had planted a small plum tree and, though the fruit was gone and the leaves sparse, there was a soft, lingering scent to this tree and Harriet sat down beside it. She pulled a carrot from the earth, cleaned it on her damp skirt, and ate it – both the body of the carrot and its green tops. The taste of it was as sweet as anything she'd ever eaten and Harriet thought that she must have been starved of sweetness for a long time because what she wanted to do now was to stay here by this plum tree, munching her way along the carrot bed.

She plucked and cleaned and ate a second carrot and then she waited. She was waiting for the gardener to return so that she could apologise to him for stealing his vegetables, but she was also waiting because she didn't want to move. The noise of the waterfall was still quite loud, but Harriet had put it from her mind because all her mind was concentrated here. She thought that this garden was one of the most strangely beautiful places she'd ever seen.

Still nobody came. The sun climbed higher and was warm and Harriet's skirts began to dry. She wanted to go into the hut, to find out who was responsible for all these thriving plants and for the hut itself, which seemed well made and strong, as though, when the winter winds came or when the fresh arrived, it alone – among all the temporary shelters that had been begun along this river – might remain standing.

But she didn't want to act like a trespasser or a spy. She ate one more carrot and then she laid her head down on the narrow grass path.

When she woke, the light had tilted away behind the mountains and the air was cold.

Harriet looked around her, but nothing had moved or changed. She got up and brushed her skirts and slowly walked to the river, where she quickly found the submerged rope and used this to guide herself safely to the opposite bank. The thought of returning to the Kokatahi camp made her feel suddenly sick, so she sat down on the shingle bank, waiting for this sickness to pass. She rested her hands on her knees and kept her head lowered. She stared at the grey and amber colours of the shingle. She told herself that she'd come back here again the next day and resume her search for Pare and the waterfall.

It was then that Harriet saw the gold.

The gold was a coarse dust in among the grey and amber stones. It shone in the blue, approaching dusk.

II

While Harriet was gone, Will Sefton returned to Joseph's claim.

'Mister Blackstone,' Will said with a mocking smile, 'I hear your wife couldn't live without you. I hear she missed you so much, she followed you all the way to this graveyard!'

Joseph let go of his windlass handle and looked at Will. The boy wore a new jerkin. His curls looked clean and soft. He stood with his legs apart and his hands in the pockets of his moleskins.

'What are you doing here?' Joseph asked.

Will took out his penny whistle from one of his pockets and caressed it softly, making the familiar small shrill sound.

'Go away, Will,' said Joseph, turning his back on the boy, to resume winding the windlass.

The whistling stopped. 'I'm going,' said Will. 'A few more weeks and you'll never hear my whistle no more on the Kokatahi. Going to Scotland, I am, with Mr McConnell. Dress me in a kilt, so he will. A fine *kiltie*. And nothing beneath, and all that cool breeze between my legs. What d'you say to that, Mister Blackstone?'

Joseph half turned. The sound of Will's voice, the least prepossessing thing about the boy, summoned back a familiar feeling both of longing and of wretchedness.

'It's all one to me where you go,' replied Joseph.

'Not true, though, is it, Mister Blackstone?' whispered Will, moving a step nearer to Joseph. 'For if I'm gone, then you can't go where you long to go, can you, for don't tell me your wife lets you –'

'Leave me alone!' said Joseph. 'Go to Scotland. Go wherever you like, Will, with whoever you like. But leave me in peace.'

'Aye, I will. Isn't that what they say there? *Aye*? I'll leave you in peace, Mister Blackstone, soon enough. But I thought, before I leave, I could be introduced to your wife and tell her what "services" I performed for you in her absence. Then, everything would be straight and true, eh? I don't fancy leaving till everything be straight and true.'

Joseph kicked out at a slab of pine, sent it scudding over the mud towards Will, but the boy stepped daintily aside.

'If you think,' said Joseph, 'that blackmail can work with me, you've overlooked one thing, Will Sefton. I have no gold. Not an ounce. Not a speck. Nothing. Look all around, if you don't believe me.'

'I believe you all right. I can see it in your face. No colour. But you still have money, Mister Blackstone. You still buy your stores at Hokitika and your new Miner's Right. I know you do, for I saw you there. And you never paid me a cent for all that I did. Never a cent. And I told Mr McConnell, "I'm angry with Mister Blackstone. I'm angry with a man who promises to pay and never keeps his promise." And Mr McConnell agrees with me. He says to me: "You go and get your dues, Will, for you're the sweetest little prick-sucker in the southern hemisphere, and if you're not given your due, then I'll come after Blackstone." He called you "Blackstone", not *Mister Blackstone*, you see, so I think he despises you. "I'll come after Blackstone myself and get it off him with my bare hands."'

Now, Joseph felt that he was falling.

He felt that there was nothing underneath him to save him from this endless, terrifying fall. He saw a rat arrive at the edge of the shaft he was working on and go down into the hole. He saw Will watching the rat and grinning, his mouth red and damp as Rebecca's had always been. He saw that the distance between him and a shovel lying on the mud was no more than an arm's stretch.

He knew that he was under-nourished, that he was becoming weak and lacked speed – speed of thought and speed of action. He knew he had to feint at what he was about to do, as though he intended some slow retreat towards his tent – as if to find money for Will. So he took out a piece of rag from his pocket and began wiping his hands. Will didn't take his eyes from him.

Then Joseph lunged forward and picked up the shovel. With all the strength that was left to him, he raised it high into the air. He felt it reach its arc and then he brought it down, down through the heavy, stinking air of Kokatahi, and he waited for the sound of the iron shovel crashing into the skull of Will Sefton and silencing him for ever.

But Joseph was slower even than he realised, his actions more predictable. He heard Will shriek and then he realised that the boy had leapt away, leapt backwards, well clear of the intended blow. For a moment more, they regarded each other, eye to eye, then Will turned and ran away over the pocked ground, towards the rope that marked out Joseph's claim and he vaulted the rope and sped on, jumping the piles of stones and mullock that lay all around until he was gone from Joseph's sight.

Joseph threw the shovel aside.

He was aware that, on the adjacent claims, men had stopped work and were now staring at him as at a man who had taken leave of his mind.

III

In the night, Harriet came to Joseph's tent.

He lay without moving, pretending to be asleep because he dreaded that she'd come to ask for love.

He heard her open the tent flap and close it behind her and crouch down beside him, where he lay with his head in the crook of his arm and his shotgun within his reach. She touched his elbow and he made as if to wake from one of his nightmares.

'Joseph,' she whispered. 'Light a candle. I have something to show you.'

She was wrapped in her red blanket, with her face severe and half turned away from him, so he knew by her look that he was safe from her embrace. He lit a candle and set the light between them. As she bent forwards to open the small bundle she was holding, Joseph remembered that she used to have long, wild hair and that he had once liked the touch and feel of this on his face and shoulders. But then she had emulated her friend, Dorothy Orchard, and hacked the hair away; she and Dorothy liked to believe they were modern women, exemplary colonial pioneers, and didn't seem to care if they made themselves ugly.

He watched her closely. She untied a damp rag and the smell of the river came into the tent and Joseph saw revealed in the candlelight a heap of muddy shingle, through which Harriet began to run her hands. She brought the light nearer and whispered: 'Do you see it? I'm not mistaken, am I?'

Joseph Blackstone found himself looking at grains of gold.

Barely breathing, he reached out and touched them, then picked a few of them up and rolled them between finger and thumb, feeling their weight.

'Where?' he asked.

Harriet explained that she'd walked up-river, a long way beyond the Kokatahi diggings, towards the sound of a waterfall, and on the way to the waterfall she'd found an extraordinary garden . . .

'Scurvy Jenny,' said Joseph quickly. 'Was this gold on his plot?'

'Who's "Scurvy Jenny"?'

'Chinaman. Sells vegetables. Was this his gold?'

'Ssh,' said Harriet. 'Or you'll wake the –'

Joseph let the gold fall and grabbed Harriet's wrist. 'Where did you find this? *Where?*'

Harriet stared accusingly at Joseph, holding him in an icy gaze until he relaxed his grip on her arm. Then, she said: 'Not on the Chinaman's garden, Joseph. On *this* side of the water. There's a flat piece of land, where the river widens ... and that's where I found it. I just scooped it up in my hand.'

So then Joseph let himself look at it again and touch it and begin to pick out the grains of gold and set them to one side. And something rose in his heart which threatened to choke him and he thought he might weep or begin babbling pure meaningless nothings and it seemed to him as if all the blood that flowed through him had been filtered of its poisons and was fresh and bright again and his limbs were strong again, like the limbs of a younger man.

'The colour,' he repeated. 'We found the colour.'

Already, he was estimating the value of what lay before him here. He thought there was enough to take him into the Bank of New Zealand and bring him out again with a smile on his face. But he needed to know that there was more, that this wouldn't be like the dust he'd found on the creek, a find to tease and tantalise him; he needed to know that this gold was just the beginning ...

He made Harriet describe the site, the texture of the earth, the disposition of rocks and trees, and he learned that here, at a bend in the river, there was this wide curve of shingle and that the gold had lain there, in what had looked to her like a rich scattering among stones at the water's edge, and that the soft mud where the river lapped had a yellowish sheen. And so he recognised that this was that most precious of all finds, a surface claim, an easy beach-working, needing no shafts, but only a pan and a cradle, and he thought that after all he had suffered how strange it was that the colour had come up from the depths, come towards him, as though to say: Enough, you've endured enough.

Joseph lay down on his back and shut his eyes. Through the

closed lids, he could see the dark shadow that was Harriet, kneeling by him. In the morning, he thought, he would leave Kokatahi, abandon everything here to peg out the new claim. He'd send Harriet back to Hokitika with money for a new licence, but the gold he wouldn't sell yet, in case he was seen at the Bank, in case questions were asked about where these beautiful grains had come from, in case the hordes from Kokatahi took it into their heads to follow him ...

And this was when Joseph felt the first worm of agitation enter his mind. Though Harriet had said that the new site was two hours' walk from Kokatahi, it was nevertheless almost opposite the Chinaman's vegetable garden. And Joseph knew that the Chinaman – if he chose – could betray the find to all the diggers along the river, inform every miner from Kokatahi to Kaniere that Joseph Blackstone was dredging gold from a shingle beach. In days, or hours, perhaps even before he'd been able to survey the terrain and decide on his pegging, Joseph would be surrounded by the rabble and they would encroach on his plot, try to shoulder him away, pan close to his section of water and steal whatever they found. And then he'd end up with less – always so much less – than he might have had, if only the world had not been so crowded, if only it had not been so blighted by the sameness of people's longing ...

At this moment, Harriet, as though she could read what was in Joseph's mind, began talking very quietly. She said: 'I've devised a plan and you must tell me what you think of it. I know that if you move up-river and there is any sniff of gold there, you will be followed and all that squalor that has been created here would very quickly be re-created in the new place. So, we should surely buy ourselves a little time, shouldn't we? And I believe I see a way.'

Joseph said nothing. He only opened his eyes and looked at Harriet in the flickery light. He had always mistrusted her cleverness, as though it had been a hard rock on which he was fated to stumble and bruise his feet.

'I will go upstream, Joseph,' she said. '*I* will go. And you will remain here. I will go secretly, at night – tomorrow night – taking just my tent and the dog and some supplies and a pan. And in the morning you will tell the other diggers that

Kokatahi was too much for me to endure, that I hadn't the stomach for it, that I've gone back to Hokitika. And they will never suspect any other thing, for why should they? No one will see me, for I shall travel in the darkness and I shall walk down-river towards Kaniere and then cross to the other side and make my way along that bank and not cross over again till I come near to the Chinaman's garden.'

Joseph was silent for a moment. To think that he could outwit the other miners, stay ahead of them, even if only for a while ... this was the very thing he'd longed for. But then he sighed and said: 'The Chinaman is the flaw. He will betray the plan.'

Harriet sat very still. Then she said: 'I do not think he is the flaw. I think there is no flaw.'

'He is the flaw,' Joseph repeated. 'He will see what you're doing. He travels up and down the river twice a week. The first part of your plan is cunning. But all its weakness lies in the nearness of the site to Chen.'

'Is that his real name? Chen?'

'I've heard him called that.'

'Trust me. I do not think Chen will spread any word about what I am doing. For I saw his garden. I don't believe whoever made that garden longs for a hundred men to arrive and blight the land around him. Trust me, Joseph.'

She'd said it twice: *Trust me.*

But Joseph thought: After all that's passed, knowing how separate we've become, why should either of us trust the other? For wasn't she – who had let him go from her heart, who preferred the company of her dog to him – wasn't she capable of taking the gold for herself and never returning? Might she not creep down to Hokitika, sell whatever she found, take a boat for Lyttelton, a boat for Australia or Shanghai? Might she not sail away and deprive him, finally, of all the future lives of which he dreamed?

Tired, in the cold, bleak hour of the early morning, Harriet lay down beside him. She wrapped herself tightly in her blanket and looked at him. She saw by his hard and lightless eyes that he was a man who had grown to doubt everything and everyone.

After a long silence, during which the candle began to burn very low, Harriet told him the last part of her plan. 'Keep the gold I found today,' she said. 'It's yours. In a few days, pretend you have found the colour here. Raise up a little stir. This way, you will keep all the diggers round you here at Kokatahi.'

The Power of Dreams

I

Harriet took with her as many possessions as she could carry, including the bulky canvas tent and her scarlet blanket and a dented pannikin. As Joseph helped her strap these things to her back, she found herself wishing that she had her horse with her, to let him shoulder the burden. Billy would have picked his dainty way round the wash-dirt and the shafts and the stones of the river. But Billy was far away, munching clover on the Orchard Run.

Harriet left the camp after midnight. She sensed that some of the Kokatahi diggers were still awake and heard her leave. One face peered out at her as she whispered goodbye to Joseph, touching his cheek with her hand, so she let this inquisitive man hear her say: 'I'm sorry, Joseph. I'm sorry. You were right when you told me that this is not a woman's world.' And she knew that the man was still watching as she walked away, but she was walking away towards Kaniere, towards Hokitika and the sea. When she crossed the river and came back along the other side, she would take care to follow a path out of sight of the Kokatahi goldfield.

The night was cold, with a thin moon up, and silent. Only the river kept up its eternal conversation with the sky.

Harriet carried a staff in one hand, a limb of black beech, cut by Joseph, so that she wouldn't stumble or slip when she crossed the water, and in the other hand, she held on to Lady's leash. The dog seemed enthralled by the moonlight and the shadows, distracted by scents, biting the air, as though she, too, knew that she was leaving Kokatahi far behind and making her way into a green and soundless place, where there would be fish to lap at the river's edge and kingfishers to startle from the trees.

Though Harriet knew that what she was doing was daring, even dangerous, she had no other feeling, as she walked, than one of elation and she thought that to be moving forward, to be travelling in expectation, was the thing which – after twelve years of being a governess, yoked to a room, frozen behind a wooden desk as time kept passing and never stopping for her – she enjoyed beyond all other.

She felt buoyant and steady through the long trek towards the mountains on the north bank of the river. She didn't know what time it was when she crossed the water for the second time and came at last to the shingle where she'd found the grains of gold. She felt only that the night had begun its slow descent towards morning, and that she was tired now and her skirts were wet and her feet were aching with cold and she longed to wrap herself in her scarlet blanket and sleep.

But she walked on. She'd promised herself that she'd set up her tent out of sight of Chen's garden. The shingle bank ended at a turn in the river, but beyond this another small beach appeared, with low vegetation at its back, and though the moon was almost gone, Harriet could see, by the milky light on the water, that the ground was level here.

She set down her heavy bundle, heard the pan clank against a stone. Lady went in circles, shaking water from her coat.

'Here,' said Harriet to the dog. 'This is our camp.' The sound of the waterfall came distantly to their ears.

Harriet took some charred, fibrous kūmara from her knapsack and she and Lady ate it, and then Harriet spread the canvas tent flat on the ground and they lay on this and Harriet held the dog to her as she might have held a child, with its warm back against her chest, and they slept until the light came.

By mid-day, her camp was set up.

Though the river flowed only yards from the place where her tent was pitched, the spot was dry and the ground yielded to the tent pegs. Harriet collected brushwood and dry branches and set a new fire in a circle of stones. In the earth covered by the tent she dug a deep hole and filled this, too, with stones. This would be the place where she would keep her gold.

Fantails and silver-eyes arrived at sunrise and caught insects hovering in the white mist that spread itself over the water. The bush creaked and clattered as the light grew bright.

Harriet took out the gun Joseph had given her at D'Erlanger's Hotel and examined its workings and loaded it with two bullets and laid it by the place where she would sleep, with its barrel pointing away from her into the scrub. Then, she made coffee and fried bacon on the fire and wondered whether the gardener, Chen, would see smoke rising and cross the river to investigate, or whether, before the next night came, she would pay a visit to him. She thought that she would give him money for a head of cabbage and onions to fry with the bacon and carrots and leeks to make a vegetable broth that would keep her fed for a long while.

And this 'long while' displayed itself before her, a slow feast of solitary days, each one like the one before, except that the dark would arrive a little earlier, except that the niche she'd crammed with stones would quietly fill with gold.

She knew that every miner on this river was in a race with the coming winter, that her survival here depended upon the temperature of the air, but she felt, on this first morning, that time and she were walking in step, that she had a little space – to rinse gold out of the river, to travel to the waterfall in search of Pare, to stare at the stars – and that when the snows came in, to drive her away and obliterate her camp, she, who had dreamed for so long about the mountains, would have travelled far without moving: she would have framed a question about her life and all that remained then would be to try to answer it.

Harriet panned for gold all through the warm afternoon on the shingle opposite Chen's garden. There was no wind or bite in the air and Harriet felt hot and excited and alive. She collected a fistful of golden grains in a tin cup, and washed and rinsed them until they shone. And the ease with which she had gathered them, so that the little beach was barely disturbed, struck her as miraculous. She also felt the unfairness of it. Only two hours away were the deep shafts and excavations and all the squalor and disappointed hopes of Kokatahi. Here, a child could have sat down on the mud and picked up the little bright nuggets, like shells from a Norfolk strand.

There was no sign of Chen until the sun started its decline and then Lady began barking and Harriet looked up and saw the Chinese man standing on the edge of his garden, watching her. She hadn't seen him arrive; he must have crossed the river lower down. Now, perhaps he had been going to check his fishing net and then he had caught sight of her – a stranger in his isolated world – and he stood there without moving. He wore his fur hat, but his clothes looked as though they were made of thin material, like cotton. He was holding the scarlet-handled hoe. It seemed to Harriet that he wasn't looking directly at her, but at the ground on which she was standing.

Harriet stood up. She let the tin cup lie where it was on the shingle. She wiped her hands on her pinafore. Then she called out: 'I have money to buy vegetables.'

She waited. Chen stood perfectly still. And she thought now that perhaps he was a man who never spoke, never entered into any transaction with the people of this country, except to sell them his produce in some way that required no words?

And what came into her mind, as the silence between herself and Chen accumulated and spread itself out along the water, was all the loud and monotonous babble Joseph had spent his life intoning at the livestock auctions. And she found herself wondering: did he dream about this old, chivvying language? Did he long for a life that would be more transparent in its gestures and have less need for words?

Harriet reached into the pocket of her pinafore and gathered up a few pence and she held the money out and said again: 'May I buy vegetables?'

For a moment more, Chen remained perfectly silent. Then he said: 'Yes.'

He put down the hoe and walked to where the rope lay under the water and Harriet wondered whether he'd strung ropes across the river in several places, so that he could wade across the water wherever it was quietest.

He held the rope taut for her, as she crossed the river,

holding on to her boots. Lady bounded and splashed at her side. When she arrived on the further bank, Chen held out his hand for her to take, but she didn't take it because her balance was good and she wanted to show him that she was strong and independent and free.

They stood face to face on the grass. Harriet noticed that Chen had slender hands and that his pigtail was grey and that his eyes were large and bright.

Harriet wanted to begin by telling Chen that she'd been here before, stolen carrots, slept in the scant shade of the plum tree, but she had no idea how much of this he would understand, so she set down her boots, put a hand on her collar bone and said: 'My name is Harriet.'

Lady was crouching in the wet grass, looking at Chen as if he were a stray sheep she would soon set about returning to the flock. When he looked down at the dog, Harriet saw his eyes flicker with amusement.

'Black. White. Beautiful dog,' he said.

'Yes,' said Harriet. 'She is called Lady.'

'Lady?' he said. 'Woman?'

'Like woman, yes. Lady.'

He nodded. 'Lady.'

'My name is Harriet.'

'Hal Yet?'

'Yes,' said Harriet. 'Hal Yet. And you? Chen?'

Again, the Chinaman smiled. It was a smile of exquisite melancholy.

'Chen. Family name,' he said. 'My name. Pao Yi.'

'Pao Yi?'

'Yes. Pao Yi. Panyu County. Guangdong Province. China.'

Harriet nodded. 'Far from home,' she said. 'Very far from home.'

'Yes,' said Pao Yi. 'Far home. Far away lake.'

'You live on a lake?'

'Yes. Beautiful lake. Heron Lake. Far away.'

Pao Yi looked up at the sky, as if he saw in it some shimmering resemblance to the distant lake, or as if he could fly back to it like a bird. Then, he turned and walked towards the vegetable garden and Harriet bent down and put on her boots.

*

Gold. Secrecy. How was Harriet to explain about these things?

She put all of this to one side and told Pao Yi that she was going in search of a Maori woman called Pare. She asked him whether he had been to the waterfall. He told her that he had been once. In his own language he would have explained to her that the waterfall made him uneasy, that it reminded him of the weir over which his parents had tumbled to their deaths, but he lacked the English words to say this and Harriet saw him try to tell her something else about the waterfall and then stop and look away.

'At the waterfall,' she said, 'was anybody there? Did you see a Maori woman?'

'No,' said Pao Yi. 'No woman.'

They fell silent. Harriet could hear pigeons clattering in the high bush behind them. Then she asked to be shown the vegetable plot and they walked in single file along the neat paths and Pao Yi recited in English and in Cantonese the names of the things he had grown. After a while, Harriet asked: 'Did you have a garden at Heron Lake?'

'Yes,' he said. 'Small garden. Boat. Everybody.'

'Everybody?'

'Everybody come to Pao Yi. Beautiful fishes.' And he pointed then to his net strung across the river. 'Fish there,' he said. 'Pao Yi stay alive.'

They gathered an armful of vegetables and Pao Yi put them in a sack. Harriet held out her money and Pao Yi took a few pence and then he bowed and turned and hurried away, as though this taking of money from her vexed him. She watched him take off his fur hat and go into his hut with its doorway made of sacking on a wooden frame and close the door behind him. Lady made as if to follow Pao Yi, but Harriet called her back.

Yet she waited. She thought that perhaps Pao Yi had gone to fetch something to show her and would quickly reappear. She tried to envisage what he might keep in his hut and whether he slept on a mattress or only on the hard earth or even in a hammock because he was a fisherman and could tie a net.

But he didn't reappear and, after five or six minutes had passed, Harriet felt stupid waiting there. She picked up the vegetable sack and walked back towards the river. She began thinking of the fine broth she was going to make and the long letter she was going to write to her father.

II

With his pick and with his hands, Pao Yi unblocked the entrance to his cave, stone by stone. He went into the cave and took with him a small oil lamp that burned with a steady blue-and-yellow flame. The lamp gave out a little heat, as well as light.

Pao Yi lay down, resting on one elbow and lit an opium pipe. He saw the walls of the cave begin to swell and gleam. He was filled with an apprehension of the beautiful strangeness of the world.

He began to dream of an avenue of lime trees. The scent of the trees and the vision of his own feet walking under them created in him a sense of the harmoniousness of all things.

Far away, a man hurled a fishing net into the air from a scarlet boat on Heron Lake, but the man was not he. Crabs came creeping into the net, an accumulation of whiskers and claws and eyes like seed pearls, but they were not his to sell when the man rowed to shore, for he was not the fisherman, he was not there; he was treading the long, soft road under the limes.

On he walked. And soon he saw that a woman, stately as the trees, was moving in step with him on slender, dusty feet and the lime seeds lay all about them like green grasshoppers, and in his own language he began to describe to her how, when a plague of grasshoppers had come to Heron Lake and devoured the string beans and choked the water-wheels, he had shown his ingenuity, his ability to adapt and survive, by netting the grasshoppers and roasting them in oil with salt and sesame seeds and they were as succulent as crisp, fried sea-grass, a veritable delicacy, and soon everybody was gathering them and eating them and praising him, Pao Yi, Brother of Righteousness, for inventing such a delicious recipe.

The woman smiled as she walked, smiled at his story of the roasted grasshoppers, and Pao Yi felt the attraction of this smile, which he knew to be flawed by some small detail that he couldn't identify, but which seemed to lead him, by slow degrees, to a feeling of desire.

The avenue of lime trees stretched out ahead of the two walkers in a swaying and shifting and endless green and Pao Yi knew that this garden, where the avenue had been planted, had been created on such a varied and colossal scale that he would be able to wander in it for a long, long time and never take exactly the same path nor tread twice in his own footsteps and always, as he went along, he would be aware of the woman engaged on her own journey – separate from his and yet by some coincidence in step with his – and find himself looking forward to every patch of dappled sunlight between the trees which revealed her face to him and searching his muddled head for some other story to tell her, like the story of the grasshoppers fried with sesame seeds, that would make her smile.

The day declined outside and the oil lamp in the cave flickered and burned low and Pao Yi finished the pipe and laid his head down on the hard floor.

He still walked in the avenue of his imaginings and he thought that when the trees finally ended, there he would discover a pond where pink carp swam in circles under the broad lily-leaves and where he would watch the woman lean over to wash her feet among the fishes.

III

Every morning, Joseph began work once more on the eighth shaft and its accompanying drainage bore. Bucketful after bucketful after bucketful of earth was hauled to the surface by the makeshift windlass, but Joseph didn't bother to wash any pay-dirt above the line of the blue clay, nor did he barrow it down to the water; he just tipped it out at the shaft-head, where it piled up and hardened in the late sun and the dry wind.

Though the windlass kept turning, though the heavy buckets were lifted and emptied, Joseph accomplished these tasks without giving them any thought and he knew that his life here at Kokatahi had become a sleep-walking life.

Alone in his tent, persecuted by nightmares, he examined the golden grains that Harriet had brought him, but he found he now had difficulty believing that what he held in his palm really was gold. Sometimes, he scratched at the grains with his nail, half expecting the sheen to peel away, to reveal the dull base metal beneath. He thought that this find of Harriet's had an illusory quality to it; it had been too easy, its timing too particular. He began to suspect her of some deception, knew her to be capable of outwitting him with ease, and he cursed his parents – his father in particular – for bequeathing to him a slow and unremarkable mind. If only he had been cleverer, he reasoned, then life would not have tortured him as it had.

But at other moments, he would see everything more positively.

He was able to tell himself to be patient, to trust his wife, to wait out the month that they had agreed upon and never be tempted to walk up-river to where she was camped and risk being followed by other men from Kokatahi. He thought her plan ingenious. She had understood what was needed; she had seen that their only hope lay in being ahead of the crowd.

That Harriet was panning for gold without a licence was a question which now and then worried Joseph, but he saw that there was no way to purchase a miner's right and still keep her whereabouts a secret. He tried, therefore, to 'adjust' the matter in his mind, told himself that she was only 'fossicking', that she had no real equipment, that once the gold was safe, then he would deal with the Government Licensing Office, bribe somebody if need be, or plead ignorance: 'My wife went in search of a friend of the Orchard family, sir. She came upon her bank of gold by miraculous chance when washing her feet in the river . . .'

And then at the fly-blown hotel in Hokitika, he would gather the colour into his arms and know at last that he was free. Free in the way that Hamish McConnell was free, to embark on a new phase of his life, to begin everything again. For Joseph Blackstone knew now what he wanted to do: *he wanted to make amends to Rebecca's family for his crime.*

In his nightmares at Kokatahi, he returned to Parton in the time before the crime, to the days in which he was planning it with his friend, Merrick Dillane, the veterinary surgeon, a man who had soft, red hands and a tender voice and a cold, calculating mind. He saw again the ease with which he and Dillane had done what they'd done and walked away and thought themselves clever and free for a little while. He remembered that the whole process from beginning to end had rested upon Dillane's desire to be rid of a bad-tempered Shire horse . . .

Merrick Dillane bred Shires in his spare time. He loved the greys especially. He liked to stroke the white tresses of their feet. But he had one mare, named Dido, who bit him whenever he tried to do this and kicked at her fencing and bucked like a steer in the daisy field and generally vexed Dillane with all her ungovernable behaviour.

He came to Joseph, his friend the livestock auctioneer, to say he wanted to sell Dido. The day that he came was the day that Joseph had been told by Rebecca that she was carrying his child.

These two things would be for ever and always yoked together: the child and the horse.

The plan was swift to arrive in Joseph's mind and swift to accomplish. Joseph promised to guarantee Merrick Dillane a 'pretty price' for Dido at the auctions if he would only help him with his present problem. He called it 'getting help' and never referred to it in any other way. And Dillane picked up this term for it and carried it forward through the coming days. He would help his friend. Together, they would help Rebecca. What were friends for, if they could not help each other?

Dillane promised Joseph that Rebecca would have no memory of what they were planning to do to her. He said there would be no trace of it in her consciousness, neither at the time nor in memory in the time to come, that it would vanish *as though it had never been.* 'All she will remember', he said, 'will be the foal . . .'

They took her to see a new-born Shire foal in Dillane's stables. The soft-hearted Rebecca had a weakness for small creatures. She leaned into the stall, all entranced by the foal – as Joseph and Dillane had known she would be – and cooed to it, as to a baby of her own. She reached out her hand to stroke its nose. And at that moment, she was felled to sudden sleep by the passing under her nostrils of rag soaked in ether of chloride, cut with a pearly opiate, a 'useful vapour' devised by Dillane himself and known to grateful farmers and pet owners as 'Dillane's Dream'.

'Good,' said Dillane. 'Now she will enter a cloud of forgetting.'

They carried her into Dillane's house and laid her on the operating table, where sheep and cats and bulldog terriers had so often lain, and Dillane put on his surgical apron and his gloves. He told Joseph that he could stay 'to see it done' if he wanted to, but Joseph began to feel faint, as though he had inhaled some of the vapour, and he understood that he wanted *not to know* how it was going to be done, so that he would never have to imagine it, could choose to think, if he wanted, that it had never really happened and that the events which it would bring in its wake occurred of their own accord and through no fault or design of Joseph Blackstone.

So Joseph went out of the room. It took very little time. Merrick Dillane's red hands, holding the surgical instrument, parted Rebecca's thighs, reached in and accomplished with two stabs all there was to do. He made sure the wall of the womb was ruptured. Then he came out and told Joseph that 'our part in this is almost over'.

The two men carried Rebecca back to the stables, and laid her down on the floor by the foal's stall, exactly where she had lately been. They let her sleep for a while and then patted her cheek to wake her, and when she opened her eyes they told her she had fainted. They gave her smelling salts and Dillane went off to fetch a cup of water and Joseph stroked her curly hair and she clung to him and said: 'Lord, Joseph Blackstone, that child of yours has begun to lead me a pretty dance already.'

She drank the water that Dillane brought. She stood and smoothed down her rumpled skirt and tried to smile. Then Joseph lifted her into his pony-cart and drove her home.

This was the last time he saw her.

Dillane had promised him that 'all will proceed exactly as though she were undergoing a bona fide miscarriage'.

'And then she will be as she was before?'

'Oh yes. She will be quite well.'

But Rebecca Millward never got well.

She bled for three days and died on the fourth of blood poisoning.

Perhaps the instrument with which Dillane had ruptured the wall of her womb had been insufficiently cleaned after one of his operations on an animal? Nobody would ever know. All they knew was that Rebecca Millward died of a violent, puerperal fever no doctor could alleviate.

Joseph Blackstone stood in the road and saw her coffin carried to the church in Parton and knew that there was no difference between him and a man who has committed murder.

The nightmares didn't end there.

The auction of the Shire horse never went as planned. Joseph had meant to bribe someone to stand in the crowd to talk up Dido's price. His father had sometimes used this method to sell animals and usually with good success and tankards of ale at the Plough and the Stars to celebrate afterwards. But so haunted was Joseph by the sight of Rebecca's coffin that this necessary part of the plan went clean out of his mind. And when the day of the auction came, the assembled bidders already seemed to know that Dido was a bad-tempered horse. Nobody wanted her. Joseph's gavel had to come down on a paltry sum.

And then he saw Merrick Dillane striding towards him. Dillane led him away beyond the crowd at the market. He jabbed a finger at his dusty black lapel. He told him he had performed his part of the bargain; now he wanted 'a correct sum' for his horse.

'Rebecca died . . .' was all Joseph could stammer. 'You shouldn't have let her die.'

But Merrick Dillane began to walk away. He turned only to say that he would tell the whole village what Joseph had asked him to do.

So then Joseph knew that he had no idea how to escape from the darkness closing round him, unless it might be to engineer his own death, to pass the way she'd passed, in her oak box, towards Parton Magna's Church of the Redeemer, where among the ancient graves the primroses were shining.

He was helpless. He paid Dillane, but he knew it would not rest there. Dillane would ask for more. Joseph's money began to leach away. Even Lilian, from whom he withheld so much, understood that something was wrong. She tried to tempt him back to happiness with his favourite food and with small kindnesses. But nothing could tempt him back. Nothing under the sun until he met Harriet Salt and understood that this tall young woman was in need of a husband.

He burned all the small, illiterate notes Rebecca had written him. He put the curl she had given him into his fly box. He wooed Harriet with dreams of a life far away, of a life begun afresh in the Land of the Long White Cloud . . .

A simple story, thought Joseph, as he lay in the stink of his tent. So simple in its progression from one event to the next; so lethal in its outcome.

Damage compounded by further damage.

Damage growing, expanding, subdividing, multiplying, never ceasing . . .

But now the damage was going to cease. In his more lucid and optimistic moments, this was what Joseph tried to reassure himself. It was about to become finite. *Harriet had found the colour.*

And then Joseph would allow himself to remember that, although the winter was coming in at Kokatahi, the seasons in England would revert to what they had once been and that, perhaps, when he saw Parton again and arrived at the Millwards' door to unburden himself of his secret, a stray wasp of summer, half intoxicated with death but still alive, might yet be creeping along the garden path.

Between Two Worlds

I

Pare led Flinty Fairford and John-boy Shannon along a swampy track in the valley of the Arahura River, going towards the buried forest she'd heard the Maoris describe. The squashy ground was kind to her feet; the pain of walking was less than it had been.

For a while, they could feel the wind at their backs, blowing off the sea. Then, as the river divided and they began to follow its northerly course, the breeze faltered and Pare stopped and put down her bundle and looked around and sniffed the air. She'd heard that you could *smell* the ancient trees as they slowly petrified under the black soil, a smell like fungus, tangy and dark, and she felt that she was near it now.

They went a little further and they began to see signs that some excavation had taken place here and been abandoned.

'I'm not digging where some other perisher has tried and failed,' announced Flinty. 'If I'm going to fail, I'm going to fail in a new spot.'

John-boy and Pare went on walking. She could hear frogs gurgling in the reeds. She knew that eels, too, lived in this swamp, camouflaged amid the black limbs of the buried trees, and that the flesh of these eels was so dense and oily and nourishing, it was difficult to swallow, but that it could keep away hunger for a long time. And Pare thought she would try to snare eels and kill them with her shark-toothed knife.

Pare did not know what she was going to do. She had begun to hope that, if she led the men to where the gold was, she would somehow get her share. When she went to dig for eels, what was there to prevent her from searching for the colour in the ground and, if she found it, from hiding it in her bundle? And then eventually she would barter gold for greenstone, and she thought this might be easy because the only thing the pākehā longed for was gold.

She was weary of this long walk. She felt her feet begin to bleed again, but the blood left no trace and was absorbed into the mire and she was aware of how few traces her life would leave on the earth when she died, and that although she had walked from the pā near Kaiapoi to the Orchard Run more times than she could count, no footstep of hers would remain on the miles and miles of tussock, nor any imprint of her body in the toi-toi thicket.

We fly away, she thought: Even while we're alive, we slowly fade, because for fewer and fewer of the living are we solid and important and bright. And so she realised that here lay the real reason for her long and arduous journey: Edwin Orchard was the one and only person for whom she was *necessary*.

She found the dead forest at dusk.

She saw white shadows flitting over it and believed them to be patupaiarehe, pale sprites who lived in the misty hills but who were insatiably curious about humans and coveted their treasures and were able to carve palaces and cradles out of greenstone. And she saw that the patupaiarehe were angry with her because, as yet, she had found nothing.

To try to protect herself from the patupaiarehe, Pare took out her phial of red ochre and smeared her forehead with this and neither of the men noticed because the light was almost gone.

But they, too, could smell the mushroom scent of the buried trees. Flinty took up his shovel and began digging down through the bog and sure enough he found them: arching limbs and stems, black as charcoal, hard as his own name, and he and John-boy stared at them and were struck dumb. Flinty swore.

John-boy said: 'I'd like to show my mam this. I'd like to see her flabbergasted face.'

In the fading light, the men were eager to pitch a tent, but all the ground in this part of the Arahura Valley was wet-flat swamp and no surface was stable or solid, so Pare suggested that they stretch blankets from the trees, like hammocks, and sleep suspended here, where they would be dry. Flinty complained that he couldn't sleep in a hammock, that he had to lie face down, with his nose pointing into the earth in order to get any rest 'from the purgatory of consciousness', but Pare told him that the Maori could sleep standing up if they sang a certain song to themselves and that she would teach him that song.

'What song?' he asked belligerently. 'Don't tell me it's a lullaby?'

'No,' said Pare. But the English word 'lullaby', which she hadn't heard for a number of years, reminded her of the days when she used to sing baby Edwin to sleep with Maori lullabies and his small fingers would reach up and clutch a hank of her dark hair and often he went to sleep still holding on to it and she would have to unclench his hands and lay his arms by his sides before tiptoeing out of his room. And she thought how frightening it was that her life had brought her here, to this swamp, all because, on a certain afternoon, she'd offended the spirit of Tane in the garden of Orchard House.

'So?' continued Flinty. 'What song is it? I don't want any witchcraft worked on me.'

'No witchcraft,' said Pare. 'But if you don't want to hear it, I shall sing it to John-boy.'

'My mam used to sing to me,' said John-boy. 'I can remember the words:

'Baby and I
Were baked in a pie
The gravy was wonderful hot.
We had nothing to pay
To the baker that day
And so we crept out of the pot.'

'Baked in a pie?' said Flinty. 'What kind of nonsense is that?'
'Shut up, Flinty,' said John-boy.
He began unfolding a blanket and his eyes scanned the

straggly beech trees for a limb to hang it from. He wished he hadn't mentioned his mam and her lullaby. It felt to him like a betrayal of a secret which had existed between her and him for more than twenty years and now it was let loose upon the mangling, love-denying world. 'I want to hear Pare's song,' he said.

Pare saw that John-boy was upset. She moistened her mouth, which was dry from walking on and on through the Arahura swamp, and began to sing:

'Kei whea
Te ara
Ki raro?
Kei whea
Te ara
Ki raro?'

Then, she stopped and said: 'Not many words, but when you repeat them and repeat them, then sleep will come.'

'What do they mean?' asked John-boy.

'Could be a spell,' said Flinty. 'An incantation.'

Where is
the path
to the underworld?
Where is
the path
to the underworld?

This was the true meaning of the words, but Pare knew that to Flinty Fairford and John-boy Shannon they could have no resonance.

'"Where is the path to the land of sleep?"' she said. 'That's all the song asks. But if you keep asking, then you find an answer.'

'Sounds all right to me,' said John-boy.

Cutting through the buried forest barely resembled mining. Sometimes, there was a long, vertical ooze of black mud between the trunks of the trees and this could be shovelled out and then something like a shaft would suddenly appear, going down towards a bottom which glittered like coal. But this bottom appeared unreachable. Flinty would crouch over these shafts, try to narrow his eyes, as though he were looking through a telescope, to discover what was hidden there. He had to admit, with the glimmer or sheen it sometimes showed, that these shafts looked auriferous and his mind began working on some cutting device, operated from above, to bring the coal to the surface and see what it contained.

He started on a series of drawings (made in a notebook so old and dirty that some of the pages were still stuck together with the rancid fish scales of Dover herrings), first of a simple borer to cut the shimmering rock and then of a narrow bucket, like a tin coffee pot on a long, rigid handle, to bring the chunks to the surface. In his mind's eye, Flinty could see how these devices would work, and he showed them, not without pride, to John-boy.

'What are you going to make all this from?' asked John-boy. 'Beech twigs?'

'Iron,' snapped Flinty.

'Oh, a fine idea!' laughed John-boy. 'I suppose you see iron girders growing out of the reeds? I suppose you can feel the heat of a smelting furnace just over that rise?'

Flinty turned his back on John-boy, put his notebook away, and saw with a new and dispassionate eye the black tracery of the tree-tops their excavations had revealed.

He stared at this tracery and thought it like nothing he'd ever seen in fifty-four years. There was something about it which he found beautiful, something which made him proud of it, and he tried to understand what this was, but he couldn't understand it. And he thought then that he had come to a place where he was lost: not lost in the way that he and John-boy had been lost in the dark of the Hurunui Gorge, but lost as to the meaning of things and he stood for a long time, looking at the forest coming out of the earth and wondering what it signified.

It was as though he expected Pare to explain this new existence to him. Whenever Flinty looked at her – the Maori woman whose life they had almost certainly saved – she seemed to him to be engaged on some task or other and she worked at these things as though she were in her own home, as though she'd done them a hundred times before. And yet what she was doing struck Flinty as extraordinary: she was plaiting reeds to make snares for weka; she was catching frogs with her hands; she was wading barefoot in the tea-coloured slime brandishing a knife, with which she killed eels as thick as a man's arm; she was dragging a flat stone, on which to make her fires, half a mile from the Arahura River; she was killing rats by breaking their necks with one snap of her wrist.

Pare roasted whatever she caught and Flinty ate it and never asked what it was after the first few days because he felt himself getting stronger on the food Pare found and cooked. Bush food. Flinty thought about his body, which had lived for so long on the flotsam of the salt seas of the English Channel, ingesting mussels, clams, winkles, sea urchins, limpets and oysters, and never once sitting down to any real feast or banquet, nor even knowing what a banquet might consist of or how the table might be set for it; and he understood this much, among all that confused him: that he'd always been and always would be a creature on the edge of the known world, a scavenger, and a beachcomber, and that it was too late to alter this destiny now.

Yet one thing vexed him: that he was on the verge of growing old, that he was on *the very beach of old age*. And it was for this that he longed to discover gold, so that when old age finally arrived and he had to come in from the wild and find shelter, there that shelter would be.

He didn't want this shelter to be grand because he hated grandness in all its manifestations. When he thought about Queen Victoria inhabiting all her varied and gigantic palaces, it made him want to plunge a knife into her milk-white breast. He decided that his place might be no more than a cabin. It might have a single door, painted blue. There would be no flowers along the path which led to the door, but only a garden of shingle and seaweed and stones.

John-boy had formulated few notions of what he would do with his gold. The only thing he knew for certain was that he would give money to his mother, Marie, so that she could live in a better house and indulge her fondness for bright clothes and perhaps, as a result of these things, find a man who would love her and stay with her.

All John-boy's life, Marie Shannon had talked about his father, who had been blond as a Viking, 'with a lovely fuzz on him, the colour of primroses', and this astounded John-boy, as he grew up, that his mother could still remember with such delight a man who had betrayed her – a man who had never even known of his son's existence. John-boy had told Marie often enough to forget him. She always replied that really she had forgotten him, 'but now and then it's his body that comes back to me and his eyes which were grey like the winter sea'.

And John-boy concluded that certain people resist being forgotten, as though being held in a lover's memory might be all that kept them warm or sane or capable of any tender feeling, and that this Viking father, whose name had been Jed, was one of these. But it made him rage. Why should Marie forgive a betrayal so cruel? John-boy thought that if his father ever did return, he would make sure that he suffered to the end of his days.

II

Ever since their arrival at the buried forest, when Pare had seen the patupaiarehe like ghosts flitting over the ground, they'd hardly left her alone.

She kept daubing herself with red ochre, until her pot of ochre was almost used up, but still the patupaiarehe came flickering and dancing round her like snow and sometimes stung her or flew into her eyes and kept on and on trying to steal the small piece of greenstone hanging round her neck.

They exhausted her. In sleep, she could hear them whining and buzzing, and so her nights began to be wretched and it became harder and harder to get out of her hammock when the dawn came.

Flinty and John-boy slept like the dead. Pare would struggle into the light of morning and stare at the canopy of trees emerging from the earth. She would listen to hear whether any of the patupaiarehe still lingered as the night receded, and try to flap them away if they did, and then she would stand and look at the two pākehā men suspended like larvae in their hammocks and wonder how or when they would find the colour they were dreaming of.

As each day passed, it became harder and harder for Pare to complete the tasks that kept them all alive. She would squat by the flat stone she'd dragged from the river, building and lighting her fires and boiling water for tea, but the hunt for weka and eels and the killing of rats now tired her to such an extent that she felt unable to raise her arm and for two days together she found nothing for them to eat.

'I was getting strong,' Flinty complained. 'Now, I'm half starved. If you want any reward, you have to keep us fed.'

Pare dragged herself back to the deep swamps. She gathered frogs into Flinty's bucket. Rain fell on her and she could feel the coldness of it and the way it made the ochre run down her face and into her mouth. And she felt herself sliding back into her old sickness.

She sliced the heads off the frogs and roasted them in a hot fire. Flinty and John-boy ate them greedily, crunching their bones, like quail, and this mashing of the frogs' bones seemed to Pare to be one of the most repulsive sounds she'd ever heard. She staggered away from the fire and vomited into the reeds.

She saw a black log floating there and felt the power in the log and remembered her old encounter with the taniwha who had seemed to ordain her vigil over Edwin Orchard. The log terrified her. She wiped her mouth with the back of her hand and spoke in a weak voice: 'I'm doing all that I can,' she said, 'but everything depends first on the discovery of gold and we have found no gold at all . . .'

The log moved sluggishly in the swamp, bumping against a stand of rushes, then slowly turning, as the wind moved the water. No voice came from it.

'Help me!' Pare wanted to cry out, but as she was about to speak she heard footsteps arriving at her back and turned to see

John-boy, his cheek bulging with frog-meat, wading through the reeds towards her.

'You're ill,' he said, eating as he spoke. 'Flinty and I are going to find a new place to tie the hammocks, with more shelter from the rain.'

'You *must* find gold . . .' Pare said to John-boy in a distracted voice, but her words trailed away for, near her now, she saw the log upend itself and very slowly begin to sink. Pare felt John-boy's hand on her shoulder. 'It's all right,' he said gently. 'It's the swamp makes you sick. I'll get fresh water from the river. You'll be right soon enough.'

Good as their word, Flinty and John-boy trekked into some dense bush and retied the three hammocks under the canopy of trees. The rain clattered and dripped all around them. They tried to spread out the calico tents in the higher branches, as a ceiling of shelter, and they lifted Pare into her hammock and put her bundle under her head and covered her with her blanket.

She asked them, as the dusk came on, whether they could observe the sprites, like whining mosquitoes, discovering her new whereabouts and beginning to land on her hair and on the leaves that surrounded her.

But they thought she was delirious and never answered her, only held a billy-can to her mouth, to try to let the fresh water of the river rinse away what ever it was that had struck her down.

In the night, she heard them talking about her. Flinty said she'd led them to a duffer, that the Maoris, obsessed by greenstone, knew nothing when it came to gold, that the buried trees 'might make a coal mine', but that the colour would never be found there.

'It may be too soon to say,' said John-boy.

Pare heard Flinty begin to cough. 'Maybe,' he said. 'But I'm not staying. This place will make us ill. I'm for packing and moving on.'

'Where to?' asked John-boy.

'Kaniere,' said Flinty. 'Or Kokatahi. There was talk of a homeward bounder at Kokatahi. We're wasting our time here.

And time's the one commodity I don't have much of. If I don't get gold, I'll die like a dog in some lonely place.'

'We'll find it,' said John-boy. 'We'll find it.'

They were quiet after that and soon Pare heard them snoring. The rain kept on and the music of the rain in the bush almost lulled Pare to sleep, but the vexing patupaiarehe kept landing on her and searching out her bundle and stinging her ears and she could feel their maliciousness and knew that they were never going to let her rest.

Very slowly, she lifted her aching head and reached down and took the greenstone pendant over her head and into her hand, and laid it on her chest, on top of the blanket that covered her, and waited.

She thought she could hear the sprites began to sing with their desire for the precious greenstone.

'Take it,' whispered Pare. 'Take this. It is all I have.'

She closed her eyes. She knew the patupaiarehe never took anything when observed, but only when the human eye was turned away. She could feel the weight of the pendant steady and unmoving on her chest and then she fell into a heavy, dreamless sleep and when she woke, as light came filtering through the black beech, she reached out a hand and felt for the pendant and discovered that it was gone.

The loss of the greenstone pendant brought into Pare's limbs a feeling of hollowness, as though the patupaiarehe had stolen the marrow from her bones. Now, she found that she could barely move.

She looked around to discover where the two men were. She could only see one hammock. Some time later John-boy, bringing her water, told her that Flinty Fairford had packed up and moved on.

III

Pare fell into a delirium. In her dreams, the wrath of Tane blackened the air.

She was aware, in the days which followed, of a presence

near her from time to time and she sometimes called out the name 'E'win' and began asking: '*E'win, are you there?*'

No reply ever came, yet she couldn't think who else it might be, couldn't recognise the figure leaning over her, couldn't have guessed that John-boy Shannon stayed to nurse her, stayed because he despised betrayal.

He did what he could. He'd nursed his mother through scarlet fever. He went back and forth to the river for fresh water. He laid cool rags on Pare's forehead still stained with ochre. He brushed insects from her hair. He sang his old remembered lullaby:

'Baby and I
Were baked in a pie
The gravy was wonderful hot . . .'

He killed a water-bird and cooked it and mashed the flesh and tried to spoon it into Pare's mouth, but couldn't get a morsel of it into her. He talked to her about his mother, Marie, and her coloured dresses and the house he would build for her when he made his fortune.

Pare heard very little of this. She knew that she had one last, heartbreaking task and this was to remove herself from Edwin Orchard's world. She knew that she was doomed, but she thought that if she could move far away from the solid landscape that enclosed Edwin and yet leave him behind within it, then there might be one death – her own – and not two.

So what remained of her willpower had to be concentrated into revisiting all the places she had ever visited in the pākehā world and removing every vestige of herself from them, every blade of grass still bent by her footstep, every lingering scent of her body in the air, every feeling of warmth on the surfaces of objects she'd touched.

This task didn't seem very difficult at Orchard House, where she hadn't set foot since the day of the furious wind. But when Pare arrived in her mind at the thicket of toi-toi grass, she found that, here, she could still see the imprint of her body on the grass. She tried to make the wiry grasses spring up again, to obliterate her own shape. But the harder she tried to leave this place and to eradicate all trace of herself, the deeper became the imprint of her body on the toi-toi.

She bent all her mind and will to the task of obliterating her mark, but the more desperately she strained to do this, the more sweetly did the earth call to her to let the imprint remain, and the toi-toi stems themselves whispered to her soul to remain and even the blue sky and the sun pressed down upon her, pressed down with such insistence that she had no choice but to stay and to be still, to lie down on the ground, fitting her body into the cleft it had made long ago, and close her eyes. And it was not long before she began to hear a familiar voice.

Pare, are you there? Pare, are you there?

'Yes,' she replied. 'I am here, E'win. I am here.'

John-boy Shannon dug a deep hole among the buried trees and in it he laid Pare's body, wrapped in her blanket and with her arms folded around her bundle. He marked her forehead with the last scrapings of the red ochre and then covered her with the wet, black earth.

He felt, standing there all alone in the pouring rain, that he should sing or say something, so he sang the lullaby she'd taught him:

'Kei whea
Te ara
Ki raro?
Kei whea
Te ara
Ki raro?'

Where is the path to the land of sleep?

The only things he took from her were her shark's tooth knife and her paua shell. He felt that Pare wouldn't have minded. He imagined that, with these objects, he would one day save his own life.

The Fresh

I

Harriet began writing to her father, Henry Salt. She knew a long time would pass before she would be able to post the letter, but she wrote it just the same, because she wanted to talk to her father.

I walked to a waterfall yesterday. I'm searching for a Maori woman, called Pare, and I thought I might discover her here, on a high ledge by the waterfall, but there was no sign of anyone. Yet I stayed a long while at the fall. I would never have been able to imagine the feelings both of wonder and of terror this torrent created in me. The fall spills out of a high crevice in the deep heart of the mountain and plunges down more than a hundred feet into the river where, as the poet Coleridge so brilliantly observed, it creates an eddy-rose of frothing white, which keeps blossoming up and up, 'obstinate in resurrection'.

All day, I sit by the river, panning in the steady rain that now falls from an angry sky, and every day the colour is there in my pan. I have unearthed some pieces bulkier than the knuckle of my thumb. And I feel myself begin to succumb to the 'gold fever' which has taken hold of Joseph, and look forward excitedly, each morning, to the finds I'm going to make. For gold, I now understand, is a substance truly fascinating in its allure. It's not merely the weight and shine of it that enthrals us, but its infinite transformations, its power to become whatever we choose. Yesterday, the

*gold that I found became a harness and trap, which my
horse Billy will pull along with a high-stepping trot. Today,
I am dreaming of a new house by our old creek, a house
made of wood, not cob, and situated out of reach of the
winds. But I do not see Joseph in this house. I see only
myself. But then I imagine myself walking to one of the
windows and looking out, and I see you walking along the
path to its gate, carrying a suitcase, exclaiming at the
brightness of the New Zealand light.*

The letter was laid aside at this point, but taken up again the
following day, for now that she'd started on it, Harriet found
that she wanted to describe everything that she saw and
everything that she was feeling, as though some record of all
this had suddenly become vital and that unless it were made, it
would never be recollected anywhere.

She described Pao Yi's vegetable garden and the way the
colours of it changed and yet always seemed bright, even when
heavy rain was falling, and the demeanour of Pao Yi himself
'which strikes me as very unusual, or even exceptional, because
he is so still and contained'.

Then she talked about the soups she was making from his
vegetables, 'stringing my pot on a poorly contrived little tilting
cradle above my fires', and how she felt that this was the finest
food she'd ever eaten, better than the beautiful steak-and-
kidney puddings they served at the Assembly Rooms in
Norwich, better than the succulent oyster pies that could be
bought at Wells and Brancaster.

She saw that what she'd written here amounted to ridiculous
hyperbole, but she didn't want to cross it out; there was
something about the soup which struck her as uniquely good.
She would have liked some bread – even Lilian's bread – to eat
with it, but she felt strong enough on the soup alone.

She went on to describe the diggings at Kokatahi, the crude
and leaky huts, the persistent impression that she had formed of
some 'aftermath' there, as if, without being noticed, an
earthquake had struck and the miners were now trying to
rebuild what they'd already lost. '*I know*', she put, '*that this is*

not logical and yet this intimation of a disaster, about which nobody will speak, endures in my mind and I conclude that, because I am so much alone with my thoughts, I may have begun to see the world in a topsy-turvy way ...'

II

Now, the rain, which had been drenching the high peaks for such a long while, began to seep down and down through the porous rock to fill the underground springs, and these buried springs started to converge and mingle in a complicated conversation underneath the mountain.

Nobody heard this conversation. Neither Harriet, nor Pao Yi, nor Joseph, nor the other miners at Kokatahi heard anything at all, yet with every passing hour it became noisier and more clamorous, until at last it had to escape its underground confinement. And so it rose up and broke on the surface of the rock and then the sound of it burst out into the air. For a brief moment, the wash of water bubbled and trembled on the rock's ferny edge. Then it began to fall as a roaring cataract into the river.

The dog, Lady, was the first to hear it. She was standing at the river's edge, pursuing her favourite occupation of trying to gobble up small fish as they swam within reach of her mouth. She raised her head and listened. She was attuned now to the sounds of the bush, even to the sudden crash of a tree or a cascade of falling rock, but this presented itself to her as something frightening, something new and unknown, and she started to whine.

Harriet was a little way off, wearing a shawl and her old knitted hat to try to keep off the rain. She was examining what looked like a piece of greenstone, feeling its surprising smoothness, as though it had been polished by its constant slip and roll among the smaller stones. Harriet was so preoccupied by the greenstone that she paid little attention to Lady's whining, but then she, too, heard the roar coming from the direction of the gorge, and then she looked up and saw arriving, at the bend in the river, a wall of white water like a vast, breaking wave, and before she could cry out, the wave swept down upon Lady and snatched her away.

The water crashed by inches from Harriet's feet, almost obliterating the shingle strand on which the tent stood. Behind the first wave came a second and then a third, and then the river calmed, but rose higher still, drowning the banks, frothing and whirling in a swelling tide.

Harriet unlaced her boots and kicked them off, snatched her hat from her head and her shawl from her shoulders and waded into the freezing water. She began calling to Lady, but the sound of her voice was gone instantly as the swiftness of the flood caught her in its cold arms and she fell under.

Water streamed into her mouth and she felt her heavy, drenched skirts drag her down into the weeds. She kicked out, thrashed against the pull of the skirts, tried to claw her way up towards the turmoil of light far above her, as her lungs burned and the icy coldness of the river pressed on her skin and sent shock-waves into her bones.

She felt her head come to the surface and she coughed and choked and gulped for a mouthful of air and saw the sky for a brief, white moment, but her clothes weighed her down and the sky vanished once more and Harriet Blackstone knew that she was drowning.

She was falling into a green darkness. Yet she still fought and kicked against the winding sheet of her skirts, thrashed upwards with her arms, and now at last a bright bubble of sky burst once again above her face and she struggled to hold it there, to hold the sky above her, to emulate the rose at the base of the waterfall, rising through its own drowning, 'obstinate in resurrection'.

She heard herself shrieking, as though this sharp sound piercing the air might play a role in holding up her head, but she knew that she was helpless against the icy current. And what cold was entering her veins! No cold in any snow-filled winter had been as terrible as the cold which had its grip upon her now. Harriet knew that even if she could vanquish the tug of the saturated skirts, she had no weapon with which to fight the cold . . .

Unless . . .

Unless it was her voice, her cries of ice going up into the air, so she tried to stretch these out, each one like a high note on a flute, taking all the breath that remained.

And then, as she choked again on the water and her cries were cut off, she felt her body being slammed into something yielding, like a thicket of weed and this thicket held her still as she saw the flood keep driving past her and she reached out and tried to clutch at this yielding thing and she got hold of it and found that it had some cunning pattern or design that she knew to be shaped by people and not by nature and she searched for the word to describe it, searched and searched as she let her body be wrapped round by it and felt her skirts slowly billow to the surface, as though both she and they had suddenly become weightless.

Then she remembered the word.

A net.

III

She thought the sky had been pale, despite the rain, but now Harriet saw that she was staring into darkness.

She could hear nothing.

She closed her eyes. She supposed that this was what death was: darkness and soundlessness. But after a little while, she was aware of something else: heat. She was still in her body and her body seemed to be burning.

She opened her eyes again and she saw, or thought she saw, very close to her open eyes, a face which she didn't recognise. She stared at it and she thought that it smiled at her but that in this smile was contained such measureless sadness that she concluded it belonged to the face of someone come to mourn her as she lay in her coffin. She wanted to ask: Who are you? Then she remembered that she was almost certainly dead and the dead had no voice. And she returned to sleep.

IV

Harriet turned her head and saw a small fire.

The way the flames moved without ceasing fascinated her, for what moved them? Could it be said that a flame was 'alive'? She saw shadows, shapes. There was some movement in these, or else they didn't move at all, but the firelight only flickered over them or behind them, giving the illusion of movement. She waited to see which of these possibilities would prove to be true, and while she waited felt herself spirited away into a dream of the Cob House, where Lilian was riddling the smoky range and cursing and crying, both at once, and she, Harriet, was decorating cakes that Lilian had made and on one of the cakes she laid some berries of belladonna. Lilian turned round and saw the belladonna berries, but instead of protesting, she dried her eyes on her apron and began to smile a secretive smile and to nod her head with its rope of hair like a noose. 'The belladonna is for him,' Lilian announced. 'A very fine idea. *Wulla.*'

Then Harriet woke and felt her head being lifted up and a cup was put to her lips and she took a sip. She wanted to ask: 'Is it belladonna?' But she still had no voice and couldn't declare beyond all question that she was no longer dead or dreaming. Yet the drink was warm and had a strong scent of flowers or herbs and she felt it go down into her body and begin to fill the empty spaces inside her, and it was at this moment that memory returned to her and she asked: 'Lady. Where's Lady?'

There was silence. Then a voice said: 'Lady? Black white dog?'

'Yes.'

'Fresh came,' said the quiet voice of Pao Yi. 'Lady gone.'

V

Pao Yi had been standing on his onion bed when the flood arrived.

Since the death of his parents on the weir, he always listened attentively to the changing moods of any river or lake near which he found himself, and so he heard the roar of the fresh begin far away in the Styx Valley and stood waiting to see what it was going to do here. He'd wanted to bring in his fishing net, but judged that he didn't have time to do this.

When he saw the advancing wall of water, he felt his heart quicken. Though his garden was on a plateau well above the river's edge, Pao Yi retreated towards his hut. He knew that in New Zealand a dry creek could become a brimming river in seconds and the great rivers themselves carve out new valleys in a single season.

The succession of high waves broke and pooled and the river-banks disappeared and other waves appeared, rising up and coming to their curve and falling, and all the time the level rose and rose and Pao Yi understood that the old, sluggish Kokatahi was gone – gone for this season, gone for ever, perhaps? – and the new river would be wide and angry and fast. And he saw in his mind's eye how it would rush down upon the mine workings at Kokatahi and Kaniere, flattening the heaps of mullock, snatching away the tents and hovels and streaming into the mine-shafts and bores, carrying everything onwards, tumbling and broken and drowned, and hurling it all into the sea.

And so Pao Yi knew that his livelihood here was at an end.

Some of the miners would be drowned and the rest would take whatever they had left and make their way back to Hokitika. There would be no customers left for his vegetables and they would rot in the earth.

He looked down at them, at the neat rows, at his leeks like fountains, at the blood-red beets. He felt, not fear for his future, but a sentimental sorrow for the plants themselves or for the orderly beauty of the plot which nobody except himself and the Englishwoman had ever seen. He was just imagining, too, how the routine of his days, with which he had been so strangely content, would change, when he heard screams coming from the water.

Pao Yi had fetched rope, looped it round his waist and tied one end of it to a tree. The coldness of the water surprised him and he instructed himself to work quickly, playing out the rope, holding fast to it and not to the net, in case the net gave way, then feeling his feet lose their grip on the river bottom and starting to swim. He swam like a frog, with his strong, wiry legs pushing out at a comical angle.

Harriet Blackstone was still holding on to his fishing net, but her head had fallen sideways and her face had the pallor of the drowned.

Pao Yi lifted her up and fed the rope round her waist and brought it back and tied it, so that he and she were roped together and now, as he turned to swim back, he felt the heaviness of her and didn't know whether he was too late to save her. He swam on his back, with his frog legs kicking out as strongly as he could make them, and she lay on him and to keep her head from dropping into the water, he rested her face on his.

When he felt his back arrive against dry land, he was aware of how steep the slope of the land suddenly was. He tried to stand up and to turn, so that he wouldn't topple over as he attempted to scramble out. He fumbled to release Harriet from the rope and when she was free of it he laid her on the grass and he saw the rain which was still falling begin to pattern the mud which coated her skirts.

Shivering, still looped about with the rope, Pao Yi knelt by Harriet, then turned her over gently and tried to do what he'd often done in his dreams to the bodies of Chen Lin and Chen Fen Ming – *to undrown them.*

He'd always been able to see it so clearly, this miracle of an undrowning: the soaked heads and thin torsos lying at the side of Heron Lake and his own strong hands pressing on them, on the back of their rib cages, to force the lake-water out of their lungs, pressing down again and again, and then at last seeing the streams coming out of their mouths and feeling them come alive again – his beloved parents, irascible Lin and self-centred Fen Ming – and begin to curse and spit.

And then he lifted them up in his arms and they were as light as cloth, and he carried them to their dark little house and laid them down and lit a fire to bring warmth back into their veins and heard them begin to chatter and giggle, saying:

'Oh but did you see how near we got to the weir, Lin? We were inches from it, we truly were. We were a fish's length from the very lip of the weir!' 'Oh yes, my word, what luck we had, Fen Ming! We would be dead now, Pao Yi, and you would be an orphan. How sad! An orphan's life is full of worry and confusion, ha, ha! But you saved us and you saved yourself. What a miracle!'

Despite the reality of his parents' death, Pao Yi always enjoyed this dream. One of the things he liked most about it was his own unchanging efficiency.

He'd never undressed a woman before, only Paak Mei.

In his own language, he apologised to Harriet for doing this, but was aware that she didn't hear him.

He saw that her hands and arms had been browned by the weather, but that her body was translucent white like an onion and her nipples dark as beets. Her feet were slender and finely arched and Pao Yi stared at the straightness of her toes. To warm them, he held her feet in his hands and then laid them against his thighs.

He dressed her in some of his own cotton clothes – jacket and wide trousers – and laid her on his mat, and covered her with rags and blankets.

He made a little fire, opening a vent he'd contrived in his roof with a flower-pot that would take most of the smoke up and away into the air, and crouched by the fire to warm himself, but with his eye always on Harriet. Her body seemed to fill all the space around him. Nobody else had ever come into his hut in all the time he had lived there. He began unplaiting his hair.

When he was dry and warm, he set water to boil on the fire and made a tea from mint leaves and juniper berries and tried to lift Harriet's head so that she would drink and he saw her looking at him, unafraid, but curious. The feel of her neck under his hand was intimate and troubling. He tried to smile when he looked at her, to reassure her that she was safe. She asked about the dog, Lady, and he attempted to tell her that the fresh had surely taken the life of the dog, but he didn't have sufficient words. And very soon, he laid her head down again and watched her tenderly as she drifted back to sleep.

Pao Yi felt very tired now. He fetched the last thin blanket that he had and wrapped himself in this and lay down on the hard floor. Outside he could hear the river rush onwards, leaving him and his garden far behind. His last thought before he slept concerned the piece of gold lying buried under the seventeenth onion.

VI

Harriet woke in the dark.

There was an ember of light on the earth to the left of her, where the fire had burnt low, and Harriet remembered staring at flames and forming some peculiar question about them which she'd been unable to answer.

And she felt now that she didn't know the answers to any single thing which concerned her. She knew only that the fresh had come, that she'd found herself in the river. But why had she been in the water? She was cold now, yet seemingly safe, lying in darkness by the scarlet ashes of a fire. But this was not her tent, she knew that. And how had she escaped drowning?

She pulled the blanket that covered her more closely round her and stared at the darkness, trying to see the outline of things, but her eyes couldn't make sense of anything. She thought how excellent it would be to discover within her reach a piece of wood and throw it on to the fire, so that both heat and light would increase, but she felt unable to move. Her head ached and her throat was parched. But what could she do about any of these things?

She lay as still as she could and listened. The night seemed to be calm, but Harriet could hear the river sliding by, lapping at stones, and now she began to wonder whether her tent and everything that she'd owned, including the gold she'd found, had been taken by the river, and she saw that such a thing could easily happen because she could remember suddenly, with extraordinary clarity, the way the drought and the rain and the wind had taken the Cob House and how the calico walls had lain flapping on the tussock and the door had rammed itself into the earth . . .

The sudden brief flaring of the fire, as a small twig burned and went out, brought Harriet back to the present and to her task of listening. She began to try to count the things she could hear:

No wind in the high bush.

The river travelling on and on.

The sighing of her own heart.

No other sound.

Then, the daylight came: a grey shadow of day.

She was warmer because the fire was burning again.

She turned her head and saw Pao Yi kneeling by the fire, plaiting his hair. She recognised him and knew that he had saved her from the river and that she must be lying in his hut above the vegetable garden.

She watched him without moving, feigning sleep: his face that was comically sad, the thick braid of his hair, his hands that looked nimble, like the hands of a flautist. She remembered his name. She remembered that in his other life he owned a boat and fished a far-away lake.

Pao Yi stood up and crept silently about the hut, intent on small tasks, folding a blanket, filling a tin can with water, taking dry food of some kind from a sack, breaking more kindling for the fire. And Harriet thought how she'd never seen anybody who moved like this, barefoot, making no sound. She felt that she would like to go on watching him, unobserved, all through his day: see him drink his tea or eat whatever food he was going to make; hear him whistle or sing or talk to himself; hear him go out of the hut to piss; see him wash and shave himself; observe his naked arms, which had saved her from the water, and his narrow hips and his strong thighs and his sex.

Pao Yi crossed to her and knelt down by her and Harriet lowered her eyes, wondering if he'd seen her staring at him, intruding into his life with her fever-distorted thoughts. Then she felt his hand on her brow and the touch of this was as beautiful a thing as Harriet had ever experienced and she wanted it to remain there and never move. She tried to speak, to ask him, perhaps, to stay still, exactly as he was, but she found that she couldn't say a word because she was crying. She was scarcely making any sound, yet her tears kept flowing, running down her face and neck and arriving as a pool in the cleft of her collar bone. She felt Pao Yi's hand move gently away from her forehead down to her cheek and rest there, trying to collect the tears, as though the palm of his hand could absorb her grief into itself.

'Cry for Lady?' Pao Yi asked softly. 'Black. White. Cry for dying?'

Bellbird Singing

I

When the fresh arrived at Kokatahi, Joseph was working at the bottom of his eighth shaft.

He'd already glimpsed the shine of the blue clay in Shaft 8 and had begun to feel the familiar yet futile resurgence of hope that always came when the clay bottom was reached. Then, he heard the roar of the water. He lifted his head. He'd just put a foot on to his rickety ladder when the flood arrived at the lip of the shaft. He fell back into the hole and the water came drenching down on him.

He grabbed the ladder and gripped it and climbed up and got his head out into the air, and he heard screaming all around him. Then the white waves broke against Joseph's head, as against a stone, and he was hurled backwards into the shaft.

Again, he struggled to find the ladder and held it as the freezing water rose around him. He felt his feet leave the ground, but now, he forced his body down, taking gulps of air as and when he could, knowing that being below ground in the mine-shaft had saved him from being taken by the flood. For the pace of the river was like nothing that he'd ever seen. Joseph understood that any man standing out in the open would have been knocked down and whirled away in the freezing eddies of the fresh.

The water was so cold, it was as though Joseph were being packed in ice. But he knew he had to remain in the hole until the water began to pool and calm. He knew he was lucky that this particular shaft was near the back of his claim, furthest from the river, and when he came up for air again he could see that he was only a few feet from ground that was still dry under the manuka scrub.

When he surfaced once more, he could see tents and huts being crumpled and broken apart and sailing out on to the water, and one of these was his tent, with everything that he possessed, including his gun and his cradle and his cup of gold given to him by Harriet and the precious dust he'd found long ago at the old creek.

As he watched his tent disappear, Joseph thought how, in moments, the fresh would arrive at the Scots' claim and come down upon Hamish McConnell and all his fancy machinery and upon Will Sefton. And the thought that Will might drown was, despite all that had happened, as wistful a thing as Joseph could contemplate and he imagined Will's penny whistle floating out on the tide like a miniature raft, staying afloat for a long time, bobbing on the waves until at last it was swamped and gone.

All this while, as he hung on in the freezing shaft, Joseph gave no thought to Harriet. Perhaps, some part of him knew that the fresh must have come down from the mountains high up in the Styx Valley, where she was working her shingle beach, but it was as though he imagined that its true force had been unleashed only here, at Kokatahi, and that all the deaths would occur here and at Kaniere, and they would be miners' deaths, the deaths of *men*, of old returners and new chums; and all the rest of the indifferent world would be spared, as it had been spared the days that he'd suffered here.

It was only some time later, when he could feel his blood begin to go cold in his veins and understood that he could die in the water and would have to try soon to reach the lip of dry ground, it was only then, when he had to act to save himself, that Joseph realised the full and fearful consequence to him of what had happened: Harriet and all the gold might also be drowned and gone. Her miraculous find – the only thing which had kept him from going mad with rage and disappointment – might now have been taken from him.

It was almost certainly his fury at this, pumping energy to his heart, bringing a sudden, murderous strength to his arms, that enabled Joseph to pull himself out of the shaft and claw his way on his hands and knees through the surging water to the manuka strand. He clasped a limb of the prickly scrub, knew it was tough and wouldn't snap, threw himself forward into the bushes, immune to cuts and scratches, and lay where he fell, among the thorny leaves.

After a while, he stood up. He was trembling with shock and cold and with the horror of everything around him and the dread of everything that was to come. He saw that it was no longer raining and that a cold sun glimmered on the river, moving in its new and lethal course. He saw that nothing remained of the mounds of wash-dirt that had lined the water's edge and that not one tent or hut had been left standing.

If he'd been able to make a fire to warm himself, Joseph might have tried to trek up-river, to where Harriet had pitched her tent. But he had nothing. And he knew that he could die of his drenching in the fresh if he let the cold night come on.

He took off his heavy, soaking shirt and tried to dry his neck and arms with grass. Then he began to walk in the direction of the McConnell claim and the distant shelter of Hokitika.

The path had gone. Joseph had to make his way over and around boulders, through scrub, cling precariously to trees to stop himself from slipping down into the surging water. Ahead of him, other survivors of the fresh were making this same long, difficult, melancholy journey. He saw some of the miners clinging to each other, almost as lovers cling, and it occurred to him now that men he'd thought crude and vexing at Kokatahi had perhaps been stoical and good-humoured and that he could have made friends here – but for Will Sefton – he could have become part of some camaraderie and got drunk with these people and felt less alone. But none of this signified now. They were all headed back to Hokitika. The Canterbury Government would have to authorise some assistance . . .

Joseph saw from a distance that McConnell's horse-whim was still standing as well as two or three tents behind. But the river now ran only a few feet from them and most of the

Brenner–McConnell claim was under water and there was no sign of any miner choosing to remain.

Nevertheless, when Joseph arrived there, he stood for a moment on the mud – on the very soil that had brought Hamish McConnell and his partner so much good fortune – and wondered if McConnell was still alive and would yet live to inhabit his castle in Scotland.

And he asked himself what the epitaphs of the Gold Rush would be and what would come after and how the country would be changed and who would eventually turn out to be the winners and losers. But he had no answers. All he could see and feel was the suffering that gold had brought upon the miners of Kokatahi. And although the idea of McConnell's grand establishment had once made him half mad with envy, now he hoped that the man would get it after all and live in it like an aristocrat and spit in the eye of anyone who looked down on him, but yet remember to his dying day that he'd got his whole fortune by fossicking in the earth. For if McConnell was beaten, what hope was there for him or for any of the others?

He trudged on. He saw the sun getting low in the sky and dreaded to be overtaken by the dark. As he neared Kaniere, he saw a body washed up on the wide bank. A little way from it, stood a cluster of gulls and Joseph stopped and stared at them. He shouted out, trying to frighten the birds away, but they wouldn't be moved. They were waiting for the moment when they would begin their feast. So now, like a madman, flapping his soaking shirt and screaming in just the way he'd screamed so often as a boy, Joseph ran at the gulls, and they hopped away from him over the mud and lazily took off, but only to fly in circles above him. Soon enough, he knew, they would land again.

He went to the body and turned it, half afraid it would be McConnell's body, but it was a man he didn't know, and the man had a strange smile on his face, as though he had just caught his first beautiful glimpse of the colour on his claim. And Joseph felt that this smile was one of the most terrible things he'd seen in all this long, terrible time. Barely aware of what he was doing, he began to wrap the man's head in his wet shirt. He bound it tight.

Let be, he muttered. *Let be.*

II

Now, Joseph was sitting by a fire, trying to eat a plate of kūmara that seemed too hot and too sickly and he kept laying it aside.

'Eat,' said the woman's voice. 'You'd better eat.'

He tried again but couldn't swallow the kūmara, sipped a dribble of sweet red sauce and retched.

He'd been billeted in one of the shanties that lined the Hokitika wharves. A widow, Ernestine Boyd, had taken him in, along with two other survivors, and handed out to them her late husband's patched and mended clothes and given them what she had to eat, which was the sweet potato in its crimson gravy, and let them wrap themselves in the blankets from her bed, which were frayed and worn.

As she handed out the food, one of the other men said: 'Shall we toss a coin for who keeps Ernestine warm tonight, now that her covers are all gone?' The man was in his twenties, and Joseph looked at him and saw him wink at his companion and saw the widow Ernestine smile at them both and so he thought that, when they'd eaten their fill of the kūmara, he would be left alone to sleep by the fire.

He'd encountered no one that he knew in Hokitika. The Customs House had been turned into a morgue. Volunteers had brought bodies down from Kaniere for as long as the daylight lasted. Joseph thought that he should go into the morgue, to see whether Will or Harriet was laid out there among the drowned, but he was so tired now and felt so ill that he couldn't go near the morgue, not in this frozen night, not until he'd rested and begun to get everything straight in his head . . .

For what if he found Harriet's body?

What could he do and where could he go if Harriet were

dead and there was no gold after all because the river had flooded the shingle bank and swept the gold away? And he thought of everything that he'd lost: his tent and most of his tools, all his money and his wallet that had been precious to him, his gun, his wash-box, the fishing rod Will had left, his stores, his grog, his cans and kettle, his blankets, his clothes that Harriet had washed, his pipe and his cup of gold and all that he'd brought with him from his brief time in the Cob House. He had nothing now. He was wearing a dead man's mothballed rags. He had difficulty keeping down a spoonful of sweet potato. He was finished.

Ernestine Boyd took his plate away. Joseph saw that she was good-looking in a small way, with ample breasts and the vestige of a dimple in her cheek. 'You sleep now,' she said. 'In the morning, I'll get us some eggs and a handful of tea leaves. Then, you'll feel more like a man.'

He heard the younger miners giggle, but didn't care, didn't pay them any heed, asked the widow to bank up the fire because the cold wouldn't leave him, just wouldn't go from his bones, and he didn't want to wake up beside a dead fire, and she did as he asked and while she was fetching in logs Joseph raised his head and looked out of the small window and heard the sound of the sea.

III

When Harriet woke up again, she saw that she was alone in Pao Yi's hut.

She propped herself on her elbows. The fire was still bright, and Harriet noticed that the pieces of wood had been laid in a square, symmetrical pattern, like a trellis. And the fire seemed to burn like this, obediently, with hardly any alteration to its original design.

Her fever had cooled. She lifted the blankets she was wrapped in and saw that she was wearing Pao Yi's clothes. They were grey and crumpled and smelled of her own sweat, but also of something strange, like incense. She sat up and stared at her white feet, coming out of the ends of the cotton trousers. She looked around to see where her skirts and chemise might be, but there was no sign of them. She had a sudden vision of pegging washing on a line near the Cob House and watching Joseph's shirts billowing in the wind and knowing at the time that she felt no tenderness towards any clothes of his. Love, she thought, can be measured by what we feel for items of laundry.

In the daylight that was coming through the sacking at the door, Harriet let her eye wander around the hut, trying to read, from the objects she could see, something about the solitary life of the man who had saved her.

There was a black earthenware pot, which probably contained water, and an assembly of cooking pans and a wire sieve, hanging from nails driven into the walls. There were sacks of rice and flour and a jar of oil and a stone pestle and mortar. There was a dilapidated wicker trunk, which might have contained clothes or bedding. On top of the trunk were some thick sheets of yellowed paper, tied with ribbon into a worn leather binder.

On the near wall, where the hut had been lodged against the rock of the hillside, a rough wooden shelf had been put up and on this little shelf was a tablet, also made of wood and inscribed with Chinese characters. Some stubs of candle lay near the tablet and behind these, leaning against the stone, were four faded water-colour pictures of an elderly man and woman and of a young woman and a child. And Harriet understood that this was Pao Yi's shrine to his real life, to his life on the lake, to the people he'd left and to whom he would one day return.

She lay down again. She found that she felt a kind of instantaneous attachment to the strangers in these water-colours, as though she had once known them, or as though they were here in some unselfish way to keep her company. And, more than this, she felt, in this low, dark place, that a kind of deep, indescribable tranquillity was present. And she thought that she would just lie here and not move and let everything quieten all around her and remain still. She thought that the tomorrow of her life would be harsh and lonely and long and that it could wait for her, wait a day or more than a day, wait till the river had fallen . . .

She felt sleepy, but she didn't want to close her eyes because every moment that passed seemed to possess an unusual intensity, as though it wished to draw her attention to its own uniqueness. She tried to recollect whether she had ever before felt as she did now and it seemed to her that, in thirty-five years, consciousness had never presented itself to her in precisely this way, so that the texture, colour, smell and feel of things all combined to distil her mind and body to a perfect sensation of *being*.

After a while, after a lapse of time which might have been of long or short duration, Harriet couldn't say, she heard Pao Yi taking off his boots at the door to the hut, so she lay down and pretended to sleep, pretended to be as helpless as she'd been in her fever, so that she could lie there and watch him as he moved about the hut. She thought it was still morning, but that Pao Yi might have been working since dawn in the garden and that he would be hungry. He would lay more wood on the square fire and prepare some food. When the food was ready, he would offer some to her and the taste of it would be different from any food she had ever eaten.

She heard him come quietly into the hut and close the door. She heard him fill a billy-can with water and drink. Then, it was as if he were no longer in the hut, so soundless did everything become, but when she opened her eyes again, she saw him standing in front of the shelf, where the tablet and the water-colours were propped up against the stone, and he was staring at them without moving, without seeming to blink or alter by any fraction the position of his head. But she knew that he was talking silently to the pictures, talking and then waiting, as if for an answer, always without moving or altering his gaze, then starting to talk again. And she wondered whether, in his solitary life at the edge of the Styx Valley, he was tormented by his loss of these people and by homesickness for his village and his boat and his lake.

So absorbed did Pao Yi seem to be in his conversation that Harriet continued to stare at him, believing him to be unaware of her, of her intrusive gaze, but suddenly, without warning, he turned his head and looked down at her, as though he'd been aware of her watching him all the time. And there was a new intensity to his look. It was as if he had returned from far away and brought the power of that far-away place back with him and it was now visible in his eyes.

Harriet lowered her gaze. She could feel the agitation of her heart. And as the seconds passed and she didn't dare to move and Pao Yi didn't move, she understood that what she wanted was for him to touch her.

Once she had allowed herself to admit this to herself, there was nothing but it and it alone in her mind and she thought that if he didn't touch her, if he was indifferent to her or couldn't see that this was what she wanted, her longing for his touch would only increase and increase. And yet she knew that she could say nothing, do nothing. She could only remain where she was, with her face turned away from him, but in her mind, with her will that had always been so strong, she began to call him to her.

She could see the firelight flickering on the slab wall of the hut and hear the river rushing onwards in its altered course and yet feel the suspension of time, as though the coil of a clock-spring had been wound to tightness and held there and prevented from breaking free.

She didn't hear him move. She thought that he was still standing exactly where he'd been, in front of the faded pictures. But then she knew, from the warmth and scent of him, that he was beside her and she lifted her head and looked at him. She was reminded how absolute was the sadness of his expression, yet she now saw that the curve of his mouth was sensual and beautiful beyond any other that she'd seen, and she was unable to stop herself from reaching out, hesitantly, like a blind person trying to find her way, and touching his lips with her fingers.

Even now, while she touched his mouth and he held her gaze as intently as he had held the gaze of his family a moment or two ago, Harriet was terrified that he would suddenly pull away from her, as though this moment had somehow happened by mistake, by some crude misunderstanding, and he would act to bring it to a swift and terrible close. But Pao Yi didn't pull away. He took Harriet's outstretched wrist in his hand and crushed her palm against his lips and kissed it.

After some moments, he relinquished her hand and laid it down on her breast. Then he folded back her coverings and looked at her lying there, dressed in his own clothes, and he bent over her and took her foot in both his hands. He caressed the foot, seeming to examine every tender inch of it and then he moved very gradually towards it, holding her leg aloft for a moment, like a dancer's leg, and then reaching down and taking out his sex, which was erect, and then bending her knee and bringing her leg down until her foot touched his penis and then starting to rub himself against her foot. And now Harriet saw the habitual sadness of his face transformed by an expression of pure wonder.

The feel of his heavy sex against her instep, the flagrant yet poignant intimacy of these gestures, made Harriet gasp. No moment of her life had appeared to her as astonishing or as exquisite or as overflowing with promise as this one. And it seemed to her that for all the time she'd been alive, desire had lain asleep in her and never stirred, so that she'd believed she would never feel it and would go through into middle age and old age never understanding what it could be.

But now it had been woken by this one man. She whispered his name: 'Pao Yi.'

IV

Thirty shillings each they were given, the miners who had survived at Kokatahi and Kaniere – the thirty shillings which their claims had cost them, no less and no more. A newspaper article was posted on the door of the warden's office, telling the claimants that the generosity of the Canterbury Government 'had no precedent or equal on the goldfields'.

So they queued obediently at the warden's office and took the money and wondered how long it would last. They queued again for a distribution of sheepskins that smelled of disinfectant and for tins of condensed milk, discovered in the back room of a grocery store.

Joseph stayed on with Ernestine Boyd, trying to swallow the poor meals she made, trying to gather his strength so that he could make the journey up the river to look for Harriet and her gold.

But when he contemplated the long trek back up the Kokatahi Valley, Joseph felt himself become dizzy and weak. He knew that he was a man at the end of his resources. He longed to clamber on to a ship and fall asleep on some soft, narrow bunk and not wake till the ship arrived in England. The possibility that he would never get there, never be able to make amends with the Millwards, never smell the wild flowers on Parton Green, burdened his mind so intolerably, it was as if he'd never ever had any wish but this – to arrive home in Norfolk. It was as if the man who had bought land on the Okuku and felt so optimistic about his farm were someone else, not him, someone blind and hasty and deluded whom he no longer talked to, no longer recognised.

He delayed setting out for Kokatahi.

Ernestine Boyd offered to cut his hair, which had grown straggly and long, but he refused. He wanted to remain as he was, cast out from normality and happiness, until he reached home.

He began the journey up-river on a cold morning.

Joseph thought he could see, in the flat, violet darkness of the sky, the approach of snow. So he understood that he was in a race with the weather. He might make his way up to Harriet's camp and then be trapped by snow far up the valley, unable to get back to Hokitika. And he knew, in the weak state he was in, that he wouldn't survive a winter in some makeshift shelter. He would just lay down his head and die. He would die like the cow, Beauty, without making a sound.

The river had fallen. Washed up on the banks, from Kaniere to Kokatahi, Joseph saw the familiar detritus of the diggings: slabs and wheels, torn tents, rusted buckets and chains, broken picks and shovels, and in one place, a peculiar isthmus of grey and brown rags, strung out into the shallows. Gulls squealed and bickered in the cold air.

Joseph dreaded to discover bodies. He saw rats tearing some carcass to pieces and turned his head away. He missed his gun. He felt too light, too insubstantial without the miner's paraphernalia he used to carry. He tore a stick from the bush to use as a staff and thought how, wearing the disinfected sheepskin around his shoulders and with his wild hair and beard, he must look like some mad prophet of the wilderness.

When he came to the spot where his tent used to be, he sat down on the muddy grass and drank from the river. Water and milk kept him alive these days. The very thought of bacon or mutton made his flesh creep. Sometimes, in the shanty in Hokitika, he'd chewed bread or eaten the suet dumplings Mrs Boyd had set out in a plate of thin gravy, but even these he'd found difficult to swallow. He would have liked to drink beer, frothy and strong, but had no money for beer, knew he had to save as much as he could of the thirty shillings if he was to have any chance of a passage home.

He stood up and walked on. Now, he was on new territory, where he'd never before set foot, and he felt a quietness fall on the landscape, as though, at Kokatahi, the noise of the mine had still remained behind after everything had been swept away, but that here, beyond it, where no diggings had ever been started, silence returned because everything had persisted in its wild and sequestered state. He saw kingfishers darting over the water and a heron standing motionless on a rock. The grey density of the sky began to lift and a bolt of sunlight fell on to the narrow path.

Joseph knew that, at other moments in his life, he would have been cheered by the sight of these things, but it was as though nothing could cheer him now, nothing in New Zealand, nothing that Nature or Man could contrive here. All he wanted was to sail away.

He made very slow progress up the valley, leaning more and more on the stick. He kept searching the sky, wondering if snow was beginning to fall. He didn't know how many hours he had walked when he lifted his head once more and saw, across the river, above the new line of the deep water, the Chinaman's vegetable garden.

Joseph stopped. No snow was falling. The sun was, in fact, still shining, and Joseph stared at the startling colours of the planting and thought how, after all, what had been grown here might be the kind of food he could eat – food you could swallow when life took your appetite away. And he felt, for the first time, that his rage against Scurvy Jenny had been brutish and unnecessary, a shameful corollary to his enslavement to Will Sefton, a kind of madness.

He remembered that those Chinese he'd encountered – like the men he'd observed on the *Wallabi* – had all manifested a kind of quiet resignation, as though they'd understood better than anyone else how bitterly hard it is to survive in the world and rise up in it to any degree, and so decided to put their trust and their energies into small things and dream no grandiose dreams and even be content to fossick patiently through stray corners of earth left behind by others who had moved on.

He found that he envied them their ability to do this. He saw how his own head had always and ever been roaring with schemes and desires and, even now, wouldn't let him rest. He dreaded to live his whole life like this, burning with unsatisfied longing. He looked over to the vegetable plot and understood another thing: that Scurvy Jenny no longer had any customers for his vegetables now that the diggings had gone, and yet the plot appeared newly hoed and weeded, as if Chen were indifferent to customers, as if the garden itself were what counted and nothing else were of any importance to him. And Joseph thought: This is the state to which I shall aspire, where what is important to me is already mine.

He walked on. He knew that he couldn't be far from the strand of shingle where Harriet had found the colour. But he dreaded to arrive there now, dreaded what he was going to find. He faltered on the path, his breathing laboured, the sheepskin beginning to make him sweat and itch.

Again, he looked up at the sky, which was clearing all the while. And he wondered whether he wasn't searching, now, for the snow clouds, looking for a reason to turn back. But the sky only looked pitilessly down. For a moment, Joseph remembered Lilian, standing on the flats, staring up at the rainbow, and he thought how long it was since anybody had said his name.

He went on like a sleep-walker. His heart thudded in his chest. He began to mumble some long-forgotten prayer.

Now, he had reached the river's bend. Now, he saw Harriet's tent. Bile rose in his mouth and he spat it out on to the grass.

The tent leaned at a precarious angle, but still stood at the back of the beach. Nothing moved. Joseph held on to his staff like an old man and stared stupidly at the scene before him, trying, without moving nearer, to deduce what it had to say to him. He felt petrified. He opened his mouth to say the name 'Harriet', but he couldn't utter it. And it was then that he remembered the dog, Lady. If the dog had been alive, she would have heard his approach and begun barking, but there was no sound at all, only the low, conversational noise of the river.

He forced himself to move forward again. He noticed a ring of blackened stones where a fire had once been made. He saw that the river had risen to within a few feet of the tent and then receded, leaving a flat shelf of mud on which there was no human footprint, but only lines of little arrow-like markings, where birds had trod.

Joseph took off his sheepskin and laid down his stick. He sniffed the air to see whether there was any sweet stench of death, but there was none.

So now at last he dared to approach the tent. He pushed it with his hands and it fell sideways, pulling on one rope. He lifted the canvas away and saw a careful huddle of familiar things. In the centre was the red blanket, folded in two on the flax mat, which looked clean and dry. Lying on the mat was the little gun he had given Harriet at D'Erlanger's Hotel. Near this was Harriet's knapsack and the long string which she sometimes used to tie Lady to a post or tree. There was a piece of ham gone mouldy in a muslin pouch, where a fly was crawling, and a careful arrangement of dry food in small, frayed sacks.

Joseph squatted down and touched the blanket. That Harriet

had been here alone, existing in this minute and tidy way, touched him to some degree, but his mind danced about and wouldn't remain fixed on her, but only kept insisting that the gold was here somewhere and that it was the gold that mattered.

He began to sift through her few possessions. She was dead, he told himself. The river had taken her. Harriet Blackstone was dead and gone, so all that remained here was his by right. He hurled away the pouch of ham. He emptied out the sacks of flour and sugar. He told himself that if he'd known Harriet better, he would have had a better idea of where her gold was hidden. Yet he hadn't wanted to know her better. Since the death of Rebecca, he hadn't wanted to know anybody at all.

He moved round the little encampment on all fours, like a scavenging wolf. He moved in circles, exploring the ground. He lifted up each stone blackened by the fire. He dug down beneath them with his hands.

He found no gold.

Joseph sat on the red blanket and pulled it round him. He wondered whether, if a man longs ardently enough for death, death obligingly arrives. Then he reached out idly, to touch a flat stone, to feel the continuing reality of the earth, and he heard the stone scrape against something metal. He lifted up the stone and saw buried underneath it, deep down in the mud, a tin cup full of the colour.

Joseph threw off the scarlet blanket and spread it out and heaped the golden grains into the middle of it and gathered them up into his hands and let them fall again and then laid his cheek down on them. He saw his future come towards him. He saw the dawn coming up on the beech woods at Parton Magna. He saw that he was going to stay alive.

He wanted to waste no time.

He pressed every last grain and fleck of gold into the empty sugar bag and then rolled it up in the blanket. He tucked the small gun into the waistband of his trousers. He scooped up a handful of sugar and ate it.

He looked up at the sky and saw that the day was advancing

and that dusk would overtake him if he didn't begin his homeward journey now. So he stood up and rinsed his hands in the river and then he turned and began to walk away.

He walked as briskly as he was able to walk. He knew that his tread was lighter now. Somewhere up above him, he could hear a bellbird singing.

When he drew parallel once again to Chen's garden, he stopped because he felt hungry for the first time in a long while. He wondered whether he could find some safe crossing over the river. He imagined the iron-fresh taste of spinach leaves. But he could see that the water was still deep and the current swift. No crossing would be possible here until the winter had come and gone.

So Joseph walked on. He held the gold clasped to his chest as he might have held a child. When he reached the first bend in the river, a sound made him stop and look back. He thought at first that it was the sound of somebody crying out, but then everything went silent again, as silent and hushed as it always was, and Joseph assumed that he'd been mistaken: the sound had been made by the inquisitive bellbird following his human path.

An Acre of Land

I

On the night of the twenty-fourth of May, the worm in Edwin Orchard's gut wound itself into a coil so tight that Edwin could feel his intestines bunching and twisting, and a hard, writhing cone appeared beneath the skin of his belly. He began screaming.

Dorothy and Toby came running into Edwin's room. They held him and talked to him and lit lamps round him and Dorothy began to sing him old nursery rhymes that he knew by heart. Janet crept up the stairs and stood at the door, with a handkerchief pressed to her mouth. Toby banked up the fire and went to search for a bottle of rum and brought this back to the room and tried to dribble a few drops into Edwin's mouth and to join in Dorothy's singing, because he always sang out of tune and he thought that this might make his son laugh, as it usually did.

'Can you make me a cambric shirt,
    Parsley, sage, rosemary and thyme,
Without any seam or needlework?
    And you shall be a true love of mine.

'Can you wash it in yonder well,
    Parsley, sage, rosemary and thyme,
Where never sprung water, nor rain ever fell?
    And you shall be a true love of mine ...'

In the middle of this song, Edwin stopped screaming and went quiet. The worm had suddenly uncoiled itself and the pain went away. Dorothy and Toby could see that the cone had disappeared, that the worm now lay in a U-shape just above Edwin's groin, and they watched it, as a dog would watch a rat, to see where and how it was going to move next, but it didn't move.

After a while, they gently pulled the covers back over Edwin and tucked him in. Toby was sweating in the heat of the fire. Edwin stared up at his parents and at the shadows from the firelight dancing on the wall. 'Go on with the song, Mama,' he whispered.

So while Toby mopped his face with a silk handkerchief and Janet crept nearer to the bed and perched on a hard chest that had once contained Edwin's blue sailor suit, Dorothy continued:

'Can you find me an acre of land,
    Parsley, sage, rosemary and thyme,
Between the salt water and the sea sand?
    And you shall be –'

'But I don't know where it could be,' interrupted Edwin.

'Where could what be, my darling?'

'The acre of land. There's no room for it.'

'No,' said Dorothy. 'But you remember that this is a rhyme about impossible things. For how can you make a cambric shirt without needlework?'

'What's cambric?' asked Edwin.

'A kind of material . . .'

'Like bombazine?'

'No . . .'

'Worsted. Alpaca. Chenille. I've never understood the names for materials. What are they? Do you know what they are, Papa?'

'Lord, no!' hooted Toby, throwing his head back. 'What the devil are they? I don't think anybody knows, do they? Are they materials or are they spun sugar? How do we know? Are they feather bolsters?'

The ghost of a smile passed over Edwin's face, then it vanished and he said: 'Pare's cloak had magic feathers.'

Toby looked at Dorothy and she looked back.

'You couldn't possibly remember Pare,' said Dorothy gently. 'You were a tiny baby when she was sent away.'

Edwin stared up at his parents. A look of great weariness was on his face. It seemed important to him that his mama and papa should, at last, know that there was another world, where spirits danced about on the edge of the sun or hid themselves in floating logs and where a kiwi-feather cloak could make you invisible.

'She came back,' Edwin began. 'She called to me when I was playing in the toi-toi. She used to say: "E'win, are you there?" She couldn't pronounce the *d*.'

Toby opened his mouth to speak. Then he closed it. He remembered how Pare had always referred to the baby as 'E'win'. He took Edwin's thin hand in his that was large and red and burning hot. 'Go on,' he said.

'She told me stories,' continued Edwin. 'She told me about the taniwha and the wind god and about the patupaiarehe, who are sort of fairies and they come and steal from you sometimes. And the cloak was magic, which was why you never saw her. It was only me who could see her. She had long black hair tied back and her legs were brown and thin.'

'Are you sure that you didn't dream her?' said Dorothy.

'I didn't dream her, Mama. And you have to believe in her world, that's what Pare said. You have to try to see it, like when you see a lizard, it could be something else...'

'No, Edwin,' said Toby firmly. 'You're talking about superstition. Superstition has to be resisted, not encouraged. This is why the Maoris have not got on as well as they might have done –'

'I don't know what "superstition" means,' said Edwin.

'It means,' said Toby, 'exactly the things you're talking about: believing that a lizard is a monster, when it's only a lizard. On the day that Pare abandoned you on the verandah, she thought she saw a monster, but we know that there was no monster, just a gecko. She almost let you die, you see, because of her ridiculous superstition!'

Edwin was silent for a moment, his eyes large and sad. Then he said: 'Pare wasn't ridiculous, Papa. I don't think you should say that. Especially now.'

'Especially now, why?'

'When she's gone, when she's dead.'

Again, Toby and Dorothy looked at each other. They didn't know what this story of Pare meant, or whether to believe it or whether to dismiss it as one of Edwin's inventions, like the red and yellow Moa Bird he'd drawn so many times.

'How do you know that Pare is dead?' asked Dorothy.

'I just do,' said Edwin. 'She was on a ledge near a waterfall for a long time. I saw her on the ledge and she –'

'What *ledge*, Edwin? What are you talking about?'

'He just imagined it,' snapped Toby.

Edwin now started to struggle in the bed, to try to pull himself up.

'I didn't imagine it!' he cried out. 'I saw the ledge! And Pare wanted me to go there, to help her, but I couldn't. I asked Harriet to find her, but she wouldn't go over the Hurunui, she was too frightened.'

'Harriet? You told Harriet about this?'

'Yes. And she didn't say it was silly. She believed me!'

'Hush,' said Dorothy. 'We believe you, don't we, Toby?'

'No we do *not*!' said Toby, pressing Edwin's hand. 'You had a *dream*, Edwin. Listen to me. You had some very frightening nightmares and they've made you ill. So you have to forget them and then your worm will come out and you will get well.'

'No!' said Edwin, tugging his hand away. 'Pare was real! I smelt her. I touched her. She gave me a kiwi feather. I could show you the place in the toi-toi where we used to sit. My caterpillar used to crawl up her arm. She saw Mollie and Baby . . . She was *real*!'

Edwin began weeping now and Janet, perched on the wooden clothes chest, couldn't help but cry too, as silently as she could, trying not to draw attention to herself.

'Papa is right, Edwin,' said Dorothy with a sigh, wiping Edwin's tears away with her hand. 'You have to forget this now. You have to concentrate on getting well.'

'I'm not going to get well!' cried Edwin. 'You don't

understand! Pare died. *She died*! I know when it happened because she kept calling and calling – '

'Oh my goodness!' said Toby, angry now. 'What on earth is all this? I do believe I've had enough of it. Go to sleep, Edwin. Forget your nonsense. Your pain has gone now. Try to sleep.'

'I'm not going to sleep!' shouted Edwin. 'I'm going to die!'

'No,' said Toby. 'You are *not* going to die. We are not going to let you. The worm has come lower down with the medicine you're taking. Another day or two and it will be out. And then you will get well.'

Edwin began to hit out at his father with his pale fists.

'Stop this, darling,' said Dorothy firmly. 'Lie down. Why don't we sing the song again?'

'What song? What stupid song? About impossible things? About "cambric"? Nobody knows what cambric is! Cambric isn't real. But Pare's real and I know where she is and I'm going there, I'm going to see her!'

'Ssh, Edwin, Edwin . . .'

'Because the worm died! It bunched itself into that cone thing and then it died. And that's the end of my life!'

The only sounds, now, in the room were Edwin's exhausted breathing and the weeping of Janet. Toby got slowly to his feet.

'Stay with him, Dorothy,' he said. 'I'll ride to Rangiora. I'll fetch Dr Pettifer.'

II

The daylight was coming up by the time Toby Orchard had dressed himself and saddled the horse and set out, and with the slow arrival of the light, the snow began to fall.

Toby knew the weather. It was still only May and the snow wouldn't lie for long. He didn't doubt he could get through, but tired and anxious as he was, he felt tormented, as he cantered on, by the dancing snowflakes, which stung his eyes and impaired his vision. He cursed the arrival of winter. He cursed the vastness of the land – the very thing which normally exhilarated him and reminded him how wise and fortunate he'd been to escape his old, unbearable life in London.

He'd ridden only a few miles and was still well within the boundaries of the Orchard Run, when he saw a figure, indistinct in the maddening snow, but just visible to him as a man running along with an animal. And he saw, as he came closer, that it was indeed an elderly man in threadbare coat and a dented felt hat, leading a sheep by a long piece of twine, and seeming to try to escape Toby as he came level with him, veering suddenly away northwards, stumbling on the tussock and pulling wildly on the frayed string.

And Toby knew then, without any doubt in his mind, that in this cold dawn, he'd found the man who, for months, had been stealing sheep off the run and that, urgent as was his mission to Dr Pettifer, he couldn't let this go by.

He turned his horse and again drew level with the man and rode beyond him a little and reined in the horse and looked back. The sheep-stealer stopped, yet pulled the sheep closer to him by looping the twine over his hand.

Toby could now see, through the daze of falling snow, that the man's eyes looked outwards, one to each side of his head, and couldn't focus, and this made for an expression of perpetual confusion on his face, and Toby found it difficult to decide which eye to look at when he began to speak, so he directed his gaze above the eyes towards the ignominious hat.

'That is my animal,' Toby announced angrily. 'You're on the Orchard Run – on *my* run – and that's *my sheep* you're trying to take.'

The man wiped off the snow, where it had clung to his moustache, with a mittened hand. His wall eyes looked east and west and nowhere in between.

'May be your animal, sir,' he said. 'But this sheep tried to bite me! An' I'll take my revenge on any beast which tries to do that! I'll slit her neck and eat her for my dinner and make a coat from her wool because she tried to nip me clean through to the bone.'

Toby faltered for a moment. The man's reply was so unexpected, so cunning in a small way, that Toby Orchard knew that, at some other time, if only all that was happening to

Edwin had been far behind him, then it would have amused him enough to let the man go, warn him off the run, but let him go now, let him have his mutton dinner and his armful of wool, because he was a poor cockatoo who had nothing and Toby Orchard had everything he wanted in the world. But on this icy morning, the flicker of amusement that he allowed himself to feel was replaced, in the next second, by a fury so colossal that he felt his large chest was going to burst apart.

He held the horse on a tight rein and took up his whip. He raised his arm in the air and brought the whip down in a stinging blow on the man's shoulder. The horse reared and whinnied and the man cried out and fell backwards, but all the while managed to keep hold of the string.

'Christ, love us!' babbled the man. 'Christ save me from *you*!'

'Nothing will save you!' shouted Toby, inflicting a second terrible cut with the whip. 'You're a liar! The world is full of liars and I will not tolerate it any more! People come here and they think they can take away everything that's mine, everything that's precious to me, everything I'd give my life for. They think they can come in the night and spirit it away and that I won't catch them and punish them. But they're wrong!'

As Toby raised his whip arm again, the man staggered to his feet and managed to dance away from the blow and he let go of the string and the sheep skittered off at a frantic run.

'Don't kill me!' the man cried out. 'Don't kill me for a sheep. I've let her go, see? I've let her go!' And then he tripped over a mound of tussock, beginning to be slippery in the snow, and fell into a heap and covered his head with his hands. But the lash of the whip fell on to his back, fell twice more and then a third time, until Toby Orchard's surge of rage began to diminish and he began to see the man once more for what he was – a poor creature with a sorry existence, freighted with hunger and want, bowed down by failed hopes – and at last he restrained his arm.

The man was whimpering, but Toby could barely hear this. He himself was short of breath, making a wheezing, sobbing sound in his throat, and he felt as though he were going to choke and die of misery right there, as he sat on his horse. He looked at all that appeared before him, at all that he had been unable to prevent or alter, and confronted the horror of it.

His son was going to die.

A man in a frayed coat lay on his land in agony, with his flesh bleeding.

These things he had somehow allowed to happen.

In the cold air, Toby could hear the foolish, endless bleating of the sheep and he wanted it to cease. He wanted never to hear it again. He thought it nothing but a futile serenade to dreams which had once been realised, but which had now vanished away.

III

Edwin was dreaming.

He was standing by a lake, but the lake was so still, it was as though there was nothing alive in it, nor any wind to coax the surface of it into movement. But in this glassy, silent lake he could recognise his own reflection and he could see that his face, which had been moon-white, was no longer pale, but blotched a deep, dark purplish colour, as though his blood had seeped out of his veins and come to the surface and was pooling underneath his skin.

He stood perfectly still and observed the way his appearance was changing, but after some time had passed, he saw that his face had become so dark that it refracted no light whatsoever and that where it had been reflected in the lake, there was now merely *an absence*, as though his body ended at his shoulders. The absence of his face was remarkable, but he found that he was able to accept quite readily the idea that it might no longer be there.

Yet he could still see.

This meant that he still had eyes, even if they were unable to see themselves. And now he understood that, although this seemed illogical and contradictory, he had no choice but to accept this too, because he'd entered a world where the impossible was everywhere, a world where all the rules he'd once learned were broken. And this realisation filled him with a strange excitement and he turned away from the lake to look around him to see how everything was changed.

The most surprising thing he noticed was the altered disposition of the lakeside (where he was standing) in relation to the lake. Instead of descending or curving down into the water, the land seemed to *float* in a rolling pathway, just above the still surface of it. It was solid ground, the colour of greenstone, yet behaved as though it were a skein of mist, and Edwin wanted to run back to his mother and tell her that he'd seen it now, the acre of land between the water and the sand! He wanted to reveal to her that there was no end to what was possible in the world and that, in their lives together at the Orchard Run, this realisation had somehow passed them by, so that they had done the same things in the same way day after day and year after year and never seen how each and every one of these things might have been different.

He remembered suddenly that Janet, who dreamed that a blancmange might be blue, had engineered what everyone had thought of as an impossible pudding and how the blue blancmanges had been a source of wonder and had never ever ceased to be wondrous, even after they'd eaten dozens and dozens of them. But they'd none of them ever seen, not even Janet had ever seen, that if a blancmange could be blue, then a thousand other living or inanimate things might be other than they were. And now it was too late to tell them this. The world of the Orchard Run, the world of lamplight and firelight and bounding dogs and scorched linen and crayons and books and silver dishes, had disappeared somewhere – somewhere unreachable and unknowable. It had become, in this new universe of altered possibility, the one impossible place, to which he could never return.

Edwin would never see his mama and papa again. He understood this. So, before he set off along the greenstone pathway, which, in its mysteriousness, drew him on, he also wanted to allow himself to remember them.

He saw his father, sitting in his armchair, which creaked and whined under the bulk of him, trying to light and relight his pipe, which never burned with a steady rhythm, but always threatened to go out. Edwin remembered that once his mother had said: 'Toby dearest, why don't we try to find you a new pipe the next time we are in Christchurch?' and that his father had simply shaken his head and lit another taper from the fire and puffed once more on the old pipe and said: 'No thank you, Doro.'

And Edwin thought now that this was what he'd loved most about his papa, this stubborn perseverance of his, and he hoped that, for as long as his existence lasted, wherever that existence might be, it would remain and that Toby Orchard would never give up and never give in.

And as to his mama, Edwin liked to imagine her bending over him – as though he might be a baby again in his cradle – and singing her melancholy songs.

Her voice had always been consoling and she sang with a kind of smile on her face, as though there was something amusing about the words of the verses that only she could understand. Edwin had sometimes thought of asking her what it was which made her almost laugh, but he never had and now the songs were fading, growing fainter, and all their words becoming muddled and lost. The songs would no longer be for him.

'She will sing to Papa,' Edwin told himself. 'They will sit either side of the fire and Janet will draw the curtains on the darkness and Papa will fuss with his pipe and Mama will start singing . . .'

But now it seemed to Edwin that time was passing very fast and that he had to set off along the floating path before everything became as dark and absent as his own face, for he could see in the sky some alteration, as of a coming storm or the nearness of night, and as he began to move, he understood that he was walking towards a destination that would obey the laws of the new, altered world. It might not be recognisable, therefore, as a place of arrival and he began to worry that he might not know, from one second to the next, whether he'd arrived or whether he had to go on.

But then he saw a patch of earth. It was grey and hard, and on the earth, arranged in an order that seemed to express a perfect understanding of the relationship of one object to another, was a circle of stones.

Edwin knew that Pare had put these stones there. He knelt down and touched one stone and then another and what the stones seemed to tell him was that they had been waiting for a long time.

IV

When Toby returned to the Orchard Run with Dr Pettifer, the snow was still falling and, though it was near to mid-day, the air was piercingly cold.

Dorothy, still wearing her night-clothes, with her head uncovered and her feet bare, was standing in the middle of the lawn. From the distance of the verandah, Janet, who held in her hand a mug of something hot, which might have been tea, was calling to her to come inside, but Dorothy didn't move. She didn't appear to hear Janet or to see her or to notice anything around her, not even the arrival of Toby and Dr Pettifer. She just stood where she was, seeing nothing, with the snow falling on her, as it fell on to the grass and on to the dovecote and on to the trees, turning everything to an obliterating white.

Paak Mei's Laughter

I

Long ago, in the house on Heron Lake, Pao Yi had overheard his wife, Paak Mei, telling her friends a secret.

Paak Mei had a high laugh and she loved to giggle, as though giggling intoxicated her, as though by laughing more and more, she could arrive at happiness. The secret she revealed, amid a soaring flight of giggles, was that her husband, Pao Yi, was what she termed 'a connoisseur of love'.

Pao Yi, startled as he was when he overheard this, immediately realised that the three women friends were fascinated by Paak Mei's revelation. 'If he's a connoisseur of love,' they asked, 'from whom did he learn his techniques?'

Pao Yi had to strain to listen to Paak Mei's answer because her voice subsided to an amused whisper, as though the laughter-bird had fluttered down and landed somewhere, as she said: 'He was once the lover of the concubine of a war lord. I don't remember her name. But she taught him all her artistry. When you meet Pao Yi, you see, you assume he's just a poor fisherman from Heron Lake, but in fact, in the nights, he is an artist of love!'

A cascade of delighted laughter greeted these disclosures. Two of the friends said they wished their husbands had been the lovers of concubines. But then the third friend asked: 'How do you know that Pao Yi is an "artist of love", Paak Mei, if he is the only man who has ever touched you?' And there was a moment's silence, during which Pao Yi pressed his ear even closer to the wall.

After a little while, Paak Mei whispered: 'Because he is so attentive to my pleasure. Sometimes, we never sleep at all, but make love over and over again until the sunrise. And then I feel so light and free and contented, it is as though I were floating on the tops of trees, as though Heron Lake and all the fish in it and all the water-lilies that grow in its shallows were mine.'

For some reason, this idea that little Paak Mei, with her minute and shuffling feet, could suddenly become the owner of Heron Lake amused the friends more than anything that had so far been said and the room was then filled with laughter so musical and prolonged that Pao Yi also found himself smiling.

But then, as he walked away from the house towards his boat, he began wondering where the story of the war lord's concubine had come from and why Paak Mei had decided to invent it and then boast about it.

The truth was, Pao Yi had been the lover of many women in his mind, but Paak Mei was the only one he'd ever truly known. Perhaps, he decided as he began to gather up his fishing nets, his imagination had served him better than he'd realised? Perhaps – because he had so often 'seen' the soft curve of a woman's thigh, the pearly beads of sweat between her breasts or on her lip, and had found it easy to transport himself to wherever it was this woman lay waiting for him – he had learned all a man needed to know about love from his own reveries?

It occurred to him that in these reveries, time, which is the enemy of love, had always been entirely accommodating. As a young man, Pao Yi had been able to sustain a love-reverie through all the deep hours of the night or all the shallow hours of the dawn. His imaginary concubines had had fantastic names, Indigo Bird, Scarlet Tigress, Emerald Flower, and he had always been certain that these beautiful beings would be capable of feeling sexual pleasure as intense as his own.

So Pao Yi searched their bodies to try to discover precisely how that pleasure could be arrived at, and where the true source of it lay, because he saw that to imagine pleasure on the faces of Indigo Bird and Scarlet Tigress and Emerald Flower increased by several degrees the intensity of his own ecstasy. And by the time he married Paak Mei, he had found it.

On their wedding night, he lay with his head on Paak Mei's belly, lapping at the tiny bud he found among the perfumed tangle of her pubic hair, and Paak Mei – as she later admitted to her envious friends – thus became in her mind the Empress of Heron Lake, the one who could lie on the tops of trees and look down upon all her silvery endowments.

II

Now, as the snow began falling on his garden, Pao Yi's only thought was to become the perfect lover of the woman he called Hal Yet.

First of all, he banished time.

That the snow was falling delighted him. For he saw that now, provided it kept on falling, the way back to the sea, the way back to the real world, would soon be closed. All that would remain here would be the bed where they lay and the fire which they tried to keep burning day and night, and the food that they cooked and the white light of day at the window and the cave at their backs, blocked up with its wall of stones.

Heron Lake disappeared from Pao Yi's mind. He could no longer see it, no longer imagine his boat floating on it nor his house standing on its shore-line. Even the graves of Chen Lin and Chen Fen Ming became like faded pictures, or like clothes he'd once worn as a child and grown out of and could barely remember. And from the house itself, there was no sound at all, no sign of anyone moving, no whisper of Paak Mei's feet shuffling across the floor, no flute of laughter from the place where she cooked.

And Paak Shui, too, was absent most of the time. Pao Yi thought that no doubt his son still massaged his mother's feet with lavender oil, still gathered water chestnuts from the river, still flew his scarlet kite on Long Hill, still struggled with his calligraphy, but he could no longer see him do these things, nor hear his voice, nor remember the sweet smell of his hair.

All Pao Yi knew and all he wanted to know was that he had found his perfect woman and now he would love her. For her, he would be a real 'connoisseur'. He would find the bud of her pleasure and make it flower. He would discover every inch of her and caress it with his hands and his lips and his sex and his mind. He would sleep inside her, with his head on her breast. He would press her to him so tenderly, with such human gentleness, that she and he would become like dancers, moving to the same intoxicating rhythm. Everywhere she moved, his eyes would follow. Everywhere he moved, her eyes would follow. There would be no stumbling or falling, no hurt, no shock or damage or dying. There would only be this: Pao Yi and Hal Yet; Hal Yet and Pao Yi.

That the world would disapprove of his love and would attempt to destroy it was something which Pao Yi knew with absolute certainty, but he put this from his mind. It was part of the future, and he willed himself to live in the present and give the future no thought.

The most extraordinary thing that he did (and even at the time Pao Yi knew that it was extraordinary) was to take down his pictures of his family and hide them behind the wooden board on which were written the names of his ancestors. To do this, to consign the people he had loved to the dark space between the wall and the ancestor chart, should have terrified and shamed him, but it did not. He didn't want them to see where he was or what he was doing and so he hid them away.

And it seemed to Pao Yi that Harriet, too, inhabited the room which contained their existence in a way that was absolute, in a way which refused both past and future. If he found her staring out sometimes, it was only, he believed, to reassure herself that the snow was still falling, that the paths to the sea were buried, that nothing and no one would come to disturb them.

Now and again, she put on the clothes she'd been wearing when the flood came and which she'd washed and hung to dry on the trees. But mostly she wore Pao Yi's grey cotton jacket and trousers, or she wore nothing at all and Pao Yi would gaze at the whiteness of her body, made whiter in daylight by the icy light at the edges of the sacking window which was the light of the South Pole, of a clean vastness, of a glittering, empty, untravelled world. He knew that this sight would live in his memory for as long as he was alive.

III

As Pao Yi guessed, Harriet, too, understood the role played by time in their love. She knew that in the Land of the Long White Cloud she and her lover had arrived by pure chance at a sequestered place and that the past had no business there.

Sometimes, it infiltrated her dreams, that recent past of the goldfields, and an image of Joseph drowning when the fresh came down upon the Kokatahi mine. She seemed to see his ghostly, suffering face. But when she woke up and discovered that she was lying, not with Joseph, but in Pao Yi's arms, she put everything else out of her mind.

Harriet was too wise, too rational a person not to understand that, one day, a different future would arrive. Sometimes, when Pao Yi went out of the shelter, closing the makeshift door behind him, Harriet forced herself to imagine that he had gone for ever. She imagined walking alone the long and difficult miles to Hokitika and the sea and waiting for a boat and then getting on the boat and not caring whether she survived or whether she drowned because her lover was gone. And sometimes the anxiety that she felt was so great that she would open the door of the hut and look down on the snow-covered garden, just to see him, just to hold him with her eyes. But there were times when even this wasn't enough and she had to call to him or go to where he was, as though he were about to disappear, as though, if she didn't feel the warmth and solidity of him and enfold him with her arms, he would vanish away into the snow.

The smallness of their world, its absolute simplicity, marked every object within it as precious to Harriet. Even the fire, which seemed to embody the ceaseless flickering of time, was touched with significance, and Harriet fed the fire as tenderly as she would have fed a child, to make sure that it wouldn't die. And beyond the fire, the arrangement of cooking pots and sacks and panniers and garden tools was etched on Harriet's mind with such clarity, had about it such an intense primacy, that it became in her imagination *the only arrangement* her life would ever require. She was amazed to remember what a quantity of furniture, objects and commodities had cluttered the rooms where she'd once lived and that even in the Cob House, she had considered as necessities things which now appeared to her as valueless.

And she concluded that passion of this kind effects an alteration on the material world so absolute that it could be said to resemble a long hallucination or dream, from which the lovers hope never to wake.

IV

It snowed for a long time and then it stopped.

Harriet looked out and saw the sun begin to melt the icicles on the solitary plum tree. She had no idea how many days and nights had gone by, nor what month they were in. She remembered that, after Beauty's death, the deep snow had melted away very fast.

So now it seemed to her that she and Pao Yi were no longer sufficiently hidden and walled away in their shack and she went to him and told him that they should move their bed into the cave.

Pao Yi remembered his opium reveries. He remembered the yellow flickering of the candlelight on the roof of the cave and the things he saw in the shadows and it frightened him. Deliberately, he had never lain with Harriet in the cave, because he was afraid that in there, in that silent space which nobody but he had ever entered, carnal love would become ungovernable and have no end and that it would feast upon itself until it died.

But now, all he longed for was to go there.

Stone by stone, he unblocked the wall. He placed a candle on a rocky ledge and together he and Harriet pulled the thin mattress into the narrow space that was just wide enough for their two bodies to lie side by side. It was so cold in the cave that Harriet almost faltered and changed her mind, but then she asked herself which she would choose – the icy darkness of the cave or the loss of her lover – and she told herself that she would get used to the cold, that she and Pao Yi would keep each other warm, that nothing mattered, only that they should not be discovered.

But Pao Yi knew that the cave in winter couldn't be endured except with the help of opium. He lit a pipe and they lay down together and the pipe passed from the one to the other and Harriet felt for the first time that stretching away of her being into fragments of extraordinary lightness which could rearrange themselves into any shape or form she might desire.

And she desired to be a white bird with warm soft feathers and a heart that beat in time to its own song and as a bird she lay on her lover's body and covered him with her wings and she felt him rise up in her as though he were growing there and she told him that they were one.

And Pao Yi, who had been afraid to abandon himself to her, who, until now had held on to his separate and private self, now called to her to kill him, to let him pass to oblivion through desire, and she acquiesced, and he felt come into him an animal rage to mate without ceasing, like the wild stags on Long Hill in the springtime, and in a torrent of language he cursed her as a demon, as a reptile who had tempted him away from all that had been precious to him and now he was lost in her, lost in darkness, and all that remained to him was the horror of his own dying.

When Pao Yi woke, the candle had gone out.

He could taste blood on his mouth.

He had no notion of day or night or any passing of the hours. His body felt impossibly heavy, as though the floor of the cave were pulling him down.

He sat up at last and saw, from the remnants of the firelight outside the cave entrance, that Harriet was awake. She was lying beside him and staring at the ceiling and she reached out and touched his shoulder and then she pointed upwards and her long arm almost touched the roof of the cave and in a voice which sounded melancholy and quiet, she said: 'There is gold.'

Pao Yi was shivering. He pulled a blanket round himself and lay down again and tried to pull Harriet to him, to warm him and she held him for a moment or two, but then she said again: 'Pao Yi. This cave is made of gold.'

He understood the words. He looked up and saw what she had seen and his gaze wandered there, but he refused to marvel.

In his own language he said that, when the winter ended, when the snow was all gone, when the river fell, when the way to the sea was open once more, then would be the time to consider whether the cave was made of gold. But until then, they shouldn't concern themselves with it, just as he had never concerned himself with the golden nugget that he'd buried under the seventeenth onion.

Pao Yi doubted whether Harriet could understand any of what he was saying, but he kept on talking and she lay beside him and listened and he told her that all the while it was becoming clearer and clearer to him that the yellow light he'd seen in opium reveries and which he'd thought had been made by the candle-flame, had been a golden light. But now it had to remain as a light and nothing more because he knew – he, the fisherman Chen Pao Yi from Heron Lake in Guangdong Province in south-east China knew as surely as he knew his own name – that the day on which they decided to steal that light would be the day on which they would have to part.

V

After this, they returned to the shack and made their bed again close to the fire. Pao Yi walled up the entrance to the cave. He put the opium pipe away on the high shelf, next to his ancestor chart.

The weather taunted them with its wild variety. The winds of June and July came funnelling down the makeshift chimney, blowing smoke into their faces, tearing at the sacking on the door. The snow melted and the smooth tops of the cabbages emerged like a line of old men's heads, not dead, not quite; only patiently waiting under a shroud.

Hail pelted the roof, like falling shingle. Violet and orange rainbows shone an ethereal light into the room. The river roared one day and was almost silent the next. Rain seeped into the thatch and began dripping on to the floor. Then they heard the trees sighing and clicking and knew that the rain had turned to ice.

Now, the cold began to torment them. They went outside only to relieve themselves or to claw vegetables out of the ground or to bring in firewood or fish from the nets. They wondered if they would die here. They knew that the fire kept them alive. They longed for furs or sheepskins, but had neither, only their arms to wrap around each other.

After their night in the cave, their passion calmed, as though they had crammed into one night the experience of a year, and what they settled into now was something which resembled an affectionate marriage, one without prudery or secrets or shame. Together, they fussed over the fire, prepared their soup, tried to comfort each other when one of them was ill or in pain, taught each other songs, told stories, suffered boredom and sadness and joy, made love slowly and tenderly and tried, above all, to keep the cold at bay.

They began listening for the thaw.

When the thaw came, they knew that the spring wouldn't be far behind.

VI

One morning, Pao Yi was walking down to the river to see what fish had been caught in his net, when he heard a familiar sound in his mind, one which hadn't surfaced for a long time; it was the sound of Paak Mei's laughter.

Pao Yi pressed his rabbit-fur hat more firmly on to his head. He strode on and took off his shoes and waded into the water. He thought, to his relief, that the laughter was fading, but then when Pao Yi's hands came into contact with the fishing net, he found that the familiar feel of it transported him back to Heron Lake so vividly, it was almost as though he had arrived there. And when he looked around, all he could see was devastation.

His house, once brightly painted, appeared faded and neglected and there was no smoke coming from its chimney. The door was closed and the hinges looked rusty and the dark heads of dead sunflowers knocked against the window frame.

Pao Yi's boat was resting in the water some way from the quayside, but its red hull had turned a dull greenish-brown, and sitting in the boat was a thin, dejected figure Pao Yi was appalled to recognise as his son, Paak Shui. He tried to call to Paak Shui and Paak Shui looked up for a moment, just as though he *had* heard a voice calling to him, but then the boy resumed his former posture and remained there without moving.

It was at that moment that Pao Yi understood that he'd been wrong about the sound he had just heard: Paak Mei wasn't laughing, she was weeping. She was weeping for the shame of being abandoned, for the shame of being promised riches and instead losing what little she had, for the shame of being betrayed by her husband with a white woman.

The morning was almost warm, with a pale sun sparkling on the water, but Pao Yi was frozen. If Harriet had been watching, as she sometimes watched him when he went to check his net, she would have seen him put out a hand and clutch at the tree to which the net was attached and lean towards the tree, as though he were faint or dizzy, and then stay like that without moving.

But Harriet wasn't watching. She was trying to count the days that had passed since the night in the cave and to work out whether it had been on that night or on some subsequent night or morning that the baby she now knew she was carrying had been conceived. She knew it made no difference to the fact of the pregnancy, yet she wanted it to have happened then, so that whenever she looked at the child, far into her future when she would be alone again, she would be able to remember the wildness of that night and her beautiful reverie of being a bird, a bird with a heart almost stopped by desire, and the crying and calling of her lover to this bird across the darkness of continents.

So absorbing was Harriet's memory of this that she was startled when she heard the door open and she saw Pao Yi returning with a basket of fish. She saw him set down the basket and she was about to get up, to go to him and tell him her secret, which was the secret of the child, when he turned suddenly and went out again. And when he came back, a moment or two later, he carried a pickaxe in his hand. And he walked by her, not looking at her, but only at the mouth of the cave, and then he knelt down and began taking out the stones from the doorway.

She said his name: 'Pao Yi.' She tried to frame a question.

She saw that he was weeping. So she went and knelt down beside him, with her skirts on the dusty earth, and she asked him if the time had arrived to take out the gold, and he nodded and kept on with his task of moving the heavy stones and his tears ran down his cheeks and began to dampen the top of his shirt.

She wanted him to try to talk to her, to tell her what he was going to do, but she saw that he couldn't say anything. She reached up and tried to stop his hands from bringing away the stones, but he wouldn't be deflected from his task, and so Harriet understood.

She saw that the only thing to do was to help him.

They worked side by side without speaking. Pao Yi kept clawing at the rocks with the pick and Harriet tugged them away. Inch by inch, the cave was revealed to them again, their opium cave, and they felt the chill of it and remembered its darkness and its mystery.

They stopped and rested a moment and then began lighting candles and they took the candles into the cave and crouched there, staring up, seeing the veins of gold running over the ceiling and down into the walls.

It was in this moment's pause, before they began to tear out the colour from the cave, that Harriet considered telling Pao Yi about the child – his child – so that he would take this knowledge away with him when he returned to Heron Lake and hold it for ever in his mind. But she kept silent.

Now the pickaxe began smashing into the veins of gold. The sound of iron on precious metal seemed to echo all through the mountain. But the rock was more porous and brittle than Pao Yi and Harriet had imagined, yielded more easily to its breaking, so that it became possible to tear flakes and chunks of it away with their bare hands, and pieces of it split of their own accord and fell in showers all around them and into their hair, and their faces became coated with a black and shiny dust.

Their hands were bruised and their fingers began to bleed and, in the flickering candlelight, Harriet picked up a bright shard and saw the staining and mingling of the two colours, red blood upon a vein of gold, and she felt the unearthly wonder of this and its human sorrow.

She gazed at her lover, at his face turned away from her, at his back, his strong legs, his arms still resolutely wielding the pickaxe, and at the stones and dust that kept falling on to him. She wanted to cry out to him to stop, wanted to beg him to wall up the cave once more, to return with her to their shelter, to press her hand to his mouth, to enfold him, to pretend that no thaw had come and that they could live like this, on the edge of this mountainside, together for ever.

She knew that these thoughts were futile.

She thought that she should begin to sort through the jagged lumps of fallen rock, before so much had come down around them that they would scarcely be able to move. So she took up the pieces streaked with gold and laid the rest aside. She was wearing her old clothes that day, her skirt and petticoat, her chemise and shawl. She took off her shawl to use as a pannier. She crawled backwards and forwards to and from the cave, tugging the shawl, bringing the gold out from the flickering darkness into the white light of this new spring day.

She spread out the pieces and stared at them. She took up a single jagged stone and brushed the dust aside from the vein which threaded it. She tried to guess what Pao Yi would buy with this one golden vein. She could not imagine. She knew almost nothing about his life. But from far away, she could now see his son, Paak Shui, come running towards him and, behind the boy, was his wife, Paak Mei. Paak Mei was unable to run, but she came shuffling as fast as she could towards her husband

and she held out her arms to him. And Harriet could hear a
melodic sound, like bubbling water, and she knew it was the
laughter of Paak Mei, echoing round a wide bowl of hills.

Houses of Wood

I

The names of the miners who had died in the Kokatahi fresh were now posted on a list in the warden's office at Hokitika. The list proclaimed itself to be 'a complete and true record of all bodies recovered at Kokatahi and at Kaniere'.

Harriet stood and stared at the list.

Knowing where Joseph's claim had been, she'd presumed that his name would be here. She couldn't see how, working at the river's edge, he could have escaped being swept away. She had sometimes wondered how long he had survived and whether the hopes he'd had of her gold would have made him struggle and fight against the pull of the river. Perhaps he had fought very hard – in the way that he always fought with destiny, with a selfish desperation – only to be hurled to his death against a boulder?

But now, his name wasn't on the list.

Harriet walked away from the warden's office and went down to the beach and sat among the driftwood and looked out on the sea, which was a fine blue that day. But all she could see was the one and only thing she would now remember about this ocean: she saw the ship that had taken Pao Yi away.

She tried not to think of it.

She had the puzzle of Joseph to solve. If Joseph wasn't dead, then she had to find him. She had to give him a share of her gold and tell him that she could no longer live with him as his wife.

*

Hokitika town was still busy. Men were still arriving and departing. The hotel was building on more rooms. The Bank of New Zealand had a new, much larger sign and other, smaller, private banks had come clustering into tilting shanties, to proclaim their 'advantageous offers for the meanest find of gold dust'.

Harriet had hidden her gold, wrapped in a shawl, in the wardrobe of her room at the Hokitika hotel. She walked out into the spring sunlight, with one hand resting gently on her belly. She wandered the wharves and alleyways, searching the faces that she passed. She'd been told that survivors of the fresh had been billeted for a while among the families of Hokitika, so she began to ask about, to see whether anyone could remember Joseph Blackstone. The widow, Ernestine Boyd, wasn't among those she talked to.

People shook their heads. 'No,' they said. 'We'd remember that name. Black Stone. Wouldn't we? Perhaps he was taken by the flood?'

'His name isn't on the warden's list.'

'Ah,' they said, 'but then there are names missing from the list, the ones whose bodies haven't been found. The people who vanished.'

People who vanished.

When she heard these words, Harriet was suddenly overcome with the sadness she was trying all the while to keep at bay. She sat down on a low wall made of cob and the feel of the scratchy bricks was still familiar to her, but it seemed to her that the woman who'd inhabited the Cob House had been someone else, not Harriet Blackstone, nor even Harriet Salt. And this woman she pitied, for she saw that nothing had stirred or inspired her except the idea of solitude. She'd kept a scrapbook, but there was almost nothing human in the book, only papers and feathers and leaves, things which had floated down to her as she stood alone under the empty sky. This woman had never smoked opium in a golden cave. This woman had never become a white-feathered bird so beautiful and wicked she could make her lover curse and rage and want to die . . .

Harriet put her face in her hands.

She knew that Pao Yi was still far out on the ocean, yet what she imagined once more was his return to the house on Heron Lake.

This time, she saw his son Paak Shui lead him inside the house, to where Paak Mei was waiting, waiting proudly behind a table of food she'd made to celebrate her husband's return as a rich man. She saw Pao Yi embrace his son and then move towards Paak Mei, with his habitual silent and graceful step, and he was smiling, smiling with pride that he had conquered his passion and returned, that he had not lost face, that he had not inflicted shame on the family. And then he bent down (for Paak Mei was shorter than he was) and kissed her and he remembered how, long ago, she'd been his bride and that he had loved her and that he loved her still . . .

The pain of these imaginings was so intense that Harriet decided she had to do something new to combat the agony, something which would help her to make sense of her future. She got up off the cob wall and walked slowly back to the hotel and went to her wardrobe, which was made of thin slabs of wood, like poor Lilian's coffin at Rangiora, and brought out her bundle of gold. She didn't look at it. She didn't want to remember how, by breaking the rock to tear out the colour, she and Pao Yi had destroyed their cave. She just shouldered the weight of it and began walking towards the Bank of New Zealand.

A coal fire was burning there. Two employees of the bank, wearing black, sat behind a counter, on which had been placed some large brass scales and a line of assorted weights.

One of the men was writing in a ledger, in a meticulous slow hand. The other man was polishing the weights with a soft cloth. His fingers were stained black with the tarnish his polishing had brought out. He held up a five-ounce weight and squinted at it, to assess its degree of brightness.

The men looked up as Harriet came in, but didn't pause in either of their tasks. Their commerce was seldom with any woman. It was only the men who possessed gold. The bank employees presumed they would soon have the momentary annoyance of redirecting Harriet to whichever establishment she had mistaken them for.

She said 'Good morning' and then she laid the dusty shawl on their counter and untied the bundle and they saw the pieces of rock shot through with gold.

'There will be a fine, I know,' Harriet said at once. 'I paid no Miner's Right. I was fossicking on a beach above Kokatahi. I was swept across the river by the fresh and I sheltered from the winter in a cave. I was walled up there and couldn't come down to the coast or cross back to where I had been. All of this I brought out of the cave.'

The ledger was laid aside, the brass weight was put down and the two bankers reached out and touched the rocks and ran their fingers along the lines of gold. Harriet sat down on a high stool and waited. She could feel the warmth of the fire at her back and hear it hissing gently as it burned.

'You said you had no Miner's Right?' said one of the men, with a choke in his voice.

'No,' said Harriet.

'Twenty per cent,' he announced. 'That is the forfeit. I refer you to Rule Seven in the *Rules Governing the Acquisitions and Disbursements of Auriferous Matter in Canterbury County*, dated March 1865. And I quote: "Whatsoever is found of gold by any man, whether by accepted mining practice or whether by some other means not herein specified, but is wantonly got by him without a true and authentic Miner's Licence, issued by the Warden of the County, so shall this same gold be forfeit to the County Treasury as to twenty percent of its market value, this value to be ascertained by – "'

'You need not go on,' said Harriet. 'I shall pay the forfeit. I merely need to know whether you will buy the gold or whether I am to take it to another bank.'

'We will buy it,' chimed the two men together.

'We will certainly buy it,' said the man who had been writing in the ledger. 'Now, may we offer you something? Tea? Tea with a dash of rum, while you are waiting?'

'No thank you,' said Harriet. 'Give me a receipt for the gold and I will return later, to see whether I am rich or not.'

'You are rich,' said the man who had been polishing weights.

'You've brought us a homeward bounder, ma'am. Nothing less.'

Harriet came out of the Bank of New Zealand. She didn't want to return to the hotel and sit in her room. She wanted to keep walking.

She walked nowhere in particular, pondering the knowledge of her new-found wealth. And she thought again how it was Joseph who had longed for riches, not she, but that if, after all, she was going to be rich, then she would make as good a life as she could for her child. For this was all that mattered to her now. She was going to give birth to Pao Yi's son (she was sure the baby was a boy) and in this boy's sweet face she would see the face of her lover, and the child would never leave her to return to Guangdong Province, never board a ship and sail away; he would be hers and nobody would take him from her. She would name him Hal. She would brush his black hair till it shone. She would build a strong wooden house for him, protected from the southerly winds. She would tell him that she had once discovered a golden cave, deep in the mountains . . .

Preoccupied with these imaginings, impatient now for time to pass so that her child could be born and she could hold him in her arms, Harriet looked up and found herself outside the door of the Hokitika Office of Shipping. She hadn't intended to come here. She'd been walking without any destination in mind. But when she saw where she was, she thought, suddenly, that perhaps the mystery of Joseph was going to be solved here, that it lay not in the records of the dead, nor in any continuing search for bodies washed up at Kaniere, but here, in the Shipping Office.

Harriet went inside. Unlike the bank, the place was cold and the floor damp, as though salt water from the decks of the fishing smacks and the old leaky steamboats seeped in and out of the place in a perpetual tide.

She told the clerk of the Shipping Office that she was in a state of uncertainty: she didn't know whether she was a widow or not. She explained that she had money to give to her husband, if he were still alive, if only she could find him . . .

The clerk picked up his monocle and through its sparkling

lens he searched for the name Joseph Blackstone in his cumbersome ledgers. His gaze travelled up and down column after column of names. He murmured, in passing, that the quantity of people named Brown or Smith became 'vexatious in the verification of passenger records', but observed that the name Blackstone 'is not so very common'.

Then his gaze alighted in the middle of a column and remained there and didn't move. He pressed his ink-stained finger on to the page.

'I have found him!' he exclaimed with genuine delight. 'Joseph Roderick Blackstone. Here he is. He sailed for England on the Australian ship, the *Percy McKenzie*, on the last day of June.'

The clerk turned the ledger round so that Harriet could look at the column of names. And when she saw Joseph's name written there, she knew that what she felt was relief.

'Sailed home, ma'am,' said the clerk. 'Left you behind, what? Seems he wasn't bothered about his share of your money?'

'Yes,' said Harriet. 'It seems he wasn't.'

For a moment, Harriet thought how strange it was that, after all that had happened, Joseph had decided to go home with nothing except the few grains he possessed. But then she remembered that the river had still been running fast and deep when she and Pao Yi had begun their long trek to the sea; she hadn't been able to cross over to her little beach to recover her store of gold. But Joseph could have walked up there on the north side of the river. And perhaps her brimming cup had still lain buried in the shingle, still reachable above the new water line? She imagined Joseph squatting down and digging it up and holding it out to see its contents gleam in the sunlight. *The colour.* Perhaps, as he stowed the cup away in his swag, Joseph had decided that his wife was drowned, or perhaps he had simply told himself that – as his wife – whatever was hers belonged rightfully to him?

II

Through all the weeks of the voyage on the *Percy McKenzie*, Joseph Blackstone willed himself to survive.

He kept to his small cabin, roped himself to his bunk when storms blew, lived on biscuits and water, counted his grains of gold, rehearsed the words he was going to say to the Millward family. He felt that he was living only for this, for his moment of confession.

He spoke to no one. Sometimes, in the dead of night, he walked on the deck and stared at the stars or made his way to the stern of the ship and watched the wake streaming out behind it. He had the notion that he was being pursued, even across these vast oceans, and he longed for this pursuit to end.

Not until he arrived at last in Parton Magna did Joseph understand how strange he looked, how ill he had become. As soon as he glimpsed himself in the altered light of England, he found that he could no longer hold himself up.

He took a room at the Plough and the Stars. He lay in a narrow bed, listening to the doves on the roof. He slept a dreamless sleep.

He sent for a barber to cut his hair and shave off his beard. He mourned his mother and wished he had been able to bring her body home, to bury it here, in the shadow of the Church of the Redeemer.

Joseph had planned to go to the Millwards straightaway. He'd believed that his confession, so often rehearsed in his mind, would be made in the first days of his return and that, once he had made it, once he'd submitted himself to the anger and grief of the family and given money to them, he would be free to go on with his life.

But now he found that he wasn't yet strong enough to go anywhere near the Millwards' house. He told himself that he might become strong enough, when more days had passed. But then the days did pass and kept passing and he was no nearer being able to say what he'd come to say. Every morning he asked himself: 'Shall I go today?' And every morning he answered: 'No.' As the weeks accumulated, part of him began to admit that he would never be able to do it, that the words he would have to say were beyond saying.

One afternoon, walking with slow steps to the mere, he saw a figure standing there, feeding the ducks.

It was Susan Millward, Rebecca's younger sister. Joseph turned quickly and began to walk away, but she came after him, calling: 'Joseph Blackstone! Joseph Blackstone! Won't you say hello to the likes of us any more?'

So he had to stop, couldn't scuttle away from her like a thief, had to let her catch him up. He stood and looked at her. She'd become more than ever like Rebecca. The same brown curls, the same teasing smile. The same snaggled teeth. He managed to bow to her and she laughed at the awkward formality of this and Joseph heard Rebecca's laugh. He knew that he should prostrate himself in front of Susan Millward, here on the pathway to the mere, start babbling that he'd kept himself alive for this, to make amends. But he was incapable of doing it.

'What would you like?' he blurted out. 'Tell me what I can give you.'

'Beg pardon?' said Susan.

'I have a little money now. I found gold in New Zealand. Perhaps you heard? Tell me what gift you would like.'

'What?' she said coyly. 'What wedding gift?'

'Yes,' he said, but he was confused now. For what 'wedding' was she talking about? Was it possible ... was it conceivable that Susan Millward had set her sights on the man her sister had loved and lost?

'Well,' said Susan, 'my mam says people have already been far too kind.'

He stared at her. Confusion blurred his vision of everything, as though the day were suddenly darkening. And she seemed to him so young, so almost like a child, that surely it was impossible she should think of him, who now looked so much older than he was, as a man fit for her ...

He waited for her to say something else, but she only smiled and squirmed and turned her head away. He saw the sun falling on her shiny hair and on her hands, which held a crumpled handkerchief. And then he saw the ring there. A small, brilliant stone set in a gold circlet and he understood.

'So tell me,' he said, recovering himself, 'for I've been away so long . . . tell me who you are to marry.'

Susan Millward blushed and pushed the hair from her face and smiled at him again. 'Marrying above myself, so my mam teases me,' she said, 'marrying the veterinary, Mr Merrick Dillane.'

Joseph wondered, after that, as he lay listening to the doves in his narrow room, whether he should leave Parton, leave Norfolk, go to some other county where he knew no one, where he could lead an invisible life. But he understood that he was incapable of this. He had travelled across the world to return here. He didn't have the strength to leave.

He bought a low, thatched cottage that had belonged to a toy-maker. In the small out-house, which had been the old man's workshop, the tools still hung on the walls. Over the brick floor, a pale and scented tide of wood shavings drifted towards the walls. The garden had long ago been abandoned to nettles and ground elder.

Joseph left everything as he found it.

He purchased new linen, but he slept in the toy-maker's bed and read the books which had been stuffed into the shelf above it, *Gulliver's Travels, A Short History of India, Famous Dolls' Houses of the World.*

Gulliver made him too anxious and he laid this aside without finishing it. The *History of India*, likewise, seemed to him too filled with an unsettling anger and gave him dreams that he was being pecked to death by some peculiar animal, just as his father had been pecked to death by ostriches.

Only the book about dolls' houses gave him any consolation. He would stare for a long time at the pictures, intensely aware of how the human mind finds agreeable and wondrous everything that is a miniature replica of something else. And after a few weeks had passed, Joseph decided that he would try to make a doll's house – to give to Susan Millward and Merrick Dillane, for the children they would one day have.

He cleared the toy-maker's work bench, but left the sea of wood shavings on the floor, not only because he liked to walk in it but because he was able to imagine all the years of work of which it had been a part – as though this had been *his* work and all his labours in New Zealand had been a dream from which he'd now woken. He bought plywood and slate and nails and a glass cutter. He bought tins of paint and varnish and glue and slabs of putty.

Now, when he woke in the morning, this was what he thought about: his doll's house. He drank a mug of weak tea and sometimes heated a muffin in a blackened pan and ate it with jam. Then he made his way to the workshop and, with a patience so infinite it surprised him, went on with the task of building an elegant little Georgian dwelling, modelled on that once owned by the eldest daughter of the eleventh Duke of Hereford.

The house had five bedrooms. Joseph read in *Famous Dolls' Houses* that the floors of the hall and drawing-room had been paved with miniature parquet and the kitchen floor with slate and he knew that his house wouldn't be complete until all of this had been installed. He thought that the cutting of the parquet blocks and the tiny slate slabs might take him his whole lifetime, but he found that he didn't mind.

The marriage of Susan Millward to Merrick Dillane came and went and nobody invited Joseph Blackstone, but from the workshop window he saw the wedding procession pass and heard the bells ringing in the church. And it was on this day that he decided he would never give the doll's house away, neither to Susan and Merrick nor to anybody else; the doll's house was his – *his house* – and it would be the place where he would take refuge from the world.

As the winter came, Joseph worked more and more slowly. The house now had its roof of slate, and ornate chimney-pots made of clay, and fourteen windows. He began on the parquet. But he understood that what hope he had left resided here, in this house made of wood, and that when it was finished, in all its last, tender detail, and he closed its door for the last time, his world would fade to silence.

III

Early in the New Zealand summer, Harriet arrived at the Orchard Run.

She walked arm-in-arm with Dorothy round the garden and Dorothy said: 'I hate summer. I don't want to see the shine on the grass. I don't want to feel the sun on my face. I don't want to see flowers growing.'

When the women passed the titoki tree, and saw the remains of Edwin's tree house, they clung together and wept. Dorothy stammered: 'He was spirited away. I know he was. I look for him everywhere, in everything. I look for him in the dust on my shoes.'

Upstairs, the door of Edwin's room, which had been left exactly as it was the morning he died, remained closed. Dorothy told Harriet that on a slate by his bed was a single word: *bombazine*. She said that the room smelled of him and that it always would. She said the old, faded drawing of the red and yellow Moa Bird was still glued to the wall. She said: 'Janet is mourning, too. She puts salt into cake and sugar into gravy. I should sack her, really, but I don't suppose I will.'

As for Toby Orchard, the two women barely saw him. He slept very little and got up at dawn and went out. The only way in which he could combat his despair was by riding horses at a wild gallop over the sheep-run; not with any purpose, not to round up his sheep or inspect the dipping pits or talk to the hired hands, because he was no longer interested in any of these things, no longer knew what purpose a sheep-run or the money he made from it could possibly serve, but only to keep moving, always moving under the vault of the sky, to wear himself out, to wear the horses out, to go on until he could go on no longer and a blessed unconsciousness smothered his mind.

Dorothy sometimes tried to reason with Toby by saying he would kill himself, kill the horses, bring about more tragedy if he went on leading his life in this way, but Toby appeared not to hear this, not even to listen to it, as though Dorothy could have been reading from a sentimental novel he knew he would despise.

'I can't talk to him,' said Dorothy to Harriet. 'And he can't talk to me. I suppose that now we shall be silent until the end of time.'

Harriet knew that Dorothy had been glad when she arrived, that she, who was now alone so much, valued her companionship, yet Harriet knew that, despite this, she couldn't linger on in this household. She'd promised herself long ago that she wouldn't become a cuckoo in the Orchards' nest and now she saw that she had to honour that promise. And besides, she had her future to build: her future in her new house.

She would site it lower down the flats, not far from the pond and the southern arm of the creek, where it would be sheltered from the wind. It would have a wide verandah, Harriet decided, and a tiled roof. There would be five or six rooms with floors of totara pine and bright colours on the walls and one of these rooms would be for her father, Henry Salt. Already, Harriet could imagine him there, sitting at a desk, making sketches of birds and plants that he'd never seen before.

Next to her own bedroom would be a room for Hal and Hal would have a cradle of wood and soft curtains at the windows to keep out the light. And when he was old enough to run, she and her father would make him a kite out of scarlet paper.

When she told her plan to Dorothy and Toby, Dorothy said: 'I don't want you to leave. I want you to live here with us. You and the child.'

But Toby, who was for once sitting with the women by the fire, said: 'Take no notice of Dorothy, Harriet. Everybody has to live their own life. Just remember drainage. Drainage is the first necessity of human comfort. Dig a cesspit and run your pipes into it. I can find men to help you.'

And there and then, Toby got up and found paper and pen and ink and drew an elegant plan of a drainage system, with water carried in a box flume from the river to a water tank on iron stilts, and underground clay pipes running down into a pit.

He laid the plan in front of Harriet. She saw that his fingers were stained with ink, like the fingers of the shipping clerk in Hokitika.

'Your land has a natural fall,' he said. 'You can site the house looking any way you want, provided the tank is above the roof line and provided the drains follow the inclination of the hills.'

The following day, laying her hand gently on Harriet's large belly, Dorothy whispered: 'That cesspit was the only thing Toby has shown an interest in since Edwin died. And then in the night he made love to me. Perhaps, if we can become a family again, we can survive after all?'

IV

Harriet was reunited with her horse, Billy. One morning very early, she saddled him and began to ride towards the land on the Okuku flats which Joseph Blackstone had bought for £1 an acre and where, now that he was on the other side of the world, she would build her house.

As she rode, she remembered the pleasure of the empty valleys and the shadows of clouds moving with her across the earth. When she crossed the Ashley River on the ferry, Billy swam beside it, and Harriet remembered the donkey and the donkey cart of her first season in New Zealand and she remembered Lady washed away in the fresh. And then she remembered what was always in her heart.

When she came to the place where the Cob House had stood, she saw that the tussock-grass was long and green and that it had come clustering round the old range, as if to try to hide this embarrassing human invention, so that the winds would no longer see it, no longer try to destroy it, but only howl around it and pass on.

Acknowledgements

My grateful thanks to Chris Price, Jenny Patrick, Harriet Allan, Tilly Lloyd, Fiona Clayton, John Glusman, Sylvie Audoly, Roger Cazalet, Mary Gibson, Caroline Michel, Vivien Green, Alison Samuel, Penelope Hoare and of course Richard Holmes.

I also acknowledge a debt to the work of Denis Glover, Judy Corbalis, James Ng, William F. Heinz, Margaret Orbell, Philip Ross May, Lady Barker, Keith Sinclair, H. A. Glasson, G. J. Griffiths, June A. Wood, Rona Adshead and Jillian Johnson, and to the inspirational singing of the St Joseph's Maori Girls College Choir.

Rebecca Millward successfully achieved immortality in this book by bidding at the 'Medical Foundation for the Care of Victims of Torture' 2000 Immortality auction. The Foundation would like to thank Rose Tremain for taking part in the event and supporting the Foundation. www.torturecare.org.uk